YOUNG FLAME

BOOK ONE

YOUNG FLAME

BOOK ONE

J. B. Oro

Podium

This is a work of fiction. Names, characters, places, and incidents are either products of the author's imagination or used fictitiously. Any resemblance to actual events, locales, or persons, living, dead, or undead, is entirely coincidental.

Cover design by Mario Teodosio

ISBN: 978-1-0394-7908-1

Published in 2025 by Podium Publishing
www.podiumentertainment.com

YOUNG FLAME

BOOK ONE

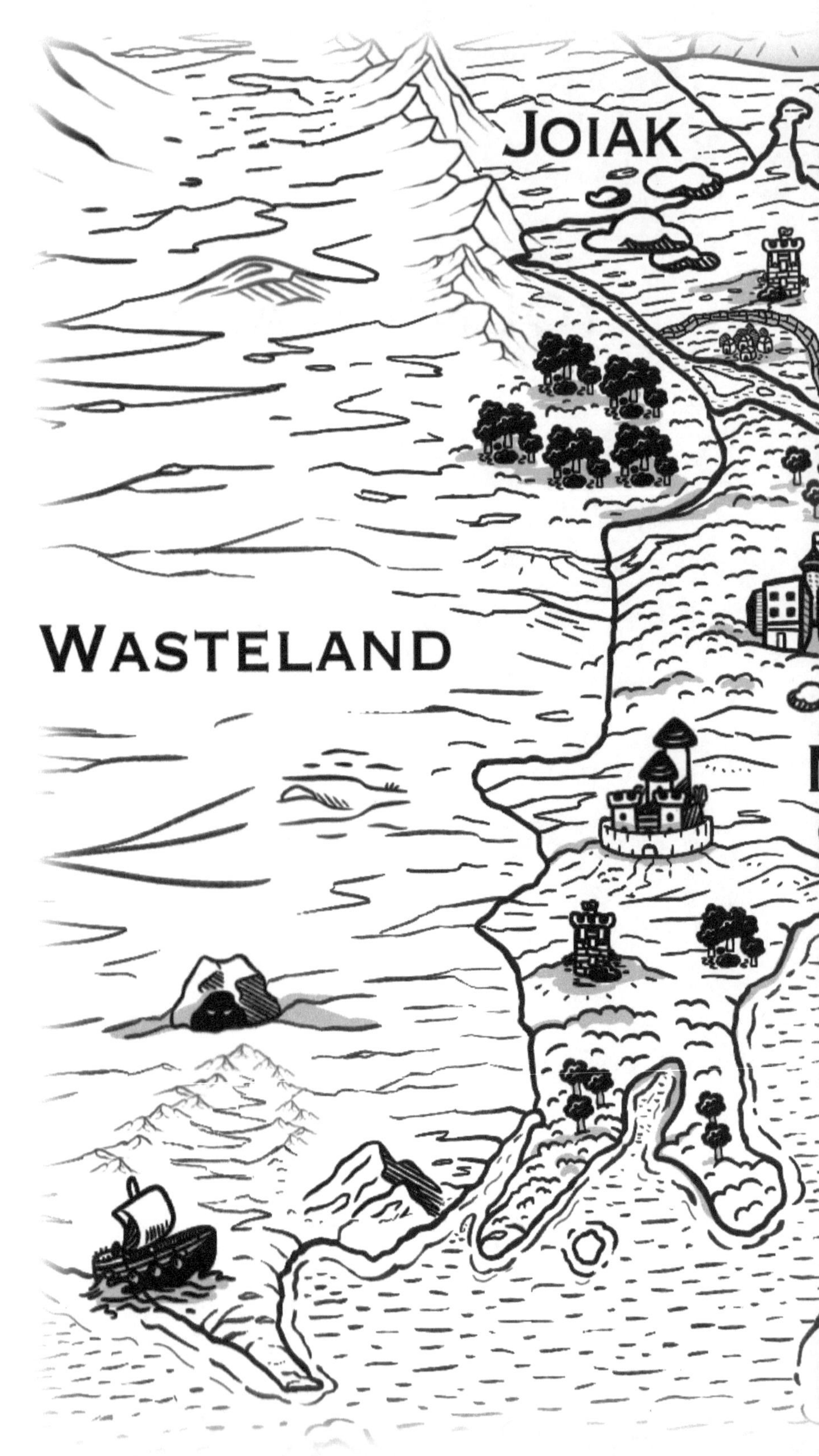

JOIAK
WASTELAND

THEOCRACY
DOK
W VETUS

CHAPTER ONE

Funeral Pyre

Life can't get worse.

I don't understand anything anymore. Why does the world have to be unfair? Why do I feel so empty? Everything is numb. I know I should be bawling, but the wisps refuse to come. I want nothing more than to run to my mommy and cry in her warm embrace. I want to; I want to so much, but she is no longer there for me.

Without her I don't know what to do; I don't know how to do anything without her. I wish to just go back to before when I could run to her warm arms and forget the world as I sleep in her hold. But I can't. I can't deny her death. Not with the unquestionable funeral pyre consuming my attention.

The inferno burns brightly in contrast to the dark, sandy landscape. Fiery flares rise high into the air above, the moon having hidden away not long past. My tribe sits in silence around the pyre, patiently waiting for the Ember Moon's appearance. The elders of our tribe sit closest to the flame, ready to begin the ritual.

A cinder catches the wind, blown away from the pyre. It ebbs and sways unpredictably, following no predetermined path. It floats before me for a moment, and I reach out for it. The wind, as if knowing my intent, whirls the ember out of my grasp and around my arm, its motion teasing, before the wisp drops to the sand below my feet. Its glow is gone as the desert consumes it.

My gaze locks on the remnant cinder. Now ash, indistinguishable from the surrounding sand. Unable to reignite. Unable to reunite with the flame from which it originated.

Once again, I am confronted with the fact there is no way for her to come back to me. I should be crying for her, but I can't. What would she think of me being unable to cry for her at her funeral? She must be so disappointed in me, maybe even as much as I am in myself.

A subdued red light catches my attention from the corner of my eye. Turning slightly, I'm embarrassed to realize I've been so focused in my own head that I have lost control of my fire again. My hair, hanging from the side of my face, is lit in bright red flame, exposing my lack of control to everyone around. I clamp down on it, returning my hair to its physical form.

I am ashamed of myself. Nothing but a disappointment to the tribe. I should have enough control to stop an outburst like this. I'm already ten—I should have been on top of this a year ago. But still, I fail.

The sudden touch of a hand on my shoulder startles me. Turning, I see my Uncle Rivin. His somber expression stares down at me. Is he disappointed in me too? I can only be glad he isn't yelling at me for losing control like he usually would.

Instead, he only nods toward the pyre and I realize I've been lost in thought for a while. I stand and walk toward the pyre with Uncle beside me. The Ember Moon has appeared in the night sky above, its glow tinting the desert a deep red.

I glance up toward Uncle. His blue-and-black hair is short but is still the same color as mine and my mom's. The slight motion of his hair makes the blue flicker like flame, but he hasn't lost control, that's just how it looks. Just the same as my mom's does.

Did.

I stop a few steps from the fire. It burns many times my height, fueled by the ring of elders encircling the pyre. I hesitate to take the next steps, unsure how I can ever willingly say goodbye. I'll be saying goodbye for good, but I don't want her to leave.

I know she is gone. I know that in my head, but I don't want to accept it. I don't want to lose any more of her. I want to cling to everything I have left of her, even if it's simply her memory, and it scares me I might lose that if I accept her death.

I feel Uncle put his hand on my shoulder. "Solvei, I know it's hard, but you need to do this. Just say whatever you wanted to say before we lost her," he says, giving me a slight push.

As much as I don't want to do this, I feel like not doing so would be somehow worse. No, I *know* avoiding it will be worse. I will regret it if I don't say what I can the last time she might ever be able to hear it. Once she returns to the Eternal Inferno, there will be no more chances. This is the only time I have.

Settling my thoughts and gathering my courage, I take the last step through the blazing wall into the pyre. The flames are warm and they embrace me completely. At the center of the flame, I see the remains of the timber used to ignite the ritual pyre, now barely charcoal. The elders' efforts are now the sole source of these flames.

I make my way to the bed of charcoal and lower into a seated position. I let the comfortable heat of the flames nestle into me and let my body shift into flames. My form retains the same shape but takes on the appearance of the flame around me. No longer do I suppress my nature. I push my inner flame out to mix with the surrounding pyre, the flames of my elders ceding control to me.

My tongue twists and nothing comes out when I finally try to talk; too many words want to come out at once. So I try to start simply.

"Mommy, I wish you weren't leaving. I don't know what to do without you. I want to properly wish you on your path to the Eternal Inferno, but I also don't. I don't want to say goodbye to you yet. I already miss you too much. I'm selfish and greedy, and even though I know you'll be in a better place, I still want to hold you back."

I feel myself choking up. It's a struggle to continue as involuntary sobs make their way out with my painful speech.

"But, as much as I don't want you to go, you still need to go. So, good-bye, Mommy. I hope Eldest Ember guides you on your journey to the Eternal Inferno. I will always remember you. I'll miss you and I love you."

It hurts so much to say my farewell. An emptiness swells within me. I push everything I have into the flame, stirring the surrounding fire and forcing it to grow to greater heights. I push everything I have into the flame, hoping the hurt will go with it.

The blaze spins around me and I stare up at the Ember Moon through it. If I don't get to keep my mom with me, the best I can do is hope the eldest áed can help her on her way.

I can't help the wail I let out as I burn through as much of my energy as I can, trying to push the pyre's flame to my limit. The deep red of my fire rages and flares into the sky.

I push myself 'til I'm exhausted, to where the pain of my body hurts more than that of my soul.

I gather my thoughts and control my emotions like my mother always taught me, and I regain my form. I pull my energy back from the flame and allow the ritual pyre to return to the elders' control.

I step out of the fire and see my uncle there waiting for me. Feeling battered and exhausted, I hug him. I know it's over now. Mom is on her path and I've already let her go. I know it was the right choice and I can't turn back on that now, even if it feels so much worse than before.

Uncle embraces me before lifting me up. I push my face into his shoulder, trying to hide my crying from anyone that can see.

Uncle carries me back to a spot far from the flame. He sits down with me in his arms, and I feel his inner flame encompassing me. His heat mixes with my own flame and supports it. The Kindling process fills me with warmth and I can't help myself but relax. It's not as good as when Mom did it, but it still feels nice.

With heavy eyes, I watch as the pyre grows. The blaze sears high into the sky and shifts to a light shade of orange.

The fire is much hotter than two minutes ago. I know the elders probably reduced the rank of the fire when I went in, but considering it is Auntie Kay I see in the pyre, the heat and strength of the inferno are probably all her work.

I'm momentarily amazed at the show she puts on, and I stare in awe at the twirling fire as it reaches far into the sky above. My admiration is interrupted when I hear Uncle grumble from above me.

"Must she really show off even at a time like this? The elders are going to make her regret it later."

I glance up at him questioningly. "Is it really so bad?" I ask.

Uncle catches my eyes and ponders my question. "No, I guess not," he responds after a moment. I feel him rubbing my head, so I relax into the warmth of the Kindling, letting it soothe my exhaustion and smother my conflicted emotions.

When I wake up, it's to the jostle of the furs beneath my chest. I look up from my lying position to see we have already packed up and begun traveling from our campsite last night. The furs and carpets we use to decorate our ger surround me, as do the familiar repeating patterns of lines and dots etched in the wagon.

Uncle Rivin is pulling the cart ahead of me, so he must have let me sleep here. That's kinda weird for him. He usually wouldn't let me anywhere near the furs, what with the lack of control I have over my flame. Maybe he is feeling generous after last night?

Well, I best get off before I do make a mistake and set everything alight. It should be fine as we have ways to fireproof a lot of the stuff we have, but it's not completely foolproof. I know better than most, considering how many of my own clothes I've burned through. Moments I really wish everyone else in the tribe would forget.

The last thing I would want is to accidentally burn through everyone's bedding. As forgiving as most of my tribesmen are, I doubt I would get off without punishment. I wouldn't forgive myself either.

Landing in the sand, I enjoy the heat of the grains as I dig my toes in. For some reason, I feel much more refreshed than I have in weeks.

I catch up to Uncle, greeting him amongst the quiet chatter of the rest of the clan. It is only apparent to me now how silent everyone has been since the disaster occurred. Last night's ritual must have been more helpful to everyone than I would have thought.

The same is true for me as well. Despite how painful it is thinking about how I will never see my mommy again, I feel like I can move forward now. It feels like the world isn't going to end anymore.

Smiling a bit at the thought, I ask Uncle Rivin, "Hey, where are we going now?"

I know we were traveling south for a week after the tragedy with us losing so much of our family, but now that we have held their memorial ritual, I'm not sure what the plan is.

"The elders have decided we will check out an old mining site the records show is in the area. They hope to find some minerals there," he says.

I look in the direction we are traveling and then back at the moon looming low behind us. "We're still moving south?" I ask.

"It's too risky to travel back the way we came when we have no knowledge of those who attacked us. We figure it will be safest to travel southwest for a time before going north again. It's already uncomfortably close to the coast as is."

I'm not usually interested in where we end up going, as lots of the desert looks the same. Rock-lands and mountains can sometimes be unique, but the desert is the same no matter where you are. So when Uncle mentions the mysterious coast I've always been told is a terrifying and horrible land of death, I can't help but be interested.

"Have you been to the coast before, Uncle? What was it like?" I ask. I've been told some crazy things about it, always how bad and scary it is. Even if I'm told it's a terrible place, I can't help but want to see it. It sounds so different I can hardly imagine it.

I guess my excitement is pretty visible because Uncle gives me a glare. "Solvei. Get that thought out of your head. We will do our utmost to avoid it at all cost, and you shouldn't be so curious about such dangerous things."

His attention returns forward, continuing to pull the wagon as he answers my question. "I've been there once before, but far west from here. It differs greatly from our lands; there are many dangerous plants and animals there, but the weather is the most terrifying thing. Even if you find cover to protect yourself completely from the storms or mist, you can't do anything when the air you breathe begins cutting at your throat." The look he gives me makes sure I know he is being serious, and I gulp at the idea.

The air itself attacking you? How is that even possible? It sounds ridiculous, but Uncle doesn't lie, especially not about things like this.

To mask that his warning only makes me even more interested, I divert the conversation. "Where is Auntie Kay? I haven't seen her."

Uncle smirks. "She's off hunting."

I look around the caravan, trying to find anyone else missing. "Who went with her?" I ask.

"No one. She's not allowed back until she brings her own weight in meat," he says, chuckling.

I gape in shock. Everyone knows how hard it is to find creatures out here. Well, maybe not that hard, but it would take forever to catch enough sandworms and jerboas to reach her weight. The only other thing I can think of that she might catch is scorpions or snakes, but they are impossible to find unless you are right on top of one.

Dingoes or fennec foxes are also an option, but I haven't seen any in days, so I'm not even sure they come this far south.

Uncle Rivin just laughs at my reaction, his voice booming louder than I have heard from him in a week. Calming his humor a bit, he continues. "I said last night she would be punished. She was much too wasteful, so of course the elders are gonna give her a hard job while she's trying to recover."

I feel bad for Auntie, but I can't say anything about it. I mean, I had less energy left last night than she did, and I don't want to get in trouble too. So keeping quiet seems like the best idea.

It's not much later when Elder Cyrus approaches us. "Morning, Solvei, did you sleep well?" he asks.

"Yes, Elder. I feel very energetic today," I answer. With Auntie Kay still on my mind, I don't want him to think I'm still tired from last night. Who knows what kind of hard work he might make me do?

Elder Cyrus is one of the five remaining elders in the tribe. All of them make decisions for the tribe together, but Elder Cyrus is usually the first one to take action in emergencies.

"Has your grandfather spoken to you recently?" Elder Cyrus asks.

I look at his face as he asks. I think he looks a bit hesitant to ask, but it is harder to read his emotions than others.

"No, Pop hasn't spoken to me since that day." And it's true, my pop has been avoiding me since Mommy passed. If I didn't have Uncle always by my side this past week, I'm sure it would have hurt more. But even so, I have always loved playing with Pop, so it hurts a bit that he doesn't want to see me.

"Well, you shouldn't worry too much, he'll come around. He still loves you. He just needs time, I'm sure." Elder Cyrus tries to encourage me.

"Ah!" He looks directly over my head, opposing the direction of travel. "Looks like Kay was quicker than we expected. What do you think she caught?" he asks Uncle.

Both Uncle Rivin and I look behind us. I can barely even make out the dot. How does Elder Cyrus know it's Kay?

It appears I'm the only one having trouble, because Uncle points out, "She's carrying a sack. Maybe she got lucky with a couple of foxes." Uncle shrugs, but still seems interested in what she might've brought back.

When Auntie Kay finally catches up with us, she has a large self-satisfied grin on her face. She throws the sack at Elder Cyrus's feet and smugly states, "My weight in game, as requested."

She's acting suspiciously. Both Rivin and Cyrus's eyes narrow at her. Instead of acknowledging the two, she just winks in my direction, and I can't help but grin with her, even if I don't know what she's being so mischievous about.

Elder picks up the sack with hesitance. Acting like something might pounce at him the moment he opens the bag, he unties the neck and lets the contents fall to the ground.

What drops out is hundreds of black charred . . . things. I can't tell what they are because they are already all burned to a crisp.

"What . . . is this?" Elder Cyrus seems more annoyed than confused. Maybe he already knows what the black things are.

Auntie's smirk seems to grow with the question and she repeats herself. "My weight in game, of course."

I try to stifle my giggle but fail.

As if emboldened by my humor, she continues. "I didn't think I would have to repeat myself to you, Elder."

I look over at Elder Cyrus and he does not look amused at all, but I see Uncle trying to hide the small twitch at the corner of his mouth.

"I understand that. But I want you to tell me why you have brought jerboas that are in such a terrible condition. Really, is there any flesh left on any of these rodents?" Cyrus interrogates her, but Kay's smile never wavers.

"Well, you said to bring back my 'weight in game.' I don't remember you specifying anything about its condition." She picks up one of the charred jerboas and continues. "It's not like we can't make use of them anyway." She swallows the animal whole as if to prove her point.

Elder Cyrus just sighs. He seems more exasperated than angry. "So, what? You just found a swarm and fried them all? You were supposed to work for this."

Auntie puts on a face of fake annoyance and replies, "Hey, do you even know how hard it was to pick up all these rodents? There's hundreds of 'em there. It took me so long."

"Obviously not long enough," the elder comments before giving her a command. "Add them to our supplies, then. And don't try to skirt your duties next time." After saying this, he walks back to the front of the caravan.

Once he is gone, Auntie offers me a jerboa, which I take after she cuts it up.

"Isn't it bad to anger Elder so much? What if he makes you do something worse next time?" I ask Auntie, worried about how much she provoked Elder Cyrus, even if it was funny.

Instead of Auntie, it is Uncle Rivin who answers. "I'm sure she'll be given a harder task next time, but Elder Cyrus isn't mad. I'm sure he finds it just as amusing as we do. Why do you think she isn't being punished right now?"

I see Auntie Kay nodding along. So maybe they are right. But why wouldn't he laugh if he found it funny too?

While I chew on half a jerboa, Auntie groans, realizing Elder left her to pick up all the rodents once again.

CHAPTER TWO

The Chthonic

We stopped to camp for the night about an hour ago. It took a while to help the adults set up the gers, but now that our shelter for the night is set up, I have some free time.

No better way to use it than angling.

I grab my angler line, check that my knife is secured to my waist, and walk until I'm a couple hundred paces from camp. Sand spreads in all directions around me, the desert extending far beyond my line of sight. The mountains in the north are the only remotely interesting difference along the horizon.

Well, as boring as the desert is, at least angling is always kinda fun.

Crouched low to the ground, I unsheathe my knife and hold it in front of me, ready to strike with a twitch of my arm. I dangle the angler line from my other hand, slowly dragging a small rock along the sand. My angler is a string made from a bunch of animal hairs tied to a stone at one end. Uncle showed me how to make them myself a year ago, and ever since I've been forced to remake my angler whenever it breaks. It was better when he let me use the one he made; his don't break as easily as mine.

I make sure to keep the angler at arm's length from my body. I've had my fingers bitten enough times to have learned my lesson.

I tug on the string, teasing the rock along sand for almost ten minutes before, finally, I get a bite. With a burst, sand flies everywhere and a sandworm bites at the stone of my angler. As its teeth latch around the stone, I bring my knife down and cut through the soft flesh.

The worm, almost as long as my forearm, squirms around on the sand without its head. It always creeps me out how they twist and wriggle when they die, although it doesn't take long for the worm's erratic movements to still.

Mom told me once that the sandworms misunderstand the movement of the stone as that of a jerboa. Because of this, we can mislead them into thinking they can get an easy meal, which allows us to have an easy meal.

I still think it's amazing that they can feel movement through the sand. It's no wonder you can find them everywhere, because jerboas are everywhere. It must be like a free lunch for them whenever a swarm of jerboas runs along.

I catch two more sandworms, these ones slightly smaller, before the sun sets and I have to rejoin the tribe. I quickly show off my catch to Uncle Rivin. After receiving his praise, I get to skinning the worms. We could just eat all of it, as they are super delicious, but the skin can be used in the lining of our tarps. We could use it for other stuff like clothes, but to create a tarp needs hundreds of worm skins. So after skinning the worm and storing the meat for myself, I toss the skin in a cart piled up with them and other unused animal parts.

A few days later, rocky ground finally replaces sand. While the color of everything stays the same, at least the landscape itself differs from the horrible repetition of the sandy desert dunes. Not by much, though. While the features of these rock-lands can sometimes be impressive—massive boulders balanced in seemingly impossible ways or vast valleys and canyons—most of the time, rock-lands tend to just be the same as the desert, but with rock instead of sand.

Fortunately, today seems like a lucky day. The sheer walls of the canyon rise high around us as the elders lead us through the wide, bowl-like valley. The rattle of our wagons as they roll over hard rock echoes around us, overwhelming the quiet chatter from a few of my tribesmen. Many of them have their eyes glued to the surrounding canyon, wary of an ambush or pursuers.

The attack over a week ago was not the first, but it had been—by far—the most devastating. We lost nine of our own and I'm ashamed to admit it, but I hardly paid attention to any of the losses besides my mom. My chest hurts even thinking about her, and I know many of those around me feel the same way.

My tribesmen are worried. The first time we fought off our attackers without issue, but they tracked us down within the week and slaughtered a third of us.

My elders tell me nothing, thinking I cannot handle the news. But they talk, and they don't always realize I can hear them; they assume I'm asleep or just not paying attention. I've overheard them talking about the concerning ability our pursuers have of controlling water.

Water is . . . not really something I know anything about except how "dangerous" and "scary" my elders tell me it is. But, when I see even the strongest of my elders shifting their eyes in paranoia, I can't help but feel a knot in my chest.

I look up at the walls of the canyon closing around us the farther in we go. The canyon slowly closes into a ravine with towering cliffs blocking the sky from all but directly above.

A shrill whistle echoes around us and we slow to a stop at Elder Cyrus's signal. I look to the sky in search of the source of the whistle. It is rather easy to spot the bright glow of the fiery bird. Her wings, each as long as I am tall and flaming an intense yellow, are unmistakable from this distance.

She flies at an envious pace until she reaches our caravan and lands on the wagon at the front with the other elders.

Elder Enya is one of the most amazing áed I know. Her binding with fire has reached the highest rank our tribe has seen in generations. At least that's what my mom said. She idolized her, so of course I think she's incredible too.

Everyone gathers around Elder Enya, wondering what she has found. Because of her ability to alter her form, Elder Enya has the greatest capability for scouting. We don't rely solely on her, but she can cover so much more ground than anyone else.

"Everyone, I have found a cluster of chthonic. They have dug themselves into the walls of the gorge ahead of us and are likely to ambush us should we push forward," Enya says. I've always found it strange to hear her voice coming through her beak in this form.

"Is there any way around?" Elder Cyrus asks.

Enya was probably expecting his question, as she is quick to answer. "There is, but it would delay us a few days at minimum and it would take us through crocodile territory."

The elders seem thoughtful, and unsurprisingly, Auntie Kay is the first to give her opinion. "If there is risk either way, then why not just push through the gorge and take on the chthonic? At least we know we'll get something from wiping them out. I'm sure their tunnels are filled with ore."

Her broad smile and the fact that she is almost bouncing on her feet make me think she's motivated more by excitement at the idea of a fight than any interest she may have in the ore.

Uncle does not agree, though. "If we go through the sand crocs' territory, then at least a fight isn't guaranteed. If we are careful, those fat lizards won't even bother to move."

Ready to defend her opinion, Auntie turns to Uncle Rivin. "You know what those things prey on, right? What happens if—"

Auntie Kay is interrupted by Elder Cyrus. "Stop, stop. Yes, we all know what would happen if there is a nest of those around, so we will proceed with our current path," he says, then looks at Uncle. "Objections?"

Uncle shakes his head, nonplussed, and then we are off again.

Elder Cyrus approaches Uncle and me once the caravan is moving.

"Solvei, I believe now is a good time for you to learn to fight. I'm not going to have you fight just yet, but I want you to be there watching when the fight starts. Make sure that you stick close to Rivin now, okay?" Elder Cyrus says.

"Really?" I ask.

I have always been kept as far away from fights as the tribe could keep me. I always hate that I am the only one who isn't allowed to take part. If we ever need to fight, everyone will join in. No one in our tribe wouldn't fight for the protection of their family. Of course, some are stronger warriors than others, but everyone knows how to wield a weapon, and our flames when needed. Everyone except me, that is. I've always been told to wait until I am older, no matter how much I try to prove I am ready.

So if I am finally being given the opportunity to be included, I will happily jump at it, even if it's only to watch.

Unfortunately, Uncle doesn't seem to agree with me. Dropping the shafts of the wagon, he raises his voice at the elder. "You can't! It's still much too early for her. And it hasn't even been two weeks since we lost a third of our tribe. Why would you risk her now?" he pleads.

He simply wants to protect me, but it annoys me he won't give me the opportunity to prove myself. I want to contribute my part to the tribe. I want to show everyone that I am valuable, even if I'm not as strong. And if I can learn to fight too, I might be able to prevent any more deaths in the future. At the very least, I won't be a burden on those who would protect me.

I know I can't do much now, but if I try, I might find a way forward for myself. I might discover a way to be beneficial to the tribe.

As I'm about to argue against Uncle Rivin, Elder Cyrus does it for me. "It is exactly because we had such loss that she should start. There is a greater need for her to learn now than ever," he says sternly, locking eyes with Uncle. After holding his gaze for a moment, Cyrus sighs and continues. "Besides, what will happen if we get into another conflict we can't handle? She should be able to protect herself should she find herself in a situation where we cannot help her."

At Elder's words, Uncle turns away, looking toward the rest of the caravan that has now opened up a generous distance between us. He snatches the handles of his wagon from the ground and begins moving again without a word.

Elder Cyrus shifts his attention to me. "After you have seen the way we fight for the first time, I'll have Kay begin your weapon training. You want to learn the spear, right?"

I nod emphatically at him. "Yes, Elder!"

The spear is the weapon my mom used. She was the best in the tribe with it and was even allowed to use one of our tribe's special relic weapons. Her spear is made of dark silver metal with pearly white engravings lining its length. The three relic weapons we have are unique, as they enhance our control and power over the flames pushed through the weapon. Mom described it as the weapon becoming like an extension of her being.

Now that I am finally allowed to train with the spear, I want nothing more than to make my mom proud and earn the right to use our tribe's cherished spear, just as she did.

"Good." Satisfied, Elder Cyrus nods and walks off.

I run back to Uncle's side and settle into a comfortable stride beside him.

We walk in silence for half an hour before Uncle speaks up. "Solvei, stop here for a second." He puts down the handles of his cart once again and removes a small red pouch from his belt. He turns and hands it to me.

"I should have given this to you a while ago now."

I gingerly take the pouch and pull the strings to look inside. Mom's dark glass marble is held within. She always kept it close when she was still with us; she thought of it as a lucky charm. The marble fits easily in the palm of my hand. The glass is impossibly dark and I'm unable to see out the other side at all. Despite the marble's incredibly black glass, the focal point at the core of the marble is clear to see.

A bright pink flame frozen within is completely visible from any direction, as if the marble is not even there. The flame is incredible to look at. It doesn't move at all but still seems to burn strong. The color itself is unheard of. I've seen Elder Cyrus reach a blue flame, but never anything like this pink.

"Solvei." Uncle Rivin snaps my attention away from the marble. I look up and lock eyes with him. "I need you to promise me you will keep yourself safe. I need you to promise that when we engage the creatures, you will do nothing but stay by my side and put yourself at no more risk than necessary."

I don't want to worry Uncle, so I give him an immediate response. "I promise, Uncle."

Uncle has changed a lot since Mom passed. He no longer raises his voice in every conversation and his temperament has become much calmer. I appreciate everything he has done since she left us. He's stayed right by my side ever since Mom was taken, and moments like this show how much he cares.

I wouldn't have thought the same before the incident. Both he and Mom taught me to control my fire. He used to get angry at me a lot when I failed in the tasks he gave me, and afterward, he would give me harder and harder objectives to reach.

I thought he hated me.

I feel guilty for having thought that. He has proven he cares. I was probably sulking because his training was so hard. I hope he stays this way, though; an angry Rivin is a scary Rivin.

Nodding in contentment—and probably not knowing about my inner thoughts—Uncle returns to pulling the wagon along as Elder Cyrus calls for everyone to fall into position.

The last of Elder Enya's feathers merge into her arm as she finishes her transformation. Having spent the past thirty minutes changing back into her more standard form, she'll probably be joining the fight this time.

The elders all concentrate at the front with a few more of our better warriors. Kay is walking there beside them, holding her poleaxe casually over her shoulder.

Me, my uncle, and the three other wagons are concentrated toward the center of the formation.

As we move farther into the ravine, a group of three on each side separates from the caravan and begins scaling the sides of the gorge, following our caravan from above. As we advance, our formation solidifies. The better warriors take the front with their weapons while everyone else takes a position behind them.

The line of tribesmen curves around our wagons, covering the front and sides while only leaving a few at the rear. Or at least that's how it should have gone from memory. Now the loss of so many members is so much more obvious than before. Whereas previously, a wall of áed stood at the front and still left some to guard the rear, now we have four at the front and only Enya left to defend our back. Of course, if a fight actually starts, Uncle and the three others pulling their respective carts can easily join in. I have seen each of them effectively wield their own weapon, after all. But with so many missing, it feels empty.

We travel like this for nearly half an hour. I try to watch along the gorge walls for the chthonic or the tunnels they are known for. I don't see anything, but the elders must, because Elder Cyrus calls for us to halt.

With a flick of his wrist, Cyrus sends a flare into the sky and then commands everyone, "Defensive positions."

Still not seeing any enemies, I cast my gaze around the gorge. I don't see any tunnel openings or anything else we should be worried about.

The other wagon carriers around us drop their handles and join Auntie Kay and the elders at the front, forming a line across the ravine. Uncle leads me behind the carts to join Enya, who hardly acknowledges us and keeps her eyes scanning the walls behind us.

This is usually where I would be taken away by Uncle and another tribesman until the fighting is over. The few times our tribe has been surrounded and we couldn't run, I've been hidden under a wagon where Uncle would make sure I never had the chance to actually watch any fighting myself.

When everyone is in position, a flicker of movement attracts my attention to the top of the right ledge. The flanking groups on both sides of the canyon descend with hurried steps. When did I lose sight of them? I haven't really been paying attention, and I will get grouched at by Uncle if he finds out, saying I don't focus enough on my spatial awareness. He'll say my senses won't grow stronger if I don't train them.

As the flankers reach about a third of the way down, they disappear from sight. From where I am, it looks like there can't be a gap large enough to hide even an arm, and yet three áed easily disappear. On both sides.

I look up at Uncle, but his face remains still; he doesn't seem surprised at all. Turning back to the ravine walls, I finally realize what they found. It must be the chthonic tunnels. I never thought they'd be so well hidden. How did Elder Cyrus notice them so quickly?

I cast my gaze across the rest of the valley ahead of me. How many are hidden from sight? Is there one right beside me? I glare at the closest rock wall, daring it to hide a tunnel from me.

Shrill, high-pitched shrieks crash through the silence. Smoke billows out of the tunnel entrances, both the two that our tribe used to enter and far more along the walls ahead of us. I spin around, making sure the wall beside me doesn't suddenly become a tunnel.

The shrieks pick up in intensity, and a creature that can only be one of the horribly ugly chthonic surges out of a tunnel ahead of us.

The creature's long arms and wide shoulders stand out above its scrawny legs and slender hips. Terrifyingly long claws grow out of its thick hands and scratch deep into the rock underneath as it throws itself toward our defensive line. Its wild, erratic eyes twitch upon its scratched-up face, scanning over my tribe as it charges. The chthonic reaches incredible speeds; its long, bladed fingers dig into the hard stone with each leap of its hands.

I grab at Uncle's arm as the creature literally throws itself toward our tribe with no hesitation.

It doesn't even come close. The chthonic is burned to a crisp the moment our tribe hurls our fire toward it. Scorched ash is all that remains.

While the single chthonic was early to the fight, its brethren are not far behind. Hundreds of the monsters erupt out of the tunnels, their legs almost unnecessary as their powerful arms carry them forward. They quickly fill the gorge, rushing with unwavering bloodlust toward us. Their mad fixation has them clawing over one another, cutting into many of their own in their attempt to get to us as fast as possible.

The sight drains the strength out of my legs and I hug myself to Uncle's side. He is quick to put an arm around my shoulder and hold me close. I appreciate Uncle's protection; he places himself between me and the charging monsters.

The chthonic are throwing themselves into the constant stream of fire our tribe throws out. So many of them die immediately. But plenty still break through, either flinging themselves over the streams or shambling over the walls at the sides. Those jumping over the wall of flames are immediately cut down, preventing the chthonic from breaching my tribe's formation. The creatures climbing the walls suddenly screech in pain as their very platform ignites. Most are burned on the spot. The chthonic that survive launch themselves at my tribesmen, only to have their bodies pierced, cut open, and delimbed before bursting into flame.

Over the sound of the shrill chthonic screams, a loud roar cuts the air. The wave of monsters stills for a moment, then splits down the middle. A chthonic larger than any other stands amongst them all, holding itself with its arms, legs barely touching the ground below it. Its claws are longer than the entire length of my arms, and they slice through stone beneath the monster's weight.

One more roar reverberates in my ears as it charges through the other chthonic, shredding any of its brethren that don't get out of its way in time. Its claws tear apart the stone, sending earth flying in its wake. Its speed increases with every swipe of its long arms.

Both my pop and Elder Angarika run forward into the path of the monster. Pop holds his long saber, while Angarika readies his halberd for the gigantic chthonic charging toward them.

Both weapons are burning a bright white, the flames hot even from as far as I am from the fight.

The giant chthonic catapults itself toward the two elders, both claws poised to strike. I am only able to see Elder Angarika block the claws, but Poppy's arm moves too quickly to see. It's obvious what happens, though; Pop cuts the massive chthonic right down the middle. Both elders step out of its path and let it collapse behind them before moving deep into the chthonic crowd. The fallen chthonic screeches and lashes out at the closest of its kin for a few moments before the life finally leaves it and its movements slow to a stop.

Pop and Angarika push through the chthonic, dismembering or killing with each swing of their respective weapons, sometimes launching waves of scorching hot flames through the horde.

The fight does not last much longer; the remaining chthonic scramble to escape. Our flanking units cut the stragglers down as they come out of the smoking tunnel system.

I shiver a bit at the remaining bodies buried and burning within piles of ash. The chthonic are terrifying, horrible creatures. But they could do nothing, even with them outnumbering us by an incredible amount. They attacked and were all slaughtered. How could something so scary be dealt with so easily? How can we take these insane creatures out with such ease, but lose so many to a small group of strangers?

Thankfully, it doesn't look like anyone was injured in the fight. Uncle Rivin nudges me and I realize I am still clinging to him. I loosen my grip on his body and grab his hand as he leads me to the burning pile of corpses.

I am hesitant to go toward such an ugly scene, but Uncle is insistent, pulling me along. Once he considers us close enough, we stop, and he says to me, "Remember, we have taken their lives, so it is up to us to make sure they have not perished for nothing. Take their energy, Solvei. Send out your inner fire and consume them."

I do as he says and send out as much of my inner flame as I can. It coats the ground as it approaches the leftover corpses. My darker red flame, much weaker than everyone else's fire, slowly eats away at the flesh of the monsters.

I have to look away because of how disgusting the view is, but as much as I look away, my inner flame is still a part of myself and I feel the creatures burn away, fueling my flame and enhancing me. Really, I'd get a less detailed image of the disgusting creatures if I only had to look.

I've killed hundreds of sandworms myself and consumed plenty of creatures in the same way, but it feels different this time. These creatures that had such bloodlust for our deaths, creatures we slaughter without hesitation aren't normal. They are more savage than most beasts, and yet they are cohesive. They live and fight together. Like us.

It's not like I regret that we killed them. We have to do what we can to survive. And if we try to leave them be, it's unlikely the chthonic will return the sentiment. So why do I find it hard to watch such a scene? Why is it hard to watch their deaths if it is for our survival?

Maybe I pity them, or maybe the deaths in our tribe have shown me how sad death is.

I finish burning through the corpses I've been allowed and move away as everyone else burns a portion for themselves.

I return with Uncle to the wagons to set up our ger. With a tunnel network to explore and many needing time to rest after the fight, we'll be here for a few days.

CHAPTER THREE

Spear Training

After Uncle and I set up our ger, Elder Cyrus and Auntie Kay come to talk to me. Elder goes over the battle and explains the process. He shows me the signs in the area that indicate the presence of the chthonic. Elder Cyrus explains that we hadn't stopped where we did solely because he noticed the tunnel entrance. He explains that the geography of the ravine would funnel the enemies into a concentrated point, which allowed us to fire upon them without being wasteful. The flank group's task was to create as much fire in the chthonic tunnels as possible to force them out, which led them toward us.

After a long lecture about the battle, he leaves me alone with Auntie Kay to learn spearmanship.

"Olvy. Are you ready?" she asks.

"Yes! Let's start. Let's start!" I exclaim. Jumping on my feet, I am so excited to finally start, especially after having sat through Elder's boring lecture.

Auntie laughs and passes me one of the wooden poles she brought with her.

"A stick?" I can't help but ask.

It is a straight bit of wood without even a sharpened point. Any attack from an adult would destroy this thing in a second.

"Of course," she says, as if it's obvious. "A proper spear will be too heavy for you, so you get a stick."

"But won't we burn it when we attack?" I ask.

She seems amused by my words. "Oh, I didn't think your control was that bad."

I know I have poor control, but I don't want Auntie Kay to think of me that way, so I immediately deny her accusation. "It's not! But don't we coat our weapons in flame? How would that not burn the wood?"

Auntie is smirking at me now. "Of course, by controlling your flame. How else?" She proceeds to show off and coat her own wooden stick in fire, before stopping the flame and showing the staff is still in the same condition as before.

I know I can't do that, so I look at my feet, disappointed I will not be allowed to learn the spear. It'd be easy if we treated the wooden stick with patterns like we do our clothes—they can handle some heat—but tinder like that would burn in a moment in my hands. I've been so excited to learn the spear. I'll be letting my mom down if I can't learn her weapon.

"Ah. Olvy, sorry. I was just messing with you. You don't need to control your fire that well yet. Keep your flame in your grasp and you'll do fine," Kay says.

"Really? But how can I attack without fire?" I ask, relieved but still not understanding.

"Well, the base of spear arts doesn't use fire. We enhance our weapons with flames because it is natural for us. There are races out there that use these same weapons but cannot use fire."

It seems strange—another race that is intelligent enough to use weapons yet can't wield fire? I imagine a cute fennec fox standing only on its hind legs and trying to swing a saber in its forelegs. I giggle to myself at the strange image.

"Why don't you show me where you are in your control, Olvy?" Kay asks.

I bring my eyes away from Auntie and stare at the dusty stone below. I don't want her to think I suck at it any more than she might already.

I am about to refuse, but her expectant face makes me reconsider. She is trying to help me. The least I can do is be honest with her.

So while I bring up my arm, I try to lower her expectations. "I'm not that good, I still lose control sometimes."

I start by creating a flame on my hand; the crimson flame pops into existence without issue. I grow the flame in my palm until it reaches about as high as my hand is wide, and I concentrate.

It is easier to make larger flames than to control the minuscule changes to the flame. So I want to try to push myself to do something I still struggle with. I try to keep control over the flame while also separating it from my form.

At the edges of my palm, it begins to separate. I raise the flame until only a strand is left connecting me with the flame. I take a breath and concentrate, focusing with everything I am to remain in control for the next part.

I cut the thread, splitting my attention into parts. I struggle to keep control over the flame hovering above my palm. It is a lot like dividing myself into sections. I need to focus on this now-separate flame, but I also need to focus on myself at the same time. The flame flickers and falters under my watch. Not wanting to fail with Auntie still watching, I push more of my attention away from myself until the flame steadies.

Success! I did it! I have a small bit of flame hovering a finger length above my palm. It may not be very impressive compared to the others in the tribe, but this is the first time I've properly been able to do this.

I proudly show it off to Auntie Kay, grinning up at her.

She shares my grin. "That's amazing Olvy! Good job."

After holding for a moment, her smile becomes sheepish and she breaks eye contact. "That's great, Olvy. But, uh . . ." She doesn't continue. Instead, she moves her hand to pull some of my hair from behind my ear.

The hair she pulls into my sight is blazing with red flame. I gasp, and the small ball above my hand dissipates as I grab at my hair, forcing control over myself again.

It's so embarrassing. I was so happy to have succeeded, especially with Auntie Kay there to see. But having lost control of myself like a little kid, I can't help but feel ashamed.

"C'mon, you did well. You still separated your inner fire from your body. That's a great achievement. I'm sure in no time at all you'll have better control than me," Auntie says, trying to cheer me up.

I am relieved a bit that she doesn't think too badly of me, and I can't help but imagine a time when I can get control as good as hers. Everyone knows she's extremely skilled for her age, only losing to the elders who have decades of experience.

"Come, why don't I show you how to hold a spear?"

She has me pick up the wooden stick again. I put more effort than necessary into making sure I don't lose control of myself again. Embarrassing myself in front of her once is enough.

"The first thing you should know is that there are different styles for fighting with the spear. The core of these styles is the stance you should take."

She picks up her stick and places her hands near the blunt end.

"The first stance is the simplest, used with a basic style focused on thrusts."

She moves her feet and body into a stance and I try to imitate her, placing my hands on the bottom of the makeshift spear and spreading my legs like Auntie.

"For this stance, keep your legs about shoulder width apart and keep your hands an equal distance apart along the spear shaft."

She relaxes from her stance and comes over to me. I try to hold the stance as she inspects me.

"Bring your front leg back a bit and turn your foot to face where you're look-ing. Your back foot should point outward to keep your balance."

Kay twists my body with her hands so I'm facing in the direction my left leg is pointing. Moving up to my hands, she pushes my rear hand farther back on the spear.

"Your hands should be far back on the spear but do be careful to keep some sticking out a bit so you can readjust without losing your grip. For this stance, you want to keep your left hand on the pole with your palm facing away from your body, while your right palm should face inward."

She flips the direction I am holding my left hand in the way she says. Holding it like this feels a bit unnatural; I would usually keep my hands facing the same way when picking things up. I know Auntie Kay knows what she is doing, though, so I let her move my hand without complaint.

"Finally, you want to keep your back hand at your hip, and you have the basic stance," she says, giving me a once-over before continuing. "Good. Now we can move on to how to properly thrust. The first thing you should know is the task each hand has. Your forward, left hand is your guide and will be what you use to control the aim of your spear. The guiding hand helps you target either an opponent's head or chest."

Kay shows this by moving her left arm up and down while in her stance. I mimic her, moving my stick up and down.

Tempted to try striking, I push both my arms forward, trying to thrust like I'd seen done by others.

"Nice try, but you're doing it wrong. If you had let me finish, I would've told you how to strike correctly."

Worried that I have annoyed her, I look up as she tries but fails to suppress her smirk.

"You don't want to thrust with your forward hand, just leave that to control your thrust. Your back hand should be where all the strength comes from. Keep it at your hip and try to move it as little as possible until you thrust. When you do thrust, you should be twisting your body to give yourself more power."

As she tells me what to do, she guides my body through the motions slowly with her hands.

"Now I want you to try a thrust yourself," she says, and I do as told. I stop myself from pushing with my left hand and only push with my right. When I do so, it feels weak, even in my hands.

"You're not twisting your body, Olvy. Try again. Move your hips and legs."

And so, for the next few hours, she teaches me to throw a simple thrust.

I am disappointed we spend so much time on only one move, but Auntie seems happy. She compliments me whenever I do the strike correctly and eventually moves on to introducing footwork into the strike. It is essentially just taking a step with the thrust, but Kay says it increases the strength a lot.

By the time the sun sets, my body feels like lead, and the moment I make it to my bedroll in our ger, I am out.

It's been a few weeks now since I started my spear training with Auntie. She's had me working until exhaustion every day since. The rest of the tribe was busy mining in the chthonic tunnels for whatever resources they could find.

Those first few days of training were intense but mostly filled by doing the same few movements over and over. It was tiring and boring. On the second day, Auntie taught me a few more attacks achievable with the basic stance, which I was then forced to repeat until I couldn't feel my arms.

I thought learning the spear would be fun. Memories of watching my mom dance with her spear made me want to learn it. I found it interesting. Even if I thought it would be challenging, I never imagined it'd be as boring as it is. We eventually moved on to a new style, this one far more interesting.

At least it was at first.

This new stance and style rely much less on thrusting attacks and more on sweeping strikes. Auntie Kay says this style is better when fighting by yourself, compared to the thrusting style, which is best when standing side by side with allies.

As interesting as the style sounds, the process of learning it is the same as the first. Many long hours of repeating the same movements, until the boredom almost hurt more than my arms.

Well, I complain about the boredom of it, but it's not much different from the tedium of walking for ten hours straight. Once we began traveling again, my training time reduced to a few hours in the evening after we set up camp.

Apparently, the tunnels the chthonic dug were much more beneficial than expected. There were deposits of both cobalt and coal, which is an incredible find for us. The elders even said we could skip the mining site we planned our next stop at, much to everyone's relief.

Those hunting us had been waiting at a few of the áed's communal resource deposits in the area. Somehow, they have information exclusively shared amongst áed. Considering we aren't local to this part of the wasteland, we have to rely on information from generations ago. This is particularly annoying because there are some places we found completely stripped of resources.

Enya had spotted the enemies waiting in ambush a few times. Finding supplies now is great, as we were running low and the location we planned to go has a decent chance of us running into our unknown aggressors again.

It is a good thing we found coal. My reserves were near empty, and relying only on hunting animals is not reliable. Of course, it is possible, but I'd spend most of my day angling to get only barely enough. Other animals can be hunted, but I can't do that myself yet.

For me, and any other young áed, coal is important. My inner flame is not yet hot enough to sustain myself from other rock types like cobalt as the rest of my tribe does. Coal burns at a low enough temperature that even my flames can burn it. If I consume enough coal, I can easily go a week without eating again. We can consume animals to strengthen ourselves, but they aren't the greatest for actual lasting energy.

Now we're heading toward a known timber-acquisition site. With as scarce as wood is in the wasteland, there is an understanding held between all the tribes to only take what is necessary.

This is especially important because the charcoal created with this wood makes up most young children's diets, when they are too young even for normal coal.

The timber site is west, so I only have a few more days to enjoy the rocky landscape before we are back in the sands of the desert.

I can only hope that we will be given a few days again to rest when we reach it. I don't enjoy having to continually travel, even if I am used to it.

CHAPTER FOUR

Kenna Tribe

I can finally see it. Our destination is on the horizon, a large pointy thing unmissable amongst the featureless sandy wasteland. Uncle calls it a shipwreck. A ship that had been wrecked. He was cagey about what a ship actually is, but something that big can only be some form of shelter. Maybe the eastern races lived out here at some point. No áed would be silly enough to build their own homes from timber, no matter how heat-resistant they manage to make it.

Timber is an important resource for us even if it is more prone to accidental damage than any other type of material besides some furs. It is an extremely easy-to-use crafting material that doesn't require us to set up entire workstations to use, as most ores do.

We use wood in our traditional rituals that require us to let the fire begin naturally. These fires, like the funeral pyre, are given no direct interference to allow the will of the world to determine if it is the correct time for it. If the pyre doesn't start, we would try again somewhere else the next day. After the fire reaches a certain strength, we then oversee and control the flame for the rest of the ritual.

The most important use for wood in áed tribes is the production of charcoal. As the youngest member of the tribe, I have seen no one but myself consume it. I remember being told how important it was for me to eat it when I was first trying to be allowed to have normal mined coal.

Now, as much as I want to move on from coal and consume other rocks and metals like everyone else, I know I can't. My flame is still far too cold to burn through them and I would only give myself indigestion.

Unfortunately, I'm speaking from experience.

Turning my attention back to the shipwreck far in the distance, I struggle to make out any features besides its outline. Objects in the desert have a weird way of obscuring their size and distance. Some things you'll see don't change their size for hours, making you think they are really far away and huge. Which then turn out barely bigger than they appeared hours ago. Then there are the times when you only notice something minutes before you come across it and the thing turns out to be massive. Most of the time it happens because of the dunes of sand blocking sight, but I doubt that's all there is to it.

Elder Enya returned from scouting the shipwreck not long ago. Turns out it's one of the former circumstances; we still have many hours of trekking before we reach it. The other news she brought was that she'd seen an encampment of another áed tribe already set up.

This comes as a surprise to everyone; almost a year has passed since we last interacted with another tribe. I am excited to meet them. Have they been to the ocean? The coast isn't too far south from here, so it isn't impossible, especially if they frequent the area.

It is odd to see another tribe this far south. Our tribe only came down so far to keep out of the reach of the murderers of our tribesmen. And we had been traveling farther south than ever before. The elder's plan now is to head west and place the mountain ranges between us and the known search area of our threats.

I hadn't been close to the fight that day. Elder Enya had not noticed the ambushers within the mine, and by the time our first scout checked it out, we had already gotten too close. A group of our elders and the better warriors of our tribe engaged them after they came charging out toward us. Uncle led me away, keeping me from seeing the fight.

When our tribesmen came back, they were nine members short, four of our elders missing. My mom didn't come back. A pained tightening pulses in my chest at the memory of that day.

They had been waiting for us. Water wielders slaughtered many of our tribesmen before we even realized what had happened. Nobody expected it. The monsters had too many able to control water for us to fight without losses, even while we had the advantage of numbers.

My elders found maps on their bodies. They contain markings denoting many of our race's most common resource collection and camping locations in the area. They had more information on the local area than we do.

It was also determined they weren't working separately and there is a larger supporting structure for this group. We found notes confirming that there are many other groups and that they are definitely hunting áed.

Nobody told me this directly. Everyone still believes I don't hear when they talk after my bedtime. They prevent me from listening when I am around. They try to make me think we are heading south because of the "untouched resources" we can find in this area.

I feel uneasy about them keeping this from me; do they not trust me? My thoughts have been consumed with grief since my mom's passing, but now? They still keep the biggest issue we face from me. Do they assume I can't handle it? It is irritating.

It has been on the minds of everyone in the tribe for the entire month since the attack occurred. Whenever they believe I'm not listening, or I'm not around, they talk. It's all they talk about. They speak of their fears of what lies behind us. They speak of the uncertainty in the path before us.

While in my bed, overhearing their subdued comments, my thoughts resonate.

Why did they attack us? What are they after? Are they following us?

The information taken from the group that attacked us confirms they are targeting áed. But why?

It is a good thing we will interact with the other áed tribe soon. Giving them the forewarning not to head north might save their lives.

The ship is enormous. At least a hundred of me tall. The front is flat, but the sides curve to a point at the back. The walls of the ship taper to a sharp spike at the top, pointing into the sky.

The foreign tribe's camp is set up a short distance from the shipwreck. Their ger are familiar and of the same style as ours, but their wagons are odd. They are huge; way too heavy for an áed to reasonably pull without tiring themselves in minutes. The space in the wagons is double, maybe even triple, that of our wagons.

Each wagon has this strange box at the front with padded seats on top. Thin metal tubes poke out of the box at random points and curve back in. It looks like someone took several spears and bent them out of shape before shoving them into the thing.

The weirdest thing is that the wagon does not have the long handles at the front that allow for easy pulling. Do they have to push it from its rear? It looks inconvenient.

They have three of the things, and I don't see any standard wagons around, so they must be able to push them somehow. Even if they would be incredibly heavy with three carts worth of storage.

The elders go off to give their initial greetings and discuss trade while those who don't go with them, including Uncle and me, move to set up our own camp for the next few days.

I don't notice until I try to set up the framework of our ger that Uncle's attention is on the other tribe.

We learned they are the Kenna tribe. Not a name I am familiar with, but I'm sure those older than me had interactions with them or heard things in the past.

I can't set up the ger by myself. I am too small to reach the parts necessary to bind it in place.

I am going to call my uncle's attention back to helping me when I see Serafi watching the Kenna tribe in much the same way. Glancing around, I find myself to be the only one not paying attention to the interaction between our tribes. My tribesmen look unsettled. Many of their faces contort into frowns as they look on in concern. Very few tribesmen are helping to set up the gers, instead waiting for the elders to finish their introduction.

Does the Kenna tribe have some unsavory history with our tribe? Nobody looks hostile at least, so it's probably nothing too bad.

Raised voices from the interaction between the leaders of our tribes reach my ears. Looking toward the elders, Elder Cyrus is loudly berating the Kenna elders, who look back at him with wide eyes and pale faces. The other elders seem just as furious as Cyrus; my pop has a deep scowl and seems to give off smoke. It is the closest I've ever seen him to losing control. What could possibly make him so mad?

"What kind of absolute fucking morons do you have to be to make such a dumb mistake!? Your greed and misjudgment have and will cause disaster to . . ." Elder Cyrus's angry tirade is muffled by the hands abruptly covering my ears.

I scowl up at my uncle, who looks back at me unapologetically. I'm old enough now that he shouldn't be covering my ears because of a swear word. It's embarrassing that he thinks I'm not mature enough.

I try to remove his hands from my head, but it is a futile effort; he won't let go.

When he finally does let me go, I hear the words of Elder Cyrus as he and the other elders rejoin the tribe. "We are leaving. Pack your things back up. Those not packing, go and collect as much timber as you can before we leave."

Apparently, our history with the Kenna tribe is worse than I thought. I don't remember Elder Cyrus ever being so mad. I've seen him yell before, of course, but he is usually pretty careful with his words, so to hear him swear is rather shocking. It frustrates me being the only one not in the know, so I ask Uncle Rivin, "What did they do? Why are we mad?"

"Something bad" is all he gives me. I wait a moment for him to elaborate before becoming impatient.

"Well? What is it?"

Uncle just remains quiet, not giving my question even a thought. Anger flares within me. Why does he not trust me? This is something important to our tribe, so why does he want to keep me in the dark?

Irritated, I storm off, planning to ask Auntie Kay. I'm sure she'll tell me— she's pretty bad at lying.

As I approach her, I can tell even she is mad about what the Kenna tribe has done. "Auntie!" I call. "What did the Kenna tribe do? Uncle won't tell me."

Auntie Kay looks at me, then over my shoulder. Turning around, I see she is looking at Uncle.

"I'm sorry, Olvy. I shouldn't say." She looks at me sadly, but it irritates me more. Why does nobody trust me? I ball my fist and grit my teeth. My hands tremble in anger, and a sense of helplessness washes over me.

The urge to run to my mommy and cry into her lap washes over me. But that does nothing but amplify the tangled knot of emotions within me. Anger, frustration, and sadness well up in me, and before I know it, my legs are moving. The sand passes beneath me as I run.

Straight out into the desert, I run. I don't know what I'm doing or where I'm going, but I want to be alone. I run until my legs tire and slow; dropping to a walk, I keep moving. My body feels sluggish, exhaustion dulls the sharp edge of my ire. As I drag my feet across the sand, my dejection only stings more. I'm not truly a part of the tribe. They try to protect me, but it feels more like they see me as a burden than a valued member.

I look back and see that I've run a fair distance from the shipwreck. Our tribe has begun traveling to the left of the wreck. Looking toward the moon, I see I've been running north, so the tribe must be heading east.

Why east? Didn't we come from that direction? Aren't we heading west?

I can see Auntie following behind me, still almost a hundred paces away. Even if she comes to take me back, I don't want to yet. The cold silence beckons me to return, but the frustration is likely to overwhelm me again should I not try to do something for myself, even if it is simply to travel by myself for a bit.

I turn my walk to the east, not enough that I close the distance with my tribe, but enough that I can keep them in sight.

I say nothing when Auntie catches up with me. I just continue walking. If she wants to take me back, she will; there is no way I'll be able to stop her if she wants to carry me back forcefully.

Fortunately, she doesn't do that. Instead, she matches my pace and walks beside me.

"Olvy, I'm sorry. We only want to protect you, ya know."

"I know." And I do know, but I don't want them to protect me. I want them to be honest with me. I want them to trust me.

A few minutes pass with both of us walking in silence. I don't want to talk, I want to walk and forget everything right now. I'm still hurt by Auntie's decision not to tell me, so I don't pay attention to her.

Auntie Kay eventually breaks the silence. "They gave them information."

Not sure what she's talking about, I can only let out a "huh?"

"The Kenna tribe sold the location of all our major resources to some strangers for those wagons they now have." She looks me in the eye with a seriousness I haven't seen in her before. "Those wagons are of similar design to the weapons the group that attacked us had. The Kenna tribe gave the most likely locations any áed may travel to a group that is now hunting us."

I look back at the shipwreck with disbelief. They are the reason my mom is dead? It's unbelievable. Did they sell out our race for a couple of shiny wagons? No, it is unreasonable to believe they did it on purpose, but we lost so many because the attackers knew where we would be.

As horrible as it is to know that some of our own are the cause of our suffering, or at least contributed to it, it changes nothing.

"Thank you." I appreciate her telling me, even if it's bad news; I prefer to know than not to.

"For what?" she asks, confused. Maybe she never actually realized how I feel. Then why tell me?

"You trust me enough to tell me. Nobody will trust me with anything. I am never expected to do anything for the tribe, and when anything important happens, no one will tell me. Everyone protects me, but I can't help but feel they do it because they have to, not because they consider me an actual part of the tribe." I let out my concerns, clutching my arms together as I tell her.

Auntie pulls me into a hug, and I bury myself in her stomach.

"Olvy, of course we think of you as part of the tribe. You're family," she says while rubbing my back. "I'm sorry we didn't trust you. We wanted to keep the truth hidden so you wouldn't be any more hurt or worried. Also, you are still young. Nobody in the tribe is expected to participate until they reach adulthood. It's still early for you." She pauses for a moment, reaching forward and tilting my head up to meet her eyes.

"Look at your spear training. We have you learning so that you can do your part in the future. So whenever you feel neglected or rejected, focus your feelings on improving yourself. You should never worry about not being a part of the family. Even if you take years to contribute anything, you will never be an outsider. And you will never be unwanted."

I look up into Auntie's eyes and see the concern she has for me. Maybe I am being silly; there is no reason to believe they don't consider me family. But since my mom passed, I can't help but feel like this.

My value to the tribe is nothing compared to those that we lost. It's been constantly nagging at the back of my mind: I am scared they will see me as not worth the effort to keep around. I am scared I will be abandoned.

Maybe I've doubted myself and my position because of the way Pop has been treating me. I used to talk and play with him every day before the incident. But now? He won't even look at me anymore. After losing Mom, that feels like twisting a knife in the wound. It stings thinking about it.

I talk about them not trusting me, but I haven't even done the same myself, have I? I haven't trusted that they wouldn't abandon me. But should I have ever worried about that?

Looking back, both Uncle and Auntie have done a lot for me without needing to. Uncle has been looking after me in a similar way my mom did. He makes sure I am eating and kindles my inner fire every night. Auntie has been trying to keep me happy and attempting to turn my thoughts away from Mom.

I may still have doubts about how some in the tribe may see me, especially Poppy, but I still should have trusted Uncle. I overreacted, and I should apologize to him.

But first I should do the same to Auntie Kay.

"I'm sorry, Auntie."

She smiles at me and rises to her full height.

"C'mon, do you think you're ready to head back?" she asks.

I nod and we turn toward the tribe. It'll take a while to return, so at least I'll have some time to think about how to apologize to Uncle Rivin.

CHAPTER FIVE

The Coast

It has been a few weeks since our interaction with the Kenna tribe and my ensuing tantrum. I don't like to refer to it as such, as it makes me sound childish, but it was. I am embarrassed about how I acted, but Uncle has been more open with me since, so I consider the situation positive.

I apologized to him when I made it back to the tribe, but other than a simple nod, he pretended like it never happened. Even though he acted this way, he has been willingly telling me things he would've refrained from mentioning before.

He explained to me what they had found on the bodies of those who had killed my mom. We had confirmation that they were hunting áed. Most of what he told me I had already pieced together from the conversations he didn't know I'd been listening in on. But there were parts of what he told me I hadn't known before.

The weapons they used were strange, causing almost as much confusion at the beginning of the fight as those with water bent to their will. It is unfortunate that their weapons had been mostly made of wood; there was barely anything that remained for investigation after my tribe's retaliation. Uncle hadn't been in the fight himself, so even he doesn't know what to think about the odd weapons.

We are traveling in the opposite direction we originally planned, now heading southeast. The elders shook down the Kenna tribe for all the information they sold. Every destination or route we could take in the west is already in our enemies' hands. We can avoid all the places they know about, but that would require us to travel for months without restocking. It is possible, considering our lucky haul at the chthonic mines, but extremely risky.

The elders decide that taking the path along the coast is safer. Mom, Uncle, and Pop always regaled me with the dangers of the coast and the ocean that lies beyond. They always pounded it into my head that there is no worse place to be than along the coastal region within breathing distance of the ocean. The terrifying tales only ever tempted my interest. So what if it is dangerous if it is new and unique?

Despite my own—secret—thoughts about the coast, it goes to show how dangerous this enemy group is if the elders would prefer to travel to the source of innumerable horror stories than to come in contact with them.

Our gers usually take about an hour to set up, but for the past few days, the elders have had us set up a single ger in as little time as we can manage. They encourage us to do so faster with each attempt. The elders are concerned about possible rain that may occur at any time closer to the coast. They decide it will be better to have everyone crowd in one ger than to waste time constructing the others.

With our practice, we can get a ger up in a bit over a quarter of an hour if everyone is helping. For the sixteen remaining members of the tribe, it is a tight fit. But safety is worth a bit of discomfort.

While we expect to be forced through the coast eventually, the elders plan to avoid it as long as possible. The path we need to travel has us following a line of cliffs that extends the length of the coast. There are few places to climb the cliffs, especially with the wagons we need to take with us. Our intended route is through a cave system that allows passage to the top of the cliff. After that, we will travel as far north as we can, out of the reach of our enemies.

I swing my stick in a long strike from right to left, knocking Auntie's stick out of its path as she attacks. It continues to the ground to my left and I take a step forward to take advantage of the opening. As fast as my hands can move, I bring my spear back before thrusting it forward into Auntie's chest.

Auntie Kay doesn't take it, though; she steps back, keeping away from the tip of my stick. I reach farther, pushing my arms out, trying to hit her as I lean in with my body. Unfortunately, it isn't enough. Auntie moves to the side and swings her own wooden pole into my side, making me stumble forward, off-balance.

"Olvy, you keep making the same mistake. Stop trying to force an attack, it's making you overextend. If your attack doesn't hit, pull back. Your defense should always be more important than your offense. It's good to see you take advantage of openings, but do not open yourself to counterattacks."

I have taken Auntie's advice about putting my thoughts into improving my spear training. She's even started to spar with me, not going much further than a few attacks or blocks at a time. Auntie has shown me how to block or deflect and then how to counterattack. I'm not very good yet, only able to do it when she slows her strikes. Slows her strikes more than normal, I mean. I've seen her training with her poleaxe, and I struggle to even see the weapon with the speed it moves in her hands.

Unlike before, when I had been jabbing at air, I can now feel myself getting better. Having a point of comparison makes it much easier to see if I am doing well. I can tell it will still be a while before I will fight Auntie properly, but improvement feels good. And I enjoy sparring with her.

"Once more, Olvy. Don't extend this time, just defend and counter. Defend, then counter."

From all the stories I have been told about the coast in my life, I expected it to be different from the wasteland. I expected to see an entirely new area filled with plenty of interesting wildlife, constant heavy rainfall, and plants. Oh, how I've wanted to see what a plant looks like. Instead, I am disappointed to find that the coast isn't that different from the desert. Sand as far as the eye can see. Ugh, the last thing I hoped for was more sand. The only thing that indicates that we have made it to the coast is the white splotches littering the sky to the south.

"How do we know if one of those will rain on us?" I ask my uncle, who is, as usual, pulling his wagon beside me.

"They usually get darker before we need to worry. Also, we have a few days before we reach land where rain will be a concern," he says. Why does he even bother to call this the coast? There isn't anything different. Obviously, the actual coast is still to the south.

We've been traveling alongside the cliffs for days now, following it southeast closer to the ocean than most of the tribe is comfortable with. We expect to have to spend about two weeks traveling along the coast. Most dread the journey.

I feel a bit guilty about it, but I am excited to explore somewhere new. It's disappointing that the coast doesn't start with an entirely new landscape, but I'm holding out hope for something interesting closer to the ocean. I make sure my excitement is well hidden from everyone else, though; I've already been told off by Uncle a few times for it. And he remains cranky for a while if he thinks my mind stays on it.

As much as I want to see something interesting, I know better than to go looking for danger. We wouldn't have so many horror stories of water and the places associated with it if there wasn't something dangerous about it. So, not only for the good of Uncle's stress, I suppress my curiosity and listen.

We have finally reached the dangerous area of the coast. Earlier today, we had a scare where it looked like it would rain and we had our ger set up in minutes. A record. The shimmering wall reflected light as it approached from the south. The sky above darkened as dark gray clouds condensed and closed in above us. That was the last I saw before Uncle snatched me up and forced me inside before the walls were properly bound.

Our preparation was needless. As the sound of rain approached, it gradually slowed before vanishing entirely. After the elders had called all clear, I walked outside only to see the dark gray sky had returned to its normal blue. It was as if there had never been rain to begin with.

The elders say it is the desert protecting us from the rains. But I don't understand what that means. How can the sand beneath our feet stop rain coming from the sky?

We packed up our ger and were on the move again soon after, treading dry sand once again. Fortunately, other than that small scare, there has been little need to worry about rain. The skies stay mostly cloud-free.

I notice in the distance a few odd shapes appear, all retaining the same color as the sand they sit on.

When we are close enough to touch them, I discover it is a plant: the fabled growths that live outside the wasteland. Uncle, with me beside him, breaks off a piece and holds it out to me. "I've told you of plants before, yes? We call this type an acacia shrub. Do you see it is made of wood? This is where all wood comes from."

Of course, I know wood comes from plants, but this is my first time seeing one.

"They made the ship from these plants?" I ask, shocked. How many of these plants would they need to make something that big? How do they keep it all together? The small bit of wood in my hand crumbles with barely a touch.

"No, they used bigger plants. Trees. In areas with water, plants can grow freely. This also means that if we ever run out of sources of timber, we would have to expand our search outside the deserts, endangering ourselves in the process."

I'm pretty sure I've been told plants are mostly green, but the plant in front of us has the same hue as the desert that surrounds it.

I don't think I could be more disappointed. I've been expecting huge looming trees with colors I could hardly imagine. But instead, I get this twiggy-looking sand shrub. The surrounding land is still barely different from what we always travel. I can only hope there will be some of these trees I've heard about or new wildlife to see.

Hopefully, the coast has a lot more to show than these shrubs.

Eldest Ember would be laughing down on me now if she was watching. When I asked for more, I meant variety, not quantity. Well, at least the land looks different than I am used to.

I cast my gaze around the dense shrubbery that now makes up the desert landscape. If only the acacia shrub wasn't the only plant to see, it might be amazing. The plant has turned out to be much more flammable than anything I've seen before, having vaporized the moment I tried to chew some. Only once have I seen anything burn up that quick, and that was when Auntie Kay convinced Elder Cyrus into a competition of flame strength. The poor dingo didn't last long under his blue flame.

Considering his flame is so much hotter than mine, I am curious what would happen if he had some of this shrub.

Actually, with how dense the shrubbery has become and how easy it is to ignite, we've had a few accidents that caused a surprisingly fast spread of fire amongst the plants. It was only due to the fast reaction of a few tribesmen that it didn't spread out of our range of influence.

I wonder what it would look like if we set it all alight? I'm sure an entire landscape of fire would be amazing. I can feel a part of myself yearning for such a sight. The elders are decisively against it. They would rather keep the option as a way to protect us, I think, in case we come across another of the groups tied to our family's murderers.

We only have about a week until we expect to reach the passage, and so far we've been lucky to not have to deal with any actual rain. There were a few scares, but the clouds dispersed before they could reach us.

Although we were lucky not to have rain, the constant setting up and taking down of our ger has cut into our travel time. It is decided that we need to extend the time we travel, so now we spend half the night moving as well. As much as I try to stay up with everyone, I always find myself sleeping on the back of Uncle's wagon.

The first time rain hits us, we already have a few gers set up for the night. I snap awake at the loud slam of the door. The thrumming sound of sand impacting the walls of the ger in the wind can be heard beneath the surrounding chatter. It is only when I shake off my sleep that I realize the ger is not fluttering as it would with a usual sandy breeze.

The worried faces of those around me are my indicator that it isn't sand impacting the outer tarp of our ger. I look up at Uncle Rivin, who happens to be sitting beside me, and ask for confirmation. "Is this rain?"

"Looks like it," he says. "It's not too heavy for now, so hopefully it lets up soon."

I want to peek out the door. I wonder what the rain looks like, but the concerned expressions on my tribesmen's faces stop me. It's unlikely they'll let me even approach the door. I look up at Uncle and see him watching me; his eyes narrow at me and he puts a hand on my shoulder, pushing me back down into bed. Yep, no getting past Uncle right now.

We have people tasked with watching the walls for leaks, but with how tense everyone is, it won't be necessary. They'll all be watching.

For now, I give up on any adventurous thoughts and snuggle into Uncle's side as I once again fall asleep to the warmth of Kindling.

All in all, the trip through the coast wasn't as bad as everyone kept saying it would be. While I can tell there is still some stress running around the tribe, it is mostly due to the little sleep everyone is getting. We aren't too far from the cavern pass now. It should be amongst the rocks ahead. Elder Enya claims we will be inside the cave system within the hour, which is good because we have pushed later than usual into the night. We hope to make a proper camp once in the safety of the caves.

It's been a rough few weeks of travel until this point and I can tell many are wearing thin. At least with the target in reach, we find the energy and excitement to make the final push.

We were lucky not to have much rain. When it came, we had plenty of time to prepare ourselves. I never did get an opportunity to watch the rain, though, other than seeing it in the distance. I was always the first to be hidden away inside and out of sight. Uncle somehow knew of my interest and wouldn't let me out of his sight. It's been annoying. A few times I'd tried to sneak a peek out the front door when I thought he was distracted, but he would always put a stop to it.

The land is currently bathed in the pitch-black darkness that always occurs before the Ember Moon's appearance. The bright stars and our fires are the only light around. Usually, our tribe likes to keep a clamp on showing our flames unless in a fight, but the dark night between the bright moon hiding and the Ember Moon's appearance is much too hard to traverse without light.

I am walking with Auntie for now, having slept the past few hours in Uncle's wagon while everyone walked. I've long since given up fighting against Uncle Rivin to let me stay up, especially when I find myself not remembering how I fell asleep half the time.

Auntie Kay once again helps me with my spear forms. Well, the forms that rely on movement, at least. The constant walking prevents me from practicing more stationary moves or styles, but Kay insists it is better than wasting our time. I spin my stick in the flowing motion Auntie taught me before I pivot into a thrust. A dim red shade is cast over my spear, and the landscape around gradually becomes visible as the Ember Moon finally reveals itself for the night.

The Ember Moon's light sweeps the darkness of the surroundings and redefines them in a deep shade of red, like burning cinders. The Ember Moon is the manifestation of the Eldest Ember and brings her protection and good fortune when it appears in the sky. It is a good sign to finish the last leg of our journey through the coast under her protective eye.

* * *

"What is that?" The question brings my attention toward the ocean. I don't know what I am looking at. It's like a cloud but seems to cover much of the southern horizon. The wall of cloud, tinted red by the moon, begins from the ground and covers much of the sky in the distance.

"That's fog. How much time until we reach the cave?"

So it's called *fog*? Must be similar to rain; everyone seems worried but no more than when we have to deal with rain.

"Be calm, everyone, we are not far from our destination now. We will increase our pace for now, but we should have time to spare once we reach the pass," Elder Cyrus reassures everyone.

Following his words, the tribe picks up the pace. The faster clip means I can't continue my spear training, so I throw my stick into the back of Uncle's wagon alongside our furs and dismantled gers before running to Auntie's side.

Casting my gaze back toward the fog, I can't stop a chill from running through me. I'm not sure why, but it unnerves me. I was fine with the rain, and even seeing the clouds coming never worried me. At most, I have been worried about being told off when trying to have a look at it.

But this cloud, or fog—something about it has me worried. Jitters in my leg tempt me to sprint away as fast as I can. Instinctually, I need to be as far away from that fog as possible. The feeling only gets worse the longer I watch it. I'm not the only one who feels this way; many of my neighbors toss fearful glances over their shoulders. The tension in the tribe increases by the second.

Even Auntie Kay is worried. I always thought she wasn't scared of anything. I've seen her take on a colossal-worm without batting an eye.

As I watch the fog, it looks a lot bigger than before. The wall of water seems to reach higher into the sky. With each step I take, the more it seems to spread.

"Is it getting bigger?" I ask Auntie. I think she already notices as well. She holds her gaze on the coming fog for a while before she responds.

"No. It's moving," she says to me before raising her voice. "Cyrus, we should pick up the pace, it's closing on us faster than it should. It's unnatural," she calls to the elder.

He nods back before giving the order for everyone to rush. Auntie Kay picks me up as everyone increases their tempo to a jog. I resist a bit against her hold, not wanting to be carried again, but settle after I realize how worried she looks. I reach my arms around her neck and hold on.

With the fog approaching from our back, I have the perfect view of it over Auntie's shoulder. The loud breaths and heavy footsteps are all I hear as we run from the looming threat. The fog moves closer and closer as the minutes pass, covering more of the sky than ever.

I can see the point on the ground where the fog begins now, which makes it much easier to tell how fast it is moving, and the speed terrifies me. What would take us hours to pass, the fog does in barely a minute.

There is a collective cry of relief when Elder Cyrus calls out, "The cave is in sight, not much longer now. Keep moving!"

I feel Auntie pick up her pace as I jostle in her grip. She runs to the front of the tribe, and I watch as the elders fall back to our rear. Uncle and those pulling the carts are helped by their tribesmen, allowing them to keep up despite the weight.

The fog closes in terribly fast now. The cliffs block the sky to the north, and our south is cut off by the impending fog wall. We will be squashed between the two soon enough. In the distance, back where we came from, the fog finally reaches the cliffs. It doesn't so much as slam into the wall as it consumes it. There is still some distance remaining until it reaches us, but we don't have long.

I squeeze myself tighter into Auntie as I watch the fog rush closer to the back of our caravan. The elders unleash powerful streams of flame, hoping to hold it off as long as possible.

Fighting water with fire is difficult, but the elders know what to do. They can't have their inner flame in the fire that contacts the water at all unless they want it to be vaporized, which would be like cutting off an arm. The flames they create fling forward fast and with intensity. They then cut their inner flame from the fire, leaving it to rocket forward and burn long after it has left their control. This prevents harm to themselves but still helps to protect everyone from the encroaching fog.

The torrents of fire launched behind us do well to keep the fog at bay, but it doesn't take long for it to push at our sides, edging ever closer. My arms stay clasping tightly around Auntie's back as I tremble. I push my head into her neck to hide from the fog as it moves closer than ever.

My eyes are blocked, but I still hear when the others in the tribe throw their fire into the fog. I'm sure otherwise by now we would be completely enveloped in the fog. Only the fire being spent in all directions is keeping the terrifying vapor from reaching us.

A scream accompanying a sizzling noise rings out amongst the sound of the roaring flames. My head shoots up only to see Elder Angarika recoiling in pain while steam rises from his affected arm. Others are quick to cover him, and before long he returns to burning away at the fog.

I look behind me at the cave opening; we are so close now. If we keep our pace, we should be able to reach it in a dozen seconds. The fog already surrounds us, and it becomes more apparent the farther we go that we cannot hold off the fog for much longer. The only air we can breathe anymore is becoming filled with mist. My throat stings. Holding my breath doesn't help, it just agitates the rest of my body instead. If this keeps up, our situation will crumble.

It all seems hopeless until a fierce cry from the back of our scrambled caravan pierces through the roaring blaze and panicked shouts. I watch in awe as the fire surrounding us twists and writhes on its own. The flames engulf us all as a clear, fiery tunnel is created. I feel Poppy's inner fire within the blaze, protecting us all.

Everyone rushes through to the cave opening. Looking back, I see Poppy being held upright by Elder Cyrus, struggling to walk through the pain. The tunnel of flame lasts until he reaches the cave opening and others take over. They keep their flame streams burning away the fog trying to push into the cave system with us.

A bit of coordination between tribesmen allows a tarp to be set up over the narrow opening and everyone can relax.

I watch in hopelessness as Poppy collapses.

CHAPTER SIX

Collapse

Now that we are within the safety of the cave, many collapse in either exhaustion or relief. Maybe both. The patterns on the tarp's edges seal off the entrance, blocking any encroaching fog from following us into the cave.

Everyone has been accounted for. Not all escaped the fog without injury, though. Some have charred, blackened skin on their exposed arms or faces.

Pop has it the worst. He is alive, thankfully, but unresponsive. The amount of his inner flame burned away by the fog is immense. It will take a long time for him to recover, assuming he recovers at all. An áed's flame is their soul, their sense of self, and their entire being. If he loses enough of it, there is a risk he will lose a part of himself.

It is shocking to witness the true horror the coast can bring. I've been warned about the rain and water before, but they never explained how dangerous it can be. Er . . . well, they have, but I didn't truly believe it. I haven't been able to picture the possibility of some nonphysical thing able to bleed through my tribe's ever-impervious flame walls.

The fog replaced the very air around us. What sort of damage could it do if we hadn't found the cavern pass in time? Would our gers have been enough to keep it out? Or are they only effective against the rain?

The warnings they gave me always highlighted the danger of rain rather than fog. Thinking back on it, nobody was too worried until we discovered the fog moved so fast. Is this fog different from what they have encountered before?

Auntie is quick to place me on the ground before checking me over with hasty eyes.

"You're not hurt anywhere, are you, Olvy?" she asks while moving my limbs to her whims.

"No, Auntie, I'm fine." I'm a bit shaken up after the ordeal and my chest still stings from breathing in the fog-tinged air, but I'd rather not say that at the moment. There are others who might need help more than I do.

Uncle appears not long after I reassure Auntie Kay, looking just as worried. After I relieve his concerns, I notice Uncle's cart behind him. It is burning.

"Uh . . . Uncle? Your wagon is burning."

"Huh?" he says as he turns around. "Oh, shit!" and he is off running.

Auntie just laughs as we follow.

Uncle Rivin attempts to salvage some of the animal pelts and skins that were set ablaze. The tunnel of fire must have burned through a lot of our less fire-resistant equipment. A glance confirms my practice spear is unusable now.

How unfortunate. Now Auntie will have to let me use a real spear.

Smothering my growing smile, I turn to the growing pile of charred pelts. A fair few are thrown out. Uncle was putting off applying fireproofing treatment to many of our collected pelts until we reached somewhere safer. That decision is coming back to bite him. Still, better the pelts than us.

"Was that fog different than normal?" I ask, wondering if he's experienced it before.

He stops and turns to me. "Yes. It was unnatural, faster than it should have been."

He returns to his work, contemplation clear on his face. "Also, I am not sure why, but I struggled just looking at it. It was like I was staring death in the eye. I have never felt that before, not like that."

"Yeah, I'm the same. Last time I felt like that was when I was a little girl near the western sea," Auntie Kay says.

Uncle's wagon isn't the only one that lit up in the run for the cave. The other carts' contents all experienced damage to some degree. One ger will be unusable for the foreseeable future, having lost much of its outer tarp. The two remaining ger will be rather uncomfortable—with eight áed per ger—but it isn't the worst. As we are already in the safety of the cavern, we don't need to set up our ger and simply organize our sleeping arrangements on the sand.

I want to approach my pop. I know he hasn't wanted to talk to me in a while, but I still care about him. And anyway, he risked his own life for everyone, so he must still care somewhat, right?

As I approach his sleeping form, I see he is being tended to by my cousin Serafi. Serafi is the youngest in the tribe besides myself and yet she is still double my age. She has him laid on a bed of cobalt, but his flame has yet to consume it.

"Is he going to be okay?" I ask, sitting beside her.

"Probably," she replies in monotone. Serafi's odd, grumpy attitude usually scares me away from her. She tends to be rather harsh with her words, and I've learned to keep my interactions with her short. She voluntarily takes up the role of carer when anyone in the tribe is sick or hurt, but always gripes about it. A "probably" is a rather favorable response from her.

I watch as she places more cobalt around him, almost burying him with how much she loads onto him. She is using a good part of our stockpile, but she would've gotten permission from the elders. The quicker Pop recovers, the better, after all.

"When will he be better?" I ask. I shouldn't have, because she turns to glare at me.

"He'll be better when he's better. Now go annoy someone else."

I quickly do so to not agitate her any more. I'd think she dislikes me if she didn't treat everyone the same way. No, maybe she doesn't like anyone. I don't really get her, but she has taken care of me when I used to get sick on chilly nights, so she probably cares somewhat, right?

A few days pass with everyone recovering after such a stressful ordeal. After weeks of nonstop travel, the elders decide it is a good time to relax for a few days. Of course, there will be a great need to hunt once we leave the confines of the cave system, but for now, they are satisfied with letting everyone recover.

We move farther into the cavern pass to get away from the opening. We can paint our tarps with the strange patterns of our ancestors to keep the fog at bay, but nobody truly knows how the odd assortment of dots and lines actually works, just that it does. A repeating pattern encircles the edges of the tarp, creating a tight seal between it and the rock, but not even the elders are certain if they will hold out the fog permanently, so we stay away just in case.

Scouts have been watching the other end of the tunnel and have reported the fog to be equally as thick on that end as well. It was only earlier today that the fog receded to where it is safe to leave. The elders are fine with allowing another day of rest, even with the possibility of continuing.

When Auntie continued my spear training, I was extremely excited to use an actual spear. So when Auntie Kay tossed me the stick she's been using—the stick I forgot about—my disappointment must have been palpable. She laughed for a good while at my expense, clutching her stomach and wheezing. She actually wheezed!? It wasn't that funny!

Of course, she'd found my anger even funnier. I'd been close to storming off when she calmed herself and brought out another spear, a real one this time. She'd been messing with me about the stick. I was conflicted about being toyed with, but the allure of finally using a real spear attracted me too much.

The spear is a lot heavier than I expected, and it took me a few hours to adapt my training to it. My greatest difficulty with the added weight of the spear is that it's hard to change direction and speed on a whim as I could with the stick. My first wide sweep attempt didn't stop as easily as I was used to, and the spear dragged me along with it.

I wish it had been anyone other than Auntie Kay who saw me trip over myself; she's never been one to hold back her laughter. At least she was the only one to see.

I get exhausted much quicker using the weighty spear than the stick. After this last extensive session with Auntie, I drop onto my back and just lie there.

With my head low to the earth, I catch movement out of the corner of my eye. Turning to my side to find what caught my attention, I see . . . nothing. Just the thin sheen of sand covering much of the stone cavern floor. My eyes scan over the ground. When nothing catches my eye, I consider maybe it was my tiredness playing tricks on me. That's when I see it again.

The sand is moving.

Well, it does for a bit. The floor almost looks alive for a moment when the small grains of sand hop along the surface before returning to rest.

I watch as the barely noticeable rhythm of moving sand continues.

Standing up, I realize I can't even see the dance from this high. I need to show Auntie; this is so cool. I run up to Auntie Kay and grab her arm.

"Auntie, Auntie, you have to see this. The floor is dancing."

I pull her with me to the spot where I saw the sand moving.

"All right, Olvy. All right." She gives in to my will, smiling.

I lie down and drop my chin onto my hands, patting the ground next to me so Auntie will lie with me. When she joins me, taking the same position, I point to the ground in front of me. A second goes past and I almost think it isn't going to happen when the sand dances once again.

"See?" I say.

"Huh. That's neat," she says, increasing her focus on the ground. "I wonder why it does that," Auntie continues. "All right, I think it's time to get back to your training. You look like you have plenty of energy."

A few hours later, the dancing sand seems to grow in intensity; the ground vibrates under my feet. I'm not the only one to notice either. The elders decide it is best we move, worrying that the shaking might increase.

Without our gers set up, it takes much less time than usual to pack up. After about an hour of walking up the incline of the tunnel system, we reach the opening at the top of the cliff.

It is dark when we finally breach the surface. It's strange, though; I thought for sure it should still be daytime. A glance at the sky shows the moon isn't visible and the stars are gone. Instead, the sky is a dark gray, barely noticeable in the dim light. I don't know what it is at first. My attention focuses more on the low groaning hiss that seems to grow louder the longer we are outside.

"Everyone, get back into the tunnels." Elder Cyrus's words are sharp. His eyes are glued to the skies above, and it is only then that I realize the entire sky is an enormous cloud. Its dark gray color covers every point in the sky from horizon to horizon.

We are about to follow his direction when the hissing noise explodes in intensity. The sound of an eruption of sizzling whips our heads to the ocean. An immense column of steam billows out from the body of water visible in the distance. The clouds above grow darker still as the steam rises.

The ground trembles. It trembles so much more than the measly shaking that occurred up 'til this point. The world seems to drop from under my feet as I lose my footing. I regain my balance and run to Uncle's side, holding on to him as the world continues to shake.

I'm too unsettled to focus on anything but the shaking. Uncle puts his hand on my back, which helps me steady myself immensely.

When I look up again, I'm met with the shocked, gaping, terrified faces of those surrounding me. Looking back toward the ocean, an intense icy shiver floods my body. I immediately lose control of my form—all control I had disappears as the icy, instinctual dread consumes me.

The wide pillar of steam rising from the ocean hides a bright red glow within. The glow rises within the mist and another thrum of the earth echoes in my chest. The steam splits, and for a moment I refuse to believe what I see. From within the steam steps a titanic beast. The impact of its claw on the ocean below sends another crashing tremor through my legs. I lean entirely on Uncle to keep upright, and my arms blaze red, but I'm too terrified to care.

I'm frozen in my place, I can't focus on anything but the calamity. My chest wretches and coils, and a sob bubbles its way up my throat. My lips quiver and my inner flame curls in on itself, trying to hide away from the world. An otherworldly terror. Its size dwarfs mountains and its sheer mass creates tsunamis. Immense, razor-sharp teeth line its jaw. Its large skeletal spines sear with bright glowing magma rolling down its sides into the water below.

The sizzling sound of water boiling slowly settles into a constant reverberating rumble. My chest trembles as the sound rolls through me.

"Back into the tunnel. Now!" Elder Cyrus yells.

I hold on tight to Uncle as we move back into the depths of the cavern. Another step from the crocodile Titan, another tremble of the ground. I'm only able to keep moving with Uncle keeping me upright.

A quake knocks many to their knees once we are some distance into the tunnel. Away from the exit, they are content to huddle and hide.

I hug my face tight into Uncle's side as we sit on the earth. I can't get the image of that horrifying, gigantic creature out of my mind. Every time the earth shakes, I'm scared we are about to be crushed under its gargantuan foot. I try to remain as quiet as I can, smothering my sobs before they can make a sound.

The ground continues to periodically tremble. The intensity of each quake only increases as time goes on. Each time the earth around us shakes, a spike of terror runs through me. I clutch harder, hoping for Uncle's protection and comfort. His hand rubs my back reassuringly, but I can feel him shiver too.

The tremors grow louder, stronger, closer. Horrific apprehension for each upcoming quake makes the time between stretch endlessly.

Cracks and fractures form in the tunnel walls, growing with each subsequent tremble. A crevice opens up far down the tunnel, the cave ceiling collapsing above it.

Then, when it seems like the seismic beating can't get louder, it stops.

We wait with bated breath. Each moment more unbearable than the last. Until a quake, somehow infinitely more intense than any previous, fractures the tunnel. Fissures materialize all along the walls. The cave ceiling crumbles under the massive movement of earth.

I don't know if someone calls for it or if it is decided unanimously, but everyone is up and running for the surface. Uncle picks me up and runs for the exit, leaving his wagon behind.

Another quake hits. This one feels like my inner fire is trying to be squashed. Uncle stumbles beneath me and I find myself thrown to the side of the cavern.

The ceiling caves in above the lagging members of my tribe. I let out a cry as I watch so many of my family crushed beneath the stone. My breath hitches and I'm unable to look away as they are buried before my eyes.

"Solvei!" I hear Uncle scream as he tries to make his way toward me on the unstable ground.

I move to stand up when another crash rocks the world around me. The ground under my knees crumbles and I panic—my arms flounder to find something to hold onto. By luck my body halts, wedged between the walls of the new crevice.

I can't move and the panic in me surges.

"Uncle! Help!"

Terror overwhelms me. I try to escape, but I'm stuck too tight. I scream, but that doesn't help. Trapped and scared, I can't stop myself from bawling.

"Solvei! I'm coming!" I hear Uncle call. I see him at the top of the crevice, quite far up. I've fallen so much farther than I thought.

He is climbing down the fissure when another thundering shake rocks the earth. The cave above collapses, closing up the crevice I'm now stuck in. The sounds of screams and panicked shouts cut off completely.

"Uncle?" I call once the shaking stops again.

I don't hear a reply.

"Uncle?" I repeat. He can't possibly be gone, right?

"Uncle Rivin? Please!"

I wait and wait, but I never hear a response. He must be blocked behind the cave-in. There's no way he didn't get out, right?

I keep trying to tell myself that he is still fine. I don't even want to consider that he isn't. I can't handle it if he isn't.

Another quake hits and the fissure frees me from its grip.

Only now I am falling into the abyss below.

CHAPTER SEVEN

Only One Step

'm alive.

In a lot of pain. And at the bottom of a fissure. And stuck.

But alive.

The fall hurt. I collided with the walls of the chasm many times on my way down. The impact with the stone below almost snuffed out my flame altogether.

It is only when a boulder dropping from above crushes my leg that I truly feel pain. The agony slams through me, silencing any other aches I gained on the way down. I try to pull my leg out, but it won't budge. Lightning jolts up my leg and through my body with each attempt.

The rumbling of the earth is reducing in intensity now. I am still scared; I don't know whether I will be buried alive or if the ground will break open underneath me once again.

I don't move. Not because I can't—although with my leg stuck that might just be the case—but because I can't bring myself to do it. The world closes in on me, the walls closer than ever. Every cluster of rocks falling from above makes me clutch my arms tighter. The next stone to fall could be my end. The pain and fear freeze my body, and my arms feel like they have been replaced with brittle shrub sticks.

I am alone. Stuck down here away from my tribe.

They are still alive, we only got separated, I'm sure of it. There's no way they'd die because of a little rockfall. I didn't, and they are all much stronger than me. It's impossible for them to be gone.

If I wait here, I'm sure Uncle or Auntie will find me. I need to wait for the tremors to stop, and then they'll come and help me and everything will be back to normal.

I'm overcome by a wave of nausea, and my inner flame pulls in on itself. My eyes struggle to remain open as another, now subdued, quake drops a pile of gravel and sand over me. I'm exhausted and the gravel weighs down on me. The impacts from the fall took a lot out of me. I'm in too much of a battered state to do much at the moment. So I try to ignore the intense throbbing in my leg and let my consciousness fade into darkness as the earth continues to rumble around my body.

I don't know how long it's been since I went to sleep, but I can't feel the tremors anymore. So at least that monster isn't nearby.

I will never be able to get the sight of that Titan out of my head.

Hopefully, enough time has passed since it left that they might have started searching for me.

"Uncle? Auntie? Anyone? I'm down here."

I wait for a minute for some form of response. Hear nothing but the echo of my voice.

I am completely alone. I don't know if I am buried underground where they can't get to me or if they think I am dead, but for now, whatever the reason, I am alone.

Moving my attention to my trapped leg, I find I can't feel it anymore. I dig away the gravel and sand covering my leg and much of my body until my leg is visible. It doesn't look good; it's gone black like charcoal below my knee. My inner fire won't flow back into it no matter how hard I push. I try to tug it out with what strength I have, but it shows no signs of coming loose.

Thinking positively, at least it doesn't hurt much anymore.

The next thing I try is to push the boulder off me.

It doesn't budge.

I would be closer to pulling off my leg than moving that boulder. My fingers scratch at the gravel and stone to try and dig under my leg, but that only gives more room for the boulder to crush my leg. The short knife is useless and hardly scratches the surface of the stone when I hack away at it.

I give up and lie back, staring up into the darkness of the fissure above. I wonder how far I fell. How far underground am I now? Will I ever get out of here? Despairing thoughts circulate in my head. I can't help but feel the situation is hopeless. I have nobody to help me for the first time ever, and I am stuck in a position where I need them more than ever before.

In the hours that follow, I regularly call out, hoping for anyone to be there to hear me.

I am desperate now. I am starving and lack energy from the fall. My knife continues to scratch away at the boulder despite the futility. A frustrated jab at the rock dislodges the knife and drops it on my blackened leg. It is then I realize the only option I have.

With trembling hands, I grip the handle of my blade and bring it to where my leg is wedged under the boulder. I push the sharp edge against my blackened leg, or at least I try to. All the strength leaves my arm as I try to cut into it. It's too daunting. I can't push myself enough to go through with it.

If I am going to be able to do it, I need to be quick to stop myself from hesitating. I pull the knife away from my leg before swinging down as fast as I can.

I cringe at the feeling. It isn't painful, which is a relief; rather, it is odd. I push myself to saw away at the charred remains of my leg, trying to pretend that it is anything but my own body I'm cutting through. Each movement of the blade in my leg sends reverberations through me, causing uncontrollable shivering and revulsion.

The unpleasant sensation continues as I struggle to tear through my leg. Ash puffs out from the cut as the blackened parts of my leg crumble under the knife. It is a lot like charcoal in the way it fractures and crumbles from my efforts. A loud screeching noise rings out whenever I push the blade through it. The noise echoes through my leg and makes me squirm as I force myself to continue.

The sudden freedom of my leg takes me by surprise and I roll backward. I hadn't realized I was getting close to cutting through. Looking down at the new black stump of my leg in discomfort, I can only hope it won't take long to regrow. I've seen Auntie grow back her finger after it was cut off once, but I have no idea how long an entire leg will take to regrow.

With my freedom gained, my stomach lashes out at me, letting me know how hungry it—and I—am. My inner flame flickers as if ready to pounce on the nearest morsel. But first I need to find a way out of this crevice. Missing a leg will not make it any easier to escape.

I raise myself to my only leg while leaning against the wall of the fissure and hobble along the bottom of the crevice. I go in the opposite direction to the boulder. Climbing it will be too much for me right now.

Stones and boulders lodged between the angled walls of the chasm provide a path stable enough to walk on. Now and then, I glimpse through a gap in the stones underfoot. The ravine below goes down farther than I can see. The walls are close enough that I could likely stop myself from falling, but looking down still makes my leg wobble.

I hobble along for only a few minutes before I get my first lucky break. I find one of our wagons wedged between the walls above my head. The wagon turns out to be one of our pelts-and-skins wagons. It's disappointing, but my hunger demands sustenance, so I send out my inner flame to consume them. I go through a pile of sandworm skins and dingo pelts before I burn through the fennec fox furs. It's unfortunate there isn't much else. I really like their fur.

As wasteful as it is to consume the pelts, I am too hungry not to. I imagine I'm going to be a lot hungrier than usual until my leg is back, however long that will be.

It doesn't take me long to regret eating the pelts. All the abandoned wagons must have fallen into this crevice, as in front of me is a graveyard of our broken carts. Including, of course, our cart loaded with coal. If I had been patient, I could have saved a few of the fox pelts.

Ah, well, what's done is done. I fill the satchel at my hip with coal so I have enough to travel with before gorging myself until I feel satisfied. I am tempted to take some cobalt too, but I still can't burn through it, so it is worthless to me. If the others need it when I find them, I'll bring them back here.

I find Auntie's practice stick underneath an overturned cart, so at least I have something to help me walk. There are no actual weapons around, but I consider that a good thing; it means they are still with their owners. I might think the worst if I find a weapon by itself; áed bodies don't retain their forms long after death.

I follow along the fissure for a few hours at a sluggish pace, barely able to move a few steps before having to climb rocks or scale the walls. My passage is made all the harder with my missing limb. Eventually, I reach a point in the crevice where light breaks through the rock and bathes me from above. The crevice breaks into open air a short distance up. After so long, I've found an escape.

I search for a way up before deciding the best option I have is to scale the walls. It's slightly terrifying to think about it, but it is my best bet. There are plenty of ledges and small grottoes I can use to rest. Even if I fall, I'll be fine . . . probably. I survived a fall from much higher, right? I'm going to ignore the fact that said fall made me an amputee. I should be fine.

So I begin my ascent. The faux spear makes the climb much easier than it would have been otherwise. I am able to wedge it between the walls and use it to pull myself up with little issue.

About halfway up, I reach one of the grottoes lining the wall. While it's wide, the ceiling is a bit too low for me to fit in. I move my arm to continue up the wall, placing my hand in a small pocket of the rock wall. Stinging pain assaults my fingers and I fling my hand away. My fingers are steaming and already the tips have gone black, steam rising from them.

Alarmed, I look up the wall I've been climbing. Thin streaks of water trickle down the side of the fissure. I flinch away, almost losing my balance before I grab hold of my stick. How can I keep moving up if there is water above? I don't know whether I should make my way back down or try to continue up while avoiding the water.

Before I can make a decision, though, a bright light briefly engulfs the world around me. I look toward the sky. Hardly a second passes before a loud crack booms through my chest. It doesn't reverberate through the ground as the Titan's steps did, but it is similar enough to the sound that I fall into a panic.

Fearing the Titan is back, I dive into the grotto and hide as much as I can. It is an impossibly tight fit; both my back and chest scrape hard against the stone while I am forced to twist my head. I push in as deeply as I can until the tight clutch of the earth brings almost as much of a chill through my body as the Titan did.

The Titan does not appear. I do not feel the heavy quaking through the ground like I did before. Instead, the recognizable pelting sound of rain begins. Even though I hid away for the wrong reason, it still saves me, as the sky unleashes a torrent of rain greater than I've ever imagined. Water pours down into the crevice in incredible volume.

Squashed as far back into the grotto as I am, I tilt my head enough to see out into the fissure I was in not ten seconds ago. Already it is hard to see the other side, the incredible flow of water cutting it from view.

Well, I got my wish to see rain. Now I would really like for it to stop.

Please?

Unfortunately, the world isn't willing to appease me. Though, the rain isn't making its way into the small hole I find myself in, so I can be glad for small fortunes.

I once again spoke too soon. As the rain picks up, I notice the air becomes more stifling. Soon enough I feel stinging in my throat, followed not long after by all my exposed body. It feels like the fog has returned. Every breath now comes with agony. It feels like my skin is being rubbed with knives all over.

Is the air coated in water? But there is no fog, so why?

I am having trouble thinking straight now. The pain blinds me from everything else. Each breath feels like my chest eating at me from the inside.

My body aches worse than ever before. I lack the energy to even open my eyes. My body is cold. Colder than I thought was possible. My body has already reverted completely into flames, but I still feel cold. All over my body, I can feel hardened lumps where my flames won't reignite. I can't think straight with such a pounding headache, but considering where I passed out, I need to make sure I'm safe.

I open my eyes and the first thing I see is the sickly black marks over most of my exposed body. Attempting to ignore the pain, I glance out into the chasm. There is no waterfall over the opening to my grotto, which brings me only some relief. It is hard to be too happy when my body feels like this. It looks like the rain has stopped. I can still hear a constant flowing noise, though. I am too tired to do anything, so I orient my arm enough in the tight space to grab some coal to eat before allowing myself to relax into a nap.

At least there isn't any immediate danger.

The second time I wake, I feel much better. Munching on some coal, I struggle to drag myself out of the tight hiding hole. I can hear the loud rushing sound from down the crevice. Down below, the entire bottom is replaced with an immense flow of water. Suddenly nervous from the knowledge that I'm sitting directly above certain death, I move away from the edge.

I peer up. What little of the sky I can see is clear. Hopefully, there will be no more rain to worry about.

I've already gone through so much, it is difficult to push myself to resume my climb. My body aches and it feels like I barely have enough energy to remain awake. But I need to move; I can't stay here any longer. Feeling for a handhold, I force my hand to steady its shaking and hold tight. With my spare hand, I raise the stick above my head and lodge it in a ridge before jerking it tight on the opposite wall and pull myself up.

I continue this until I'm almost at the top. I only have a body length left to climb when I find the chasm has opened too wide to wedge my stick anymore. I'll have to climb the rest without it, but I don't want to throw it away, because I will need it to walk. So I throw it over the ledge above me and hope it stays.

Climbing without the support of my stick is much harder. I hold myself steady with cracks in the wall and try to hop from one foothold to another. On my first attempt, I jump too far and miss the ledge. My chest slams into the wall, but I am saved by my wrist wedged in the crack. It cuts into my hand, but I haven't fallen to my death, so for the first time today I'm thankful for the pain. My eyes fall down to the ravine below and I'm struck with vertigo. The sight of rushing water makes me cling tighter to the wall.

Learning from my mistake, I only make small jumps as I proceed. It is exhausting and time-consuming, but I finally make it. I sprawl out on the ground at the top of the crevice, praising the solid, flat earth beneath me.

When I raise my gaze to my surroundings, for a moment it looks like I am in a completely new place. It doesn't take me long to realize I am back at the bottom of the cliffs. The entire area is decimated. The ground has massive fissures all around, and the cliffs themselves are by far the worst. They have crumbled and collapsed in some places, looking like the entire cliff face has slipped off.

In other areas, the earth has torn apart with such force there are canyons where there were none before. The starkest difference from before is the river of lava that flows from the top of the cliff. I can't see the other side of it, so the flow of magma must be as far across as an hour's walk.

It is, without question, the path of the Titan.

The entity climbed the cliffs so far to the west from here and still caused this much damage? How is that even possible? I thought the creature was climbing above our heads, but the proof before me says otherwise.

The path of the crocodile is far more than devastated, it just isn't there. The area doesn't even look like there ever was a cliff; a slight incline is all that's left to show what it used to be. Lava flows from the higher ground down the molten river all the way to the ocean. From where I am, I can't see the ocean, but the steam rising from that direction is telling. The cliff has disappeared, melted from the direct contact with the terrifying being.

I search the cliff face for hours for a way up, but any option I come across is far too unstable to attempt climbing. My tribe has to be up there. If they can't come down either, then how will I reunite with them?

The first place I look is the path of the Titan. It is an hour-and-a-half trek to reach it. When I try to get close to the flowing lava, the intense heat wraps me in its warmth. The Titan is long gone, but the heat it leaves in the area is still far hotter than my flames even a day later.

The lava river looks like the best way to scale the cliffs, but the closer I get, the more unstable the earth becomes. It crumbles under my foot as I walk, my wooden stick breaking through the surface as I lean on it for support. I fear the ground will collapse under me again, so I give up on that path.

Now I have nowhere to go except east; the west is blocked by the molten river, the south by the ocean, and the north by the cliffs. I can only hope I can find a way up the cliffs soon.

I miss my family.

CHAPTER EIGHT

New Path

A week has passed since I escaped the crevice and the devastated remnants of the cavern pass. It has taken until now to find a path up the cliff. Narrow and steep, it is incredibly difficult to scale with a missing leg. I hold the pseudo spear in both hands and lodge it into the stone underfoot so I can hop with some level of stability. With the energy of my inner flame dipping so low, there is little chance I will survive another long fall. Honestly, I should feel lucky I got away having lost only a leg.

I hoped my leg would be quick to heal, but there has been no regrowth. The blackened stump has cracked, showing the red glow underneath. Soon, the coal-like black coating will peel off and free my leg to the air once again, but the limb still has a long time to recover.

I stumble my way along the path that zigzags up the tall bluff. It is small, barely my shoulder width in most places, but it is flat enough that I can get a good purchase with my stick to keep me moving.

No rain has come since my time in the chasm. Thank Eldest Ember. But I know there is no guarantee that it will stay that way, so I move as fast as my one-legged hobble will let me.

Making it to the top of the cliff, I look down at the land a few hundreds of me below. The ground is so far away; it is hard to imagine that I am this high up. The lingering image of the Titan returns to my mind. No matter how tall this cliff is, that thing was far taller.

To rid my mind of the horrid being, I sweep my gaze to the horizon. The distant ocean is a darker reflection of the sky above. The blue of it is such a charming color, so different from the oranges and browns that tinge the rest of the world. It is incredible how such a beautiful thing is so horrendously deadly.

To the east, the ocean closes in much closer to the cliffs than here. It is a good thing I was able to find this path when I did. If the east is blocked off, then I don't know how I would have gotten out of the coast.

Checking my bag of coal, I see there is only a little left. I've tried to ration how much I eat, but my inner flame is gluttonous, never sated until I regain the energy I am comfortable with. At most, I expect the coal to last a couple of days. If everything goes well, I'll find my tribe waiting for me at the exit of the cavern pass, and then everything will be all right again. I just have to make sure I get there in one piece.

Without needing to constantly look for a path to follow and having become accustomed to walking with the aid of my walking stick, I make it back to the top of the cavern pass in only three days. The cracks in the landscape are clear as I close in on it, but it is the sight of the still-flowing lava river in the distance that confirms where I am.

Newly created chasms and ravines litter the landscape, more so than at the base of the cliffs. The large tears in the ground left the area difficult to navigate. I struggle to find a proper path to the opening of the cave system. Frustratingly, I have to backtrack each time I reach a dead end, which delays my reunion with everyone.

I recognize the cavern exit the moment my eyes land on it. It looks almost the same as I last saw it. Minimal damage to the exterior of the tunnel keeps it in much the same state, especially compared with the surroundings. Excited to reunite with my family, I rush as fast as my tottering single-legged walk allows me.

Nobody is waiting.

Not Uncle. Not Auntie.

Nobody.

I search inside the opening, but it doesn't lead anywhere. There has been a cave-in near the entrance. I can't even find evidence my tribe was here. Neither indications of gers having been set up nor wagon trails.

My inner flame churns with dread. Did they not make it out? I feel the hard pull of anxiety tugging at my soul. No! They are still alive. They have to be. It's been a week since we were separated; maybe they found a place on more stable ground. Or maybe they thought I died. I don't want to consider the idea that they haven't looked for me or that we might have even missed each other in our search.

There's not going to be a clear sign of them, anyway. I saw where our carts ended up. Without our wagons, they won't have any ger to set up. Most likely, they'll be traveling almost as bare as I am.

The most likely direction they would have taken if they thought I died would be north, as we initially intended. I might find them if I travel that way. I don't know the exact direction of where we were heading, and I don't have a map for guidance even if I knew, but hopefully, I will find something if I look. If they do think I am dead, I should be able to spot the smoke of the pyre and find them that way. With no other ideas, it is best I leave as soon as possible. I don't want to fall any farther behind than I already am.

Before I leave on my journey north, I need to leave a mark to let them know I was here and am still alive should they return. I line a collection of rocks in a straight line pointing north. If they come back, they'll easily be able to tell where I went.

So, I hold on to the thin glimmer of a chance everything will be okay and begin my stumble north.

I've found nothing.

I'm hungry, my stupid leg is still gone, and I haven't found a trace of my tribe. I don't know what I'm supposed to do anymore. It's been weeks since I left the cliffs and I've found nothing but the empty desert.

I now spend most of my days angling. Without my coal, I've had to resort to eating only sandworms. As tasty as they are, they're hardly nourishing. I have to stop almost every thirty minutes to keep my hunger at bay. This cuts into my already slow walking speed. Now I can hardly travel any distance each day.

My leg hasn't regenerated at all. Without a proper source of sustenance, I doubt it'll start anytime soon. The nutrition-starved worms are barely enough to keep me moving. How did Auntie Kay regrow her finger in only a couple of days? I wish it was that quick for me.

The lack of progress I've achieved is wearing down on me. I was hoping for at least some confirmation somewhere that would help me believe everyone is alive. My nights have become restless too. Being unable to get much sleep during the night makes it even harder to travel far during the day.

The thought that I was wrong and that maybe everyone is dead from the collapse of the tunnel keeps entering my mind. I crush it any time it enters my head. I am not about to even consider the possibility. What do I have left if my tribe is gone? I have already lost so much with the death of my mom; what will I have to live for if I am alone forever?

No. They have to be alive. I won't accept any other world than the one in which they are alive. I have to find them, wherever they went.

So, I keep moving. Eating enough sandworms to keep my body trudging along. Trying to find any sign of a path is futile, as the sands cover any possible remnants left behind. But still, I try. I aimlessly travel north, sometimes straying east, sometimes west.

The longer I travel, the less focused my thoughts become. The repetitive movements day after day are the only concerning matter my mind attaches to. My focus drifts, barely keeping a grip on my form. Only the ingrained memories from my family stop me from bursting into flames.

I don't know how many days pass. The landscape never changes. All I know is the same desert I have always known. It's possible I've hardly moved, my faltering hop of a walk slowing me down more than I'd thought. The only thing I know, and know for certain, is that I am not wandering in circles. The moon remains in the same position as always.

What am I even doing anymore? It is obvious I am alone. My tribe is all gone, they aren't coming back, and they aren't coming for me.

Uncle's comforting care as he Kindled my inner flame. Auntie's teasing smirk as she dodged my spear swings with ease. Even Poppy's old games before Mommy was gone.

Mommy's warm, loving hugs.

I can't help but remember them all. I can't help but grieve that I will never experience those moments with them again. They are all gone, and I am all alone.

I continue stumbling along. I don't have a reason to keep going, but stopping means death. Even if the thought of giving up calls for me, I can't do it. I am terrified of dying, so I just keep pushing. I keep moving through the pain, using physical exhaustion to hide from my despair.

Incredible pain assaults my mouth, snapping my consciousness out of the repetition for the first time in an eternity. I let out a scream as steam billows from the front of my face. My mentally drained thoughts barely connect it to the pain inflicted on my tongue.

It takes me much longer than it should have to notice the arguing happening above me.

". . . absolute buffoon! How could you have given an áed water? Are you trying to kill the girl?"

"Oh, shove it, you didn't know either. Besides, this is the first I've seen one."

I try to raise my head to see who these two voices belong to. I'm immediately disappointed at the sight of them; they aren't my tribe. Instead, they are towering creatures, near triple my height and wider than I am tall.

My mouth still aches, and I can't close my jaw.

"Fuck me, Barrett. You've ruined that tongue of hers," exclaims one of the two giants above me. He bends over me where I can get a better look at him. Thick fur covers him, like the dingoes or foxes we sometimes hunt—even his face is veiled in it. His fur is a dark brown rather than the common lighter colors I am used to.

It is difficult to discern the man's neck, if he has one at all, as his wide, fat head blends seamlessly into his torso. Similarly, his arms are wider than my entire body.

Unsure who or what I am looking at, I attempt to greet him. *Attempt* being the key word. Not only do I hardly make a gurgle of noise, but the stinging sensation in my tongue intensifies at the attempt.

"Sorry, girly, my friend's a bit of a moron. Here, try this, it's dried fruit and meat. You think you can eat some o' this?" The man leaning over me offers me some weird multicolored rock.

Unsure, I give a hesitant nod. He breaks a bit of the rock into small pieces. My arms feel heavy, but I push myself into a sitting position and take some of the offered food. He is quite intimidating; my hand is scarcely the size of his finger and the portion of the bar he gives me is deceptively large. The large rock fits easily in his hand, while the crumb he gives me is nearly too large to hold.

The dried meat and fruit—whatever that is—are rather tasteless, or is that because my tongue is numb? No, even when I eat with my inner flame, it lacks flavor. More energy runs through me from the strange food rock than a dozen sandworms would give.

"Huh, your body really does flicker like fire when you look close enough," the man above me mentions.

I realize he's right. My fire doesn't emit light, but it's still discernible. I clamp down further so the flickers aren't noticeable.

Looking around, I see the man who must have forced water on me, Barrett, has walked off and now talks to a third man. Both other men look remarkably similar; it is hard to make out many differences between them. Their height and the coloration of their fur are the only variations, and even those differences are insignificant. It might be difficult to tell them apart.

Observing myself, I notice my clothes are in tatters, almost completely threadbare. My leg still hasn't recovered. It hasn't even grown in the slightest, although the charcoal-like stub has returned to the same color as the rest of my skin.

"So, what's a young áed doing without her tribe, huh?" the man above me says.

I don't want to think about my tribe. I know now that there is little chance any of them survived. I've only survived myself because I wasn't crushed. My eyes fall to my missing leg. Well, not completely crushed.

I am still empty from their loss. The more I think about them, the bleaker my future seems. I don't know what I'm going to do without them. While I've been wandering in my absent mental state, I was unable to parse my actions. I kept moving with no plan, no logic, and no thought toward what I was doing and where I was going. It started with a search for my tribe and devolved into a mindless march as I tried to refuse the world.

Unable to talk with the state of my mouth, I indicate toward my leg, trying to show I lost them like I lost my leg.

He misunderstands.

"Oh? They cut your leg and left you to die? How barbaric. What truly savage people," he says.

I'm dumbfounded at this misunderstanding. How is that the first thing your mind jumps to? Angry and irritated at the slander of my family, I punch his leg, hitting slightly above the ankle.

He doesn't even notice it, or if he does, he doesn't react. Instead, he just chuckles into the air and stands straight, once again intimidating me with his size.

"Ha. You are with us now; we'll make sure to take good care of you. Unlike those primitive áed, we have proper civilization. I'm sure you'll love it once you see it."

I can't believe it. Not only has he made a stupidly incorrect assumption, but he's blatantly insulting my recently departed family. If he wasn't so big, I'd burn his fur off.

"Arthur, stop talking nonsense, have a look at her. That's obviously not what happened," the third man says to the man above me before turning his attention to me.

"Little miss, I'm sorry for what happened to your family. I can only give my good wishes for their prosperity in Rod's Domain."

I nod to him, thankful he's not making the same false assumption. Rod's Domain? What is that? I hope he isn't talking about the Eternal Inferno. The thought of someone trying to take ownership of the great flame sounds horrifyingly dangerous. Hopefully the Eternal Inferno remains as apathetic as ever, for this Rod's sake.

"Despite his rudeness, Arthur's offer was made in good conscience. Unless you have somewhere to go, we would be willing to take you to our city and make sure you have enough to eat there."

I'm hesitant to take his offer; they are strangers, after all. But I consider it. It's not like I know what to do with myself out here alone, anyway. If left to my own devices, I would follow the same monotonous life that I have been. Consuming sandworms and crawling my way across the wasteland.

Maybe I'd reach the Agglomerate one day, though it's more likely I'll be dead long before I find it.

But even if I have nothing to lose by following them, I'm hesitant to trust them. The only other sentient races our tribe has come into contact with have never had particularly peaceful resolutions.

Probably picking up on my hesitance, the giant speaks again.

"You don't have to choose to stay with us now. It'll be a few weeks of travel to Raetamen from here anyway, then only a small trip to the city of Fisross. Come with us and you can leave if you decide you don't want to stay with us. In the meantime, I think introductions are overdue," he says before straightening himself up.

"I am Gerben and these two are Arthur and Barrett. We can wait until your mouth is healed before you introduce yourself. Barrett is sorry about that, aren't you?" He directs his words to the man who somehow mistakenly tried to get me to eat water. The thought is odd to me; how can you make such an unreasonable mistake?

"Yeah, sorry, kid. If I had known, I would never have brought water even close to ya. It's too bad the only person who had actually met an áed before didn't think to mention it," he says, glaring daggers at Arthur.

Quick to defend himself, Arthur jumps in. "Oh, don't try to piss your mistake off on me; you should've known better that one with hair like that couldn't possibly be albanic."

"If it was so obvious, then why didn't you stop me? We both know you're full of shit. No wonder your missus left ya, with you always prattling on with your narcissistic lies," Barrett responds. His words seem to anger Arthur, and he gets right in Barrett's face. Seeing the rage on such an intimidating person makes me instinctively back away.

"That bitch didn't break up with me. I caught her riding another fucker behind my back. You've got some fucking balls to . . ." Arthur's tirade is interrupted by a loud cough from Gerben.

"Boys, as much as I love seeing you two go at it, we do have a guest. Would you act the same way in front of your daughter or younger sister?"

They both reluctantly back down after glancing at me. Each shoves the other, but otherwise, they don't act on their aggression.

My shoulders sag in relief. The last thing I want is to be stuck in the fight between two giants who can flatten me with a thought.

CHAPTER NINE

Raetamen

What are you doing there, girly?" Arthur asks as he approaches me from behind.

I am currently angling, using my finger in place of the rock bait as I have grown accustomed to doing. Every so often I twitch my finger along the surface of the sand, only displacing a small amount each time. Practice taught me that the worms are more likely to be attracted to sudden smaller movements. The only thing needed is patience. I'm not sure whether the worms are hesitant to bite or if it takes a long time for them to notice, but it can take up to half an hour to catch one.

"Angling," I try to respond to the man, but the noise I make is definitely not coherent. My tongue, in its unusable state, is particularly irritating when trying to communicate. Instead, I motion to my finger touching the ground and then press against my lips, gesturing for him to be silent. I only hope that his heavy footsteps or the loud thud of him sitting down beside me doesn't scare off any sandworms.

Luckily, Arthur understands me well enough to keep quiet while he observes. It has been a few days since I met the trio. I don't really have any reason not to take them up on their offer to travel with them.

Well, besides the fact that one of them almost killed me when they first saw me.

And their intimidating size.

And the open aggression between Arthur and Barrett.

But it's not like I have any more family to go back to. I can try to look for another tribe somewhere, but that will be extremely difficult and dangerous.

First, I don't have any of our maps, so even if I try to find one of the common áed campsites, I am likely to completely miss it. Second, it is a rare thing to encounter another tribe at one of those locations, anyway. I might be waiting over a year for another tribe, especially this far southeast. Finally—and the most worrying—those hunting áed know of any location I have memory of.

So of course, I am stuck with no real choice but to follow these three giants.

Arthur's oppressive height looming over me makes me tense up as the minutes pass, so it is a relief when the worm finally takes the bait and bites my finger. Without my angler line, I'm forced to endure the slight pain of the worm biting into my finger. My blade snaps down and cuts through the middle of the worm with nary a delay.

The worm takes a few moments before its wriggling stills. I pick at the worm's head to extract its teeth.

Arthur rises to his feet with sudden haste, startling me. I fall to my side and pull myself away from the man as quickly as I can.

"Death-worm. Shit, girl, that's a death-worm." Arthur looks down at both me and the head of the sandworm still locked around my finger. It only takes a moment before my arm is in his hand. I never have time to back away farther.

"Quick, girl, we need to amputate!" he exclaims, grabbing for the sword-sized knife at his hip.

Has he gone insane? Amputate? What is he talking about? No, I was stupid to trust him in the first place. I swallow my fear at his looming figure and ignite my arm. Arthur flinches back, the fur on his hand now burning. He swats his hand against the side of his leg a few times until he puts out the fire.

"The fuck, girl!? You'll die if we don't get rid of that poison!" he admonishes while cradling his hand.

He takes a step toward me again and I push away as far as I can on the ground. I hold my knife up toward him in the hopes it'll be enough to stop him from coming close. Poison? I have no idea what he's saying. He takes another step and I struggle to keep my distance.

I flare my entire body in flame, trying to threaten him not to come closer. It seems to work as he stops approaching.

"What's all the commotion?" I hear from behind me. Glancing back, I see Gerben approaching us with Barrett close behind. Not wanting to have any of them to my back, I scramble off to the side so I can keep them all in my line of sight.

"She got bit by a death-worm. She needs treatment now!" Arthur declares.

Gerben stares at Arthur for a long moment, only sparing a glance my way before replying. "Arthur. She is an áed, literal fire given life. How could she have been poisoned?"

"Huh?" is all Arthur can say.

Laughter from Barrett cuts into his confusion. "Wow, you didn't even know that? Weren't you the one bragging about your knowledge of áed only a few days ago?"

Arthur looks angry and ready to give Barrett a piece of his mind, but before he can open his mouth, Gerben cuts in.

"Why must you two always act like children? Now, Arthur, you scared the shit outta the girl. I think you owe her an apology."

"Ah, yeah, sorry, girly. I've seen too many men die to those evil little things," Arthur says after calming down.

With the giant man no longer aggressive, I feel myself drip in relief. I pull back on my flames, taking control of my form once again.

"Wait, so if áed are completely fire, then why does our little one here still have a leg missing? Shouldn't it be easy to, I dunno, conjure another with her fire?" Arthur says.

I shake my head to indicate that's not how it works. I would need my binding with fire to be a closer rank to Elder Enya to change my form willingly like that. For now, I am stuck with only my stub until I consume enough fuel to energize its regeneration naturally.

"Same way we can't just slap some butchered meat on our wounds to heal it, the world doesn't work that way," Gerben says.

I don't know about the meat thing, but at least he understands. I nod at his statement to show my agreement.

Looking down at my finger where the sandworm should still be, I find that it has charred black while I was trying to defend myself. Disappointed in the ruined state of my snack, I quickly swallow it. The lower body of the worm is still in good condition though, and I want to thank Gerben for protecting me from Arthur's overreaction again.

I hold it out to him, motioning to eat. He'll love the taste, it's one of the sweetest in the desert. I've grown so tired of the taste myself, but that doesn't mean it'll be bad for him.

He takes a hesitant look at the lower half of the worm before refusing me. "As much as I appreciate the thought, I would die if I ate that."

Huh? He would die from eating a worm? I look down at the limp worm. Is it the poison thing he was talking about? The idea that something as harmless as a sandworm might hurt a giant like the man in front of me is unthinkable.

"These little things are the biggest reason us ursu don't travel into the desert often. One bite from a death-worm is enough to kill a grown man within an hour," Gerben says.

Even with his clear fear of the worm, I can't see it as anything but a tasty treat. Chomping on the worm, I notice the uncomfortable expression on Gerben's face. Okay, it makes me feel a bit better to know I can make them feel as uncomfortable as their size makes me feel. I silently promise to store some away; who knows when it might be useful?

"We'll be stopping in Raetamen for a couple of nights until we can catch a ride to Fisross," Gerben announces, most likely for my benefit.

Ahead of us are a number of structures like the shipwreck I saw a while back. Actually, no, they're nothing alike, but I have nothing else to compare these buildings to. The town is a collection of large cubic stone structures placed along a long path. Most of them are similar, but they are all tall, reaching a Gerben-and-a-half high.

I've been told this is a small mining town. I don't know how they consider this place small; it is huge. There have to be over twenty buildings here and each one is big enough to house an entire áed tribe.

The mine itself is along the left side of the road. A tunnel dug right through the rock, leaving a wide opening into the ground covered in black dust.

Many ursu—as Gerben calls his race—lumber in and out of the mine with large wheelbarrows filled with coal. They take their coal loads down the street ahead of me. I salivate a bit at the sight. It has been so long since I've had a proper meal, and having so much in front of me stirs my hunger. My inner flame writhes within me.

Gerben leads us down the path opposite the coal mine. Taking us farther away from that tempting feast.

I want to go over there and gorge myself to satisfaction. If I wasn't being held on Gerben's shoulders, I might have fumbled my way over even with all the huge ursu around. I try to get my ride's attention by tapping the top of his head. I still can't speak, so I am left hoping he might figure out what I want.

"We're heading to the saloon, but you'll be able to eat later. We are lucky enough to make it in time for the weekly Bratchina." Surprisingly, Gerben knew what I wanted to ask. That's amazing!

"Thank fuck. I'd drop dead if I had to eat pemmican for another week," Barrett says from behind me.

"Yeah, I know what ya mean. I've been starving since the last proper meal," Arthur says.

Is that the first time those two have actually agreed on something? I'm surprised they're even willing to agree, considering they fight simply for the principle of it. I can understand it, though; that meat-and-fruit rock hadn't been all that good, and there is nothing as filling as a good chunk of coal.

We approach the largest building so far, which sits oddly separated from its surroundings. It lies in the center of a large clearing of paved stone. The building is missing the front wall all the other structures have. The large open floor has many scattered tables and chairs. Along the back wall of the inside, there is a large shelf filled with wooden barrels from floor to ceiling. The ceiling is twice as high as Gerben, so it hovers far over my head even while I am held on the ursu's shoulders.

The three ursu head straight for the rear wall, pouring what looks like water into wooden mugs they pick up from the side table. I fidget nervously as Gerben brings the cup to his mouth, which just so happens to be rather close to where I am sitting. He downs it in a moment before pouring another.

Gerben carries me to a table where he finally puts me down into a seat. The seat is much too big for me; I am raised high over the ground, and yet I'm still unable to see above the table.

Looking around, there are a few other ursu drinking, but most tables are empty.

"Ah. Good to finally get a decent drink," Arthur says as he sits down beside the other two ursu, who nod along with him.

I'm not sure what we are doing, so I sit quietly, hoping we go get the food they mentioned soon. It is awkward, sitting here not able to take part in the conversation the ursu are having, but also not having the courage to walk off by myself. I don't know what these people are really like. Wandering around might get me in trouble if the others are as aggressive as Arthur.

When the three finish their drinks, Arthur and Barrett grab their packs and walk upstairs, out of sight. Gerben grabs his pack and picks me up in his other arm. He carries me through a door in the back wall of the building, into an enclosed room. Barrels like those out in the main area fill the room. There are far more of them in here, stacked tightly on top of one another.

In one corner of the room, an ursu is working over a large tub of water. Nervous about the liquid sloshing beneath their arms, I jump off Gerben and make some distance. Do they really need to have so much water around?

Ignoring me, Gerben approaches the ursu. "Good afternoon, Administrator. It's incredible how clean you keep this establishment considering the landscape. I'm impressed."

The ursu stops their work and turns to Gerben. A satisfied smile appears on their face as they speak in a surprisingly feminine voice. "Ah, it's nice to know that some notice. Thank you. Is there something I can help you with?"

I drag my eyes up and down her body. She doesn't look much different from the men; the only difference I can tell is a lighter shade of brown around her face and down her neck. Her hide also looks softer and not as rough as the trio I came with, but that might just be because of the desert sand.

"We picked up a bit of a stray out in the wasteland." Gerben gestures at me. "Do you have any rooms for nonursu for the night?" he asks.

"Sorry, no. We're at the edge of civilization. I've never even heard of another race coming this far west," she says, looking over at me. "She's tiny! What's such a young thing doing all the way out here?"

The giant ursu woman with still-dripping hands starts coming toward me. As I back away from her, keeping my balance by holding the barrels to my side, I can't help but feel like this situation keeps repeating. Are all ursu so impulsive or is it just the ones I've met?

Fortunately, Gerben stops her by putting an arm on her shoulder. "She's an áed" is all he says while pointing at the woman's dripping hands.

"Really?" She seems amazed, looking me up and down while drying off her hands. "She's not made of fire, though?"

Unfortunately, Gerben doesn't stop her this time now that her hands are dry. I am picked up under the arms and raised to her head height. My struggles against her grasp are ignored as she continues to question Gerben.

"Poor thing, how did she lose the leg? Are you sure she's an áed?"

I should burn her, then she will know for sure. The thought of willingly letting my flame burn brings the picture of my mom and uncle to the forefront of my mind. Their lectures echo in my memory, wiping the thought away. It's better to show I'm strong by controlling my flames than to let them out.

"Well, we found out she was an áed when we accidentally forced her to drink water. The steam coming from her was quite something," Gerben says. At the lady's incredulous stare, he hastily continues. "What? We found a young kid collapsed in the middle of the desert. Who wouldn't think to give them water first?"

The woman's eyes land back on my missing leg. "So, what happened to her leg?" I want to answer for myself, so I make a cutting motion with my hand toward my leg, showing her I cut it off myself.

"Not sure. She was like that when we found her. I assume she lost it when she lost her tribe," Gerben says.

These two just continue to speak as if I'm not here, and the comment about my tribe flares the ache in my chest once again. Do I want to follow these people who manhandle me against my will and speak as if I don't have a voice?

Well, I don't have a voice, but that's beside the point. They can easily ask me yes or no questions, but they seem to prefer making assumptions rather than asking. Do they think I'm dumb?

Regardless of how they think of me, I'm stuck here for now, so I might as well follow through. It can't be worse than endlessly wandering the wasteland, right?

CHAPTER TEN

Second Pyre

The feast—or Bratchina, as Gerben calls it—is a much bigger occasion than I expected. After the ursu finish working in the mine, everyone in the town gathers in the clearing out the front of the saloon. It is an incredible sight to see so many of them in one place. There have to be over a hundred here, moving in and out of the saloon with drinks while talking and laughing with one another.

I am sitting off to the side by myself, having separated from Gerben, who is socializing with the many other ursu. I am looking forward to this meal; it's been so long since I've had a proper amount of coal. Meat can be tasty, but it can never reach the filling feeling coal brings.

The crowd of ursu splits in front of me and I watch as many long tables are brought out, evenly placed through the crowd. Not long after, a line of ursu carrying large platters walks out from behind the saloon. On each platter is a dizzying array of different food. I recognize the dingo meat, but most of it seems to be new types I've never seen before.

There are some strange colors mixed in as well, greens and whites and many other unique things that don't look like any type of animal meat I've seen before. The strangeness of each platter is shocking, but what truly shocks me is the sheer volume of food being presented on the tables.

The ursu are salivating at the sight of the food in front of them. Many have a look I've only seen in predators as they watch their prey. It is surprising to see such large beings all patiently waiting. That is until the last tray is placed and, as one, they besiege the buffet.

It's quite a sight to see, so many enormous people stuffing their faces with near their body size of food. When the crowd disperses enough for me to see the table again, there is not even a scrap left over. The hum of conversation overwhelms the sounds of those still munching. Those with satisfied stomachs walk off in random directions. Many return to the saloon for drinks, while a few wander off into the town. The majority seem content to remain in the vicinity of the tables.

With no food left, I have to think about my own hunger. Are they going to bring out some coal soon? Wait, am I even allowed to have some of their coal? I should find Gerben; at least he'll know what I can do.

The moment I stand up to look, I realize it's going to be much harder to find him than I initially thought. Not only is everyone more than double my size, blocking my sight, but I don't think I can differentiate between him and any of the other ursu around. They all look too similar to my eye to pick him out from the crowd without hearing his voice.

A convoy of ursu appears from around the back of the saloon with yet another assortment of food platters. It appears to be just as large as the last range they brought out. Do these ursu have bottomless pits for stomachs? I don't think my tribe could've ever found that much game, not to mention actually catching it all. I don't see any coal on the plates, though. Do they not like the taste? What else could they be mining it for other than food?

Curious about where all this food is magically being brought from, I hop my way around the nearby ursu until I reach the other side of the building. What I find looks like a perfectly round sand dune with lots of doors on its sides. The divine smell of burning coal flares my hunger and I notice smoke rising from the rear side of the dune.

Many ursu move around the door-filled mound. Some take trays of food from within an open hatch and others prepare the meals on the platters. It looks like they still have plenty more to take out.

The old practice spear helps me as I hobble my way around to the side of the dirt mound the smoke is coming from. My small size is pretty handy considering none of the ursu around pay me any attention. Although I'd feel better if I wasn't in the presence of beings that averaged a height more than twice mine.

On the other side of the sand-covered spherical dome, the ursu are much sparser. Some steps away from the base of the mound, there is a stairway leading down into the ground. Much of the smoke seeps out of a hole at the mound's base, but some finds its way out the stairway entrance. Overwhelming hunger takes me as the scent of the coal fire down the stairs blows into me. I know I might not be allowed inside, but I can't stop myself from approaching the scent of ambrosia.

At the base of the stairs is a huge stone door larger than any other. The hatchways in the hill above look like ant holes in comparison. It is already wide open, and I stumble forward as if in a dream. The mountain of burning coal is as beautiful as it is nostalgic.

I throw myself on top of the pile and shove a burning piece in my mouth. The bliss of searing energy floods my body. I relax back into the comfortable heat encasing me and loosen my form to the surrounding flames.

Thoughts of my family cut into my mind. The last time I felt so comfortable, I was with my tribe. Even though I lost my mom, I was still surrounded by those who loved me, but now I've lost them too. The warmth of the coal fire around me is comfortable and warm, but it is lonely, lacking the genuine care and emotion of those I yearn for.

I suddenly realize I have never given them a proper farewell. My selfishness kept me from giving my family a true path toward the Eternal Inferno. I have locked them here because I didn't want to admit their death for so long. My own denial prevented them from reuniting with the rest of our family in the Eternal Inferno, denied them their rightful new beginning.

I don't know what my future holds. I don't know if I will get a suitable chance to create their funeral pyre. It makes me feel incompetent, but this might be the only opportunity I have to let them move on.

I can't make the pyre here, though—it can't be underground—and I need to wait a few hours until the Ember Moon. But the coal here will be a good base for the pyre. Timber would be more in line with ritual rules, but I don't have that luxury right now. I don't know if the ursu would let me use their coal in the first place, but I can only hope they won't notice. I can't ask them in case they deny me, so doing it without them knowing should be for the best.

First, I need to make sure the coal I use doesn't burn before the time I need it to. I grab as much of the coal from the burning pile as I can, and using my inner flame to control the heat within, I stop the coal from burning. Carrying enough coal up the stairs will be hard, but I have a few hours to do it.

Reaching the outside with my handful of coal, I am thankful that nobody is nearby. Looking around to see where all the ursu have gone, I notice one of the ursu's large wheelbarrows from the mine parked near the stairs. I'm not sure how I could have missed it on my way down, but a glance over the side shows it is full of coal. I must have been far too focused on the smell on the way down. At least this makes my job a bit easier.

I am still a fair distance from the buildings in the town. The food mound is wedged closely behind the back of the saloon. With my stick in one hand and the other clutching a handful of coal to my chest, I struggle to walk a short distance away from the saloon and mound.

I would have preferred to set up the pyre far from where the ursu might see, but I won't be able to carry the coal all too far in my current one-legged state. I've already dropped half the handful I started with. Reluctantly, I settle with placing the pyre in the open space between the ursu-made hill and the surrounding buildings.

As I make my first trip of what I expect to be many, I notice there are no ursu around the mound they took food from anymore. Looking toward the saloon, I can see there are still plenty of them around and behind it, probably still conversing over their feast.

Well, it is fortunate for me; not having their attention on me can only be a good thing. I don't know how they might react to me taking the coal they worked for.

The sun has long since set and the moon is a bit more than a quarter full, so I have a little over an hour before I need to start the ritual.

I use the time to carry as much coal as I can, but the end product lacks compared to the pyre that was set up for my mom and those that died with her. I want to keep working to make the pile bigger, but the time for the Ember Moon is almost here.

The moon is darkening once again. The darkness on its surface, which has receded farther to the left during the night, retakes its hold once again, gradually but noticeably consuming the light. The Ember Moon shouldn't be more than ten minutes away now. I ignite the pile of coal in front of me and hope it will burn into a proper flame without any more input on my part.

Mom used to tell me that the moon is in a constant cycle of being consumed by the darkness. Each night the darkness will come, and it is the Eldest Ember's flames that relight the moon.

The moon and Ember herself are the protectors of the lands and the áed, caring for us as long as they are visible in the sky. Eldest Ember will always appear in the most difficult of times and guide those within her light. The Eternal Inferno—the sun—on the other hand, is an apathetic existence. Only showing on its own schedule and holding no bias between life and death. Mom has always said that while the Eternal Inferno is neutral to all, it still provides for those under its watch. It will always allow for our flames to live on after they are extinguished.

The flames grow before me as the moon disappears completely. The world around me enters its dark prelude, the small flame of the coal fire lighting up only the immediate surroundings. Not too long do I need to wait until the landscape once again bathes in dim light, this time the deep red of the Ember Moon.

Taking my cue, I step into the disappointing flame. I'd hoped it would grow larger, but this will have to do. I free my inner fire into the pyre and encourage it to grow. Soon, I am completely encompassed by the flame. I let my form relax into the blaze, control my breathing, and gather my thoughts. This is the second time I have to go through with this in far too short a time, but there is nothing I can do about it. I need to do what needs to be done for the sake of my family.

Unlike last time, I have to make sure I give all my tribesmen a proper goodbye. I can't fixate on only those closest to me as I did when my mom passed. They deserve a proper passage at the very least. I go through everyone in my family, beginning with those I'm not as close with, saying their name and a short eulogy for each one.

I want to give everyone a proper extended farewell, but with only me to send off the fifteen lost members of my tribe, I don't have time to devote to each. The Ember Moon only lasts so long.

I struggle to continue when I finally reach Auntie's and Uncle's turns. They have done so much for me, especially after I lost Mom. I find it almost as hard to bring myself to send them off as it was for Mommy, but at least now I can move forward. I don't have much time left, but I still want to say so much to them.

"Uncle Rivin, you've always been important to me, especially after Mommy passed. You took care of me, and even though you were hurting just as much as I was, you always put me first. I love you and appreciate everything you've done for me. May you be reignited in the Eternal Inferno.

"Auntie Kay, you've always been so good at making me laugh, I was always happier when you were around. You were a great teacher too. As soon as my leg is better and I can find a spear for myself, I'm gonna keep practicing what you taught me. I promise I'll become just as good with a weapon as you and Mommy. Please find your way well to the Eternal Inferno."

With my eulogies done, I push as much of my inner flame into the fire as I can, trying with all my might to replicate the impact Auntie was able to make when she did it. As much as I would have liked for it to be spectacular, I am unable to even reach the size I managed to for Mommy's pyre. Going for so long without proper sustenance has left my inner flame in a depressing state.

I'm almost immediately exhausted after pushing everything into the flame. I try to push in more of myself to make up for my lack of strength. My limits are being stretched, I know, but I just don't care right now. I may have accepted they have moved on, but the emptiness that remains from their departure is suffocating. The only thing that calms my soul is that I know everyone will soon be together in the Eternal Inferno, waiting for my turn to join them.

Collapsing into the burning coals below me, I don't even try to regain my form. I'm too tired to bother crawling out of the pyre, not that I see a reason to. The heat of the coals is comfortable but is hardly a remedy for the loneliness in my soul.

CHAPTER ELEVEN

Morning Ride

I wake up to pressure on my cheek. Opening my eyes, I find myself in the odd position of being poked. An ursu sits before me with a stick in its hand, poking me. I slap the stick away in irritation. Looking closer, I can tell it's Barrett, or at least someone with the same-colored hide as Barrett.

"You're finally awake. Hurry and get up, we're leaving," Barrett says before rising to his feet. I push myself into a seated position amongst the remnant burning bed of embers. I feel more refreshed than I have in ages. It is far too wasteful to sleep amongst smoldering coal, so it's usually only ever done when someone is in critical condition. But, having now done so, I'm invigorated.

I revel in the comfortable heat and swallow some of the remaining coal while I can. If Barrett let me sleep in this coal bed of mine, they mustn't have had too much issue with me using their coal, which is a relief. I hadn't been paying attention to the possible consequences when I did what I did; I only cared about giving my family their proper send-off so that they could move on. Should I not find another chance in the future, I wouldn't have forgiven myself if I let the opportunity pass. What I'm going to do now and where I am heading are not things I know.

"How long are you gonna sit there, girl? I told you we are going. Now hurry up and stop your flames so I can carry ya," Barrett says.

I realize I have been ignoring him while lost in the comfortable heat. Doing as he asks, I retake control of my outer form and pull my flames back into a physical body. The moment I move out of the fire, Barrett drapes a large rag around my body and tosses me over his shoulder.

An indignant squeal escapes me as he holds me tight in the uncomfortable position. The ursu is quick on his feet and soon we are on the outskirts of the town. Before I know it, I'm dropped to the ground and my breath is knocked out of me. I toss off the rag and look up to see the trio who brought me here. Barrett is shaking his hand in pain for some reason while the other two are watching him with apparent mirth.

It miffs me how blatant Barrett's disregard for my body is. This isn't the first time he has handled me with such little care, and I can only hope that this will be the last. I move closer to Gerben, as I have learned over the past week he is the best of the three by far. Neither of the other two truly understands how much bigger and stronger they are when we interact, but at least Gerben can be gentle.

Gerben approaches before briefly touching my shoulder with a finger and flinching away. As he shakes the hand that touched my shoulder, he asks, "Kid, as funny as watching Barrett in pain can be, I need to ask you to try and cool down a bit."

"Huh?" What is he talking about?

"You're still too hot for me, and I'll need to carry you onto the train. Can you do that for me?" he says.

Oh, I thought it was okay as long as I wasn't on fire, but they can't even handle this much heat? Kinda weak of them, honestly.

. . . I should probably not mention I thought that.

Well, if he needs me to lower my temperature, I can either reduce the heat on my consumed coal or increase my control. I haven't improved at all since I was with my tribe, and I'm sure Uncle would be disappointed if I don't continue to try to improve myself. Also, I really don't want to give up the sated feeling of coal's heat energizing my body.

I bring the focus on my physical form to the forefront of my mind. I spread my awareness and force my focus to condense at the edge of my body. At the parts of my form that touch the surrounding air, I exert my will and command them to cool down. The change occurs easily, dropping the heat of the outside of my body to a level the ursu should be able to manage. The warmth of my body inside this outer layer remains at the same heat, and I'm able to keep the coal burning within me.

It is when I try to move the thread of focus to the back of my mind that I have trouble. Controlling my body while I have full awareness on it has never been hard. The hard part comes when I have to keep that change under control indefinitely. It is nearly impossible for me to multitask on more than a couple threads of thought at once. Only in the past few years have I gotten used to holding my physical form permanently, but even then, I have been dropping it on a few too many occasions.

Splitting my attention back on the ursu in front of me, I struggle to maintain my outer temperature. I can hold this for a while if I'm not distracted, but it will be too hard for me to hold for a prolonged period. It looks like I'll have to settle with a lower burn and practice while we travel. I'm gonna miss the extra energy and warmth.

I motion to Gerben that I'm ready to be picked up, and once again on his shoulders, I lay eyes on the huge . . . thing that sits in front of us. It looks like a long connection of metal houses, but they sit on wheels rather than directly on the ground. Sweeping my head left, I see each metal box is identical. Gerben carries me to the right toward a strange contraption. A large cylinder, similar to but much bigger than the barrels at the saloon, is attached to wheels of its own. Two large tubes connect to the large barrel. One on top and one at the front, bending upward.

"She's a beaut, ain't she," Arthur declares. "Finest bit of ursu genius you'll ever see."

Uh, sure, but what is it? All it looks like is a huge waste of metal.

With me still secured to his shoulders, Gerben approaches the ursu waiting beside the odd wheeled cylinder.

"So, you ready to go?" the man asks, looking at Gerben.

"Yep, we appreciate the lift," Gerben says.

"It's no issue. Wouldn't want ta make ya walk the entire way." He glances up toward me. "Now, your little bonfire there ain't gonna start no fires on all that coal back there, will she?"

"No, she'll restrain herself. Won't you, kid?"

I nod twice. I'm not so bad in my control that I'll let a fire start in my presence.

"That's good, then. Welcome aboard my train," the ursu says before jumping onto the tubular thing.

Gerben doesn't wait a moment longer; lifting me off his shoulders, he raises me higher until I'm over the ledge of the first of the metal boxes. As I go over the top of it, I realize there is no roof; instead, my leg lands on a massive pile of coal. It is incredible—I've never seen so much coal in one place. The size of the fire this could make has my stomach grumbling greedily. Wait, is this why they told me not to make a fire? 'Cause they know how tempting it is? Maybe they won't notice if I take one or two chunks, or a few more.

The huge open box of coal almost tips when Gerben, Arthur, and Barrett climb their way over the side. I feel everything underneath me tilt to the side as they all clamber over the ledge at the same time.

"Oi! One at a time, you lot! You'll be the ones fixing the railcar if it tips," the ursu from before yells.

Gerben shouts back an apology before he digs away some coal and settles down for a seat, with the other two following suit. Why are we sitting down here? Didn't they say we were moving out?

I can smell burning coal. I look around to make sure it isn't me causing it. A pillar of smoke rises from the tube poking out of the top of the contraption the other ursu climbed onto. Wait, no. Looking closer, I see the smoke is actually steam. More water? At least I have a wall of metal and coal between it and me.

A loud whistle cuts through the air as I feel the coal beneath me jerk forward.

"Ah!" I let out a startled yelp as I fall to the side.

I look around to find out what is going on. Is the earth collapsing again? I catch sight of the stone buildings over the edge as the world seems to settle under me once again. Everything is moving to the right. What? I stand and approach the edge of the large box. Everything is moving. The buildings, the ursu, and even the ground are speeding up. Looking to the rear of the "train," as the ursu before called it, I finally understand. It really is a "train" of wagons, all hauling their load of coal and moving along the sand. I never would have imagined it could be possible for such an obviously heavy load to be mobile.

"Whoa," I let out as the wind picks up along with the speed of the train, fluttering my clothing about my body. Leaning over the side, I see the wheels turning over a path of iron tracks I hadn't noticed earlier.

"Yeah, it's quite something, isn't it?" Arthur says, looking smug, as if he made the thing himself.

"You got your voice back," Gerben states from the other side of the railcar to me.

"What? Oh, you're right! Finally!" I cheer.

Now that I can finally communicate, I can ask everything I've been wanting to know about. What should I ask about first? The place we are going? Maybe their lives? Or maybe I should ask if they know about the Titan? Wait, no, there is still something much more relevant to ask.

"What is this thing?" I ask, looking over the edge again as the surroundings fly past us.

"I told ya. It's a train. The best ursu creation in the past hundred years," Arthur says.

So it's something they made? I'm surprised a race of such insanely strong people even need to make something to pull their wagons. I can't deny the speed of the thing, though. It moves along at the speed of a dingo despite its size. I'd hate to get caught in front of the thing.

"Now that you can speak, how about you tell us your name? We can't go around calling you *girl* forever, you know," Gerben says.

"I'm Solvei," I tell them. "From the Vatra tribe."

"About them, your tribe, I mean. How did you lose them?" Gerben asks, leaning forward with his back to the wall of the railcar.

"It was a monster," I say. "A titanic beast bigger than anything I'd ever seen, bigger than mountains. It didn't even notice us, but it destroyed everything. The earth broke open in fear of it. My . . . my tribe died when the ground we were hiding in collapsed around us."

I take a moment to settle the choking feeling in my throat. My chest aches as I remember the events of that day. I hate thinking about what happened. I hate my naivete at the time. I saw them crushed with my own eyes; I knew they were already gone when I went looking for them, but I couldn't accept it. If I had accepted it earlier, if I had considered my options while I still could, I wouldn't have fallen into that mindless grieving state I had.

Gerben continues before I can get too lost in my thoughts. "I'm sorry to hear that. What happened to your leg?"

"Oh, it got stuck under a rock. I had to cut it off."

It's comical to watch the typically stoic Gerben's eyes widen. "That is . . . incredible but horrifying. I would find it near impossible to push myself to go through with it, even if I was stuck in such a situation."

Arthur butts in too. "Yeah, girly, that's some impressive balls you got."

"Ah, no. My leg had already died and gone black, so I could barely feel it." I try to wave off their praise. "Anyway, I should be able to grow it back as long as I can eat enough coal."

Hint, hint. Please take the hint. I can't help the small glance at all that precious stuff around me.

"Oh, you can do that? Is that what happened with your mouth?" Barrett asks, bringing himself into the conversation.

I just nod, slightly confused as to his meaning. Of course? How else would I have been able to talk again?

"Back to the Titan you saw. Could you describe it for me?" Gerben asks. "We were sent out in this direction to investigate reports of it. What did you see?"

"Well, it was big, really big. And hot too—the ground melted all around where it walked. Even a week later, the lava river it left behind was probably too hot even for me to cross. It looked like a crocodile, but it had large spines on its back that glowed with heat. Uh, what else should I say?"

"Where did it come from? Which direction did it go? Did it seem angered? Or was it aggressive? Anything else you can think of will help," Gerben urges.

"It came from the ocean. We didn't notice it until it was almost upon us 'cause there was a heavy mist. I didn't see it, but when I escaped from underground, the path it left went north," I say, and Gerben nods along as if expecting such.

"Um, I don't know if it was angry or aggressive, we were trying to hide at the time," I say, trying to think of anything else about the monster, but coming up blank on anything that isn't a way of calling it terrifying.

"You were trying to find it?" I ask. They said they were searching for it. Ursu look strong, but I don't believe for a second that they'd live long around it. They'd probably burn up just in its proximity with how they struggle with the little heat I give off. That's not to mention how far the Titan has probably traveled by now; it'd be insane for them to try to follow it. Wait, do these trains need to follow the tracks laid out?

"No, we just needed to confirm the reports we received. We already came across the path it left in its wake before we found you. We couldn't get close, though," Gerben says.

"Do you know what that thing was?"

"This one in particular? No. I don't know anything about it, but we have records of the Titans. Whenever they appear, chaos always follows. Always."

CHAPTER TWELVE

Fisross

So, what sort of place is Fisross?" I ask from the opposite side of the railway wagon to Gerben.

Being able to speak to someone again is great. I find myself continually looking for new things to talk about, to keep the conversation from going quiet. Barrett got annoyed at me rather quickly, telling me to shut up, but I don't want to. It is a good way for me to get a bit of retribution on him for pouring water in my mouth. I am still angry at him for that. Now that I've been around the ursu for a while, my fear has calmed to the point I am comfortable giving him his deserved punishment.

Well, as long as Gerben is around, at least.

Gerben is accommodating of my questions, patiently answering everything I ask. It feels a bit like I am back with Uncle, and as sad as that comparison makes me, I am happy Gerben responds so sincerely.

"Fisross is a rather unique city in New Vetus. It's part of a long-term national project to convert the arid area bordering the wasteland to fertile farmland. The city runs almost entirely on imports from other parts of the country, while the mages slowly make the land arable. It's rather small compared to most other cities, but no less important," Gerben says.

"Are the other cities bigger than Raetamen?" The town we just passed was huge. There can't be too many places with hundreds of giant ursu living together, right?

Gerben lets out a chuckle at my question.

"Of course, even Fisross is far larger than that small mining town. A city is on a different scale compared to Raetamen. Imagine that town, but a hundred times larger."

"Whoa! How do you feed that many people?"

"That's what the farmland is for. Many of my brethren dedicate their lives to growing crops and raising livestock to fill the bellies of us ursu. As I'm sure you've noticed, we eat a lot," he says, chuckling.

"What about coal? Do you eat that too?" I have been wondering since I never saw them bring any out during the feast last night. They mined a lot of it; what else could they want it for?

"No, we can't. I didn't even know you áed could eat it until you had your little bonfire in the middle of town." Gerben smiles, but his gaze burns a little too harshly into me.

I avert my gaze, pretending I don't notice.

"We can eat anything as long as our flames are hot enough to burn it," I proudly proclaim before deflating a bit. "Although I'm still not strong enough to burn through much more than coal. But if ursu don't eat coal, then why do you mine so much of it?"

"Mainly for our ovens, but with the increasing number of trains in service, much more coal is going toward powering them."

Oh right, that underground firepit I found must be an oven.

"Talking about ovens, my wife's friend runs one in Fisross. I might see if she can spare some for you if you'd prefer that to the food at the Bratchina. Well, first I will need to ask at the continae what we are going to do with you, but I'm sure there won't be any issues."

That sounds great! Maybe I'll be able to regrow my leg quickly too. Wait, I shouldn't be too greedy. I'm already imposing on these people's lives. I should make sure to pay them back for everything they do for me.

"Ah. There we go, look ahead. That's Fisross," Gerben says.

Forward, over the train's ledge, I see the many rectangular shapes silhouetted against the horizon. Even at this distance, it is clear that the place is much, much larger than Raetamen. A city is what he called it. Yeah, something like this definitely needs its own name.

I can't see many details from this distance, but I am very much looking forward to seeing the city up close.

I gape up at the towers as we pass through the main road into the city. These are many times higher than the biggest building from Raetamen. On the outskirts of the city, the enormous stone structures are far more tightly compressed and randomly placed than the ones I can see in the heart of the city. As we walk closer to the center of Fisross, the buildings grow taller and far more organized.

The entire city looks like it is cut from stone. From the ground underfoot to the large rectangular walls of each building, almost everything is made of tan stone. Unique metals and fabrics decorate the fronts of the main road's buildings. I even recognize the silvery-blue cobalt framing a large wooden door.

As we head into the central part of the city, we come into a large open area. The place looks like it could fit the entirety of Raetamen within its confines. At the far end of the circular space is a building with a similar open front to the saloon back in the mining town. The open front is the only similarity it shares with the saloon. It is far larger than any other structure I've seen. It shares a similar square stone shape to the surrounding buildings until about halfway up. Higher than that, the walls curve almost into a sphere. The top half of the sphere curves into a sharp point far in the sky.

The spherical section of the building is made entirely of unique metals. The bright green color glistens under the direct shine of the sun, making the tower stand out even more amongst its tall but simple surroundings.

As if expecting my wonder, Gerben proudly introduces the tall structure. "That is what we call a continae. All our cities have at least one, as it is an important place for hosting our Bratchina, our feasts. It is both a place of appreciation toward the elder spirits, Deivos and Rod, and a place of governance."

"It's big" is all I can say. The more of the world I see, the smaller it makes me feel.

The bulky ursu chuckles. "That it is." He looks up at the tall structure for a moment. "How about I introduce you to my daughter? I'm sure you two would get along wonderfully. I can hold off giving my report until afterward," he says as he walks down a street to the right of the continae.

"You have a daughter?" I'm surprised he hasn't mentioned her in all the days we've been together.

"Yeah, she's a smart girl. She even made it into the mage academy. Leal's a bit older than you, but I'm sure you'll get along great."

A few minutes later, we finally approach one of the many buildings in the street. It looks identical to many of the other buildings we passed on the way here. The only differences I can spot are the decorations on the front door and wall, this door containing inlays of some sort of silver metal. I don't know how Gerben can differentiate the buildings. If I have to make my way back to the central courtyard on my own, I'll probably struggle.

Gerben grasps the handle and pushes the door open with ease. It is dark inside, the only light coming down from the steps leading upward at the end of the hallway. Passing up the stairs and through another hallway above the last one, Gerben stops at the second door on the right. He raps his knuckles against the large wooden door a few times, then steps back to wait.

The dim hallway brightens as an ursu appears in place of the door.

"Gerben!" the feminine voice exclaims, embracing him.

I suddenly feel rather awkward as I'm still on his shoulders while these two ursu smooch and clutch each other. Even when they finally separate, it seems the woman hasn't noticed me and Gerben has forgotten about me.

I don't want to jump down myself, so I tap him on the side of the head, trying to get his attention. He doesn't even notice it, but luckily the lady does.

"Oh? Who is this?" She drags his attention to me.

He picks me from his shoulders and lowers me to the ground as he answers for me.

"This is Solvei. We found her alone in the middle of nowhere. She's an áed."

"An áed? Not an albanic? Oh, my!" she exclaims. "Wow, your hair flickers like candle flame, how pretty. Oh, where are my manners? I am Calysta. It is nice to meet you, Solvei," she greets me.

"Hello," I say, untying my walking stick from my back. Hopefully I don't have to rely on being carried much now that we stopped traveling.

"Gosh, what happened to your leg? How horrible," Calysta says.

"I cut it off," I state. As inconvenient as only having one leg has been, I don't regret doing so. After all, being alive with one leg is better than being dead.

Calysta gapes at me. I think there's some water that wells in her eyes as she turns back to Gerben.

"Later," he says suddenly before continuing, "She says it'll grow back in time."

"Oh, that's good, then," Calysta says, somewhat subdued.

We are interrupted by the sudden call of "Daddy!" from somewhere on the other side of the doorway. Another ursu appears and throws themselves at Gerben. He catches them and laughs as he hugs them tightly. This new ursu is the smallest I have seen, more than a head shorter than Gerben. Well, I say the smallest, but they are still almost twice my height.

This must be the daughter he talked about. She is far more slender than the other ursu I've seen, even considering her height difference. Her arms and neck are closer in proportion to that of an áed rather than an ursu. Not that you could ever mistake her for anything else; the thick coat of fur beneath her thin clothes and still large proportions are impossible to deny.

It is uncomfortable to watch the sight of this joyous family reunion. Not only do I feel like I am intruding, but it also brings a pang to my chest, reminding me of what I can never have again.

I scoot away a bit to give them some space, but it seems that Calysta has become more aware of her surroundings after her initial reunion with her husband. My movement only turns her attention to me.

"Solvei, why don't you come inside, sweetie? We can get you something to drink. Would you like some juice?" She holds her hand out to me, inviting me to take her arm.

"Juice?" I ask, unfamiliar with the word.

"Honey, remember, she's an áed," Gerben interrupts, not looking away from his daughter.

"Oh, right, how silly of me. How about some cookies, then? They should be all right for you."

Unsure of this other new word, I look to Gerben for confirmation.

"Yeah, that should be fine," he says as he sets his daughter down.

I go to hop into the house with my stick, but not even a step through the doorway, Calysta has me picked up in her arms.

Stop! Please, let me walk on my own. I can do it.

I don't complain aloud because I don't want to seem ungrateful, but I can't wait for my leg to heal. This is so frustrating.

The room we enter is not unlike the interior of the ger I'm used to. A small fireplace and the walls to separate the sleeping areas are the only differences from the home I grew up in. The floor is lined with rugs, a table is surrounded by chairs, and a couch is set against the wall for comfort.

Calysta sits me on the couch and walks to the other side of the room. The size difference between our races is once again readily apparent. When I lie back on the cushion, my leg doesn't even reach the edge of the couch.

"Hello." A voice comes from my right. The daughter takes a seat next to me and introduces herself. "You're Solvei, right? I'm Leal. Nice to meet you."

"You too" is all I can manage, not knowing what else to say.

"Daddy mentioned you were an áed. I read about them at school. Is it true you are made of fire?" she asks excitedly.

I nod to her. It's not that strange, is it? Then again, I also found it strange when I first met the ursu. I thought people who aren't formed by fire were strange, even if I already knew áed are the odd ones out rather than the norm. I've always found it weird. Mom told me that almost every other sentient race is made of meat and blood like the animals we hunt, but having never met one before, I found it hard to believe.

Leal doesn't consider my nod a good enough answer. "Well? Can you show me?" she asks expectantly, with a glint in her eye. I can't tell if she is curious or if she is eyeing me hungrily.

Making sure to keep my hand away from anything flammable, I raise it between us. I engulf my hand in flame, but she asked if I am made of fire, right? I might as well take the extra step. Limiting it to only my hand, I let my form relax into visible flames. I can't change its form to anything other than the shape of a hand, but the solid look it had before is gone.

"Whoa, that's amazing! How hot can you make it? Do things pass through you like a normal fire? How well can you control fire compared to fire mages?" she babbles, her excitement palpable on her face and in the way she jumps on her knees on the couch beside me.

Wary of accidentally burning something while I'm their guest, I regain my form and snuff out the remaining flames. It would be a crime to damage such a comfortable couch.

After she's finished asking her questions, I try to answer as much as I can. "I can't make it too much hotter, I'm still weak. Uh, my form is a bit different to normal fire, so things can't pass easily."

The last question I remember her asking I don't understand. "What's a mage?" I ask. I remember Gerben mentioning the term, but I forgot to ask him.

She looks shocked, and maybe a bit insulted, by my question. Just as I think she's about to yell at me or something, Calysta interferes.

"Here you are, girls, take as many as you want." She places a plate of what I assume are the "cookies" on a small table in front of the couch.

"Thanks, Mom," Leal says before taking one.

Copying her, I say, "Thank you," as well. I am about to get off the couch to reach for one, but before I can, Leal grabs one for me. Handing me one, she says, "How about I tell you all about mages, then?"

CHAPTER THIRTEEN

Welcome to Gloria's Home

Mages are those that can control the elements through the markings engraved on the skin." Leal turns her arms so that her palms face upward.

"I've only been to the academy for a year, so the only markings I have are the beginner guiding marks." She points to an area from her wrist, up her forearm, and reaching her elbow. Sure enough, there is a branching black line coloring the pale brown fur of her arm.

"These marks are the foundation for controlling an element, as they allow the body to become accustomed to the flow of elemental energy. The more I practice sending the element through the marking, the better I become at controlling it." Leal clenches her fist and I watch as the markings on her arm become a clear, near-blue glow that sparkles as if moving. I watch in amazement as even the fur colored by the marking becomes translucent.

"My teacher says that my control is good enough now that I'll be able to have my first spell marking tattooed by the end of the year." She reaches for another cookie, taking her third, while I still try to get through my first. They are pretty big and tasty. It gives off many short little pops of energy over my tongue with each bite.

"What is a spell marking?" I ask, still curious about the strange lines on her arms.

"Oh, they are what lets a mage control an element. To use them, you need to understand them completely, which is why it takes so long to learn to be a mage. Simple spell markings might allow you to make a stream of water, which is what I'll be getting first, where the only thing that you can control is its strength. More complicated spell markings require so much more complexities to be considered. They occupy more space on the body and are harder to learn, yet they offer greater flexibility in their utilization." She speeds through her explanation, enthusiastic to share.

One part of her description stands out to me, though, and I need to know.

"You could make water with this spell mark?" I ask, trying to keep my sudden concern from showing.

"Yep, my guiding mark is for the water element, so I can use water-based spells. The most common elements are water, ice, earth, and air. Any others are either too dangerous, difficult, or confidential for most people to use."

A chill floods through me. Have I entered the stronghold of my mother's killers? Those who attacked our tribe could wield water in the way Leal said their mages do. Now that I think about it, the train was also notably similar to the metal wagons I'd seen with the Kenna tribe.

I make sure to keep my thoughts from showing on my face as I consider the possibility. Are the ursu the ones who have been hunting áed in the wasteland? Did I follow them into a trap? Will I be able to escape if I try to run now? My thoughts continue to circle as my fears amplify.

"Is everything okay, Solvei?" I hear beside me. Maybe I'm not as in control of my face as I thought. I crush my worries as much as I can to not accidentally lose control of myself and burn their furniture. The last thing I want is to make my potential enemies enraged. If they truly are my enemies, then I need to keep them thinking that I trust them. Otherwise, I won't have a chance to escape.

But first I want to be sure. "Um, are ursu the only ones who can become water mages?" I ask, trying not to be too obvious that I'm asking whether it is the ursu who are hunting áed.

"No? Any race can become a mage. Ursu are proud of the strength of their bodies, so very few of us become mages. There are more mages amongst the other races," she states, still concerned about how I'm acting.

That . . . is both relieving and terrifying. It's a lot less likely I am surrounded by those out to kill me, but it could be any race. It's terrifying to think that every race has an ability that can kill an áed with ease.

Leal's face twists from a concerned look to a wince. "Oh, sorry. I don't know if áed could use water markings, but I doubt it would work well."

"Huh? No, I'd rather stay as far from water as I can."

Leal calms down again. "Oh, okay."

"You know trains, yeah?" I ask.

My change of the subject befuddles her. "Yeah?"

"Have you seen wagons made similarly?" I ask.

"No? Why?" she answers with confusion, worry seeping back into her expression.

Sweet relief. As long as she isn't lying to me, then there is little reason for me to believe they are the ones responsible. I feel a tad silly for jumping to such a conclusion, but the confirmation it was just that, a misunderstanding, is relieving.

"Are you sure you're okay?" Leal asks, still looking worried.

I smile at her and respond. "Yeah, I'm okay now. Sorry, I was troubled over nothing."

She watches me for a moment, and I feel like she is seeing much more of me than she should be. I shiver at the hungry look that reenters her eye.

"Have you had an issue with water mages?" she asks.

"Huh? How?" How does she know? Did she just read my mind?

"It's okay if you don't want to talk about it. I'm sorry I brought it up. You just seemed so worried after I spoke about water mages, and then you asked about other races," she continues.

She didn't read my mind? That's reassuring. But it unnerves me how she guessed correctly. Am I not as discreet as I think? Well, there's no reason to worry about it now.

"Um, a group with abilities similar to those of a water mage you mentioned killed my mom." I was stupid to jump to conclusions about the ursu. So far, they've been nothing but welcoming, even if Arthur and Barrett are rather violent.

"Oh, I'm sorry. I'll stop talking about mages, okay?" she says.

"No, it's fine. I'd rather know as much as I can." I don't want to leave myself open if they are looking for me. There isn't any reason to believe that they would hunt me rather than any áed they can find in the wasteland. They didn't find me during the entire time I stumbled through the desert as a cripple, after all. But there is still the possibility I might encounter them again one day, and I'd rather know what I am facing when that day comes. I don't have my tribe to protect me anymore.

Leal takes my words as encouragement. "Well, you can rely on me to tell you all I know." A smug smirk appears on her face. "You've chosen the best person for the job. Now, what about you? How do you control fire? It obviously doesn't work the same way mages use it. You have to promise to show me what you can do. Deal?" Excitedly, she grabs my hand as she throws out her request.

"Sure," I answer. "But I don't want to burn anything, so somewhere else."

"Great! Somewhere else is good." Leal cheers, jumping up to her feet and ready to charge out the door.

Before she drags me out of the room, Leal's mom holds her back.

"Just where do you think you are going, young lady? We're going to talk with Gloria while your dad finishes his work at the continae," Calysta says before picking me up and grabbing Leal's hand.

As she leads us out the door of their home—Gerben in tow—Leal whines, "Do we have to, Mom? I wanna go out with Solvei."

"Yes, Leal, I need to ask if she'd be able to organize some coal for Solvei while she's in Fisross. I doubt the nonursu housing facility accounts for diets this peculiar," she says, indicating toward me.

"Huh? Can't she stay with us?" Leal asks. I'm surprised; I never would've expected to be welcomed so easily.

Calysta sighs at her daughter's question. "I would love to let her stay with us, but I can't look after more than one child, as per the order of the council. Solvei will have to stay at the facility until they find her a job."

I'm not sure what to make of it all, and even less sure if I'm allowed to have an opinion, so I remain quiet as we walk down the stairs and out into the open air again. Thankfully, once down the stairs, I'm allowed to walk by myself.

We travel back toward the continae, separating from Gerben as he leaves to climb the tower. We walk around the right of the continae to its rear. At the back of the continae are five stone structures similar to the oven back in Raetamen. Each is placed in an even separation surrounding the continae. These ovens are much larger, constructed with stone blocks rather than the sand-looking clay of Raetamen's. With how much larger the population of this place is than that of the mining town, it's not surprising there are more ovens.

I look at my surroundings, noticing that, other than these ovens and the continae, the buildings are placed in an almost perfect circle around the open space. I didn't notice before as I was dazzled by the splendor of the continae, but the identical height and appearance of the buildings surrounding the city center make it seem like we are encircled by a wall.

Calysta leads both Leal and me to the building behind the center oven. This building, as well as those behind each of the four other ovens, is bare of any decorations. The lack of decorations only emphasizes the identical nature of these buildings.

Where Gerben goes straight through the door of the other building, Calysta stops to mess with something on the side. She presses an indent in the wall, and surprisingly, it lights up. As I look closer, I see the light is a number: 14. Other indents show many other numbers, but only the number she touched is lit.

Calysta stands back in front of the door, remaining still and seemingly expectant of something. I turn my attention back to the number indents. Around each groove in the wall is a bunch of engraved lines that seem familiar. I can't put my finger on what they remind me of.

Before I can figure it out, the door opens to an ursu only a finger length shorter than Calysta. One of mine, not an ursu's.

"Caly! It's good to see you." The woman embraces Calysta. "Hello, Leal. How are you?" the woman asks as she moves on to hug Leal.

Even though she is much larger than me, it seems Leal also struggles with the strength of the ursu's hugs. She squirms in the woman's arms for a moment until she is released.

"Come in, come in," she calls to us, leading us past the stairs to a room on the ground floor. I'm pretty sure she hasn't even noticed me yet. Are all ursu women this restless? I hope wherever I'll have to stay isn't surrounded by people who would crush me with a burst of excitement.

As I enter the room, the woman has already disappeared. Calysta invites me to the couch as the woman's voice comes from around the corner of the room.

"Would you like drinks?"

"Oh, yes, please. I'll have coffee, and do you have any juice for Leal?" Calysta calls back, making herself comfortable, with Leal taking a seat beside me.

The interior of the room differs far from the outside. Each wall is decorated with strange images of unique landscapes. The images look like they are made from a pelt, but I'm certain an animal couldn't grow such detailed fur naturally.

A few of the images depicted in the tapestries catch my eye. One shows a large white spear—encircled by green worms climbing its length—piercing the moon from the earth below. Another shows a large ring of what must be water circling a deep pit.

As intriguing as these tapestries are, the last image I can't take my eyes from. At first glance, it appears to be a wooden structure amongst a range of large, jagged mountaintops. The small cabin sits at the edge of a valley, which makes it almost picturesque. But the longer I look, the more something about it just feels . . . wrong. Unable to put my finger on what unnerves me so, I drag my eyes to other tapestries that depict other colorful imaginary landscapes.

"Oh! I see you're intrigued by my paintings of petrifying places!" the woman says, startling me.

She carries a few cups over to Leal and Calysta. Nursing a mug for herself, the woman looks at me with wide eyes before she shakes her head and continues on about the images on the wall.

"Or maybe I should call them the terrible territory tapestries? I can't decide. I picked them up from some albanic while I was in Morne. The man came to trade without realizing we didn't use one of those silly currencies the northern countries do. Can you believe it?" The woman huffs as if she can't.

She moves toward the images mounted on the walls and begins pointing them out. "This one is called the tower of evil. This next one is the whirlpool of evil. Oh, and of course this is called the mountains of evil," she says.

Leal nudges my side before whispering into my ear, "She does this every time Mom drags me here."

"Oh, and how could I forget the star of my collection?" she says, pointing to an image above the couch behind me. "This one is called the fog of . . ." She pauses for a moment. I guess she's trying to make it sound cool. "Evil!" And there it is.

The image is of a black fog half engulfing a city. Unlike a shadow, the fog is a uniform black, unchanging across the pelt. It makes the image appear corrupted by a mark, rather than the black fog actually being something depicted. I look at it a moment before leaning back into the soft couch padding.

Leal whispers in my ear. "That's not what it's called. It's called the Void Fog."

"Now, who is this one? Am I right to assume she's an áed?" the woman says, giving me a comforting smile.

Calysta responds before I can. "You can tell? Ah, right. Gloria, this is Solvei. Gerben found her all alone out in the wasteland. We wanted to ask you if you could organize some coal for her. It seems she prefers coal to the normal food we eat. Gerben has gone to ask at the continae what should be done with her, but she's likely going to the facility for the moment," she rambles.

The woman, Gloria, smiles at me for a time. Feeling self-conscious as her eyes dig into me, I'm tempted to turn my head to keep my eyes anywhere other than the odd, happy stare the woman is giving me. But I remain resilient and keep eye contact. I don't want to come across as anything but polite.

"I'll be happy to. In fact, I'll take care of her myself. It will make organizing the coal more convenient," Gloria says, turning to Calysta.

"Huh? You will? Didn't you not want a child?" It's not only Calysta who is surprised. She wants to take me in? Just like that?

"Well, I didn't think I did, but look at that face, she looks so cute," Gloria gushes, making me feel uncomfortable.

She leans in close to Calysta and I overhear her whisper, "Plus, she's already past the toddler years.

"Solvei, right? I'd be happy to take care of you. I work with a large supply of coal. I'm sure you'll love it," she says.

I'm all but certain my eyes light up at the mention of coal. Having all I can eat will be amazing. Even back in my tribe, I could only eat so much or we would run out in the middle of nowhere. After having relied on sandworms every day for so long, I'm excited; can I gorge on their endless supply?

"Thank you, Elder Gloria." While she's not a part of my tribe, I still want to show my gratitude with a term of respect used for those older than me in my tribe. Although it seems she doesn't like it, as she winces at the term.

"Please, just call me Gloria or Auntie," she tells me.

I don't know why she would react that way to me calling her Elder, but I am fine with referring to her by just her name. I won't call her Auntie; I may be thankful, but she can't compare to my aunt.

"Okay, Gloria."

In my peripheral vision, I see what I think is an eye staring at me. Turning, I find myself looking back at the unnerving tapestry of the cabin in the mountains. There is no eye. Nothing is looking back at me, only a small wooden house at the edge of a valley. I still feel it, though; just looking at the cabin in the mountains makes me feel tiny and insignificant. Like the world looks down on me and considers me less than a grain of sand in the vast desert.

CHAPTER FOURTEEN

Leal

A few days have passed since Gloria gave me a bed in her house. She's lived alone until I moved in, but there is plenty of space to share, especially considering the design of the building accommodates ursu, not áed. The bed Gloria gave me is huge and softer than anything I've ever felt before. The room is large enough that I have to be careful not to let the door shut, otherwise I won't be able to reach the handle.

It is a unique experience having an area to myself, my own room. The past few weeks I've had no space away from the trio that brought me here, and before that, when I was with my tribe, I always shared a ger with three or more tribesmen.

Gloria has been very nice and welcoming to me, almost overbearingly. The first afternoon I stayed with her, she even treated me to a bowl of coal topped with a sweet golden syrup that tasted divine. If I am to complain about anything, it would be that she treats me like a kid. Is it my size that makes them think I'm younger than I am? I'll have to bring it up at some point.

The coal Gloria brings me is great, but I have to hold myself back from eating all of it. I only eat to where I can still control my external temperature to a low enough level that I don't burn my new bed. I can eat it all and keep my body heat low, but I'll be throwing away almost all the coal's energy to do so. Like Uncle always said: I shouldn't be wasteful.

My missing leg has finally seen some improvement. The stump grew two whole finger widths since I began my new diet. It is exciting; soon I will walk again with my own strength, instead of relying on my crutch or being carried around by others.

It is a bit of a relief to see it will regrow. As it has remained unchanged for so long, I feared that I'd be stuck that way, even if I knew it was only because I hadn't been eating enough. Another issue I had was that without another áed to support my growth with Kindling, I didn't know how much longer it would take me to grow. Mom emphasized how important it was for her to Kindle my flame for my growth. Will I even grow without it? I hope I don't have to stay this small forever. I want to grow up already.

From the satchel hanging around my neck, I pull out the pink flame marble. The last physical memory I have from my tribe, of my mom and Uncle. Losing myself In the motionless flame, I drown myself in the memories of those already gone. It hurts every time I recall them, my time with them, the wistful memories of everyone I miss. I hate the pain that comes when I recall these moments, but I would hate far more to forget them.

A knock at the door grabs my attention. Leal sticks her head through the gap of the door, waving a hand at me. I rush to put the marble back into the pattern-lined satchel around my neck and give a smile to her.

"Hi," I say, patting my bed beside me to invite her to sit.

She doesn't; instead, she grabs my arm and leads me out of the room. "C'mon, you promised to show me your fire. Let's go, I wanna see."

I'm dragged off the bed and try to land on my foot, but with Leal still tugging at my arm, I'm unable to stop myself falling.

"I'm so sorry. I was in a rush and got too excited. I didn't mean it. Are you okay? Are you hurt?" Leal panics.

I swear, none of them know their own strength.

I push myself up into a kneeling position and reassure her, "I'm fine, but please don't pull me anymore."

Leal nods in rapid succession and stares for a long moment at my stump. She turns away from me and drops into a crouch.

"Hop on, I'll carry you," she says, turning her head toward me.

And once again I'm being carried around, this time by a girl my age. A girl my age that is heads taller than the tallest adult from my tribe.

I wave goodbye to Gloria on my way out. I want to tell her where I am going, but Leal doesn't give me a chance and is quick to escape the building, not making a noise until we are once again alone.

My first assumption is that she will take us to the wide-open area in front of the continae, which would be a perfect place to show what I can do, but she runs off in the opposite direction. It is the midafternoon now, and many ursu wander the streets. Leal must have come to pick me up the moment she finished her day at the academy. She came by yesterday trying to get me to go out with her, but it had already been dark, and Gloria wasn't willing to let me go out during the night.

Leal is studying to be a mage at the academy, but how much do they have to teach if she is there all day? There must be a lot.

"What's it like at the academy?" I ask Leal as she is walking.

I'm pretty sure I hear her say, "Good," but it is so quiet and mumbled that I might be mistaken. So, thinking she didn't hear me, I ask again.

This time she ducks her head as if to hide from my words. She dashes out of the street with high pedestrian traffic and into a side alley. She jogs along smaller, more disorganized buildings than are common in the central part of the city. Leal passes through a narrow passage and we soon find ourselves in a rather large space hidden away between buildings. I only see one way to enter the area, which is the gap we just entered through. I doubt an adult ursu could ever make their way back here. Leal struggles to fit, and she's the thinnest ursu I've met.

"Solvei, welcome to my secret paradise," Leal announces, lifting her chin and throwing her arms out to emphasize her words.

"Um, you asked about the academy, right? Sorry, I was . . . distracted." She seems unsure of herself before shifting back to her restless excitement. "I love it. The academy is great. There are so many interesting things to learn. The teachers are amazing. Mr. Humbert is a rare lightning mage who created an incredible marking to increase muscle movement speed, and Miss Berne has an amazing collection of water manipulation markings. Oh, and the library is enormous; there isn't a bigger one in the city."

I zone out as she continues to talk about how great the academy is and why she's so happy to attend. I am still being held, but I don't want to be, so I push myself from Leal's back and let myself fall to the ground.

With the weight on her back gone, Leal's talk about the academy is interrupted and she turns to find me sitting on the ground. It surprises me she even notices. Gerben has a tendency to not notice if I push myself down from his shoulders. And it's not like he is the only ursu oblivious to minor changes in weight or small touches. What they can't see doesn't exist to them.

"Oh, right, we are here to see your fire, not to talk about school." Leal then smiles at me expectantly. "Well? Well? Please show me."

I guess I should humor her. I'll disappoint her with my lack of strength and she won't ask again. First, I point my arm skyward and let free a stream of uncontrolled flame. Not putting my inner flame into it means the most I can do is create a pillar of fire only a few times my height. I can create this stream from any point on my body, but using the arms is a habit from when Mom taught me to aim.

Next, I focus on pushing my inner flame into the pillar. Now able to freely control the fire, I push it farther. I allow it to reach for the roofs of the surrounding buildings but hold back to stop it from going above. Leal mentioned this place is secret, so I'd rather not shoot off a beacon for everyone in the city to see.

With a firm grip over the pillar of flame, I change the shape into a spiral and lower it down until it surrounds us both, spinning with lazy motions. This is easy stuff. Any áed can do this before their eighth birthday. Well, that's how it's supposed to be. It took me until I was almost nine to reach the strength and control necessary to do so.

The last part I want to show her is nowhere near as flashy as the rest, but it is by far the most difficult. At least for me. I was close to succeeding while I was still with my tribe, only I couldn't do it without losing control of my form.

The scorching spiral settles back into my palm. Careful not to allow the flame too close to Leal, I compress the flame down into a size I believe I can manage. I grasp the ball of fire in my hands as if it were physical; I control my thoughts and temper my emotions. I calm my mind and let the ball free, focusing on separating the ball while still maintaining control, both of it and my body.

As the ball leaves contact with my body, it loses its spherical shape and naturally reverts to the familiar flickering of a flame. I leave it be, not taking full control over the orb in order to not distract from controlling my body. Slowly, I move the flame around my body, concentrating hard to force it to remain under my control, while it remains almost at the peripheral of my mind.

With a full rotation of my body, I let the orb dissipate, relaxing my tensed body back into a comfortable position. A quick check over my body shows no sign I lost control of myself again. I jump on my one foot and celebrate a little. This is my first genuine success at remote inner flame control. Sure, there are improvements to be made, but it is an achievement I haven't been able to accomplish until now.

Leal shares my enthusiasm. She grabs my arms and starts jumping along with me. This time she's careful not to pull me any way that might have me falling over, which I'm grateful for.

"That was amazing, Solvei! You're so young and yet you can already do what older students struggle with." Leal stares at me with stars in her eyes. "And you're able to separate your element from your body and still control it? I don't even think that's possible with markings!"

"Huh?" Her exuberance cuts into my celebration. Can mages really not control their element without it being connected? I know how hard it is to do from experience, but every áed can control their fire at a distance from their body. For an adult áed, there is almost no difference between being in contact and remotely controlling their inner flame as, well, it is a part of themselves.

Wait, she just mentioned my age. I guess she sees me as a lot younger than herself. I don't want her to treat me as if I'm a kid, especially if she's as old as I am. But I also want to avoid embarrassment in case I'm wrong and she knows my age. How should I do this? Hmm.

"Leal, how old are you?"

"I'm twelve."

"Wow, that's so close to me. I'm ten." I point out how close we are, putting more emphasis on the *wow* than I intend. Wait, am I even still ten? I was alone for months. "Actually, I'm probably eleven now."

Leal's face is almost comedic, the amount of shock that she shows. I guess it's pretty obvious now that she thought I was a lot younger.

"Huh? What? But you're so small."

Her shock morphs into apparent nervousness and she holds herself a bit more reservedly. The sudden change in demeanor worries me. It's like how she acted while we were on our way here from Gloria's house.

"Are you all right, Leal?" I ask.

"Ye-yes. I'm sorry I treated you like a kid."

She was treating me like a kid? It feels more like she's been treating me as some new toy that caught her interest. Wait, is that how ursu treat their own children? Maybe it'll be best not to think too much about it and forgive her already.

"It's all right, we can still be friends, yeah?" I say.

"F-friends? Are we friends?" Leal asks, still nervously stumbling over her words.

"Are we not?" I didn't think she disliked me, so I already thought we were friends. Does she not think the same?

"Yes. I mean, we are. I'm happy to be friends with you." Leal's demeanor flips once again. Now humming in excitement again.

She is odd. I might just be unused to talking to others my age or maybe it's an ursu thing, but I find her entire personality strange. Well, it's obvious she doesn't have bad intentions, so we should be able to get along great. I am honestly excited about what she might show me about the ursu country. The things I've seen have already been incredible. As much as I'd love to return to my old life with my tribe, I have always wanted to see the strange sights of the world outside the wasteland, and this is my chance.

It's just a shame that I'll be alone to do it.

No, that is wrong. My tribe is gone, but that doesn't mean I have to be alone. The generosity of the ursu has already shown me that. And looking at Leal talk about her interests and how she is happy to be my friend gives me hope for a proper future.

CHAPTER FIFTEEN

The Herald

With some time before needing to be home for the night, Leal shows me around the city. Of course, the first place she wants to show me is the academy. Despite there only being a couple other students her age that attend—which Leal proudly brags, might I add—the school is incredibly large, taking up the space of four typically sized buildings. The main building of the academy is a wide, circular stone structure larger than most residential buildings in the area, with four connected square towers surrounding it.

I'm not able to enter the building. Leal tries to bring me with her, but a guard at the entrance prevents my access. It is disappointing, and I think Leal is even more depressed than I am that she can't show me the ins and outs of the place she spends most of her time.

Leal points out the different sections of the academy while we circle the structure from the outside.

"I'm not very far through my studies, so I spend all day in the lecture halls of the main building. The towers are laboratories for research. I really want to look in there myself, but they only let the older students and teachers enter," she says with a pout.

It blows my mind that it is even possible to build something this big. The academy doesn't just cover its buildings with decorative metals and threads. Every part of the stone exterior showcases expansive artistic etchings. The carvings depict ursu in strange stances or somewhat confusing scenes of battle.

"What are all the images in the stone?" I ask as we pass another scene, this one not of battle or some grand discovery, as with the others. The illustration shows a sea overflowing with ships.

"Oh, those. They're major historic moments, so battles, discoveries, and the revolution. This mural shows the ursu landing at New Vetus after abandoning Vetus. It wasn't called New Vetus at the time, mind you. We were refugees then, and the country that was once in control of these lands took advantage of us."

My tribe had stories of our past, but a lot of it was unknown. All our history came from the words of my elders, who themselves gained the knowledge from their own elders. We had maps and documents of rarer rituals and crafting methods, but storing information like that consumed cargo space and we could only allocate so much toward it. The elders sometimes talked about the Agglomerate far to the north and how they would travel there every few decades to share information with the other tribes. I have always wanted to see the place. Mom grew up there and would sometimes tell me stories of the beautiful, glistening home of the áed.

We find it hard to continue the tour of the academy without actually being able to explore it, so Leal takes me to the next destination in the city.

She takes me past the continae, down the main road, then through one of the branching streets in the central, organized section of the city.

I see where she is taking me the moment we turn the corner. A sizeable area blanketed in green stands out from the gray stone of the surroundings. While I have seen the color in the city, the sheer volume is blinding. I am so used to landscapes being brown, red, or orange that I almost can't recognize what I am seeing.

"This is one of the city parks. The life mage Willow Eden created it. I really want to meet her. She's the only mage in New Vetus who can use nature markings," she says, looking down at a bed of colorful, oddly shaped plants at our feet. "The grass, trees, and flowers here need water mages to manage the ground. The desert drains water from the soil far quicker the farther into the desert you go."

So this is what true plants look like. They're much more amazing than those lame shrubs on the coast.

The grass beneath my foot feels much softer than the sand I am used to, almost like walking on a rug of fennec fox fur. It is so nice I decide it is a good place to lie down. As I roll onto my back, I invite Leal to sit next to me. She doesn't join me. Looking up at the ursu girl above me, I can tell she's nervous and worried about something.

"Do you mind if we sit beside the trees over there?" She points to a dense cluster of thick brown columns, each supporting a huge amount of green above.

"Sure." I nod to Leal and take her hand for help walking over to the shaded area. Belatedly, I notice the brown pillars are wood. These are the trees I've always wanted to see.

My awed gaze upward brings a giggle from Leal beside me. She helps me sit down, and I notice she makes sure we are out of sight of anyone else inside the park. Is she nervous around other ursu? I mean, I can understand. Their entire race is large and intimidating. But she is one herself, so should she be this nervous around them? Maybe it's because she is so much skinnier than others I've seen. I don't see another reason she might act the way she does.

"This place is amazing." There is a sweet smell in the air. A light breeze flutters the leaves above. "I could fall asleep right here."

Mostly, I am trying to distract her from her nervousness around others. She is still looking around at those who might see us.

"Yeah, it's great. It reminds me of my grandparents' place. In Morne, it looks like this almost everywhere. They've been expanding the range of fertile land into the wasteland for over a century now. Too bad it takes forever. I hate the desert," Leal says.

We lie there in the comfortable shade of the trees for a while, talking about different things and playing games Leal teaches me. One such game involves creating images from the leaves fallen from the tree and then letting the other guess what it is. I am pretty bad at guessing, but it turns out to be a good way to learn about a lot of new things I haven't heard of before.

A lot of Leal's shapes gravitate back toward things to do with mages or her mage training, but there are plenty of things that I think are helpful. One of the things turns out to be inscriptions. She goes on a full tirade of it but explains it's what makes the "doorbell" work. The inscription will ring a bell inside the house when someone presses the associated number on the outside panel.

She says inscriptions are like a mage's markings but work on a different principle. She also admits to not knowing too much about it, but what she knows is enough for me to realize that the inscriptions they use are similar to the patterns that decorate our clan's relic weapons. When I tell her about them, she doesn't seem very surprised.

"Inscriptions, like a mage's markings, aren't exclusive to New Vetus. The teachers and books don't mention it, but I'm pretty sure our inscriptions all come from other countries. I only think this because there isn't any reference to a creator or any mention of where they originate in the books I've read."

So, our best weapons are common knowledge for these other races? Hopefully, that isn't the case. They are important for the best fighters in our tribes. Well, it matters little, even if our weapons are common amongst other races. Water mages still pose the greatest threat, regardless of whether our weapons are good.

Now that I think of our weapons, I realize both my mom's spear and the other two are still under hundreds of tons of rock at the bottom of the collapsed cavern pass. One day, when I am strong enough—and find a way to dig through that much rock—I will return and find her spear. I feel it will be disrespectful to my ancestors if I don't.

Soon we move on. We spent enough time here and Leal wants to show me the continae, even though I have already seen it. Despite that, the building still amazes me, so I don't oppose the idea.

As we approach the building, I notice a congregation of ursu, not anywhere near as many as during the feast in Raetamen, but quite a few. An ursu yells over the hum of the crowd, standing on a pedestal above the others. Next to him is a raised board with writing I can't make out.

I nudge Leal and point it out as I hang from her back. "What's going on there?" I ask.

She looks toward the crowd and the yelling man before responding, "He's the herald. He makes a speech whenever the continae members want to announce something or share news," she says, steering clear from the crowd.

"Can we see? I'd like to look." I push her to go toward the crowd, my curiosity too much to be considerate toward Leal's apprehension of others.

Leal, as expected, is reluctant. "Can we not? We'll be able to find out what they said from the adults later." This is hardly the answer I want. Why is she so worried around her own people?

"Please?" I plead. I won't push her any more than this if she doesn't want to go, but I'm too interested in what the yelling man might say.

Leal turns to face me, her conflicted eyes darting between mine and the crowd. With a small sigh, she gives in, and I celebrate inside.

"Okay, but just for a bit. I don't want to stay around too long," she says.

I give her a smile of gratitude as she makes her way until we are close enough to overhear and no closer.

The ursu finishes speaking as we arrive. Many ursu laugh as they chatter amongst themselves and move away. Leal and I step to the side and wait along with a few ursu that also hadn't heard the entire spiel. A minute passes before a large enough crowd has gathered again.

Soon the herald speaks up, raising his voice over the collective in practiced ease, his wide chest allowing him to bellow loud over everyone.

"Attention, please, my fellow Vetusians! Please, your attention!" he calls. "I stand before you all with dire news from the far east. Our brethren have been attacked! The despicable Henosis Empire has launched an ignominious surprise attack on our shores near Wrusten. This invasion is unwarranted and shameful. They have pillaged villages, slaughtering ursu farmers, miners, wives, and daughters. The Henosis cowards have murdered many of those unprepared to protect themselves, hiding away from the true might of the New Vetus people." He speaks with a face of solemnity, and the crowd breaks out in a babble of outrage.

The ursu then looks up, giving an air of determination, before continuing.

"But fear not, my comrades. For the Henosis mice will soon feel the might of our collective ursu wrath. We will not forgive this transgression against us and we will obliterate them." The ursu pauses, letting the crowd cheer in agreement.

"Our brethren in the east are, at this moment, marching to crush these invading mice and thrust them back into the seas from which they came. How dare these rodents tempt the snout of the beast that has, until now, ignored them? My fellow Vetusians, I stand here today to inform you that our mighty nation is at war!" The man stands tall as he speaks the last of his speech. The crowd cheers, many amongst them laughing.

I overhear many saying the Henosis Empire is foolish. Many believe the war will be short, and from what I have seen from their numbers and strength, I believe them.

Leal is quick to carry me away, so I can't hear much more from the crowd. She moves away at a fast clip, creating distance between us and the crowd as fast as she can.

I don't have a good understanding of what war is, but from the murals Leal talked about earlier today and the context given in the speech, I can take a guess. It is essentially a fight, like when our tribe fought the chthonic, but on a massive scale.

When we are far enough around the side of the continae, Leal mutters, "This isn't good."

"What's wrong?" I ask.

She looks at me with a frown and scratches at the back of her hand.

"My dad will have to fight," she says, then bites her lip.

Her concern has me worried about her myself, so I try to cheer her up.

"You heard what the man said; those people, the Henosis Empire, are going to be beaten easily. You ursu are really strong," I say, encouraging her to see that there isn't anything to worry about.

It doesn't seem to work. She disregards my words, so I try something a little more direct.

"Leal. Is your father strong?" I ask. I already know the answer. Gerben is stronger than both of the other hotheaded ursu I traveled with on our way here. He is wise too, which is something my elders always emphasized: intelligence over pure power.

"Yeah." She nods, looking at me once more.

"And is your father smart?" I ask.

"Yeah," she responds again, with more strength this time.

"Then you have nothing to worry about. Trust that your dad can keep himself safe," I say. Even as I say it, though, I know it isn't true. Just because someone is strong and smart doesn't mean they can escape anything. My tribe could not avoid their own deaths.

I make sure my own negative thoughts don't show on my face. Cheering her up is my goal, after all. The death of a family member is something I don't want her to even consider. I wouldn't wish that for anyone.

But, regardless of my dark thoughts, it is a relief to see her relax a bit. I plead to Eldest Ember silently in my head for Gerben's safety, for Leal's sake.

CHAPTER SIXTEEN

Furnace

Where were you?" is the question demanded of me upon my return to Gloria's home.

"Out with Leal. You saw me go?" I say to Gloria as she stands above me at the front door. I have only just returned, Leal leaving before I rang the doorbell. Gloria gave me permission to come and go freely, but I can't reach the doorknob.

"No, I didn't." Gloria looks at me, concerned. "You promised me you were going to help me out today, and I've been waiting," she says.

I have no idea what she is talking about. "I did? With what?" I'm not opposed to helping her out, especially as she opened her home to me. I will be happy to return the favor, but I don't recall her ever asking for my help, nor my own agreement.

"You don't remember? You were going to help me work the oven. Come, Solvei, I'm sure you'll love it. It's a noble job." She grabs my hand and leads me to the oven between Gloria's building and the continae. Gloria walks a bit too fast for me and I struggle to stagger along with one hand in her grasp and the other feebly trying to support my weight on my walking stick. I don't complain. If she's been waiting for me, she must be in a hurry to start now.

I'm brought to the stairway leading down to what I assume is the furnace. Rather than a simple hole in the ground like Raetamen's oven, this stairway leads to a large storage room with massive piles of coal along the walls leading to a hatch in the far wall.

"Now, I want you to keep this furnace going while I organize the cooking above. Adding coal to the fire will make this gauge go up. Keep the needle in the green zone for me, okay? Don't let it drop to the red." She points to a circular panel on the wall beside the furnace hatch. A needle is etched with glowing lines I recognize as inscriptions. Three triangular zones paint the panel behind the needle: white, green, and red.

"Oh, and you are welcome to as much coal as you want while you're down here," she says with a virtuous smile as she closes the furnace storage room door above me.

Okay? I guess this is fine. It's dark in here with the door closed, but a simple thought sets my hair aflame, giving me light to see.

This entire situation is kinda sudden, but it's not the worst. It might be pretty comfortable being able to nap in the furnace. How long am I supposed to keep the fire going for, anyway? I wish Gloria was more specific about my task, but I don't want to interrupt her since she is in a rush. She must be late because I wasn't there when she needed me.

I move toward the large stone door blocking the heat of the furnace. An ursu would have to crawl to fit inside, but it is the perfect height for me. It has the added benefit of having the handle low enough that I can actually open it. I grab the handle and pull.

Only to realize I have misjudged the weight of the door. The hatch doesn't budge. I hold the handle and put my leg up against the wall beside the door for leverage. Pulling with all the strength I have gives me only a sliver of movement accompanied by a deafening screech as stone slides across stone. Once the hatch opens a bit, the resistance reduces. It is a lot easier to move when the stone isn't grinding.

The heat of the already burning oven flows over me like a comfortable blanket. I ignore the inviting warmth and check the gauge. The needle is in the white zone, far from the green it should be. So, I need to add coal to the fire, right?

I try to lift the shovel left on a pile of coal. The unwieldy tool is twice my size and too heavy to lift, so I am quick to give up on using it. I settle with carrying armfuls of coal back and forth. It takes a considerable number of trips before the gauge reaches the middling point of the green area, where I am satisfied.

Trying to move that much coal has me exhausted, mainly because I have to hop around to move; I left my stick far enough away from the flames that it wouldn't burn when I wasn't paying attention. I also made it harder as I dropped most of the coal each trip, making it necessary to work longer than I should have. Eventually, I find it easier to just push coal along the floor and throw it in from the furnace door.

With the needle holding firm in the center of the green region, it is time for a break. As I enter the furnace, I close the stone hatch to an ajar position, not wanting to lock myself in.

I sit upon a mass of coal within the small interior of the furnace. The cramped space makes me feel uneasy, reminding me of my time trapped underground. The fire is a cure to the tightening in my chest, making the enclosed space hotter and more welcoming with its cozy heat.

I don't know how long I stay within the furnace. Any time I get comfortable, I worry that the gauge has changed and step out to check again. After the gauge drops to the white zone for the second time, I finally realize it is a measure of temperature. I don't know why I didn't figure that out immediately, but now that I know what it is for, I don't bother checking it anymore. My natural sense for temperature is more accurate than the needle, so I can tell when the furnace needs to be fed. Not having to stress about keeping the temperature sensor within range, I relax into a comfortable nap in the flames.

The insulation of the stone walls and the burning floor of coal allow the furnace to reach temperatures higher than I can achieve personally. It is a perfect temperature for me. I would benefit and grow while confined within this heat. It is a bit like Kindling in a way, albeit lonely.

I'm not sure how many hours I'm down here before Gloria descends the stairs to tell me my job is done and to thank me for helping. Excited, I hurry out of the pit into the dark night outside. The oven feels great and all, but I am uncomfortable being underground. I don't like it at all. It prods too many thoughts of the chasm and that day's events.

I don't mention my worries to Gloria, though. I am glad to help. If I couldn't do this in return, would she continue to shelter me?

Soon, I am once again on my bed in Gloria's home, losing myself to a proper slumber.

An update on the war comes months after I begin living in Fisross.

Every week, I spend a couple of days before the ursu's Bratchina tending to the oven furnace for Gloria. Whenever both Leal and I are free, we meet in her hidden paradise—as she calls it—talking or playing in our time together. She often teaches me about the world outside the wasteland.

Gerben's departure for the war has left Leal feeling depressed. I try to keep her spirits up, but sometimes nothing I do can keep her mind off her father.

I spend the day at Gloria's waiting until Leal's school finishes so I can have something to do. Usually, I go wandering; I'll walk around the city, or angle in the sands beyond the paved streets. But I'm not allowed to do that anymore.

After an incident where an ursu from the military conscription agency raised a fuss at the continae about nonursu wandering by themselves, Gloria hasn't let me go out by myself anymore. It makes little sense to me. Regardless, I am confined to her house unless Leal accompanies me or I am working in the furnace.

While I haven't seen any, Gloria mentioned other nonursu in the city need to follow the new restrictions too.

In my free time, I try to practice my flame control, but when Gloria sees what I am doing, she flies into a panic. "Are you trying to burn my home down?" she says, raising her voice in anger. She comes up to me and grabs the satchel from around my neck.

"If you can't behave, I'll have to take away the things you enjoy."

I feel distressed. I can't lose it. The orb is the last thing I have left from my family.

"No, you can't! Give it back! Give it back!" I demand as panicked sobs build in my throat.

Suddenly, Gloria's face shifts. The anger flees her face and she raises an eyebrow at me. She looks at me as if I am odd. "Why are you so angry? I simply don't want you burning my house," she says, calm. She gives back my satchel with the marble inside, which I clasp to my chest. I am indignant, angry, and confused. Gloria's temperament changes from moment to moment, and it always puts me off. I remain quiet, and she walks off like nothing happened.

Later, she jokes about my reaction, saying, "You overreact so much," laughing at my earlier outburst. It is embarrassing to listen to, but I can't refute her.

I'm not sure what to think about Gloria at the moment and I just want to enjoy my time with Leal, so much so that I keep jumping when I think I hear her.

Only after my tenth time running to the front door today do I find her waiting for me.

"Let's go," I say, grabbing her arm, and walk out the front door, not giving her time to talk.

That's right, walk. My leg has regrown. A good diet has done wonders for my regeneration. I can walk again. I can run, skip, and jump. It feels amazing. I want to spend all my time running around, but I was disallowed from roaming the city alone at the same time I stopped relying on my walking stick.

Once clear of the building, I tell her how happy I am to see her. "You're finally here! You don't know how bored I was without you."

I'm going to keep my confusion about Gloria's actions to myself. Leal is worried enough with her father at war. I don't want to add concerns I'm not sure aren't all in my head.

Leal smiles to me as we walk. "It's good to see you too," she says before picking me up and running toward our little spot. Indignant at being carried again after finally having the freedom to walk, I pound at her back. I can't help but laugh with her as she giggles at my attempts.

We make it to our hidden space, squeezing through the gap once again. Leal drops me and I am quick to land on my feet. Happy I don't trip and fall on my face, I flash a smile at Leal. She returns it for a moment, then drops it as she bites her lip in concern.

"Have you heard?" she asks.

Makes it kinda hard to guess when she doesn't specify what she's talking about.

"About what?"

"The war has moved farther south than expected. They weren't particularly clear about this in the announcement yesterday, but I've heard in the academy that the enemy has taken Wrusten and is nearing Wrine." I don't know where Wrine is, so I just look at her.

At my dumb stare, she seems to get frustrated. "You know, it's so stupid you're not allowed to go to school. This stuff should be common knowledge," she gripes. I watch her as she thinks for a moment, and I can tell the exact instant she has a horrible idea. Her face lights up and she grins at me. The last time she wore that smirk, we got stuck on a roof for hours. We were lucky that someone investigated the noise we were making.

"They announced yesterday that the New Vetus Council will withdraw maintenance support to cities and towns bordering the wasteland. We'll all be moving to cities closer to the heart of the nation soon enough, so why don't we get you a little look into the academy while we still have the chance?" Yep, a horrible idea indeed. I am interested in visiting the place Leal almost never stops talking about, but I can't go against the will of my hosts. They have been nice enough to provide a place to live when I had nowhere else.

Also, I really don't want to be the target of an ursu's anger.

"Leal, I can't. What would happen if they found me there? What would Gloria do if I was caught there?"

"Come on, Solvei. You'll never get another chance. Plus, I really want to show you what the world looks like." They know what the world looks like? Ugh, no. No, don't be tempted.

"I can't be back too late, okay? I don't want Gloria mad at me." Wait, why am I agreeing?

"Yes! You're going to love it, I already know," Leal cheers. Oh, that's right, I just enjoy my time with her too much. This is gonna cause me issues in the future, isn't it?

And so, I am dragged back out of our hidden paradise, and we are on our way to break into Leal's mage academy.

Nothing will go wrong, right?

Right?

CHAPTER SEVENTEEN

Mage Academy

The academy is far easier to break into than I expected. While guards stand at each of the building's entryways, there is a distinct lack of them on the academy grounds. I climbed the stone brickwork of the building in a shaded area out of sight. The stone slabs are large and have just wide enough separation to allow me to use them almost like a ladder. The deep carvings in the stone simply make it easier.

I reach a windowsill on the second floor and take a glance inside. Not seeing anyone, I try pushing open the glass. It doesn't budge. Considering my own strength—and how heavy the ursu tend to make everything—I wouldn't be surprised if it isn't even locked. I'm not too worried. Leal went the official way when she realized it would be far too difficult for her to scale the outside wall. I trust her to open the window with haste and not leave me hanging out here long enough to get caught.

Though I have confidence in her, it's still nerve-racking being here. Every time I see an ursu, I worry they'll look up. Leal assured me I was well hidden before she left, but it doesn't stop my anxiety.

I am so lost in watching the people pass in the distance that a click from the window startles me so much I almost let go of my handholds. I am quick enough to steady myself and hide how startled I am when the window opens beside me. Leal is giving me a knowing grin, which makes me scowl at her. She was watching, wasn't she? Not wanting her to see my embarrassment, I push past her and fall through the window.

Ugh, why does everything have to be so high? The window is almost two meters off the floor. *Meters*: Leal taught me the way her kind measures distance. Makes things much easier than comparing to travel times or body sizes.

Groaning and rubbing the arms I used to break my fall, I rise to my feet.

"The library is two floors up. Stay behind me and hide if I tell you." Leal leads me toward the exit of the room.

I want to look at the lecture hall I've fallen into, but Leal is already dragging me out the door. We come out into a hallway devoid of decorations. Each doorway has been carved with intricacy, not artistically but more simplistically and efficiently. Someone built the corridor with a clear animosity of sharp edges and an affection toward smooth corners. Even the transition between walls and floor is seamless.

The most important thing is that it's empty, not an ursu in sight. I hear nothing that might indicate there are others here either.

"Is it normal for it to be this empty? And are you sure it's okay for you to be here so late? They won't think it's weird?" I ask, keeping my voice quiet.

Without turning, Leal responds, "Anyone who would still be here would be in the labs, so it's unlikely we'll encounter anyone unless the guards decide to do a sweep of the building. Actually, before I started meeting with you, I spent most of my time after classes in the library." She ducks her head as she mumbles, but I can tell she is watching me, as if expecting a reaction. Whatever she is expecting, my lack of reaction, or maybe my silence, is enough for her to breathe a sigh of relief before continuing.

"The library is empty for most of the evening, but the academy caretaker shows up to clean a bit after sunfall and the librarian would have already quit for the day. So, we have a couple hours of free time to roam without worry." As she says that, we surmount the last steps into the library.

The place is enormous. Long bookcases extend out from the walls of the massive rotunda, reaching up toward the ceiling above the double-floored hall. Tables and workstations are arranged at the center of the rotunda, systematically placed between the odd display piece, bookstands, and easels. Small balconies line the spaces between bookshelves. There is no visible way to access them. Maybe on the next floor there is a way to come down?

"Whoa," I can't help but blurt. My tribe didn't have enough books or papers to come close to filling even one of our carts. This vast room dedicated to knowledge is like comparing a mountain to our pebble. I do note, however, that the bookshelves are nowhere near filled, but it is still more than I ever imagined I'd see. Had they planned for expansion?

"I know, right? I've been here for nearly two years now and I still feel like that," Leal gushes, then drags me toward one of the large bookshelves near the back of the library. She must already know where the book she wants is, as it only takes a few seconds to browse the shelves before she grabs one of the thick, hardcover books. With the book in hand, she once again drags me farther into the gap between shelves. Along the back wall, in a nook almost devoid of light, is a pile of parchment scrolls. Without taking any time, Leal takes one before leading me around to another nook between shelves.

The dark alcove turns out to lead to another set of stairs, these much smaller than the main ones, that takes us up to a narrow corridor connecting all the balconies and encircling the library.

We find a table to sit at on the balcony farthest from the stairs, which has an amazing view over the entire library and which I imagine is a difficult space to see from the lower floor.

Leal unrolls the scroll on the table before us. Its identity as a map is obvious. I have seen the ones the elders used when planning our travels. Compared to the ones I've seen in the past, though, this one is missing much of the northern and western regions of the wasteland and only shows the farthermost east of it. Even the small part of the wasteland it shows lacks any details. What it has is a lot more range from south to northeast.

Honestly, I should have expected as much. Of course the áed and ursu would have far different maps. We almost never cross into each other's territory as far as I know. Many of the ursu I've met only superficially know of the áed, and I hadn't even heard of an ursu until I met one.

I wonder if my elders knew about them. They spoke of other beings to the east in their tales of our past, but they never mentioned the size or fur-covered visage of the ursu. The stories usually mention a race that looks as we do in our controlled forms but is far separate from our connection to fire.

Leal drags my attention back to the map, pointing to a dot labeled with the name of this city, Fisross, which is only a touch to the right of a line which I assume separates New Vetus and the wasteland.

"This is where we are, and this is New Vetus." She moves her finger to circle an outlined area of the map.

New Vetus is huge. I've traveled for as long as I can remember, so I have a good idea about the distances this map shows. New Vetus is mostly two separate sections of land to the east and west of each other, split by the ocean from the south and another from the north. The lands connect, barely, by an isthmus that bridges the land between the two bodies of water.

The western section of the nation is bordered by the wasteland and a place labeled *Zadok Kingdom* to the north. On the eastern half of New Vetus, the landmass is surrounded on most sides by ocean or sea. Only on the far southeast does the land extend into an area that is not within New Vetus borders. This land seems to contain many small countries and one that controls the entire coast.

There are many smaller-sized countries scattered around to the northeast of

New Vetus. Detail is less defined in places farther from the ursu nation. It ends at the mountain range that passes a considerable length along the northwestern lands.

The map doesn't cover the mountains going into the wasteland, but from my tribe's maps, I know they extend far to the west. Uncle Rivin called them the Titan Alps. They are considered impassable and far too dangerous to traverse. He told me of their impossible height, and I believe it. You can see their incredible peaks regardless of where you find yourself in the wasteland. Now I know that extends even farther than the wasteland. It is an incomprehensible elevation. And somewhere at the base of that extensive mountain range is the Agglomerate. The home of áed.

Leal has been commenting on a few different cities while I wasn't paying attention, saying something about which city her grandparents live in. I am reminded of one of the main reasons I wanted to come here, so I ask about the place where the war is taking place.

"Leal, where is Wrine?" I ask, trying to find the name amongst the many, many cities labeled within New Vetus.

She points to the eastern half of the country. "It's at the complete opposite side of New Vetus to us." Leal moves her finger to point above Wrine. "And this is where the Empire invaded. This northern region is where the war is taking place."

The area she shows is rather small, and I can see now why many ursu have been taking this war as less than a concern. Well, at least on top of the confidence in their own strength.

Leal continues to point out interesting titbits about the geography of the surrounding area. She shows me the land the ursu originally come from in the south, the Henosis Empire in the far northeast, and even a cluster of small islands she calls the Warring Isles to the southeast.

The hours pass as she teaches me many things from the books she collected until, before I know it, the light in the library dims. I hadn't noticed it until then, but the library doesn't have any windows, so how was it so bright? Before I can ask Leal, the sound of footsteps echoes through the library. On the main stairway is, of course, an ursu.

I hide away from the ledge in case they look up. I glance at Leal to see what we should do.

"Damn it. He isn't supposed to show up for at least another hour," she mutters, careful of being overheard.

"What do we do?" I ask. The last thing I want is to get caught here after they put so much emphasis on keeping me out.

"We'll just wait until he's working in an aisle, then we'll make our way out, all right?" Leal says, trying to keep me calm.

Leal keeps her eye on the school caretaker while I stay out of view. Soon, she directs us to make our way down to the library's main area. I'm told to wait in the dark alcove while she returns the map and books back to their original places.

I feel the tension within me rise as I lose sight of her. It has been a long time since I had to hide like this, and while nowhere near as terrifying as the last time, it still frays my nerves thinking about the possibility of being caught.

Everything is going well, though. Soon enough, Leal rejoins me, and we make our way to the stairway.

Just as we are about to reach the stairway, a voice echoes from an aisle of bookshelves we just passed.

"Leal?"

I am quick to dive behind a chair in the center of the hall. I make sure my body is hidden before the ursu turns out of the aisle and approaches Leal.

"Oh, it was you!" the man says. "You're not out with your little burner friend today?" he asks.

"N-no, Mr. Orsen." She fumbles with her words, nervous. "S-she is working again today."

"Oh? Is that right? Well, good that she is contributing. It'd be a shame to waste our resources on a burner if they didn't give back to the community."

From my hiding position, I can only see Leal, and the longer she interacts with this Mr. Orsen, the more visibly nervous she becomes. She won't give me away, will she? Even if it isn't on purpose, she's obviously acting like she's up to no good. There is no way he's gonna look at her and not think something's up. She can't even give a proper response to his last comment, instead ducking her head and mumbling incoherent words.

Once again, I am powerless to do anything. It is so frustrating not having any control. I was powerless to protect my mom, powerless to save my tribe, and powerless to protect myself in all situations that followed.

I find myself at the whim of those around me all the time, never making my own decisions. And most frustrating of all is that even knowing this, there isn't anything I can do. I have to rely on the generosity of the people around me, even more now than with my tribe. The outside world is unknown to me, and the more I learn, the more I feel I know nothing.

Now I can tell Leal will crumble under the pressure of the situation if it stays as is. I have to help her, either give her confidence or distract the ursu.

"Leal, I know it's hard, but ya really need to stop bein' so shy. You're one o' the smartest kids I know, by far the most dedicated. You'll be unable to do much in the world unless ya overcome it," the ursu says.

Good, he doesn't think she is acting strange. It is odd to hear more confirmation that Leal acts differently around me and her family than she does around all other ursu, but that isn't important right now. While it is a relief that he thinks there is nothing wrong, he is far too close for comfort. He only needs to take a few steps forward and I'll be in clear sight.

What can I do? Do I try to create a distraction or keep myself hidden? A distraction won't be hard to make. I can throw something or light a brief burst of fire behind him to attract his attention, but the issue would be that any distraction I can do will make him suspicious and think something is wrong.

I make eye contact with Leal for a moment before she returns her sight to her feet in front of her.

"I'm sorry, Mr. Orsen, Mom wants me home by dark tonight and I'm already late," Leal manages to say, still staring at her shoes.

Good job, Leal, I cheer internally. Let's hope he'll just go back to his own work now.

"Oh, of course, let me help you on the way out." He then begins walking toward the staircase.

No! Damn, can't you just go back? I glance around for some way out and notice that, while most of the rotunda has grown dark, there are small spherical objects on the ends of each bookshelf that engulf most of the central tables in light. Each orb is just a bit bigger than the size of my hands. I can feel the flames within flickering in a steady, controlled burn.

With little time until the ursu will spot me, I act. Before I realize what I am doing, I have a thread of flame sent toward the closest orb out of the ursu's vision. I push the flames as quickly as I can into the orb, merge my inner flame into the fire within the orb, and snuff it out.

But the moment I withdraw my inner flame from the orb, I feel the flame coming back, and sure enough, the sphere is glowing once again.

I am running out of time, so I throw my flame back into the orb and suck the life out of the flame, this time feeling for its source. I find a trace of energy and latch on. This must be what keeps the orb alight, so I suck all the fire out of it. Take all the energy powering the orb.

The library goes dark.

I smother the flame connecting me to the orb, extinguishing the last light in the hall.

"What in Triglav's . . . !" I hear the ursu shout as Leal lets out a panicked squeak.

I was hoping to stop that orb from remaining lit, but for some reason, all the orbs expired. Well, this still works as a distraction. Actually, it works even better than I hoped. It's not pitch-black, as some light is coming from the stone ceiling itself, but it is dark enough for me to hide, especially as the ursu is now making his way to the closest orb.

I make my way out of cover, grab Leal's hand, and run to the stairs. Hopefully, this won't come back to bite me. It shouldn't. Nobody knows it was me, anyway.

CHAPTER EIGHTEEN

Trapped

Our escape from the academy turns out to be much harder than finding our way in. My little trick with the lighting orbs seems not limited to the library. Many mages have left their labs and now chatter in small crowds outside the towers.

This leaves me in a bit of trouble. Once again, I am on the exterior of the main building, holding myself to the stone beside the window I climbed through. The issue is the increasing number of mages appearing on the grounds below. There are a lot more ursu around than the empty halls Leal and I walked through would suggest.

I am lucky that I'm not in direct moonlight, so unless I ignite, I should be impossible to spot. Though, with the heavy activity on the ground, I can't see any reasonable escape.

It is already dark as it is. I really don't want to get caught on Gloria's bad side by getting back late. She says she worries for me, and I'll feel guilty if I make her wait.

Leal has gone down to see if she can figure something out from the outside. I hope it won't end up being my only option, but for now, it looks like I have no choice but to be patient.

Now that I think about it, why did Leal act so differently in front of that Orsen guy? Was she scared of him, maybe? No, it wasn't just him. She acts that reserved around all ursu. She only opens herself to me and her own family. Even with Gloria, I don't remember her saying more than greetings.

If I didn't know better, I'd say she feared her own people. Whatever her actual problem is, I hope she will trust me enough to share. If there's something I can do to help her, I will.

The scrape of the window being pushed out of its stone frame snaps me to attention. I hug the wall as close as I can without losing my grip. Leal is supposed to be downstairs now, and I have yet to see her. Did someone stop her? Do they know I am here? I tense and hold my breath as I see a silhouette of a head poke out the window.

"Solvei? You there?" I hear Leal's voice whisper.

My shoulders dip in relief as I whisper back. "Yeah. What happened?"

"Sorry, I couldn't find a way to get you down with so many people down there. We'll have to wait until they all calm down," she says.

I give her an okay, and the silence surrounds us for a time.

"What did you do?" Leal asks, and while I know what she's referring to, I have no idea myself.

"I don't know. I was trying to distract him by putting out the flame in that orb thing, and suddenly they all turned off. I didn't even touch the others, only the one behind him."

"Oh," Leal says, her eyes widening. It seems like she knows something.

"Oh?"

"Um, did you happen to put out the source of the fire in the lamp and not the fire itself?"

"I put it out, but there was an energy that kept relighting it, so I pulled the fire out of that."

"Whoa, I thought that was impossible," she says. "You know inscriptions, yeah?"

"Yeah." I give a quick assent.

"Well, a network of inscriptions supplies the lamps of the academy. I think you just drained the source of the lamps. Luckily, it shouldn't take the professors long to reignite. Everyone will be back in their labs soon enough."

Almost as she says so, a soft glow grows in strength from within the tower across from us. Leal steps back into the now dimly lit building. "I'll see you at the bottom when everyone is back inside." And like that, she is gone again.

Sighing, I adjust my stiff arms and legs to a more comfortable position. I just hope there are no more issues tonight.

I haven't spoken to Leal since the night of that incident. When I made it home that night, Gloria was furious. I had to spend an entire week in the furnace to make up for it.

The sudden announcement that the population would be moved out of the city come next Bratchina only made it worse. I was stuck working, keeping the oven burning for Gloria. She never gave me the opportunity to find out if Leal was going to the same place as us.

The council declared that the war had become too resource intensive to

continue to support the desert city Fisross. They gave each household directions for which city they would be relocated to. This announcement had, of
course, ignited widespread rumors. I couldn't talk to anyone but Gloria in this
time, but from what she told me—or complained about—there was a common
understanding that the war hadn't been going as well as they were told. Some
claimed that the Empire had already annexed the entire northern region of the
east landmass.

I struggle to push the heavy suitcase over the high steps of the train. The bag
is almost bigger than me and no doubt heavier. With difficulty, I get it up the
first step. I clamber over it and try to pull it up the next two. I almost lift it to the
next step when a large—or rather, standard-sized—ursu brushes by me, knocking me off my feet and dropping Gloria's suitcase back off the train.

The ursu doesn't stop. He continues on his way like I am beneath his attention. With a sigh, I lower myself down the steps, ready to try again. As I get into
position to lift the weighty luggage, a shrill feminine voice stops me.

"What is this? A midget thinks they can travel with ursu? Have your blasted
kind not already caused enough problems?"

I turn around but scuttle backward as the woman steps far too close. She
towers over me, and I freeze as my back hits the train wheel. She bends down
until her face is right above mine. I do nothing but stare up at her, unable to back
away any farther or escape.

The ursu sneers at me. "It's because of your kind that we are at war in the first
place. It's your fault that we have to leave our home."

"Leave her be. I'm looking after her." Gloria's voice couldn't have come
sooner.

I send silent words of gratitude toward Gloria, who has stepped down from
the train beside me. The ursu towering over me frowns. She makes a disgusting
hocking sound with her throat before spitting on me and storming off.

The spittle lands in my eye and sizzles. It hurts. Nothing close to the pain
water brings, but it still stings. I ignite it, trying to burn away the disgusting
thing as quickly as possible.

My head lurches forward and the back of my head throbs. I look up at Gloria,
who just whacked me.

"No fire," she says, then picks up the baggage in one hand, effortlessly carrying it onto the train.

I wipe at my eye. The spit is all gone, but it aches, and I can't see out of it. At
least I don't need to worry about trying to get that heavy bag on the train anymore. I lift myself up the steps of the train and join Gloria in the seat beside her.

Gloria and I are moving to Morne, where Gloria's parents live. The city is
supposedly much larger than Fisross and closer to the capital. I don't want to
leave, though. I want to at least have a chance to say goodbye to Leal. We have

become good friends during the time I've been here, and it feels wrong to leave without her.

I look out the window, watching the people milling about. I hope to see Leal amongst them, but no matter how many times my eyes pass along each ursu, she isn't there.

The train lurches, almost knocking me from my seat. We are moving. There will be no chance to see Leal again. I rub at my eye and watch Fisross shrink into the distance. The speed of the train is incredible, traversing what would take hours in mere minutes. I would gush at the experience if I didn't feel so hollow inside.

"Which city is Leal going to?" I ask Gloria again, hoping I'll get a better answer this time.

She just sighs at my question. "I've told you: I don't know."

"There's a chance she's going to Morne, though, right?"

Gloria shakes her head. "Unlikely. Calysta's family lives down south. They're more likely to have been sent down there."

It's so frustrating. This wouldn't have been an issue if Gloria hadn't stopped me from seeing her.

"Why couldn't you have let me see her, just once, before we left?"

Gloria's eyebrow twitches once before she responds. "Solvei, you need to get control over your anger. You can't let every little thing make you mad," she says before sighing again. "But okay, I'll tell you. I did it for you. All mages, without exception, are being conscripted. Right now, Leal is probably on the front, making use of her talents."

Before she can continue, I interrupt. "But she doesn't even have any spell markings. What could she do?"

"They started speeding up the process due to the war. Look, I did this all for you. I was worried that it would hurt you knowing your friend is at war. You were better off forgetting about her. Everything I've said and done was for your benefit. You saw how nonursu are being treated at the train station. I've sacrificed a lot to keep you safe. Are you going to be mad at me for keeping this from you?"

I bite my lip and turn back to the window, spotting the first signs of green in the distance.

"No," I say.

I can't be mad at her for trying to help me, even if the entire situation leaves a sour taste in my mouth. Gloria has already shown she's here for me. She'll stick by my side even when everyone else turns against me.

I watch the scenery for a while. The sandy desert of the wasteland is replaced with expansive green farmlands with scattered trees and cattle. I'd always wanted to see a sight like this: something so distinct from everything I am used to. But I find I don't care. The landscape doesn't move me as I thought it would. If I didn't have to lose a friend, I would be fine with staying in the boring desert forever.

A laugh from Gloria interrupts my ruminations. I glance at her, but she just waves me off.

"Sorry, sorry. Just thinking about how you get mad over the smallest of things. Don't mind me," she says, and laughs again, her voice grating at my ears.

I clasp my hands together, fidgeting with my fingers as I return my gaze outside the moving train. This isn't the first time Gloria has found my attitude laughable after our arguments. It makes me feel worthless when she does. I've learned to ignore it, though. It hurts more to laugh along with her.

The next few months are tough.

When we make it to Gloria's home, her parents are not welcoming. They are reluctant to allow even their own daughter to stay with them. They don't even consider me. Fortunately, Gloria is tasked with taking over management of one of the outer ovens in Morne, so she allows me to sleep in the furnace underneath.

Morne is an almost identical city to Fisross, only at many times the size. While Fisross has only one continae and associated central clearing, Morne has six. Much of the city looks the same: highly organized in the center but diverging farther out. Timber is a far more common construction material than stone here, especially in the buildings farther from the center.

I am shown, rather quickly, that my time in Morne won't be fun.

The city often experiences rainfall. The first time it falls, I am sitting at the entry to my furnace. The sudden stinging pain in my back sends me sprawling down into the underground furnace for shelter. The pain and sound of the rain increasing in intensity send me into a panic. I crawl to the back corner of the smoldering furnace, closing the hatch to lock myself away from the water. The water will fill like it did that crevice so long ago. I'm going to die.

I don't bother keeping the furnace burning. So, Gloria eventually comes to check on me. She opens the hatch and takes one look at the furnace, bare of flames and heat, before exploding in anger.

"Why have you stopped the fire? The food up top is ruined because of you!" she snarls.

"I . . . It was raining. I was gonna die."

She snorts and rolls her eyes. "You aren't going to die. Stop overreacting. The furnace is designed to stop rainwater pooling. You are safe as long as you remain down here and do your part."

"I don't want to be down here anymore. I want to go somewhere else," I say. My voice trembles as I plead. Every day I stay underground, it feels like I am being swallowed ever so slightly more. The walls tighten and the ceiling lowers. The comfort of flames becomes less effective every day.

I am suffocating.

"No. There is no other place for you. This furnace is the only safe place. The rain isn't the only thing you should worry about. Public opinion has soured far more against nonursu since we arrived. You shouldn't let yourself be seen outside the furnace again," she says before I am once again left on my own in this horrible underground furnace.

I believe her for a while, not showing myself to anyone but Gloria for over a month. But she visits less and less frequently. I start to doubt her. I think it would be fine just to talk to another ursu once. So when the workers come down to restock the coal for the first time in weeks, I can't help myself. I want to know what is going on outside. I want to know what is happening with the war. Is Leal all right? Gloria doesn't visit anymore, so I can't ask her.

So, I leave the confines of my furnace to talk to the ursu piling up coal.

I wish I hadn't.

I shouldn't have doubted her. She's already done so much for me, so why didn't I believe her?

Now I never leave my furnace. At most, I send out my inner flame to sate my hunger, but never more than that. I've long since realized running the furnace with my own heat is far more efficient than letting the coal burn around me.

The war is going horribly, or at least that's what I assume. Why else would the attitude of the ursu change so wildly? They were such friendly people when I first met them. Loud and unaware of their own strength, but friendly.

Now they are anything but. I am too afraid to leave my cramped tomb. I want to leave. To wander west until I find the desert again, but I am scared. Scared of the rain and scared of the ursu that will find me.

We were on that train for hours. If I am going to run back to the wasteland, I will be walking for weeks, at least. Maybe months. And I will have to do it through the homeland of the ursu that hate anyone that isn't ursu. Land that is also prone to rain.

Of course, that is an impossible scenario. So, I keep the furnace burning, hopeful that one day Gloria will come down and tell me what a good job I've been doing. I don't want her angry at me again.

Now I spend all my time doing the only thing I can do anymore, improving my control. It is the only thing that takes my mind away from the walls encroaching on me. I lose myself in it, blinding myself to the world around me.

There is nothing else I can do.

CHAPTER NINETEEN

Escape

I hate repetition.

I hate it, but it seems my life is destined to fall back into it.

First, when I lost my tribe, I went near-mad with grief. I pushed myself into a painful, endless cycle that I couldn't see the end of. Lost and directionless, only moving forward because there was no other choice.

I find myself in the same repetition. Every day spent in a cycle without possibility of ending. Maybe life is doomed to repeat, going on and on until death finally claims me. I am lonely. I miss Leal like I do my family.

"No," I say to myself. "You're not alone this time. You have Gloria." While she has her flaws, Gloria hasn't abandoned me. She has been with me while all those I care about are gone.

Even if she doesn't visit often.

Like when I aimlessly traveled the desert, I've lost track of time. I am more conscious now than I was back then, but there is no day or night to track the passing weeks. There are ursu that supply coal every so often, but the time between visits feels like years.

I never let them see me, instead hiding out of sight in the furnace. It would be so much easier if I could just lock myself away, but doing so is dangerous.

During one of their visits, the ursu closed the hatch on me, and while I could open the lock from the inside, I lacked the strength to open it again. I grew exhausted after slamming myself into the hatch for hours. Eventually, I couldn't keep the furnace burning any longer. Gloria's anger is not something I wish to experience again, but at least the door was opened and I didn't starve. Now I make sure I have coal wedged between the hinges to stop the ursu closing me in any time they come down.

In the brief moments she comes to visit me, Gloria still talks to me. She is the only one I can talk to, so it is particularly painful when she is angry at me, even if she's never physically violent.

The monotony has been horrible but not unproductive. Constant flexing of my flames has increased both my capacity and my control. I can keep my flame going for much longer than I used to without a fuel source, which I'm not sure is because of either the large amounts of coal I consume or the constant use of my flame.

My control has reached a point where I'm sure my elders would be proud. I can now freely control my inner flame within the bounds of the furnace, even while separated from my body. Are my flames hot enough to eat cobalt or any of the other adult ore yet, I wonder? I know my fire is hotter now. It is a lot more orange than the bright red it used to be. Next time I get my hands on some, I'll have to try, not that I imagine that time will come soon.

I create a ball of flame in my hand, putting effort into making it as spherical as possible and suppressing the fire's nature to flicker. I throw it at the wall, where it bounces, then passes over my head and bursts against the wall behind me.

For a while now, I've been trying to make my flames act contradictory to their nature. This exercise is supposed to give my fire a more physical property, so that it bounces like a leather ball. My body is essentially that: a fire with a physical form, so I assume it's possible.

The way I've been doing it, I doubt it will help me toward that goal, though. I kind of cheat by changing the flame ball's direction myself on impact with the wall. It looks physical at first glance, but it doesn't have the weight, nor has it interacted with the world as anything but fire. All I've succeeded in is creating an illusion.

I have no other actual idea on how to get it to work, though, other than imitating how physical things work. My body's physical form is the only reason I think it is possible.

So, for now, I continue to throw the imitation ball to distract myself from my surroundings while I keep the room at a constant temperature lest I attract Gloria's wrath.

At least, that is my plan until I hear footsteps from the other side of the hatch.

I hurry out of sight from the doorway, hopeful of avoiding a confrontation should whoever it is decide to open the furnace.

And open the door they do, although it doesn't seem like they were smart about it.

"Ah! Ow! Ow!" I hear a girlish cry of pain. A moment later, they open the stone hatch. The clatter of coal dropping from between the hinges enters my ears. I hope they don't shut the door on me now.

I am already out of sight, having shoved myself into the corner. This isn't Gloria; she would've yelled at me to come out instead of touching the handle herself. Whoever this is, I want no part in whatever aggression they may have. It's not like this will be the first visit from an angry ursu. I have long since learned never to even let them know I am here.

"Solvei? Are you there?" the voice calls.

Of course, my dedication to hide crumbles when I hear that voice.

"Leal?" I cry, jumping out to see her standing there crouched over the hatch entrance.

I have to stop myself from running toward her. I don't want to burn her, and I didn't know if she has become just as aggravated as the other ursu seemed to be.

"You were actually here," Leal says, tears lining her eyes. "You were here all along."

I don't know why she is crying, but I am so thrilled to see her. I snap my form back to physicality and control my temperature to be manageable for her. Dashing forward, I hug her.

"I missed you. It's been so long," I say, my sobs rising to join Leal's.

We just sit there for a while. The loneliness I've struggled with for so long is finally relieved. I have so many things I want to ask her; so many conflicting words try to come out my mouth, preventing any from succeeding. So, I say nothing and hug her tight like I would my family.

After we both calm down, Leal rises to her feet, pulling me with her.

"C'mon. Let's get you out of here."

I pull away from her and shake my head. "There's nowhere else I can go."

She looks at me with a frown. "I can't leave you here. I can't leave you with Gloria," she says, and tries to pull me away.

I pull my arm out of her grasp. "Gloria has been good to me. She cares about me. She does what she can for me." I can't look in her eye as I say this. "She's been there for me."

I know she went to war, but it hurt to know the one I cared for like family hadn't been with me anymore. Old wounds tear open anew. I know it isn't her fault, but it still hurts, no matter how guilty it makes me feel thinking about it.

"Gloria told me you'd run away, back into the desert, back to your own kind," Leal says, just loud enough for me to hear.

"What?" I ask, not understanding why Gloria would do that.

"She told us you were gone. She said that, but still had you trapped here, in the same city as us."

I don't understand what she is saying.

"You were here, in the city? But Gloria said they took you to the war."

"No. I've been here since they abandoned Fisross."

That can't be right. Gloria lied? But why?

"Why would she lie?"

"I don't know, but you need to come with me. I'll take you somewhere safe."

But is there anywhere for me to go? This furnace is the only safe place for me, doesn't she know that? It is horrible and I wish to be back in the desert where I could just wander off, but I am petrified that I will be caught out in the rain or come across an unfriendly ursu. I don't want to go through that pain again.

"But it's safe here. I don't know where I can go out there. It's too far away from my home."

"You can stay at my home. I'm sure there's some room. But I'm not leaving you with Gloria."

"Would your mom be okay with that? The ursu I've met have become more and more angry when they see me. Would she not be the same?"

As the thought comes to me, I am once more glad Leal is here. She hasn't become as hateful as the others.

Leal's reaction isn't very reassuring. She breaks eye contact with me and looks into the still-warm furnace behind me.

"I'm sure she'll be fine," she says. "She's already met you, after all."

She doesn't seem certain about her declaration, but I'm not given a chance to refuse as she drags me out into the open air by the hand. It's incredibly unnerving being out in the open once again. I feel vulnerable under the glaring, spiteful eyes of the ursu we pass. I am thankful that Leal doesn't shy away from their attention as she usually would; instead, she pushes past them to get us out of their sight as fast as possible.

She pulls me into a side street, away from the harsh stares piercing my back. With some reprieve, I finally ask the question I've been puzzling over for the last while.

"What happened? Why is everyone so nasty now?"

Leal gives me a conflicted expression before bringing me into a tight embrace. I hold her, comforted by the caring touch. Over my shoulder, Leal murmurs, "I'm sorry, they blame the nonursu. The war hit us harder than anyone imagined. In a single day, we lost the entire eastern half of the country. All of our army—my dad—had been out there. They were encircled, trapped, and slaughtered. Almost all ursu know someone who died out there. When the herald began proclaiming the nonursu as enemies, as infiltrators of the state, so many ursu—the fools they are—were ready to burn them in vengeance. Now all nonursu are in hiding, dead, or worse."

Leal takes a moment to steady her breath. I try to comfort her at the mention of her father.

"Since then, things have only become worse. There is less and less food every Bratchina, leaving many to go hungry. The council allocates jobs to unsuited ursu, and conscription is incontestable. If you're chosen, you are required to go. All the mages with even a basic spell marking have long since left. I never got my first, so I was exempted, but only barely."

It must have been hard for her. I know how hard it is to lose someone so close to you. If I can stay with her, then I will do everything possible to help her move past it.

Reflecting on what Leal said about the perception of nonursu, the safest place for me really is down in that furnace. I don't know why Gloria lied to us, but I'm sure there is some kind of misunderstanding. Well, even if Leal misconstrued the situation, it is still great to see her again. It may be stressful and terrifying being outside my furnace, but I'll push through it if I can enjoy some time with her again.

"How did you know I was there?" I ask as we walk through the scarcely populated streets.

"I, uh, didn't," she says, scratching her ear in embarrassment. "Most ovens have been struggling to get enough fuel to run them in the past couple of weeks, what with most of the coal and usable wood being sent to the front lines. Word has been going around that only a single oven was running nonstop all week long. So, when I found out that it was the one Gloria happened to manage, I became suspicious."

Her willingness to look for me, even without knowing I was here, is moving. She found me when I had no other option but to remain trapped in my furnace.

"I'm sorry I didn't realize sooner. If I'd known, I would've come immediately. I'm sorry for not being there." It seems Leal thinks differently about herself. I can't let her think that.

"No! You had no way of knowing, and yet you still came. Gloria lied, sure, but you cared enough to still look, and I am thankful for that." I reassure Leal that I didn't think badly about her.

I'll need to ask Gloria why she lied the next time I see her. I can't think of a single reason for her to lie, but I'm sure she has a good explanation.

Oh wait, what is Gloria going to think when she realizes I'm gone? I hope she's not too angry again. Hopefully, we can work everything out without raising her ire. The furnace will cool without me there, and I'll get told off for it, but I want to go with Leal for now. I push the tension and dread of my next talk with Gloria into the depths as I follow Leal through the side streets of Morne.

Soon, she leads me through a wooden building far smaller than her home back in Fisross. Morne seems to have many more of their buildings constructed from wood than the stone of Fisross.

Leal pushes through the front door and calls for her mom before urging me in. I watch as she glances around outside one last time before closing the heavy door.

Leal calls out once more, while I stand around, unsure whether I am welcome to move over to the couch. Heavy footsteps come from the other side of the house, followed by Calysta's voice. "Coming, honey. What is it?"

Her voice sounds the same as I remember, sweet and loving, but now laced with exhaustion.

As she turns the corner, coming into the large open area we are standing in, Calysta's eyes snap to me. Suddenly, I felt like I shouldn't have come. She looks more tired, more fatigued than even her voice had indicated. The look she is giving me isn't the one she had when I first met her. It isn't that kind smile that reminded me of my mom's. No, it is a mix of concern and fear, a mixture that makes me want to leave.

"Solvei?" she asks before turning to Leal. "Leal, what is this?" she asks as if the situation bewilders her. Maybe it does? I feel uncomfortable and try to move back to the front door, but Leal blocks me. She guides me to the couch as she answers her mother.

"I found her in Gloria's oven, Mom. Gloria lied to us. She had her locked in the furnace ever since we came here."

"Leal, that's horrible, but . . ." Calysta glances at me before continuing in a hushed voice, "We can't have her here. Do you know what they would do to us, to you, if they found her here?"

"But, Mom, we can't just abandon her! She was almost too scared to come out of the furnace after whatever Gloria did to her," Leal shouts.

"I'm sure there must be some mistake. Gloria wouldn't lie about something like this. She was probably just protecting her."

I nod along with her; Gloria kept me safe amongst rain and increasingly aggressive ursu.

"But then, why did she lie before we even moved cities? You've seen how she's been able to keep her oven running nonstop. She's been taking advantage of Solvei!"

I had to return the favor to Gloria somehow. That the oven I keep heated is the only one running all the time just means I've been doing a good job. Leal is pushing this misunderstanding a bit too far now.

Calysta audibly gulps. "But even if she did, and I don't believe Gloria of all people would, we can't take care of Solvei. I will not put you in danger!" She is tearing up as she says this. Turning to me, she continues, "Even for you, Solvei. I'm sorry." She bows her head.

Leal is getting frustrated, but I can understand her mother's perspective well. Keeping a loved one safe is the most important thing, even if it means she would toss me into a ravenous crocodile den. I understand, but it doesn't make it any less terrifying.

Leal raises her voice. "Even if we don't let her stay, at least help me get her out of the city. Help me get her somewhere safe."

Calysta doesn't respond, stuck in her thoughts. Concerned glances keep jumping between me and Leal, but it's obvious she doesn't want to put her daughter in danger.

Leal decides she has taken too long. "If you're not going to help, fine. But don't try to stop me. I'm going to make sure my friend is safe."

I am once more being led by the hand toward the front door. Leal's harsh tugging at my arm hurts as she pulls me along. This isn't like her. She's usually more careful than other ursu with her strength.

It takes until Leal is pulling the door open for Calysta to finally act. She puts her hand on the door, keeping it shut.

"No, stop. Fine, I'll see what I can do. Just, please, girls, stay here for the moment. I'll be back soon." She pushes past us and leaves us alone in her home.

Leal lets out a sigh of relief, and while I am relieved Calysta is willing to help, I don't like how much I am imposing on them. She said they will be in danger for helping me. Why? Is the hatred of the ursu for other races so great now that they would even go against their own? Leal doesn't give me time to ponder as she takes me to her room.

Whatever happens in the future, I can only hope Leal and Calysta won't be punished for helping me.

CHAPTER TWENTY

Introspection

I am awoken by Leal's hurried nudges to my shoulder. I must have fallen asleep some time ago. A heavy weight pulls on my shoulders as I sit up. I look down only to remember the rain jacket Leal gave me before I fell asleep. It is a massive thing, one of Leal's old ones that she has outgrown. Of course, that means it falls to my feet, dragging along the ground behind me when I walk.

She gave it to me to protect from the rain. I don't know how effective it will be, and I hope I won't need to test it, but I appreciate the protection. Anything is better than nothing, and this thing is large enough to wrap myself in completely. It won't be close to having a ger ready for protection, but I hope it will work well enough.

The sound of conversation from the house's living area is muffled through the door. From Leal's concerned glances, it is clear why she woke me up. She is a mix of angry and scared, and it doesn't take long to figure out why. The voices I hear are Calysta's and Gloria's. Tension fills my body. I can already tell Gloria is angry. Their raised voices easily break through the walls dividing us.

I had hoped Gloria wouldn't be mad. I had hoped she would understand. Of course I would go with Leal after not seeing her for so long. I knew it would be impossible to avoid, but I don't want to see Gloria, not while she's angry. I bring my knees up to my chest and sit against the wall. Maybe they won't make me come out. Maybe Gloria will go away, or calm down, or even let me stay. It is unlikely, but I can hope.

"What in Deivos' name is she doing here?" Leal hisses. "Mom didn't bring her here, did she?"

The voices in the other room stop, and not long after, Calysta opens the door to Leal's room. Her eyes land on me before softening.

"Solvei, honey, we should talk. Please come out with us," she says.

I don't want to; I want to hide away from Gloria, but I know doing that would just make things worse. It always does. So I nod and get off the bed, following her out the door. I have to tie the tail of the jacket away from my legs to not trip. Leal falls in line beside me, looking as worried as I feel.

As I walk into the main room, I can tell Gloria is furious. She keeps a polite smile plastered on her face and holds her body in a passive, nonaggressive pose, but her eyes burn into me. Unable to hold her gaze, I drop my head.

"Solvei, I'm so glad you're all right. When I noticed you had disappeared, I thought the worst had happened."

"Huh?" I look up. She is never this nice. I shiver as I look into her eyes. She is still furious at me but keeps that sickly sweet smile of insincere relief held tight.

"Come now, Solvei, it's time for us to leave," Gloria says, holding out a hand toward me.

I give an uncertain glance toward Leal. I don't want to leave, but I feel like I have no choice, so I give in and step toward her.

"Hold on just a moment," Calysta interrupts. "You still haven't told us why you lied about Solvei, Gloria."

Gloria snarls, the large teeth of the ursu openly displayed, before she attempts to hide her expression with her hand.

"I didn't lie. Solvei here showed up at my door a while back asking for a place to hide, and I did my best to make sure she was comfortable, without alerting the authorities," she claims, then looks down at me. "Isn't that right, Solvei?"

I am too nervous to go against Gloria, so I just stand there fidgeting with the cuffs of Leal's old rain jacket.

"Well?" Gloria taps her foot, some of her fury leaking through her words.

I nod quickly to appease her. I'm not looking forward to having to face her anger later. I can only hope she will be lenient.

"Your story doesn't even make sense! How could she have gotten here by herself?" Leal says.

Gloria only scoffs in response.

"Please, Gloria, we are friends, aren't we?" Calysta pleads. "You can trust me. Please, just tell us the truth."

Gloria doesn't hide her snarl this time. She takes a step toward me, snatches my arm, and drags me out the front door. I struggle to hold myself up by my toes as I dangle from her grip.

"I've had enough of this charade. We are leaving."

Leal jumps on her arm and tries to free me from Gloria's grasp. "I won't let you take her. She's not your slave."

Gloria, with the massive weight difference, brushes Leal off. She stops after a moment, allowing me to steady myself.

"I can do whatever I want with her. She is my property, and I will not let a child stop me."

"Property?" That can't be how she thinks of me. She cares about me, right? She protected me.

"What has happened to you, Gloria? You never used to be like this," Calysta laments. "I won't let you toy with a child's life. You aren't taking her!" Calysta moves to block Gloria's path.

As I look up, I see Gloria's eyes glaring into Calysta. Her rage, no longer hidden, is almost palpable in the air between us. Her eyes flicker to me, lips twisting into a nasty smirk.

"Well, if you want her so much, go ahead." Suddenly, I find myself thrown onto the stone brickwork of the road. A short, patronizing laugh escapes Gloria's chest as she strolls away.

"I hope you enjoy your time with the little burner while you can," she says to the two. Turning to me, she continues, "As for you, well, I'm sure you'll be happy to see your barbarian tribe soon enough." With her last words given, she strides down the street, the echo of her steps the only sound to be heard.

I'm helped to my feet by Leal. She looks anything but happy about the situation. I feel numb. I am confused and don't know what to think. Leal looks worried and waits until Gloria is out of sight before she speaks.

"You won't be able to stay here anymore," she says.

It seems her mom agrees. "Yes, she's probably going to the continae now. If we are lucky, we'll have an hour before the reksha come."

"I'm gonna take Solvei somewhere she can hide for a bit," Leal says to her mother.

"Okay. Don't be long. You'll need to be here when they come."

Taking that as an invitation, Leal grabs my hand and pulls me down the street.

I try to run beside her, but she is moving too fast. I'm tripping over my own feet just as my mind trips over the words cycling in my head. Gloria's words play on loop. My mind does its best to find reason behind them. I don't want to believe she thought that way. I want there to be a mistake or some sort of misunderstanding or anything to explain the words she used. I was property? Is that really how she thought of me? It can't be.

I am too lost in my head and barely notice when Leal picks me up. I must've been going too slow for her. I'm sorry, I try to tell her, but the words don't reach my lips.

After a few minutes of running, I'm met with the view of the mage academy. It's just as I remember it from when Leal and I were in Fisross.

Wait . . .

On closer inspection, I can see slight differences from what I remember of the carvings of the building back in Fisross, but otherwise, the building is identical. The large, circular central building with the dome on top. Even the four peripheral towers look the same as in Fisross.

Leal carries me through the front doors, running straight up the stairs and into the library, which, of course, looks the same as the last. Nobody stands guard. Although I notice the bookshelves are filled more than back in Fisross. Leal drops me on the same little balcony we used last time. No, not the same, I remind myself.

Leal holds my shoulders and makes me look into her eyes.

"Solvei, I'll be back as soon as I can, all right? There shouldn't be anyone who would come here anymore, but please be careful and hide unless you are sure it's me. I'll be back, okay?"

I don't trust myself to form the proper words, so I just nod my assent.

Leal waits not a moment more. Before I realize it, I am alone again.

I have to stop myself calling out to her. I don't want her to leave. What if I never see her again?

Silently, I lean back in the far-too-large chair. My legs dangle below, and my head barely reaches the table above. I try my best, but I can't stop my thoughts from wandering. I don't want to, but my mind keeps returning to Gloria's words.

"Property."

I don't want to believe it.

"She is my property."

She couldn't think that way, right?

"I can do whatever I want with her."

No! She protected me. She kept me safe while surrounded by danger. I pull my legs to my chest and hug them as I try to remember all the times she helped me and protected me.

She kept me safe from the rain by allowing me to stay in the furnace. She gave me a place to stay when I needed it, giving up space in her home for me. Well, she did until we moved to Morne, but her parents didn't have enough space for another body. She protected me from the anger of the ursu as their hate festered. Well, except for the times when they found me in the furnace, but I'm sure there was nothing she could have done about that, anyway.

That list is . . . admittedly, not as impressive as I thought, but I'm sure there were things she helped me with or protected me from that I don't know about. She always told me she was doing things for my benefit. Although I never understood how much of the things she did would help me.

The line of thought does not help as I hoped it would. If . . . if she didn't protect me as much as I thought she did, then why did I believe that? What made me think she did everything for my sake? Why did she always tell me it was all for my sake?

I don't like where my thoughts are taking me. I try to change course to why she lied to Leal and me. Why didn't she tell us we were in the same city? After the last time I saw Leal, Gloria said she was being sent to war. But that never happened. Leal is still living with her mom right now. Why would Gloria lie about that?

I spent so long worrying about Leal. I was scared she might get hurt or die. Now I know she said a similar thing about me to Leal and Calysta. The only reason I can think of is that she intentionally tried to separate us, but why?

When Calysta showed she was willing to protect me, Gloria almost immediately gave up on me. I hadn't paid attention to it at the time, but she abandoned me then, didn't she? Did she decide I wasn't worth keeping around anymore? I tried my hardest to do my part and repay her kindness in the past year. Did she think that was worthless? I put a lot of effort into keeping that furnace going nonstop. It became even harder when I had to strain myself with less coal than I needed to keep it going. Gloria has always told me it was the minimum I could do to pay her back, but what has she actually done to help me?

A tinge of heat fills my chest as I recall the word she spoke.

"Property."

She did, didn't she? She considered me her property? She had me working day and night without end, and I just believed her!

Indignant fury boils within me. How could I be so stupid? Why did I just do everything she said as if it was obvious that I had to repay her for her generosity? I scoff aloud. What generosity? Thinking back, even during our first meeting, she planned to make me work for her. She jumped at the opportunity to take me in when she realized I was an áed. She was planning to put me under her thumb since day one.

I don't know who I'm madder at: her for doing this to me, or myself for being foolish enough to fall for it harder than a sandworm biting an angler.

She didn't want to keep me safe from the rain. That was just another reason to keep me confined to the furnace. And I'm sure she was oh-so-happy when the common sentiment became so ursu-supremacist. It made me fear leaving the oven, for any reason. I truly didn't think I could leave. I had begun to believe the furnace was the only place where I wouldn't die some horrible death.

She manipulated me. How had I not realized before? The frustration and fury festers within me. I am too late to realize my control has slipped. The searing heat within me roils, and I feel hot for the first time in my life. The intense combustion explodes from my chest, incinerating the table and chairs. Before I know it, the bookcases and walls around me are engulfed in flames.

I know I should try to extinguish them, but the flames react to my fury as my form devolves. I am too far lost within self-loathing and my newfound hate for Gloria. I want to burn down everything she cares for. And, with that thought, I descend the stairs. I care little about anything but the object of my rancor as I step out onto the street. I walk in full view for any eye to see, ignoring the roaring blaze behind me.

CHAPTER TWENTY-ONE

Conflagration

While I have never been invited into Gloria's new residence, I know which building it is. Conveniently placed behind the oven she manages, the building is obvious as I make my way toward it. I keep out of sight as much as I can, while far more obvious to any that look my way than I would like. My form refuses to be reined in; the rage bubbling under the surface agitates my flames. Turbulent flares flick out with every lapse of concentration.

I try to keep my thoughts blank. Empty. But any time I come close, they snap back to the betrayal, the manipulation, the idiocy I've endured. I've never hated anyone like this before. Sure, I hated my mother's murderers. But they were faceless, distant. Like a bogeyman to be feared. Gloria is close, someone I trusted. I believed her to be a good person the entire time she took advantage of me. It is a dirty feeling. It is foul, and I know just how to appease it.

As I arrive into the plaza of the continae, a commotion drags my attention to the tall tower ahead of me. I jump back into the street I've come from just as a crowd of ursu charges out of the continae in my direction. I run back and hide myself in one of the side streets. I have enough sense about me to know not to be seen by such a group.

The ursu rush past me, heading in the direction I came from, shouting at each other all the while. I come out of hiding and look where they're rushing. Over the dark silhouette of buildings is a bright red glow.

Ah, she's gonna hate me for that. I send a mental apology to Leal.

The thought of Leal focuses me again, the fury building once more. I don't know what the reksha are, but Leal and Calysta were sure that Gloria would send them. Hopefully, the fire at the academy will distract them from both Gloria's house and what I'm about to do.

I toss the jacket Leal gifted me to the ground. I'll be back for it. Without it being tempered like my other clothes, I don't trust myself to stop it from burning.

After running into the small gap between buildings beside my target's home, I look up at the stone structure. I won't be able to burn through it, as this building is one of the few in the city with a stone exterior. Hopefully, the interior will have enough burnable material for this to work. Now I need to decide whether I should wait for Gloria to come back or just start burning as is. I will be satisfied as long as Gloria has nowhere to live.

With time to think, I find myself really not wanting her to get off so freely. Sure, burning her house might destroy anything she possesses, but she'd be able to move on.

I remember the visits I sometimes got in the furnace. The pain that followed.

No. I want to make sure the fur gets burned off the face she is so proud of. I want to disfigure her; then her outside will mirror the inside.

So I sit and wait, trying to cool the fury amplifying my flames as I reflect on all the moments in the past. The times she misled or willingly ignored me. The unreasonable anger, her manipulative words, the constant multiplying fear of the outside world.

Right here, right now, I cannot care less if it rains. The rage settling within me prevents any fear rising to the forefront.

I know how visible I am right now, so I hide out of sight, careful of any light I give off. Before long, the sound of whistling greets me right before the slamming of a door.

She's returned.

I picture her in my mind, walking with a self-assured smirk, pushing open the door as if everything in the world is perfect.

Incredible, searing heat burns through me. I feel hot. A raging tempest of flames whips around my body. There is no stopping now. I move toward the door Gloria has just gone through with intent. Nothing will be stopping me now.

The handle is far too high for me, as most doors in ursu cities tend to be, but I pay it no mind. My roiling flames burn around the handle and hinges of the heavy wooden door in but a moment. Without its supports, it slams against the ground with a crash. My way is clear.

I make my way up the large wooden stairway, paying little attention to the flames that spread off my form as I ascend. Once at the doorway to Gloria's apartment, I stare up at it. I don't plan to get any closer than I already am.

I flare my inner flame, inciting it to burn as hot as I can manage. The scorching heat warps the air around me, and after only a moment, I launch a stream of flames straight toward the door to that horrible woman's home. Idly, I notice the door burn far quicker than expected. Where the stream of fire impacts the wood, it takes barely ten seconds before it manages to pierce through. I plan to keep the flames going, but suddenly, the ground collapses underneath me. Panic fills me, and for a moment, I am back in that cavern with the world breaking apart around me.

Fortunately, this fall isn't as long as that one was. The blaze overwhelms the staircase above, fire already reaching the highest level of the building. Most of it is still intact, but it burns fast. I don't want to be buried under the creaking and crackling wood above, so I scramble out the front entrance into the open air.

Sudden screaming comes from within, and I hear another collapse from the staircase. It is oh-so-satisfying to watch as Gloria runs out, shrieking in pain, with her entire body aflame. I just stand there watching as Gloria tries to beat out the fire engulfing her. The moment we make eye contact, she throws herself at me. Before I can even process what is happening, she pins my arms to my side. My legs dangle, unable to touch the ground. Gloria holds me in a crushing two-hand grip. I have never felt the size difference between us as intensely as right now.

Panic fills me and I push my inner flame to surround the both of us. I push hard to increase the temperature. I try to burn through the woman's hands, but the strength of the ursu is too much. Gloria pulls back one arm, the other hand gripping tight. She lashes out at me, striking me across the face. I feel my chest cave in, and my head throbs with the impact. I keep my flames rippling into her as she continues her beating. My screams soon join hers as I force as much as I can into the flames through the agony she is inflicting.

I watch in horror as her face melts in front of my eyes, the fur covering her body long since burned away. Her eyelids are scorched out of existence, leaving a gruesome and terrifying visage glowering at me. I close my eyes, not wanting to look at the disgusting sight, but I can still see every detail. My flames show me exactly what is happening to every part of her body, but I cannot relent on my flames. I keep them swirling around us, burning at any part of her they can.

The screaming stops. Gloria's grip around my chest loosens. With my free hand, I push against the fingers suspending me, allowing me to fall to the ground. The horrible pain in my chest and the aching of my head leave me woozy. I bring a hand up to my chest. I can feel where my body crumpled under the strength of her fingers. My head drops to inspect the damage and I wish I hadn't. My torso is compressed, crushed, and the sight only makes the pain worse.

Her hand left a clear imprint on my chest, like clay clenched too hard. My arm—the one that was pinned—doesn't move. I can't feel it, but it bends at a strange angle above the elbow. I am lucky she didn't whack my head off with her hits, but the damage is still severe. I wrap myself in inner flame, hoping it might help with my recovery. The soothing it brings to my aching body is a relief in itself.

I look back at Gloria; her abominate glare cuts deep into my being. There is so much hate in her eyes, I'm left stunned. No skin remains unburned and she cannot move any longer, but she maintains her scorching eyes on me even as one of them bursts. My anger and hatred drain from me. Gone. I'm filled with disgust, not only at the sight of the woman in front of me, but also at myself for having caused it. She doesn't have long to live, but she is spending every last fiber of her being to show how far her disdain for me extends.

I didn't want this. I just wanted to get some payback for her betrayal. I wanted to burn her house. I wanted to burn off the fur she spent so long each day tending to. I didn't expect her to attack me. I never realized how easily she would burn.

The building above me is now engulfed in flames. It's horrifying how far the fire has spread. It's too much for me to stop.

Suddenly, my attention is brought back to the world around me. Cries and screams magnify, and crowds of ursu now cluster in front of the burning building.

A family off to my left cries and huddles together, watching the flames burn what I now realize was their home as well. I never even considered anyone but Gloria would be there. I was so lost in fury, I just did not think about anything else.

Gloria is dead now, but somehow her lone eye stares, damning me.

I didn't want this. I shake my head as if denying those accusing eyes. I didn't want this.

Angered shouts reach my ears and I look up once more to see a gathering. A crowd staring me down as I stand over Gloria's charred corpse. A stone flies past my head. Many angry ursu pick any odd item or stone from the ground. But what hits me more is the terrified glances I am given. None of them try to approach me, instead staring at the body at my feet.

I rise, ready to make my escape. When they decide to attack me, I want to be gone. A loud crack snaps everyone's gaze to the burning building. The stone walls contain the blaze effectively, though that isn't to say the fire has been controlled. No, the inside of the building burns with an intensity I cannot replicate, still visible through the windows in the stone. The entire interior has burned away. No chance any of the ursu's homes can be saved. I notice the flames are now breaching the roof of the building, rising above the walls containing it.

Another loud crack resounds as one of the stone walls topples into the adjacent building. I watch, unable to do anything as the inferno spreads toward the new building, easily burning through the opening made by the wall of the first building.

More panicked screaming spreads, and I notice more and more ursu coming out of their homes.

I need to leave now.

As I run, I am mostly ignored by the ursu, who likely find it too difficult to turn away from the destruction of their homes. I only receive a couple of stones thrown my way from angry ursu. I try to regain control of my form as I run away, but it's too hard, the pain in my chest now competing with the guilt for primary position in my mind.

As quickly as my aching body will allow, I sprint away.

I don't know what I am going to do now. They already hated me before this; now there is no way I will get any leniency if they find me. It is sad that I won't get to say goodbye to Leal, but I can't stay here. I need to get out of Morne, and fast.

From the cover and safety of the tree line at the forest north of Morne, I find myself unable to look away. I look down on Morne from the inclined woodland and gulp, trying to gain a hold over my fluctuating emotions. It has gone so far out of control, so much further out of control than I even considered possible.

The city is burning.

It is burning, and it is my fault.

I don't know whether it spread from the academy or Gloria's building, or both, but now it has engulfed an entire section of the city. I didn't notice while I was escaping the city, but it has become readily apparent what I have done now that I look back. It is currently limited to the central area of the city, but with how fast it has already spread, I don't doubt for a second it will continue into the outer districts. I have seen the buildings that make up the peripherals of the city: all timber structures.

I am horrified by what I have caused. Because of my anger, an entire city of people will go homeless; some might not be able to escape. Gloria's dying, burning, melting face flashes through my mind. I feel sick, but I can't turn my eyes from the sight before me.

I worry for Leal. Have she and her mom gotten out of the city safely? I can only hope so. I am already wracked by the guilt of having destroyed their home, especially as they had to leave their last not too long ago. I don't know what I would do if my actions killed Leal.

I have to leave. My inner flame still supports my chest with its soothing warmth. I will be visible from anywhere in the dark night. I need to leave, but I struggle to pull myself from the glowing city. A small part of me thinks the view is spectacular, the greatest pyre I have ever seen. The flames of the city resonate with me and I can't help but feel awe in its presence.

I squash that feeling down within me. Is a good view worth deaths and leaving thousands without homes? Of course not, and I hate that I even felt that way.

Well, I hate it, but that doesn't stop me from continuing to watch the blaze as it spreads. It grows slowly, but it never falters, incinerating everything in its path. If someone hasn't left the city yet, I don't know how good their chances of escape will be. I have already seen firsthand how the ursu aren't as resistant to fire as I thought.

As the city is engulfed by conflagration, I realize I am cutting it close. I need to leave now. The amount of ursu in the area is immense. Most seemed to be more interested in lamenting their loss, but they will chase me sooner or later, and my flames stand out in the darkness, after all. Forcefully snapping my eyes from what is both the most glorious sight and my greatest regret, I turn and make my way into the forest.

I tighten Leal's rain jacket around my shoulders. I don't know where I am going, but I need to get as far from the ursu as I can.

CHAPTER TWENTY-TWO

Wailing Woodland I

I remember the tales my mom told of the wondrous landscapes outside the wasteland. She used to tell me about the incredible forests to the east, the endless mountains to the north, and the horrifyingly vast oceans to the south. It was one thing to hear about it, but with only the wasteland as my point of reference, I had no way of truly understanding the diversity these lands contained.

After leaving Morne, I travel through the forest, following the moon northwest. I hope this will be the fastest way to return to the wasteland. I have been lucky so far—having gone almost a week without rain—but I don't believe for a second that my luck will last. Either I find shelter for when it comes, or I get back to the wasteland fast. The desert is a good month's travel from here at the very minimum. I hope the surrounding trees will be enough cover when the eventual rain finally comes.

As I move deeper through the woodlands, the trees grow wider, larger than I'd considered possible when the only plant I had seen were the brittle shrubs. It is far different from what I've ever believed possible from my mom's stories. Even the horizon-spanning views I saw from the train couldn't have prepared me for the feeling of being in this new world.

The roots of these trees grow out of the soil, coiling through the underbrush. The density of the roots below my feet forces me to walk over them rather than the ground below. Although these large roots are hard to work around, I am glad they are there. The undergrowth of the forest has become almost a natural snare. A few times I stepped on the low-lying bushes between the roots of the giant trees and found myself falling into it up to my chest.

The farther through the forest I walk, the more deceptively deep the ground below becomes. To my eyes, the weeds and bushes where I placed my foot were only a thin covering of the ground, but I fell so much farther than I was prepared for.

I, of course, did not panic and properly extracted myself from the restrictive trap without nearly burning the forest down.

The random forest fire occurring at the same time was a complete coincidence.

Thankfully, the trees themselves seem more resistant to flames than ursu buildings, so I could put out the fire with ease.

I continue my way through the forest, jumping from root to root. The trees don't look like they are growing any taller, but they are definitely growing wider, some reaching three meters in width, about the height of an ursu. Of course, the roots continue to spread almost longer than the trees themselves. At least that's what it feels like, what with the amount of entangling and knots made between the roots of different trees.

Making my way under a particularly highly arching root, I notice an uncomfortable silence has settled over the forest. The constant cacophony of humming and whistling bird tunes I've grown used to within the forest has stopped. I look around, trying to spot whether the birds high in the trees have flown off or simply gone quiet. It is hard to make out as they blend in with the foliage, but I'm pretty sure I can see a few huddling up on the branches.

Curious about their behavior but wary as to what caused it, I stay still.

An ear-piercing shriek shakes the forest and cuts right into my very being. My body stiffens as, in an instant, multiple giant trees topple not a dozen meters from where I stand, crashing and splintering to the ground. Sunlight shines through the now-missing patch of tree cover.

I look toward the damage, but still I only barely catch sight of a giant bird as it returns to the air with its talons grasping what I think are dingoes.

It all happened in a moment, but noise once again fills the forest. The trees not obliterated in the massive creature's path creak and crack as their supports struggle from the weight. The birds sing once again, almost cheering the damage caused by the giant. And the howls begin.

The sound comes from every direction. Their mournful cries set me on edge. I hadn't noticed the creatures around me until the giant hawk snatched two of their numbers. The bird itself, gone before I could truly process what was going on, was large but not titanic. It was about half as tall as the trees, but it still rammed through them with little care.

The howling stops, but that doesn't ease my nerves. I am surrounded, but hopefully after losing two of their members, the beasts will move off. A hope that is dashed almost immediately as a big wolf—they aren't dingoes, as I mistakenly assumed—moves into my sight and growls as it approaches.

The beast is larger than I remember Leal describing it, almost as large as an ursu and probably as heavy as one. The wolf moves toward me, drool dripping from its snarling jaws as it eyes me. But the wolf isn't alone, right? Where are the others? I turn my head to look for them. That is a mistake.

The wolf in front of me pounces when I look away. I jump to the side as fast as I can, which is enough to dodge the jaws of the beast as it goes for my neck. Its teeth miss me, but the weight of the wolf slams into my shoulder and tosses me like I weigh nothing.

I now have space, but my chest throbs in pain. A growl behind me. I glance back and spot four more wolves approaching, spread enough to cut off my escape. These are not nearly as large as the original but still far larger than I am. With the thought of the original, I turn to see it approaching at the same steady pace as before.

I have little time, and the space I have left to work with is steadily decreasing. I launch a spear of flame toward the largest wolf, trying to push it back. The beast yelps but jumps out of the way easily enough. That reaction is the best I can hope for. I throw out a wave of flame at the four smaller wolves and run past them as they focus on evading my distraction. I'd rather take my chances against the four smaller ones than the original. The beast just feels stronger somehow.

After breaching their line, I run as fast as I can, jumping along roots and avoiding the underbrush. I am fearful, but it is manageable. I can fight these if I have to; I'm not defenseless, not against them. Some things I'll never be able to go against—the Titans and maybe the hawk from before—but these wolves are just big dingoes. We hunted them all the time back in my tribe. The wolves will tear me apart if they get ahold of me, but they aren't unbeatable.

Turning my head, I smother the dread rising within me as I see the wolves catching up. I launch myself at the nearest tree and grab ahold of the bark lining the trunk before pulling myself up. I burn my hands into the tree where there isn't anywhere to grab and rise to the branches of the canopy.

With a foothold underneath me, I glance down at the wolves. And of course, they are trying to climb the trunk after me. Their sharp claws dig deep into the wood, letting them climb as if they are walking on normal ground.

I consider jumping off when they reach my height or maybe leaping to another tree if I can get close enough. But the sight of the original wolf sitting patiently on the roots of the forest floor makes me reconsider.

This is my best opportunity. If I can knock them off the tree while they are climbing, I have a good chance to remain safe up here until they get bored and give up.

I wait until the first wolf is almost upon me, then I surprise it with a stream of flame right into its muzzle. It yelps and flinches away; its grip comes loose and it falls to the ground below.

Without paying any more attention to the first wolf, I move the stream of fire toward the second not far behind. I don't care what I might be setting alight behind it. The second doesn't have much more time to react than the first and soon meets its sibling on the ground.

The next wolf has climbed close enough that it can leap off the trunk, flying toward me. In a panic, I send out a quick burst in its direction, which fortunately either distracts it or pushes it off course enough that it sails over my head. The wolf arcs far through the air before landing in a particularly large section of undergrowth.

Snapping myself away from the creature's descent and berating myself for getting distracted, I turn to find the last wolf missing. I twist around the branch, but the creature isn't revealed below. Where is it? Has it given up? I glance back toward the big one, who is still sitting in the same position but directing a loud snarl toward me.

Nope, the wolf didn't rejoin the original.

I snap my attention above me. Almost too late, I bring my arms up to protect myself. The wolf bites down hard on my arms as my back slams into the branch below me. If I wasn't in such a horrifying position, I would praise my luck not to have fallen into the waiting maws below.

Pain rushes through my arms. It feels like they are being torn apart. The sharp teeth of the wolf fill my vision, pushing closer toward my head. I can barely keep the beast at bay through the pain. In desperation, I push as much of my flame into the wolf's open gullet as I can. The beast yelps, flinching in pain.

The wolf's cries end and the beast falls limp on top of me. I feel the flames within it burn away much faster at the flesh than I thought possible for anyone but the elders. Gloria burned quickly too. I consider if it is possible that all creatures outside the desert are as unresistant to fire as I have seen. I remember creatures of the wasteland taking a lot more punishment before they burn.

I probably got stronger too, but I know I am still nowhere close to the strength and power the rest of my tribe had. I pull my flame from the wolf, stopping the burn and trying to retain as much of the body as I can. Uncle always stressed the importance of using everything from our kills, that we should use anything that remains of other creatures to allow them to be useful even in death.

I push the heavy weight of the wolf off myself and let it fall below. I cradle my aching arms to my chest and look down. One wolf pulls another out of the undergrowth where it fell. The original keeps its growl rolling through the air between us as it glares up at me. With a final snarl in my direction, it barks at the other wolves before marching away from my tree.

Have they finally given up? I watch as the wolf that was trapped and the one that helped it out glance at the ground below me before following the original away. I let the relief fill me for a moment before I realize that there should still be one more wolf around. Looking down, the ground around the tree is burning, but not too far outside the flames is one wolf, dead. Its head is bent at an odd angle. Did it snap its neck after falling down?

I should put out the fire before it ruins the creature's pelt. Well, I should, but I'm still hesitant to climb down with the wolves so close. Did they leave because they had already lost so many? Was it because of the fire? If I had realized how prone they were to burning earlier, this whole situation would have been much easier to deal with.

Honestly, I shouldn't even be scared of them.

A sudden jolt of pain through my arms reminds me they could still hurt me, and I change my thought.

I shouldn't have been *that* scared of them.

Well, if they are as scared of fire as I am water, then I should be fine to continue on.

My arms hurt too much to properly climb down, so I shrug to myself and jump off. Slamming onto my back on the roots below hurts more than I expected, but it is nothing compared to the jolt it sends through my previous injuries. Attempting but failing to ignore the pain, I distract myself by extinguishing the flames burning through the bark of the tree and the surrounding undergrowth.

It's kind of relieving that these immense trees aren't easy to burn; it makes preventing the spread of flames effortless. After what happened in Morne, I know I have to be a lot more careful not to let my flames spread too much. It's still shocking to me how much damage it can do.

Uncle told me I shouldn't waste resources. I should take the pelts whenever I can. But right now, being bogged down by a couple of wolf skins is the last thing I need. So, to not disrespect Uncle's memory, I send my flame out and consume the corpses. If I was with my tribe, this would be far too wasteful, but I'm not. I can't do everything how we did back then.

I take as much energy from the animals as I can before resuming my hike in the direction I believe is west. I can't see the moon anymore with how dense the foliage has become, but I hope I am heading the right way. Now I just need to pay attention to my surroundings so those wolves don't corner me again.

CHAPTER TWENTY-THREE

Wailing Woodland II

I am really getting deep into the forest now. The trees may not have risen any higher, still sitting at about ten meters tall, but they are definitely getting fatter.

I make my way through the labyrinth of interlacing roots, passing under an aerial root almost as wide as I am, and am forced to turn to my right and crawl through a tight space before reaching open air again.

I climb above one of the higher-growing roots in the area and look around to get my bearings. I hadn't noticed it, but I've been crawling through the roots directly under a tree. Although, it isn't surprising considering how fat the thing is; it is easily wider than even the furnace I lived in for so long.

Navigation through this forest is a nightmare. I would love to just walk in a straight line, but the maze created by the interconnected trees is a confusing mess. I try to keep above the roots, sticking to just the highest parts. But doing so has become difficult, often forcing me to make risky jumps to keep out of the depths. Which, many times already, resulted in hurting myself or falling deeper into the roots than I wanted.

I haven't seen the ground underneath or the underbrush in a few days now, and it is making me curious. So far, I've hesitated to go too far down, preferring to watch that I'm heading in a roughly straight line—which I can only hope is still northwest—and, well, I still dislike being in cramped areas. I don't like the idea of being closed in, no matter how used to it I have become.

But my curiosity wins out. I am moving down into the roots, using my small size to crawl between many tight gaps between roots. A sudden thought of an ursu attempting to do the same but getting stuck brings a giggle bubbling up from my chest.

I still feel horrible for what I did back in Morne, but the freedom from the furnace is liberating. It is great being out here by myself and not having the constant fear of Gloria's anger or the steps of an ursu drowning my thoughts.

Of course, that isn't to say I don't still have worries. The incident with the wolves makes me wary of my surroundings, even if I haven't had an issue with them again. No. Simply making my own choices is the real reason I feel myself untangling from stress. I never want to be stuck doing someone else's bidding again. I need to make sure I'm not stupid enough to fall for the same trick Gloria pulled on me. I need to make sure not to trust anyone who puts themselves forward as being generous.

Fortunately, I don't need to worry about that right now. All I need to focus on is finding how deep these roots go.

I push through another tight squeeze to find . . . more roots. I have already gone down as far as the trees are tall. Where is the ground? As I lower myself down from a suspended root, a soft hiss enters my ears. I spin on the spot and see a . . . snake? It's been a long time since I've come across one, but I have never seen one with such a deep green color. It isn't as big as the ones in the deserts of the northern wastelands, but it is still as wide as my arm and almost as long as my body.

The snake hisses at me, rising in an obviously aggressive pose. I don't want to bother it, so I try to move around it, careful in case it attacks. Well, it attacks, and I don't even realize it before it has already bitten deep into my hand.

Wow, it is quick. The bite stings a bit, making me reflexively burn its head off.

Okay . . . things outside the desert really burn quick, huh?

I tug out the fangs that didn't burn along with the rest of its head and pick up the now-limp body.

"I guess you're my lunch now, huh?" I say to the dead serpent. If he wants to object, now would be the time, after all.

Yeah, I didn't think so.

I take a bite from the dead snake and continue on. The roots are getting almost too tight to move through now. I poke my head through the last gap in the roots I can. A glance below shows nothing but a dark abyss. I drop an orb of flame to light the opening beneath me.

I shiver when I realize how much space is below me. I can't see anything from the light of my flame until I reach the limit of the range I'm able to control it. The undergrowth below appears, only slightly illuminated by the light of my flame. It sways as if experiencing a calm breeze.

I'm just about to extinguish the orb of flame when I feel the flame suffocated by some other force.

I'm frozen, staring down into the darkness below. I don't know what caused it, but I dare not light another orb. I move my head out of the gap only to be pelted by a turbulent gust from below. The blast of air shakes the surrounding roots, the same roots that haven't budged even with all my weight standing on them. A loud wail surrounds me, shrieking from all directions.

In a panic, I quickly scramble back upward, trying to burn my fingers into the wood of the roots as I had done with the bark of the trees. I try but find myself rebuffed by the roots. My flames are unable to burn through.

In my scramble to rise out of the depths, I don't notice the labyrinth has returned to its calm, immovable state until long after I reach the heights of the nearest tree. In that tall tree, I watch over the roots below and wait for whatever monster I hadn't seen to make its way to the surface.

A good five minutes pass before I calm enough to berate myself for my stupid curiosity. There is something down there, in the dark space under the tree roots, and it didn't like me poking my nose into its territory.

Okay . . . nuh-uh, never going inside the roots again.

I think now is a perfect time to rest. Anything to keep up here, away from the roots for a while. I glance down at the long rain jacket I am wearing, tied up at the bottom so that it hangs to my knees rather than the ground. It's probably about time I get around to fireproofing it.

I had hoped to find the proper materials I'll need for this procedure, but the forest has nothing I can use, suspended above the earth as it is. I toss the jacket on the branch before me and settle for the mediocre method.

I need to temper my jacket. I can direct my flames enough even when I let my form return to its natural state to prevent damage to my clothing, but it isn't foolproof. I was lucky to have the foresight to remove Leal's jacket before I went and burned down Gloria's building . . . and Gloria . . . and the rest of the city.

Uncle has shown me the many methods us áed use to keep our own clothing from burning up even when we burn at our hottest. Of course, tempering our clothing won't stop the flames from burning through them if that is the intention. By adding these patterns—our inscriptions—to our clothes, it is possible for us to return to our flame form without destroying them every time.

There are a few different ways of doing this. The best usually involves lots of salt and metal powder or, if possible, lining the cloth or material intended with thin strips of metal. The clothes lined with metal tend to be rather heavy, so only my elders wore them.

The method I will use is the least effective, needing to be reapplied once every week lest it wear off. But it is by far the easiest to accomplish. I don't even need to use anything. Well, anything but time and patience. The sight of roots looms below. If it means more time away from whatever that monster was, I have plenty of both.

I haven't done this in a long time now. It's been far longer than a year since I was last with my family, right? It still feels like they've barely just left me, while also feeling like it's been forever since I've seen them. I place my hand on the jacket and hope I haven't forgotten how to do it. It'd be a horrible shame to damage Leal's gift.

I hold my flame, or more specifically, the energy within. I morph it, cool it into a state that won't burn the leather as it passes through. I push it into the jacket, lining the energy into a pattern that I repeat over and over again through the entire surface.

The patterns in the jacket glow, but only while my flames etch in the inscription. My tribe never called them inscriptions, but there's no denying the similarity between our treatment patterns and the ursu's inscriptions. The biggest difference between the two is that our patterns don't need to glow to work. Whether that makes much difference, I don't know.

Now I will sit here for the next hour to make sure the patterns take hold. Using salt and powdered metal would increase both the speed at which the inscription takes hold and the time it holds for. I don't know if it can hold permanently, but I've never seen a treated object ever have to be repaired from damage caused by time. It was always external damage, like from a fight with a beast or a spar between tribe members.

After sitting up in the tree for a while, I finally relax from the stress and fear of what might be below me. Well, maybe not fully, but I have stopped sending worried glances down every few seconds. I definitely don't want to sleep here tonight. After I have finished treating Leal's jacket, I want to be as far as I can from here before night comes.

The rain jacket took a lot longer than I thought to complete. I didn't know whether it's because of its size or because I hadn't done the process in a while, but once I have finally finished etching the patterns into it, I toss it over my shoulders and move down the tree once again.

I am wary of being heard, so I keep my feet light and hesitate to make any large jumps that may attract attention.

Unfortunately, the only options I have are making those noisy jumps or crawling through the entangled roots. Once again, I try to burn my fingers into the roots to make climbing them easier, but I fail. The roots seem to be almost impervious to my flames.

Is it just the roots that are fire resistant? I try the same with the wide trunk of a tree. The bark burns as quickly as it did when I first entered the forest, but once I reach the actual timber underneath, I find it is the same as the roots. I can't ignite it no matter how much I try.

It is strange—a type of wood that doesn't burn. I assumed I wouldn't be starved of choice with what I could eat in this forest, but unless I come across other creatures I can hunt, bark is the only edible thing. And from what I've tasted so far, it isn't exactly brimming with energy.

The wolves I ate the other day filled me up, but I can't help but feel like I let my uncle down. I didn't even try to make use of their pelts, fangs, or claws. It was wasteful to just consume everything the way I did, and I can imagine Uncle's disappointed glare in my mind. He would have called me lazy.

Uncle was always a proponent for not needlessly killing, and he had made sure I knew never to kill without necessity. But what really was necessity? Would it have been okay to kill the wolf if I needed one of its claws?

It's not like I think killing the wolves was wrong. I needed to protect myself, and I was being attacked. It was simply survival. I can even say the same about Gloria. She attacked me, so I was in the right to defend myself, right?

But if I kill an animal, I need to make as much use of what that creature has given as possible to make it a reasonable trade of life. At least that's what my uncle believed. What if the creature I killed doesn't have any value? What then? Is it still reasonable? Or does that make me nothing more than a beast myself?

Why am I even thinking this? I've never cared about hunting animals before. And I didn't feel bad about killing the wolves, not really. So why? Why are my uncle's words from so long ago sticking in my mind?

I know the answer, of course: Gloria.

Her death has unsettled me. The gruesome way she melted under my flames. The sheer hatred she held for me as I watched her die. But what was I supposed to use from her death? I couldn't skin her like an animal, right? Not only had all her fur been burned away, but she was a person. That would be weird.

Was I supposed to have taken her property or something? I'm pretty sure I burned all that down before I killed her.

The only thing I can think of is if I am supposed to learn some lesson from this. Maybe my uncle wants me to learn from her death or my mistake. No, not Uncle; he is already in the Eternal Inferno. In all likelihood, it is a subconscious part of myself that realizes this, not my dead uncle who has long since passed on.

So, what do I need to learn? I already know I let my anger and hatred overcome my common sense. I realized that after an entire city burned from my carelessness. I also know now that I can't simply trust someone because they act nice. I need to assume the worst in everyone. That is the only way I can think of to stop myself from being taken advantage of. Maybe there is a better way to do that, but I don't know it.

Maybe I should think about it from another perspective. Why did Gloria act the way she did? Thinking back to the first time we met, she could tell I was an áed from just looking at me. No other ursu has done that, most thinking I'm something they called an albanic. She was ingratiating herself to me from the moment we met. Making me feel like everything she did was for me. She knew áed are more efficient at burning fuel than doing it normally, didn't she? Even I hadn't known that until later on.

I had seen the other ursu around the furnace as well. Maybe it is their thick coat of fur, but they can't handle the heat for long, having to change out often or overheat. By putting me in there, she probably cut down the effort she needed to put in to manage the oven.

So, by using me, she cut down on the amount of coal she had to use and could get me to reduce her workload. I made her job easy. Is that why she considered me her property? I was just a tool for her. She thought that of me from the very start.

Is that the lesson I have to learn? To know the value she slapped on my efficiency? I guess I can probably make a train run far longer than usual, what with how Leal told me they operate. That seems like a bit of a stretch. It could be that simply being a different race from the norm is enough to be treated differently. I have seen that enough when the average ursu's opinion turned hostile toward me simply for being nonursu.

I won't be able to pretend to be an ursu, but maybe I can hide as one of these albanics. Well, that is assuming I can't get back into the wasteland.

CHAPTER TWENTY-FOUR

Wailing Woodland III

Never would I have hoped the jacket to be as effective as it now proves to be.

Sitting here on an upper branch, huddled tightly within the rain jacket Leal gifted before we separated for the last time, I am dry. I feel the thrum of the rain pelting me and the hammering sound that fills the air from its impact against the hard wood. The world fills with a torrent of deadly water, but I am safe. Well, mostly. The humid air prickles my skin even through the large coat, but the coat is doing far better at keeping me alive than I hoped.

I am small enough and the jacket large enough to fully wrap myself, separating me from the outside world. I first noticed the rain coming from the stinging moisture in the air. I panicked. Not having anywhere to hide from the coming deluge, my first instinct was to climb the nearest tree. In hindsight, it might have been better to find a spot underneath one of the fat trees. Maybe I'll do that next time. I'm not about to go wandering around while the skies are trying to kill me.

Sitting here, tightly wrapped, I dare not uncurl myself nor peek through my safety curtain, no matter how uncomfortable or curious I get. I know better than that by now.

I hope I'm nearly through this forest. It's been almost two weeks since I entered, and I'm still not sure which way I'm going. The canopy is far too thick to allow me to see any of the sky, so I haven't been able to follow the moon as I usually would. I can only hope I haven't been running in circles. If I'm lucky, I might even end up close to the desert.

Now that I'm alone again, I need to decide what to do. The stories my mom used to tell come to mind of the Agglomerate, where she grew up. I'd like to go there, but that's a six-month trip at the very least, assuming I can walk in a straight line. I don't even know where it is. I know it is northwest, somewhere along the Titan Alps. But that mountain range covers the entire north of the wasteland. If I wanted to find the Agglomerate, I might spend years searching.

My other alternatives are all equally unpleasant. I could wander around the wasteland looking for other tribes. I might even do so while making my way to the áed Agglomerate. But the chances I would ever stumble upon a tribe are quite low. Plus, there is the danger of colossal-worms, chameleons, and other nasty creatures I won't be able to fend off myself. Unlike the wolves I had to fight, those monsters won't die just from a little fire. I shiver to think about what would happen if I stumbled across chthonic tunnels while alone.

I could also just find a spot, maybe near a cobalt mine or something, and settle. I won't have to deal with the dangers of the outside world. I won't have to deal with other people like Gloria.

It sounds good, but I know myself well enough that it wouldn't last. I'd get lonely, or bored, most likely both, and soon be out looking for áed. At most, this option would be temporary. I don't know how I would find a place like that without my tribe's maps, anyway.

The last idea I've been considering for a while now. I don't know what to think about it as it has more unknowns to it than I am comfortable with, but it is an option, at least. I can go north, pretend to be an albanic in the Zadok Kingdom. From what I know, the only difference between my outer appearance and theirs is the dark hair color I have. It should be easy enough to rub some dirt in to hide the blue shade. Hopefully, that difference won't be enough to tell I'm not one of them.

The possibility they'd discover I am not an albanic is only one risk of traveling to Zadok. I know nothing about their culture, their morals, or their beliefs. I would be walking into a complete unknown.

Unfortunately, none of the possibilities for my future look like I have any way of reconnecting with Leal. It will be impossible for me to go to another city in New Vetus, what with how aggressive they have become to outsiders. That isn't even considering how I burned down one of their cities. I have no reason to believe I'm not being hunted down right this moment for what I have done.

Okay, just on the off chance I am right, I should pick up my pace. I won't be able to fight off other ursu like I did Gloria, especially if they bring any water mages.

I listen through the rain, hoping any of the odd sounds aren't a group of hunters chasing me. Not like I'd be able to do anything but cower in this downpour.

Thinking about the Zadok Kingdom, why am I even considering it? The risk is far too great compared to the others, so why is that the option I like the most? Sure, wandering the wasteland has its dangers, but those dangers are known. I know how to spot colossal-worm nesting grounds, and crocodiles don't hunt things smaller than they are, usually. I know my way around the wasteland, even if I don't have the maps I need to find the places other áed may frequent.

My feelings on going to Zadok aren't logical, I realize. I want to go because it is something new. As horrible as my time in New Vetus became, I enjoyed the early days I spent with Leal. Simply, I want to go to Zadok because I don't want to be lonely again. I want to experience new things, and I don't want to get stuck in a repetitive loop of depression as I did after I lost my tribe, wandering the desert mindlessly. The same mental loop that kept me trapped in the furnace, working for no self-gain.

If I go on a journey—alone—where the end goal would be as far out of sight as the Agglomerate, I would risk falling back into that horrible repetition. But if I travel to Zadok, I will be risking my life. I didn't know which scares me more.

The rain stopped a while ago now, allowing me to unfurl from the uncomfortable position. I still keep the jacket wrapped tight, as everything around is still soaked, but I have a bit more freedom now that there is only a trickle of water dripping from the foliage above. Remnant streams of water flow from the branches, down into the roots below, and disappear beneath the tangles.

Soon, I lower myself down from the heights of the tree, careful to avoid any obvious wet spots that remain in my path. Any damp areas left on the roots dry from the proximity to my body before each step or grab. I only need to pay attention to pools of water amongst the roots as I continue through the forest.

I've been stuck in one position for half the day and need to stretch my legs and get a move on. Already, I've been in this forest far longer than I wanted, especially knowing that there might still be something below me.

I haven't exactly been hesitant to burn my way through the bark of the trees whenever I can, and I now realize that may have been a mistake. Assuming I am being hunted by ursu, I just left a pretty clear path for them to follow. If I am lucky, they would have taken time to put together their hunting party. If I am really lucky, ursu would find traversing this rooty mess harder than I have. And if I am really, really lucky, they will have lost track of me.

I don't dare hope for any of those, though. I quicken my pace and make sure I am moving through the forest as fast as I can, even if that means I have to crawl through roots again.

A few days later, the girth of each tree finally shrinks. The roots become nowhere near as convoluted. I even see some of the underbrush between the roots again.

It is a relief to know I don't have to worry about what is below me. And with the smaller size of the roots, traversal becomes far easier.

The canopy above thins too. The moon peeking through on my left tells me I've been traveling further east than I'd hoped. I have still gone mostly north, so I don't think it is too bad. Now I just need to decide whether I am going to Zadok or back into the wasteland.

Zadok is probably far closer to where I am now; I don't imagine it will be much farther north. The wasteland covers the entirety of my west, so if I head in that direction, I will come across it eventually. And now that I know that Leal's jacket works wonderfully, I'm not afraid of traveling such distances.

I know I should head back into the territory familiar to me, but I am interested by what differences Zadok might have from New Vetus. Intrigued, but cautious. If Zadok appears dangerous, I can always head back out to the wasteland afterward, right? I should take the opportunity while I'm here. After I head out toward the áed Agglomerate, I'll be stuck doing nothing other than walking for well over a year. I'd also rather not have to go back to relying on sandworms for food if possible.

With my mind set, I move north, passing the last of the trees of this strange forest. The plains I've moved into are much friendlier for navigating. The hills I'm approaching are dense with chest-high grass, but it is easy to see far into the distance. No ursu can sneak up on me out here. Then again, they would be able to see me nearly as easily. Although if I spot them first, I should be able to hide in the long grass. I have to make sure to keep my attention behind me often. I doubt I can outrun the giant ursu in an open area like this.

The next few days are much easier on me. I have yet to see anyone coming from behind me and the grass provides a much more comfortable bed than I am used to. The landscape itself is rather simple, reminding me a lot of a green desert. The hills—more like bumps in the land—sometimes push upward from the rest of the plains but aren't steep enough to be noticed from anywhere except at a distance.

I wonder if I have made it out of New Vetus yet? The maps I saw weren't detailed enough to label the forest I passed through, but I know Morne is near the northern border. Without landmarks to give me any sign where I am—or a map that describes those landmarks—I am stuck mindlessly wandering. Okay, maybe not completely mindlessly. I know where north is, after all. I guess time will only tell if I come across a Zadok city or one of these albanics that might direct me.

Walking through the tall grass in the gentle wind is calming. Especially after all the tension that has built up in the past days. Many times, I have to snap myself out of the feeling and force my attention to the horizon behind me.

I haven't seen any animals in the plains, but the grass has moved seemingly on its own enough times that I assume anything living is simply hidden beneath the grass. I keep clear of any unnatural motions in the grass as I travel, and in return, I'm not bothered. I know it is probably nothing like it, but I like to imagine that I made a pact with the residents; I will move out of their territory quickly if they leave me to do so.

As the days continue to pass, I make sure to keep my eyes on the horizon, watching for the ursu I have yet to see. The more days that pass without them appearing, the better. It is at one instance that I have risen to the peak of one of the shallow hills to search for any pursuers that I finally notice movement on the horizon.

I have been expecting something, but seeing them in the completely wrong direction from where I had assumed they would appear startles me. Did they go east and skirt the forest to catch me after I came out the other end? How could they know where I would come out?

From my crouched position within the grass, I watch the movement far to my east. I can't make out anything other than the movement of what I assume to be ursu passing over the ledge of a hill in the distance. From what I can make out, it doesn't look like they are heading toward me. It looks like they are walking south. Is this not a hunting party for me?

Against my better judgement, I decide I want a closer look. So, while keeping my head well hidden within the grass, I make my way toward the movement.

The closer I get, the clearer it is that I'm not looking at ursu. There are far too many; they look more like a swarm of ants and I just can't reasonably pin that many ursu in one place.

Soon, I am close enough that I can say without a doubt that these are not ursu. They are, I assume, the albanics I have heard about. And what the ursu told me is right; they look like áed. As long as the áed have proper control over their forms, they are nearly indistinguishable. The only obvious difference is the white hair. The hair of most is grown long enough that the whiteness is obvious. A rare few have gray shades, but it is day and night against my dark blue.

There are a lot of them. So many, in fact, that I couldn't count them all if I had all day. Tens of thousands march along, separated in eight columns. It is impossible to tell their numbers for sure. They spread so far from the north to the south that the hills hide both ends of the lines from view.

I may not have ever seen one before, but this is an army. There is no missing that. Is the Zadok Kingdom attacking now that they know New Vetus is struggling against the Empire? Hopefully, Leal and her mom have moved somewhere south. I'd hate for them to get caught in whatever attack Zadok is planning.

Moving with a careful step through the grass, I make sure they do not see me. The last thing I want is an army thinking I am spying on them. Well, at least I won't have to worry about the ursu anymore. I doubt they would continue following me if they saw this. If they do, I know where to run to. If I can make the army think I am one of their own, I can use them to protect myself.

That will be a last resort. If I can help it, I'd rather stay as far away from the war as I can. But for now, at least, I can follow parallel to the marching army. It should lead me in the direction they came from, and I'll have an escape if the ursu track me this far.

CHAPTER TWENTY-FIVE

River Fort

Once passing far from the main body of the army, I continue to move parallel to a long string of wagons. None of those I see near the wagons look like formal soldiers, unlike the ones I passed earlier. Sure, many of them hold the same wooden club-like thing many in the army carry, but at most these are guards and not the colorfully adorned warriors marching ahead of them.

I assume many of the wagons are supplies to support such a large army, but it is quite a shock to see that there seem to be more men along their supplies than in the actual army.

I know nothing about the albanics, so I might be mistaken, but there is a clear difference between the quality of clothing these "guards" wear compared to the soldiers now far behind me. Do they consider soldiers more important than others? I guess it makes sense; they are the ones who will be fighting. Do they not expect the guards to fight?

I keep my distance until I walk far past the last wagons. With nobody around to spot me, I follow close to the path the army left behind. The ground is in a pretty horrid state after being trampled by thousands of boots, wheels, and the strange creatures they had pulling their carts. The grass is gone, and the soil is hard. I keep off the newly made road so I can remain hidden if need be.

I continue along the path until afternoon the next day, when a stone structure appears at its end. While the color is similar to the buildings in New Vetus, the architecture is far different. The walls are bare and bulge outward near the top, leaving an overhanging section of stone.

I approach, remaining hidden in the long grass, and discover that the stonework itself is shoddy and rugged. Ursu stone was smooth and square at all points, but the stone used in this structure appears slapped together haphazardly.

The building is tall, but it's nowhere near the height New Vetus cities reach. Not even close. A large opening at the front leads into an open-air courtyard. So the wide structure isn't a building, but more of a wall? There are a few small structures, like wooden huts, within the wider stone wall. The area isn't that big, probably only fifty meters wide.

Three guards sit at the entrance and I can occasionally see others—each carrying the same cudgels as those in the army not long past—peeking over the top of the wall. Is there a reason they use such things rather than normal spears, axes, or other bladed weapons? Does it cost too much for them to outfit that many people with proper weapons?

They will be fighting the far more physically capable ursu. I feel bad knowing what they'll go up against; even if the ursu are struggling against another army on another front, I can't imagine them losing.

Not wanting to have a confrontation with armed strangers, no matter how useless their weapons may seem, I move to skirt the fort.

It doesn't take me long to realize that might be impossible. I sit crouching within the grass at the top of a hill and look down at the incredible volume of flowing water meandering between the hills.

So . . . this must be a river.

I let out an involuntary laugh, shivering a little. Of course it's not that easy. The river flows right up behind the fort. At least now I know why it's there. Moving farther around the side of the fort confirms it. A bridge at the back of the fort connects to a similar but smaller fort on the other side.

I can either follow the river west and hope it turns northerly into Zadok, or I can try to find my way through the fort. Really, it's a toss-up between safety and speed.

At first glance, following the river looks safer. I wouldn't need to risk interacting with the guards at the fort. But moving away from a direct path into Zadok is a risk on its own. What if I run into another monster like that thing hiding under the root forest? I don't know what dangers are in the area, and unlike the terrors of the desert, I don't know how to avoid them.

I think the only thing that might help is that I am obviously not an ursu, so I doubt they will be immediately hostile. It'll be up to whether they believe I'm an albanic. Maybe they won't care even if they know I'm an áed, but I feel like that is too much of a risk to hope for.

If I am to go through the fort, I need a plan. Either I come up with a story to tell the guards or I try to sneak through.

A glance up at the looming stone wall immediately discounts the possibility of scaling it. Maybe I can hide in a wagon as it passes the front gate, but considering the only ones who come this way would be the army suppliers, that might be too hard.

Okay, okay. So, do I risk wasting weeks following the river and possibly getting lost in unknown territory or do I risk the guard's reaction to find myself a secure route into Zadok?

Eh. What's the worst they'll do to me?

. . . Maybe I should prepare just in case. Worst-case scenario: I'll run after surprising them with my fire and hide in the grass. If they chase me, well, grass is pretty flammable, right?

I pull the hood of Leal's jacket over my head to cover as much of my now-dirt-bathed hair as possible and step out of the grass. I walked farther down the path before, so I wouldn't just pop out of nowhere from the guard's perspective. They keep the grass short around the fort, but I don't want to give them a reason to think I was hiding.

Walking up to the gate, I struggle not to fidget with the sleeves of Leal's jacket. When one of the guards finally notices me, he nudges the guard closest to him and calls for another. My presence obviously surprises the three of them, but they are patient enough to wait. A much better reaction than the hostility I expected.

Approaching the three, I can feel the heavy stares. The guards at the gate aren't the only ones following my approach; many eyes on the top of the wall watch from above.

"What are you doing all the way out here, kid?" one man asks as I stop in front of him. I make sure to keep out of swinging range of the cudgel he holds loosely against his shoulder.

"Uh, um . . . I—" I stammer, stumbling over my words as I try to get my lie out.

What is wrong with me? These men are nowhere near as intimidating as the average ursu. I need to pull myself together. I clamp down on the nervousness and the what-if scenarios that pop up and push on with my story.

"The ursu killed Mom. I ran away." Inwardly, I cringe at how bad it comes out. I'd always been told I was a bad liar back in the tribe, but I had hoped I'd gotten better since.

Nervously, I tug at the neck of the jacket, which must have been the wrong thing to do as two of the guards twist their faces in irritation. The other visibly winces, looking between me and his two comrades.

I quickly tug my hood tight over my head again, noticing where they were looking. It is obvious that my hair gave that reaction. I thought the dirt would be enough to cover the blue tinges. Did I not put in enough? Is it really impossible to blend in with the albanics with my hair? I back up, ready to bolt at the first sign their disgust morphs to aggression. I've already dealt with the hostility of ursu against outsiders and I don't want to repeat that.

"Ahem, I think I should probably take care of this," the guard that isn't obviously annoyed by my presence announces quickly, getting two grunts of confirmation from his fellow guards, who do their utmost to keep their attention away from me.

"If you'll come with me, young miss," he says, then turns on his heel and leads me toward a structure extending from the side of the wall.

He brings me to a rather bare room with nothing but a table and a few chairs. He gestures toward the chair opposite the table and takes one himself. I sit carefully, trying to watch him and my surroundings for any sudden movements.

"So, I need to start off. Have you ever been to Zadok before?" he asks.

Okay, get your story straight, Solvei, don't stuff this up again.

"No, I lived with Mom in Morne. In New Vetus." I hadn't seen them much, but I know there is a community of nonursu in New Vetus. Well, there had been until the war turned for the worse. I don't know what happened to them after.

"How did you travel here from Morne?" the man asks, setting his cudgel against the edge of the table. I notice a metal tube encased in the wood. Does that make it stronger than a normal club?

"I came through the forest. There were lots of roots I had to climb through." That seems to get a reaction out of him. He raises his eyebrows and widens his eyes.

"And who did you travel through the Wailing Woodland with?" Wailing Woodland? What a silly name. Well, it is better than Root Forest, I guess.

"I was alone." The man furrows his brow and mutters something under his breath. He shakes his head before looking at me again.

"What's your name?"

"Solvei. What's yours?"

The man's lips twitch upward at the corners; he seems to find something funny.

"I'm Finnigan, or Finn, if you prefer." He smiles before moving on. "And your surname?"

"Surname?" I'm unfamiliar with the term.

"Yeah, you know? Your family name?"

"Oh! Vatra." That's what our tribe called ourselves.

"Solvei Vatra." Finn writes on a piece of paper. "How old are you?"

"Eleven . . . I think."

Finn looks at me with a raised eyebrow. "You think?"

I nod. I'm not really sure how long I was in the Morne furnace for.

He just shakes his head at my response. "Okay, do you remember living anywhere else before Morne in New Vetus?"

Not trusting my voice to lie convincingly at the moment, I just shake my head.

Finn sighs before moving on. "Now, Solvei, did your mother ever tell you of the importance of hair color?"

I hope I'm not meant to know. I just shake my head in answer.

"Hmm, I'm not too surprised, honestly. Look, Solvei, in Zadok it is mostly believed that the whiter one's hair, the purer they are and the more noble blood they have. Most people use it as a measure of your worth, usually allowing those of pure hair the most privileged positions. I should warn you, your hair is . . . darker than any other I've seen. Life in Zadok will be hard. If I was in your position, I'd try to get out. There are many small countries to the north that do not have albanic majority that you may live well in. But whatever you do, do not travel east."

Well, that doesn't sound great. Maybe I should have gone searching for the Agglomerate after all.

"Why?" I ask, wanting to know what I should be fearful of if I have to go east.

"The Theocracy borders our country in that direction. While I dislike some traditions of my country, it is far better than the way the Theocracy does things. Those of the Theocracy execute any with impure hair. They believe only shades of white are given Belobog's protection. Any with shades of gray are foolishly believed to be the servants of Chernobog." Finn stands up from his chair and moves around the table, coming to a crouch in front of me.

"I don't want to see such a young girl like yourself hurt over stupid beliefs. Cover yourself whenever you can and keep yourself safe." Leaning forward, he pulls the hood farther over my head and ties the string at the neck tight.

"Thank you, Finn."

He gives me a sad smile in return. I don't trust the man one bit, but it doesn't seem like he is lying.

"I'll organize for you to travel with the army suppliers back to Serron. For now, just rest here. There's some food and water in the room down the hall," he says before leaving the building.

Well, it seems I won't be able to fit in as well as I had hoped. Should I just give up? No, I can't just stop moving because it seems hard. I have to do this now. I told myself I would, and I'll hold myself to it until it becomes dangerous. Plus, I don't know how easy it'll be to leave now that I'm already within the fort. Would they stop me if I tried to run?

If there are more albanics like Finn in Zadok, then I should be fine. One out of three isn't terrible. I'll need to be careful of the other two and I can't trust any of the three, but if I keep moving, everything should work out.

The next day, Finn takes me to the group I will travel with for the next few days. With me following close behind, Finn approaches a rather chubby-looking man who is watching over several wagons and albanics moving about. The wagons look rather empty, and most people are just talking amongst themselves, so it doesn't really look like they are too busy.

"Gavin, good morning," Finn calls.

The chubby man turns to us before returning his greeting.

"Mornin', Finn. Is this the one you mentioned?" he asks, glancing toward me.

I call him chubby, but that's compared to the surrounding albanics. Any ursu would have more width than him, assuming you can find one small enough to make a fair comparison. Even Leal is bulkier.

"Hello, I'm Solvei," I introduce myself.

"Yes, I want to make sure she is safe, at least until you reach Kelton."

"Yeah, no problem. Just make sure to keep up," Gavin says dismissively, turning to watch as the last preparations for their wagon caravan are complete. Many large animals I had seen with the army convoy are now being tied to the wagons. The strange beasts are more placid than any other creature I have seen before, easily allowing themselves to be strapped to the carts.

I feel like I use this comparison far too often, but they look like large dingoes. Wide-bodied dingoes with soft, white pelts.

I say goodbye to Finn, and he waves me off, walking back into the barracks where I spent the night. I make my way to stand beside Gavin, but he pays me no mind, either ignoring me or not noticing as he yells at one of the younger men in the group for slacking off.

"All right, you lot, it's time to move. Don't dally any longer, we're leaving."

CHAPTER TWENTY-SIX

General Mudra

Major General Brant Volerio Mudra considered himself a practical man. To him, a garden was a delicate balance of cultivation and culling; the weeds are removed to make way for fresh growth, and the flowers must be nourished and protected to reach their full potential. General Mudra applied this philosophy in all things. If one of his soldiers showed potential, a wealth of opportunities for promotion and advancement would come their way. Should one of those soldiers exhibit incompetence or disloyalty, then only dismissal or execution awaited them.

Time had proven his philosophy true, and during the last war—before the unification of the Empire—he had proven his value with incomparable achievements as a commander. After the war, he had been promoted to the rank of general, a feat nigh unheard of for those not of noble or military lineage. His new rank afforded him many new perks, not the least of which included command over an incomparable number of soldiers and that which he had been targeting for years: permission to use the inheritance ritual.

General Mudra sat behind his ornate wooden desk. The room was on the lowest floor of a building a few streets away from the central continae of this captured city. He did not believe his enemies to have the capabilities to fire an artillery strike on the city, but he felt it prudent to remain cautious; it was always possible a partisan group had scavenged one of Henosis's artillery. No, he was more comfortable operating his forward operating base from a less obvious position than the continae. What good was extravagance, after all, when planning the deaths of thousands?

Currently, he was looking over the number of casualties from the war to this point: 12,135 confirmed dead and 35,624 presumed killed in action. The numbers were far better than estimates predicted when he launched this invasion. He could only thank his enemies for their lack of technological growth; their reliance on natural strength could only get the ursu so far.

He knew the limited deaths on his side were only because the New Vetus Council was holding their elites close to the chest. There was much work to be done to strangle out the resistance groups, but he had already taken control of the entire eastern half of New Vetus. It was almost unthinkable that they still hadn't sent out their heavy hitters. Then again, the Staff Office had denied him the use of the Empire's own elites in this coming fight, so he could hardly do anything but lament the selfishness of those holding power.

To make up for the lack of elites he had under his belt, he'd been forced to acquire some . . . alternative weapons to counteract the enemy elites when they would eventually join the fight. Just the thought of the questionable project and the nutjob researchers in charge of it was enough to boil his blood.

He sent his adjutant to bring the lead mage of the project for a report. The weapon, as they called it, had been nothing but a headache for him. "Experimental technology that would soon change the landscape of war." That was the drivel he'd been given by his superiors when they denied his request for proper elite force, but it had been more a pain than it was worth. Who would ever have thought relying on something that depended on external and uncontrollable factors would be a good idea? He continued to grumble in his seat while the mage was brought into his office.

The mage saluted before letting himself fall back at ease. "Reporting, General Mudra."

The general scowled at the man's disrespect. If the mage was one of his men, he'd be cleaning toilets for weeks for that show of negligence. Unfortunately, the man had too many connections within the Staff Office and punishing him would cause far more pain than it was worth later on.

"Colonel Olipho, I hope you have some good news for me. I am tiring of your failures."

The grimace the lead researcher gave was quite telling. "Apologies, General. Another of the subjects damaged and escaped its enclosure; despite the guards' efforts to detain it, the subject was unfortunately killed."

General Mudra was not happy with the news.

"Tell me, Colonel, how many subjects do we still have left?"

"Th-three, General."

"And how many have we already lost?"

The colonel gulped. "Eighteen, General."

"So, having lost that many from the same issue, what have you done to prevent it?" The anger was bleeding into the general's voice now.

"It's not that easy. They burn through the cages of any material we can use. Even if we fill their bars with water, they still take the chance, regardless of how it cripples them. Unless you call some more of the water mages back and have them rotate shifts to keep a cage up indefinitely, the only option is to find an áed child. One that has yet to gain a dangerous thermal presence."

"Watch yourself, Colonel." General Mudra glowered at him. "And where do you suppose we should find a young áed? The last time our scouts found one, we lost an entire squad of mages. Even savages know to protect the next generation."

Before the colonel could reply, a quick series of knocks rapped on the general's office door. The general's adjutant entered the room upon receiving permission.

"General Mudra, we received intelligence from General Staff."

"Classification level?" he asked, glancing at Colonel Olipho standing across from him.

"Moderate, sir," the adjutant said, remaining at attention.

"Then, please." He motioned for the adjutant to read.

"Morne has burned to the ground."

"Oh?" The general found the city on the map spread over the table before him. The large city sat just south of the border with the Zadok Kingdom. "Huh, I never expected them to be so successful."

Inciting the Zadok Kingdom into attacking the ursu was intended to be nothing other than a distraction for his enemies. Their people were rather hateful toward the ursu, having lost most of their land to them almost two hundred years ago.

At one point in time, the Zadok Kingdom had been a major power on the continent, but now they were little more than a shadow of their former glory. It had been easy getting them to believe they could retake the land from their usurpers.

To hear they'd burned down a city was surprising, far exceeding the expectations the general placed on their capabilities.

"No, General. The Zadok Kingdom army has yet to pass the border into New Vetus. The town didn't burn because of their actions."

"What? Then the ursu burnt their own city?"

"An intercepted report to Flehullen indicates an áed child imprisoned within one of the ursu ovens was the cause. The child's current location is unknown," the adjutant announced.

"How convenient. I'm not one to believe in the whims of the gods, but it looks like Belobog has blessed us with an opportunity. Wouldn't you agree, Colonel?" General Mudra's gaze bore into Olipho.

"Of course, General. I'll organize it immediately. How much of the search force should I allocate?"

"Send them all. Their search in the wasteland has already proven fruitless. If you cannot succeed with this child, then your project will be terminated."

"Understood, sir." The colonel snapped off a quick salute and ran out the door.

General Mudra sighed as he leaned back in his chair. He wasn't about to leave this entirely in the incapable hands of the colonel.

"Major." General Mudra addressed his adjutant. "Send Lieutenant von Dunnell along with the reorganized troops. Tell him he must assure the capture of the áed and he has free rein to do so."

"Understood, sir." The adjutant saluted and marched out of the office.

His adjutant's actions pleased General Mudra greatly; the man was always professional and remained disciplined at all times. It was rare for the nobility to be this well-behaved. Most usually attempted minor rebellions to appease their pride, like dismissing themselves from attention without their superior officer's permission. None of those that pushed the boundaries remained within his ranks long.

Soldiers from the military families were often his best subordinates; their parents trained them since childhood and didn't have the same foolish tendencies of the nobility, despite the similar status. His favorite to train were those from backgrounds similar to his own: soldiers like blank canvases that he could paint into art, not blemished by prior preconceptions nor pride.

One of these soldiers had just entered his office. He stood at attention, awaiting the gaze of the general.

"Permission to speak, General Mudra," the logistics officer requested once the general looked up from the documents neatly organized on his desk.

"Go ahead, Lieutenant," he grunted, appreciating the results of good training.

"The ritual preparations are complete and ready for you at your earliest convenience, General," the man said, and remained at attention.

The improvements he had made in the training staff had definitely been beneficial to the overall discipline of his troops. Memories of a time when having noble blood was the only requirement to reach an officer's position bristled his anger. Times had changed but not nearly enough. The armies had improved, but the Staff Office was still a cesspool of malignant nepotism.

General Mudra had been attempting to secure a position amongst their ranks for the past twenty years, but despite his extensive achievements, he'd been obstructed from promotion. It had been especially galling when a fellow colonel—at the time—advanced to infantry general with a padded seat in the exclusive General Staff Office, the colonel's only achievement being the butchering of an invasion during the last war.

"It's about damn time," the general grouched. "Lead the way, Lieutenant."

One would think that as the general leading this invasion, he would get priority usage of the inheritance ritual. But whenever the nobility was concerned, fairness was never a factor. Many of the Empire's nobility had attached themselves to his invasion so they could get first pickings of the corpses. They would come and take, but did they contribute to the war? Of course not!

The greed of the nobility was a poison that needed to be bled if the Empire had any future. If he had any hope of achieving that, he needed to create his own power. He needed his own strength to fight against the noble scourge that infested his Empire. That strength was here, amongst the nation of fools that rested on their laurels and yet acted so sure of their own strength.

Once he conquered Vetus, the Empire would be next. He could only hope the emperor and empress would concede the abolishment of nobility, for he did not wish their eradication as well; reestablishing governance would be a far more arduous task, after all.

General Mudra followed the lieutenant into a large warehouse at the edge of the city. Military presence guarded this area far more tightly than even the forward operating base, the ritual and high nobility of enough import to cause such a disproportionate defensive force.

Upon entering the warehouse, the general blocked his nose as the horribly familiar scent of rotting corpses flooded the air. Laying eyes on the mountain of corpses—both ursu and albanic—would horrify anyone not used to such a sight. Thousands of the dead were piled in the center of the warehouse, surrounded by inscriptions carved into the stone underneath.

He sat within a small circle of glowing white lines adjacent to the mound of corpses and waited for the ritual to start.

Not long did he wait. The technician started the process, causing the inscriptions to light up a bright white. A few moments of silence lingered before a soft humming reverberated through the warehouse. The glow of the inscriptions surrounding both the mountain of corpses and the general increased in intensity. It was bright enough to see the patterns of the inscriptions beneath the blood coating the floor. The inscriptions tinted by the blood lit the walls in an eerie crimson.

The surrounding hum increased in intensity until he felt it in his bones. Deep thrums pounded away throughout his body as he sat and waited with clenched teeth. The sound of the hum faded, but the vibration remained. His body felt like it would rattle itself to dust if he didn't fight to remain still. His eyes ached and his vision became blurry, but that didn't prevent him from watching as the first true indication of the ritual enacted itself.

The many bodies before him began disintegrating. It happened slowly, so very slowly. But there were flakes of skin and flesh floating off many of the outer bodies, separating from the corpses and rising as if gravity did not exist. They broke up into smaller and smaller pieces the farther from the bodies the flakes traveled.

Four hours passed like this, with a constant vibration shaking his body and the corpses fragmenting before him. When no bodies remained and all blood had disappeared from the floor, the vibration of the ritual cut off, taking the glow of the inscriptions along with it.

General Mudra gasped as the ritual stopped. It was as if he hadn't slept in weeks; the ritual sapped every bit of strength he had, leaving him an exhausted wreck.

He rose to his feet and looked over the floor of the warehouse. There was not a speck of dust to be seen; every remnant of the corpses taken from the battlefield was gone, as if they had never existed. He strode toward the exit of the warehouse, tired and in need of a long rest, but contrarily, he felt more awake than ever.

Major General Brant Volerio Mudra marched down the street to his quarters. There were many things that must be done, but for now, he needed rest.

CHAPTER TWENTY-SEVEN

Kelton

I try to stick by Gavin's side as we travel. He is the one Finn introduced me to, so I assume I should stay with him. He puts that notion to an end rather quickly. Any time I try to talk to him, he acts like he hasn't heard me. It doesn't take long to realize he doesn't want me hanging around, so I give him the space that he wants.

I still have no idea of what Zadok will be like. Is it going to be the same as New Vetus? Wanting to learn more, I pull my hood tight before approaching a woman sitting on one of the rearmost carriages. She's holding a rope leading to one of those strange four-legged animals. Her clothes are thinner than the leather the guards wear, but as she doesn't have a cudgel of her own, she probably isn't expected to fight.

"What is this creature?" I ask, keeping my distance in case the animal becomes aggressive. It's a quadruped, like dingoes and fennec foxes, but looks nothing like them.

"You've never seen a pholo before?" She looks down at me, surprised.

"No."

"Hmm, well, they are smaller, fatter, and slower cousins of the horse. Lazier too." She pauses for a moment before moving to the side of her seat, patting beside herself. "Why don't you join me?"

"Thank you," I say as I climb onto the carriage next to her. This is kinda nice. Being carried around by pholo would have made travel for my tribe so convenient. Uncle sometimes let me ride on his wagon, but that only ever happened when I was exhausted.

"It's odd that you've never seen a pholo before. Where are you from?" She keeps her attention forward as she asks.

I watch the pholo trod along on its stubby legs, pulling along the carriage and both of us with ease. The wheels almost glide along the well-worn path.

"I escaped from New Vetus."

Her eyes widen, and her attention snaps back to me. "No way! It must have been horrible." She turns her head, glancing between the other carriages. "Are you alone?"

At my nod, she returns a pitying glance.

"Well, I'm sure things will get much better from now on. The Zadok Kingdom is a far better country than anything those barbaric ursu could build. I'm Bianca, by the way; what's your name?" she asks.

"Solvei," I answer. "How long will it take to get there?"

"We should get to Kelton before dark."

"Oh? That's close!" I'm not used to places being within a few days' trek of each other. Most of the time, it takes over a week of travel to get to other places. If it wasn't for the railway in New Vetus, I'm sure it would have taken months to travel from Fisross to Morne.

"Yeah, it is. But Kelton is big, it'll take the caravan a week to pass through. Serron is on the other side of the wall after that. Are you traveling to Serron?" Bianca asks.

"I don't know. Anywhere but New Vetus seemed good, but I'm not sure where else I can go," I say honestly.

"Ah. Well, you definitely don't want to stop in Kelton, it's not a good place to be. I'd say go a bit farther than Serron and reach Ashon. There are a lot more opportunities there."

I consider her words. Do I want to stop in Ashon and see if life will work out there or continue north like Finn said I should?

"Did you always live in Vetus?" Bianca asks.

"Yeah, I lived near Morne with my mom," I lie. "What's Zadok like?" I try to turn the conversation away from my past. I can't kid myself, I am not a good liar. If they ask questions, I might be in trouble.

"Well, it's got its problems, that's for sure. But what place doesn't? It can be difficult for families like mine to find opportunities for work. But family is always there to help one another, no matter how hard things become. Oh, and the food is great."

Yeah, family is always there for each other.

Apparently noticing my souring mood, Bianca realizes her words. "Sorry, I wasn't thinking. I'm sure you'll be adopted into a great family when we make it to the city. For a kid as cute as you, I'm sure you've got gorgeous . . ." She reaches to my hood and pulls it back as she speaks.

It is obvious the moment she sees my hair for the first time—her eyes widen and she looks around as if checking if anyone else sees.

In a hushed voice, she speaks. "I can't be seen with you. I'm sorry. Please get off. I'm so sorry." Her face contorts in a mix of guilt and fear. Her eyes flicker left and right, unable to hold eye contact anymore.

I freeze for a moment, unable to comprehend this change. After my initial interaction with the fort guards, I'd assumed my darker hair disgusted them, but this reaction isn't the same. Bianca acts like she is afraid to speak with me, although it's not me she's afraid of, but other people. Will others judge her for simply interacting with me?

"Please, please. Go, my family can't afford to lose any more," she pleads with me.

I jump off her carriage. The tightening in my chest is hard to ignore. I enjoyed talking with Bianca—as brief as it was—so to be cut off so soon hurts, even if I should have expected nothing more. Casting my gaze down on the ground, trying to hide my hair even more, I scamper off.

"Solvei." I stop as Bianca calls my name. Turning around, I look up at her. She's struggling to get her words out, but I hardly care at the moment. "Good luck. I'm sorry," she says. Feeling insulted and hurt, I turn my head from her and continue to the back of the caravan.

Finn warned me, but I'd hoped I could still make friends, or at least have a conversation. I shouldn't feel like this. I talked to her for not even five minutes. After Gloria, I thought I wouldn't let anyone else in as easily.

No, it's not that I trusted her or anything. I was simply happy to talk to someone again. It's stupid. I'm stupid. This is a good warning for me: there are more ways for someone to hurt you than the way Gloria had. Bianca didn't want to hurt me, but she still rejected me, knowing it would hurt me.

I fall into a trot a few paces behind the last of the carriages. A couple of guards walk behind me, but I keep out of their way. My head stays downturned as I watch the wheels roll ahead of me. I'll hide myself for the remainder of the trip; even if I'd much rather talk with those around me, I've learned my lesson.

Kelton is disgusting. It looks like a junk pile tipped over and labeled a city. After the grandeur of New Vetus, this is underwhelming. I used to think the outer areas in the ursu cities were randomly laid out and lacked the uniformity that defined the central New Vetus cities, but this is on a whole other level. Kelton lacks any order at all.

Only the main road through Kelton appears defined, and even then we must swerve and wedge our way through the street of rusting metal and shoddy brick-work. Street tenders build stalls in front of one another, as if fighting for space at the forefront of the main road, all the while leaving less to travel through.

As we traverse the road, we come across a man dressed similarly to the soldiers of the army from a few days ago. He wears a colorful mix of greens and purples as opposed to the orange and red of the soldiers. The man's hair is the whitest I've seen so far. That means he is important, right?

The colorful man stands by as four men wearing the same armor as the guards of this caravan destroy a number of small stalls that line the road. The men destroy each one they come across until the space in front of the brickwork buildings is clear. Neither stall owners nor their wares are anywhere to be found.

The destruction left behind the guards reaches far down the street. Much of the wood, tarp, and metal is ignored, left in piles beside the storefronts.

I assume those street stalls are illegal here. But it is strange for so many to litter the streets if they are actively knocking them down.

About thirty meters past the colorful man and destroyed stands, I come across several albanics rebuilding the stalls. My head turns to see the guards behind us still destroying the stalls, and my jaw drops. They are doing this while still in view of the ones who destroyed the stalls in the first place. I doubt it's been even five minutes since they were knocked down.

Each of the people working the stalls wears a covering over their head. The clamber of the stalls being built clutters the air almost as much as the stalls strew the street. The men and women seem wholly unfazed by the situation, chatting and laughing amongst themselves as if this is a daily occurrence.

Seeing their headgear, I realize I need to get myself something like that. Well, if they are hiding their hair as well, they'll be more willing to help, right?

Taking a few strides away from the caravan, I approach one of the men who forego building a stall and just lay down a cloth on the ground.

"Excuse me, where can I get one of those things to cover my hair?" I ask the man, noticing the dirty looks sent his way by his neighbors still building their stalls.

The man laughs, whether at my question or at his neighbors, I'm not sure. "My, young lady, we don't use these to cover our hair. Not at all! These are stylish expressions of our inner artisan. Don't let anyone tell you different." He laughs again. "Now, I can give you your very own quality expression piece for your petite head as cheap as twenty-four thousand gid." He brings out a white cloth hat from a bag at his side, presenting it before me.

"Gid? What's that?" I ask. Hopefully, it's something small; thousands of them will take a lot of space otherwise.

The man raises an eyebrow at me and sighs in disappointment. The other albanics around now openly jeer and laugh, but the man takes it in stride. "Well, gid is our currency. It is money. You need it to buy things."

"Oh, okay. How do I get gid?"

"For you? You can get it from your parents. That or work for it."

"How do I work for it?" The first option isn't exactly available to me.

"By getting a job." He looks at me as if what he says is obvious, but I stare back, unsure of what he means.

He sighs. "You know, you do something for someone and they give you gid for the help. That or you sell things for gid. Then you can use that gid to buy food and items for yourself."

"Oh, okay, that makes sense, I think." I don't understand it; doesn't that just add an unnecessary step in things? Our tribe didn't need it. The ursu didn't need it. So why does Zadok?

"Do you have any work for me?" I ask. If he wants me to work for the hat, I'm fine with it.

"Kid, even if I had work for you, you'd need to show your hair. Would you be okay with that?"

I shake my head and pull my hood lower over my face.

"Yeah, I didn't think so. How about this, then, trade me your dad's jacket and I'll give you both this hat and a handful of gid? It's warm out, you can't possibly not be getting hot in that thing," he says with a smile that reminds me far too much of Gloria.

"No. I'm not giving it," I say as I look back down the road. The caravan is almost out of sight now and I'd rather not lose them. I don't want to stay in this town.

As I walk away, I hear the man's voice behind me. "You know where to find me."

I'd rather not give away my friend's jacket. Especially not for something to cover my hair. The jacket is far more important to my safety than that, and it's already decent at covering my hair.

I run to catch up to the caravan and find that the caravan's guards have taken to knocking down the stalls that block the way for the large wagons. Even the rear guards decide they want a part of the fun, leaving the rear carriages open to a number of blatant thieves pinching things from the back. The man sitting with the reins to the pholo attempts, in vain, to scare them off.

Skirting the burgled carriages, I approach the front of the caravan where a plot of land is being cleared to make room for the carriages. The pholos are taken to a stable beside a building that looks of far better quality than any of the others I've seen so far. As the carriages are bundled together, the guards make a perimeter to prevent the thieves from approaching. Gavin and the rest of the caravan members that aren't dressed as guards group together before entering the well-maintained building. As I approach, I can see that, while much better than the surroundings, it doesn't come close to the standard of stonework that goes into structures in New Vetus.

I follow close before the door closes behind them and find myself in a small entry room. Well, it isn't small, but with all the people from the caravan cramming within, it feels tiny.

Gavin is at the front talking to a lady behind a large desk. After a few back-and-forths that I can't hear over the hum of conversation from the rest of the group, the lady stands up. She walks around the table and inspects each of our group. Not asking questions, simply looking over them as she finds no problem.

As she reaches me, I figure out what she is looking for.

"Please remove your hood." Of course it is the hair again.

"Um, can I . . . not?" I ask, hopeful of the slight chance she will agree.

"Just do it," she says, her tone turning impatient.

Should I just leave? But where can I go? I assume they are going to sleep in this place and I want to join them. Slowly, I pull my fingers under the hood and bring it down.

The woman winces, like she bit something foul. She turns to Gavin. I don't know what kind of expression she's making, but looking at Gavin and the rest of the group, most of them have the same reaction as the lady. A few look at me in disgust like the first guards I met, but most seem sympathetic.

"She is not with us," Gavin says, and no one contradicts him, even though I know most of them have seen me.

"Huh? Yes, I was." That seems to flare a bit of anger across several faces.

. . . Maybe I should be careful here.

"I am sorry, but this establishment does not allow those below a certain purity. Please leave." The lady once again turns to face me, her impassive expression returning.

With everyone staring intently at me, I know I can't argue. I have no friends here. I flip my hood back over my head and hurry outside. Will it be better if I just out myself as an áed? No, they haven't been aggressive yet, just . . . unfair. They have a deep-seated hatred for the ursu, but does that extend to other races too? For now, I think it is best to remain hidden. The treatment is saddening, but they haven't hurt me yet, so it will be fine.

Now I need to figure out where I'm going to sleep tonight.

CHAPTER TWENTY-EIGHT

The Slums

You are not joining us."

"What? Why?" I ask in shock. It was only for the night I had to stay away, wasn't it?

"I've already held my end of the deal with Finn, even though you blindsided me with your lack of purity. I have no more obligation to help you," Gavin grouches.

"Okay"—I try to appease him—"but how can I get to Serron from here?"

"I don't know and I don't care. I've already helped far too much for my taste. You don't realize how much we have risked with you here."

This is not how I want this day to start. I had hoped yesterday's issue would stay in yesterday. Well, Bianca said Serron is only a week away. I can just follow the caravan from a distance.

"And if I catch you following us, I'll make sure the guards aren't merciful with what they do to you." With his last threat given, Gavin stomps off back to his caravan.

I gulp. Okay, maybe I won't follow them.

For the next few minutes, I watch as they make their way down the street, once again knocking down stalls blocking their way. When they are out of sight, I grab a plank of wood from a torn down stall and take it down a tight, crooked alley looking for a place devoid of eyes. I have to go rather far, walking through the alleys until I find long-winding and empty streets. Eventually, I find a tight hole in the side of a building, which I only barely crawl my way through.

A dark room of some abandoned workshop greets me. The light shining through the hole behind me only barely illuminates the trash covering the floor. Rotten remains of a rodent similar to a jerboa lie on a worn, old workbench; its decaying corpse fills the air with a vile stench. This place is disgusting, the floor littered with rodent waste and random bits of trash, but I am alone.

My stomach grumbles and inner flame churns, impatient to consume the plank. I should have eaten something in the fort's barracks, but I'd been so worried they would take issue with how much I ate that I ended up having nothing. I light a small flame on my hand, giving the room another once over to make sure no one hides amongst the mess. Finding the room empty, I push my inner flame to devour the timber in my arms, relishing the burst of energy it gives me.

Now that I give the room another look, I realize there is plenty here I can consume while I still have the chance. The bookshelf on one wall looks like it will taste great, not to mention the floorboards below me. Timber has always been a luxury we couldn't indulge in back in the wasteland, but they have it in excess here. The place is already abandoned, so I'm sure nobody will mind.

First, I send my flame to the work desk, consuming the small rodent in a matter of moments. Idly, I note it burns much quicker than a jerboa. Really, the creatures that make their home outside the wasteland really need to get better at resisting fire. I'd be seriously worried for all life in the area had Auntie ever made it here.

The somber thought breaks through my good mood, but not as much as the screech of something heavy dragging across the floor. I turn to the sound and see the bookcase slowly turning toward me. Only then do I hear the voices.

"Fire! Hurry and put it out," a feminine voice calls.

"Shut your trap, I'm going already. Get the others safe." Another voice—masculine this time—comes from a silhouette as they push their way out from behind the bookshelf.

"Why would someone light a fire here? Do they know we're here?" This time the speaker's voice is far too soft to tell their gender. I can barely hear their voice, muffled as it is from behind where the silhouette has finally squeezed himself out into the room with me.

I realize I'm still eating my way through the desk, so I hurry to extinguish the flame.

"What the . . ." the silhouette exclaims, startling as the room returns to the dim it was before. Only a small trickle of light from outside shines through the hole in the wall.

I creep slowly away from both the light and the boy I can now see. He looks older than me but is obviously not yet an adult. Are they hiding here? There is a space behind the bookshelf that I can no longer hear the voices from, but it's too well hidden not to be intentional.

The boy approaches the now-charred desk with confusion marring his face.

He hasn't seen me yet, crouching in the corner off to his right. I may not have thought this through carefully, as he is now between me and the exit. As he moves farther into the light, his hair sticks out. It is a dirty gray, sitting almost right in the middle between black and white.

I hold my breath, keeping as still as possible as the boy casts his gaze around the room. His eyes linger on my hiding position so long that I am sure he spots me before he continues on his search.

For a few long moments he just stands there looking around, before he moves to the hole in the wall I crawled through. With practiced ease, he lifts himself up and through the hole that even I, with my smaller size, had trouble getting through.

In the corner of the dark room, I sit, listening for the others. I know there were at least three voices, but now I can't hear anything. That boy has gone, but the others are still in that hidden room. I need to get out while I can.

Slowly, as to not make a sound, I creep my way to the room's exit. I poke my head out the hole, looking both ways for the gray-haired boy. With the way clear, I clamber through the wall, landing on my arms and face on the other side.

Wanting to get away as fast as possible, I run down along the alley I came from, only to immediately run into the gray-haired boy. He jumps around a corner ahead of me and I find myself knocked to the ground. Not a moment later, he's on top of me, squashing me into the gravel. In a panic, my flame lashes out in all directions around me before something cold against my neck makes me freeze.

"Stop it now, or you won't live to see the next sunrise." I can't see what he holds against my neck, but a quick flicker of flame across it lets me feel the short blade, half the size of my hunting knife.

Unfortunately, the boy sees my flame passing over his knife. In retaliation, he presses it in harder, cutting into my form.

"Last chance!" he yells right into my ear.

Realizing my situation, I force myself to calm down. Breathing deeply, I pull the flames back into myself, extinguishing all fires I have started in the area. I let out a sigh of relief when he takes off some of the pressure on the knife at my throat.

The sound of hurried footsteps makes me look up as a small group of teenagers runs up from the other side of the alley, passing the hole to the building and stopping in front of me.

"Ash! You're hurt!" a girl exclaims as she runs up to him.

"I'm fine. It's just a little burn," he says to her before pressing down on me once again. "Now, what's one of the albicant doing down in this part of . . ." He trails off as he pulls off my hood. "Fuck me."

"Sacred Belobog shit! Guess you ain't Chernobog's chosen any longer, hey, Ashley," a girl laughs as she crouches in front of my face.

The boy still holding me down, Ash, groans, "Leslie! Will you stop calling me that?"

Not looking up from me, the now-named Leslie asks, "*Cherno's chosen* or *Ashley?*"

"Both!"

With Ash still holding the knife to my neck, Leslie puts her finger under my chin, lifting my face to look her in the eye. I notice both her and the two boys behind her have gray hair, though not as dark as Ash's. The two boys look like mirror images of one another; they have the same eyes, hair, and height. The only thing different between the two is the clothing.

"How do ya think someone with such low purity ever became a mage?" she asks Ash while still forcing eye contact with me. "Oh, wait. Do ya think she got cursed with hair like that? Maybe she was doing some illegal magic and got smote for it?"

"I think the better question is why she was trying to burn down our hideout."

Ash grabs ahold of my shoulders and flips me onto my back, where I can see him and the girl fussing over his burns. I just sent out flames in a panic with no true intent to harm, but much of his arm is blistering red and his shirt has large holes I burned right through. Sure, he jumped me, but is that enough for me to kill him? The thought that I almost gave Gloria's fate to someone who didn't deserve it stabs me with guilt.

"I'm sorry. I didn't mean to hurt you."

I feel guilt for the damage I have already caused, but I'm not about to leave my safety up to the discretion of strangers. I look around to make sure I know where each of them is.

"Why did you try to burn down our home?" Ash demands, holding his knife tight to my neck.

"I didn't, I was just looking for a quiet place to eat," I say truthfully.

"What horseshit! We all saw the fire you started," Leslie says.

"Um, I started it for light," I say, unconvincing even to my own ears.

"Oh, don't lie, you little fuckin' pyro!" She steps forward, getting in Ash's way and distracting him.

Not missing the opportunity, I push away Ash's arm and roll away from them. The blade digs into my neck before I am free and on my feet. I'm too slow to run, though; they have already cornered me against the wall. My body ignites in flame. I know they do about as well with fire as most things outside the waste-land, so I hope it will be enough to stop them from attacking or to scare them off. I don't want to hurt anyone.

The sight of my body engulfed in flames sends them staggering back more than I expect. They pass glances between each other, which I don't like the look of. It's far too much like the coordination my elders sometimes showed. They would glance at each other right before attacking the enemy, almost as if they could talk with just eye contact. I need to calm them down quickly.

"Really, I'm sorry I started a fire in your home, but I didn't know anyone was there. I stopped when I heard your voices."

Ash takes a step forward but remains a couple of body lengths away. "Okay, I'll assume that's true for now, but there is still something that I need to know. What is a mage doing here? Isn't Kelton way below your pay grade?"

I consider what to tell him. Shall I go along with his assumption and claim to be a mage, or should I be truthful? Now that he doesn't have me in his grasp, I believe I can run away easily enough if push comes to shove, so I can probably use this as an opportunity. They are already in hiding, so I can assume it won't be easy for them to spread knowledge about me, even if they want to. Plus, all their hair is darker than any of those from the caravan I'd been a part of, so it is likely they'd be treated the same as me if they approached another group like that.

So, I decide to be truthful with them. "I'm not a mage."

They all stare at me and the flames still circling my body.

"You couldn't think of a better lie?" Leslie says while everyone else stays quiet in bafflement.

"I'm not lying." I pull up the sleeves of my jacket. "See, I don't have any markings."

"But you're still using spells. So tell us exactly how you are not a mage?" Ash asks slowly, treating me like an idiot.

"I'm not a mage, I'm an áed."

"A what?" Ash asks in confusion.

"An áed," I repeat, thinking he may have misheard me.

"Ash, look at the wound on her neck," says the girl who tried to treat Ash's burns.

I touch at the cut on my neck. What is strange about it? A small flicker of flame spurts out. The cut will take a while before I'll be able to force it back into my normal physical form. The section of my form will grow black soon, and in a day or two, it will heal and return to normal. But for now, I cannot hide the flame of my body within the cut.

"What are you?" Ash asks with apprehension.

Is he dumb? "I've already told you, I'm an áed." To help him out a bit, I let my body return to its natural fiery state. "Convinced?"

Now is the moment of truth. Will they act with hostility? Or can the albanics be friendly?

"Are you one of the northern races?"

"Northern? No. I'm from the wasteland west of here."

"The wasteland? How did you get over the mountains?"

"Ah, no, I came through New Vetus."

"Hardly relevant, Ashley." Leslie whacks his shoulder with the back of her hand and takes a step toward me. "Did you know we were there when you started burning things down?"

"No, I didn't." I shake my head in denial. "I was trying to hide where nobody could see. Fire isn't exactly discreet, you know."

"There, see? It's all just a stupid misunderstanding. Now what do you want to do, Ashley?" Leslie waves her hand as if dismissing me.

With everyone having calmed down and tensions not as high as before, I stop my threatening display of fire and bring my body back under control.

"So, an áed, huh? Why don't you join us in our hideout, get away from prying eyes?"

The alley is still clear of wandering parties, but with how much noise we made, that might not last long. I nod and follow his lead back to the hole. Leslie and the twins follow behind me with a decent amount of space. Huh, revealing my race actually deescalated the situation. Maybe I won't have to hide like I thought. It'll beat how they treat their own race.

CHAPTER TWENTY-NINE

Introductions

Ash leads me through the bookshelf and lifts some floorboards in the center of the room. He uncovers a new opening and climbs down. The room behind the bookshelf is far too small to hold both myself and the three still following from behind. As I lower myself down the ladder, I hear the grating sound of the bookshelf being pulled back into its original position by the twins.

Jumping off and skipping the final few rungs, I inspect the room I find myself in. A thin, straight crack between the wall and the ceiling at the far end of the room allows in more light than the room above. The room must be mostly underground, being lower than the alley outside. We are standing directly underneath the workroom we came through. Unlike the dirty and littered floor above, this is rather clean, with a few old beds on one side of the room and an assortment of objects organized on the other.

Ash takes a seat in one of the few chairs surrounding a table with a missing leg. He motions for me to sit opposite him and stares at me, or more accurately, at my neck where the cut is still visible and burning.

I settle in the provided chair as Leslie flops onto a bed, propping herself up with one arm. The twins quietly lean against the wall behind Ash.

"I'm sorry, I've never heard of áed before. What exactly are you? And how did you make your body burn like that? I've never seen anything like it." Ash absentmindedly scratches at a rather red patch of skin.

"Wait, really? Never?" Most ursu I have spoken to have at least heard of us, even if most haven't met any.

"No." He shakes his head.

"Huh." Maybe the mountains to the west are a part of the Titan Alps, but it seems a bit too far south for that. "We mostly live in the wasteland west of here. And I didn't burn my body, I just stopped controlling its form."

"So, your body emits fire?"

"No? My body is fire." It's not that hard to understand, is it?

Apparently it is. Ash gawks at me for a moment until two knocks echo through the basement, followed by the grating sound of the bookshelf moving.

"Hey, Kerry's back," Leslie says.

Kerry? Looking around, I finally realize that the girl that had been beside Ash outside never followed us in. Where had she gone? Did she go looking for others to fight me? I rise from my seat and edge back toward the corner of the room.

When the girl, Kerry, descends the ladder, the sight that she is alone would have calmed me. That is, if she didn't happen to be lugging a bucket of sloshing water along with her. I tighten the jacket around me, pulling the hood tight over my head. My legs tense; if she throws the bucket at me, I am ready to dodge.

She doesn't even look at me; instead, she runs straight to Ash's side. She places the bucket at his side before dabbing a soaking rag against the reddest parts of his arms.

"Ow, not so hard, Kerry."

Watching the scene, I know the water isn't meant for me, but I can't take my eyes off the bucket, wary of the danger its presence assures.

"Yo, you all right, fire girl?" Leslie's voice snaps my attention away from the water-soaked rags pressing against Ash's arms.

As I turn to Leslie curiously watching me, I realize my fear is far too obvious. They don't know about áed, so that also means they don't know about how harmful water can be. Not wanting to give her any more inclination as to my weakness, I force myself to calm down.

"Yes, absolutely fine, no issues at all." I can't help the glances I keep shooting toward the bucket, though.

Leslie looks at me for a time. "You're really shitty at lying, you know?"

"Wha . . . I-I'm not lying."

She smirks, then looks toward Ash, where Kerry has torn off his half-destroyed shirt and tends to the redness on his face, which I swear my flames never burned.

"So . . . don't like water, huh?" Leslie says. "I guess that's rather appropriate for fire."

I clench my jaw and hold myself back from giving her any more confirmation.

Once Kerry finishes fussing over Ash's burns, she takes a step away from him, only to glare at me. She once again picks up the bucket. I gulp and hope she didn't hear Leslie.

Ash turns back to me. "Please, come and sit. What's your name?" Once again, he indicates to the chair I sat on before Kerry came.

"I'd rather stay over here." I keep the beds and Leslie between myself and Kerry.

Leslie snorts and sits up. "Kerry, drop the bucket. You're terrifying her."

Kerry blinks. "I am?" She lifts the bucket in my direction. I make sure not to react visibly, but I watch her intently in case she throws it. "Hey, you're right!" She smirks, looking at me sharply.

"Kerry," Ash warns.

"Fine." She cuts her glare and places the bucket next to the wall behind her.

"Right, so I'm Ash, this is Kerry and Leslie." He points to the two girls. "And these two are Demi and Medi." He waves at the mirror duo.

Ash turns to me, waiting. Kerry hovers beside him, glaring, but not otherwise showing hostility.

"Solvei," I say, relaxing now that Kerry doesn't have her bucket.

"Great! It's good to meet you, Solvei. We are glad you aren't a mage or, more specifically, one of the albicant. Now, let's put our mistakes behind us and let bygones be bygones," Ash says.

I nod in agreement. I never wanted to fight in the first place.

Kerry gives me one last harsh scowl before sighing, dragging the last seat from the table beside Ash and falling into it. She isn't pleased with me, but it looks like she is willing to talk.

"So, Solvei, how long have you been in Kelton?" Ash asks, leaning forward in his chair.

"I arrived with a caravan last night. I was planning to head to Serron with them, but, uh, it seems like my hair is rather unpopular here."

Leslie snorts while both Ash and Kerry share a glance with wry smiles.

"Yeah, welcome to Zadok. Y'know, before you came along, our Ashley here had the darkest hair we'd seen. It's a good thing you aren't actually an albanic—hair that dark would scare off an entire block." Leslie grins, turning to Ash. "That sounds like a good idea, yeah? Let's take her to the white bloods and watch them run like rats. Contamination by association, as they say."

"As great as that sounds, I'd rather not throw our new friend into the wolves' den for a bit of a laugh," Ash says, turning to look me in the eye. "No, I'd much rather do it to burn the den to the ground."

Uh, I don't like the sound of that. I don't want to be burning down any more buildings or dens or whatever. Too many got caught in the conflagration last time.

"No. I'm not burning down any more homes," I say, resolute.

"Any more?" Kerry quirks an eyebrow.

"No, no, no. There's no need to burn any houses to the ground. We would just need your help to get inside."

Leslie jumps to her feet. "You're not seriously considering that, are you?"

Ash lifts his shoulders, holding one palm upward. "Why not? Most of the guards left the city, and you know how arrogant they are about their automatic protections. Without a mage, it's impossible to get in, and guess what we just found," he says with a smirk, waving an arm toward me.

A grin slowly grows on Leslie's face, and a brief laugh escapes her lips. "Oh, that sounds great. I never thought I'd get the chance."

Kerry is appalled. Her eyes widen and jaw loosens. "Don't laugh. That's a horrible idea." Turning to Ash, she continues. "Just because some guards are away, you think we can break into the Canos' manor? Are you insane? We'll be hunted down. The albicant families hold no love for the impure, and even less for those that steal from them."

"Come on, Kerry, this is our chance. Do you really want to be stuck in this shithole until the day we can't scrap together enough food to get up in the morning?" Ash says, rising to his feet. "This is our chance! She is our chance!"

He takes a moment to steady his breathing. "If we do this, we will be able to leave the country. We'll have opportunities to earn our own luxuries that are forever cut off from us in Zadok. Don't you want that? Don't you want something more?"

Kerry bites at her thumb but nods.

Okay . . . have they just assumed I will help? I think they have. I'm no mage, but I assume Ash wants me to burn something to allow him to do . . . whatever it is he wants to do. But I would much rather not go burning through the infrastructure of the new city I find myself in. I can't see any situation that doesn't have me being labeled as a target. The only reason I'm not worrying about the ursu chasing me after burning down their city is because there is an army between me and them.

As much as I would be happy to work together with this group, I'm not about to risk my safety for them. Not that I would do it as charity either; I've learned not to trust that easily.

"I'm not doing it," I say, making sure there is no room to misunderstand.

Like a wagon wheel with a spear lodged within, Ash's speech comes to an abrupt halt.

"Huh? Why not?"

"I'm uncertain what it is you want me to do, but I know enough that my safety would be put in danger. I'm not about to get myself caught in any more trouble."

Ash stutters, fumbling over his words while he looks at me with wide eyes.

"But . . . but you have the strength of a mage. You could take on anyone and they can do nothing to you."

I shake my head, remaining firm. I can fight anyone I want? What nonsense. He has obviously never seen much of the world if he thinks that is the case.

"Okay, now, Ashley, calm down. We've just met the young . . . áed, right?" Leslie turns to me for confirmation and I return a nod.

I hear Kerry mutter under her breath, "Áed?" Right, she wasn't here for that, was she?

Leslie continues, either not hearing or ignoring Kerry. "And she doesn't know much about this cesspool of a city yet. Why don't we let her stay with us for the moment and see where things go from there?"

Ash considers it, raising his hand to his chin while he thinks. Kerry is far more resistant to the idea.

"Let her stay? After she attacked Ash?" Her face contorts, incredulous. She acts like she's been slapped in the face.

"I think it's fine, I did attack her first," Ash says.

"But she left burns all over your arms!"

"I can barely feel them. They don't hurt at all. And you've already done a great job of patching me back up," Ash says, smiling at Kerry.

Kerry's cheeks flush, and she pulls back quietly. Leslie lets out a loud groan, rolling her eyes as she falls back onto her bed.

"So she's welcome, then?" Leslie asks, looking at the ceiling and pointedly not watching the two.

Ash snaps his attention back to me. "Ah, yes. Welcome to our home, Solvei. It's not much, but it's all we have."

I don't have anywhere else to go, so I might as well accept. But this time I can't trust them like I did with Gloria. It's clear they want something from me, but that's fine. I can trade my help for them to allow me to stay, but I'll make sure to first and foremost keep myself out of danger. I know now that I need to refuse if I don't want to do something and that I should not believe everything they tell me.

"Thank you," I say.

I'm not sure if it's a good idea to stay with others again, but I have no reason to believe that Serron or Ashon will be any easier to live in than Kelton. I have seen how the albanics treat their own people. The quality of life here is far lower than what ursu experience in New Vetus, even during their wartime struggles.

The roads aren't paved, just compact dirt or loose gravel, and maybe a little cobblestone in patches. The quality of each building is horrible. On my way through the back alleys, I saw more collapsed buildings than I could count on both hands. It is strange, though; my first impression of the city is that there are many people living here, what with the size of the city and the number of people operating stalls in the main street. But moving away from the main road, it's almost empty after passing a few alleys.

I will have to check tomorrow, but I am pretty sure there are more abandoned buildings around than those that look frequented. For a moment, I consider asking the others, but dismiss the thought. I don't want to rely on them for things I can find out myself easily enough. Who knows what sort of tricks they might pull if I listen to everything they say?

"Well, I think it's time to hunt. Come, Solvei, we can show you the best paths through the city," Ash says.

He tosses me a bundle of cloth. Catching it, I'm welcomed with the sight of a hat similar to the ones the people at the stalls wore. The one given to me is a faded pale pink, looking like it might once have been red.

"Take our spare. It's better than your jacket to hide your hair." The five of them put their own hats on.

"Oh? How generous of you. It doesn't have anything to do with you not wanting to be forced into the pink one again, does it?" Leslie says as she rises from her bed.

"Of course not! I just think she looks cute in it, don't you think?" Ash says, unaware of the glare Kerry sends him.

Leslie laughs and turns to me. "Come, I'll show you our second entrance. We don't use this except in emergencies, but you should know where it leads."

I follow but keep my guard up. Gloria was generous with her gifts at the start too. I'm not about to give them an opportunity to use me.

CHAPTER THIRTY

Thieves

I follow Leslie through a tight passage under a partially collapsed wall. A pathway that's impossible to notice unless you know where to look. The alleys and buildings around the home of the five seem to be filled with these hidden paths.

Leslie spent the last hours showing me all the routes she considers necessary. Many of them are far too tight to allow any adult to traverse. I may not know much about this country or how the people live, but it is plainly obvious that the teenagers are accustomed to running away.

"What do you need these paths for? What do you need to run from?" I ask as we crawl out of the debris into a semiburned building.

"Oh, you know, the typical shopkeeper, guards, travelers. Anyone, really. People usually aren't too happy about being robbed their gid," Leslie says as she peeks through a gap between wooden planks nailed in the wall.

"You steal?" I ask curiously. "Don't you work for it?" I remember what that man amongst the stalls said about earning gid.

Leslie lets out a short, sharp laugh. "Yeah? And who would let us work?" She stops looking at the street outside and turns to me. "You really haven't been here long if you don't even know this. In Zadok, the shit-can that it is, family is everything. That extends to jobs as well. An employer won't touch those of lesser purity, 'cause it'd be an insult to his other, purer employees. Nobody's gonna hire anyone with hair darker than a certain point. It'd be social suicide. Someone who does so is more likely to have their family disown them than succeed," she says, scowling. "So, yeah, theft is the only way we can keep ourselves fed. Why do you think Ash was so excited when he realized you were a mage? One that isn't an albicant," Leslie continues.

"I'm not a mage," I remind her.

"Right, right. But you're close enough. Ya see, nobody in the city has much gid. Even those of decent purity don't have much. But to get outta the country, we need enough to pay the smuggler. Unless we go for the only rich family in the city, we'll be stuck here forever."

Finally satisfied that she doesn't see anyone outside, Leslie pulls aside a portion of the wall that isn't as connected as it looks. She pushes me through and follows close behind.

"Then why don't you just leave? Why pay someone when you can leave the city yourself?"

Leslie stops to look at me, gasping as she puts a hand over her mouth. "Sacred Belobog shit, girl. Why did I never think of that? We could've been free from this dump years ago! Oh, if only you had graced us with your wisdom earlier, our lives would have been changed for the better." She stares me dead in the eye. "Of course it's not that fuckin' easy. It's impossible to get past the wall without permission from one of the albicant," she says, turning on her heel to stomp down the street.

I hurry to follow close behind. "The wall? What's that?"

Leslie keeps her pace, striding down the street, passing many other albanics. "The wall stops us from leaving. The only way past it is through the north gate that separates Kelton from Serron. Can't get through it unless you have a proper merchant license or high enough purity that you would have been adopted into one of the high families, anyway."

So I won't be able to get through either. That is . . . less than ideal. I imagine their hair is too dark to head into the Theocracy to the east, so our positions are far more alike than I'd expected.

That is, assuming she isn't lying to me.

It is definitely possible. The wall might be a fabrication to make me stay and help them steal from the most influential family in the city. I doubt that part was a lie. The family with the most gid will also be the most dangerous, assuming money is as important to them as it is to the other albanics in Zadok. If she is going to lie about that, she won't want to scare me off by saying it is more dangerous.

It's hardly helpful if the only things I'm sure are not lies are statements of danger. Then again, even those might be lies. They could easily be trying to keep me away from something or someone by telling me it's dangerous.

I bite my lip. There is no way I'll ever truly be able to differentiate lies from truths. How do I deal with it? Do I assume everything is a lie? No, if I worry about every little thing people say, I'll never stop stressing. But if I don't prepare myself for lies, I'll be taken advantage of again. I'm not sure what I should do.

Unaware of my internal conflict, or just willfully ignorant, Leslie leads me to an alley off the main street where Ash and the others are waiting.

"Yo, Ashley. How goes the scouting?"

All four of them turn to us upon hearing Leslie's voice.

"Great, actually. With the army heading for New Vetus, there's a lot of movement hitting us at the moment. We have our pick of pockets."

"Oh? So no need for a store hit?" Leslie asks.

Ash shakes his head. "How'd your tour go? No issues, I assume?"

"None. So, see any particularly fat-looking bellies out there? Who are we hitting first?"

"What about him?" Kerry says, pointing at an angry-looking man with nice-looking clothes pushing people out of his way as he storms down the main street.

"Nah, he's already been robbed of everything he has, unless you wanna try taking the clothes off his back?" Leslie says.

"I think that one is our best bet," Ash says, nodding toward a man riding a wagon pulled by one of those pholo. Four guards surround the man and his wagon, watching their surroundings with wariness, hands on the sheathed blades at their sides.

"Ash, are you sure? We'll never get to the wagon with those guards there, even with a distraction," Kerry says, eyeing the tall stature of each male guard and the weapons they carry.

"The wagon isn't our target. After Demi and Medi distract the guards, you and I will jump the driver. We'll be in and out quick. Set up at Point B. Any complaints?"

The group accepts Ash's plan, and although Kerry seems worried, she follows along without complaint. I follow them as they move through the alleys perpendicular to the main road until I find myself alone with Leslie again. The other four walk off in different directions to wait for their target. Leslie and I stop to watch the main road from around a corner.

It's good that they haven't asked me to help. I am not as willing to take the risk against armed men as these five seem to be. But even if I will not take the risk myself, I still want to watch. The group of them are taller than me, but definitely not yet adults, so I am curious how they plan to fight against those guards.

It doesn't take long before the guarded wagon comes into sight. The pholo trot along at a pace matching the guard's stride. Loud voices fill the air as people crowd the wagon in hopes of a sale before it passes. The guards never allow them close, pushing them away if they try.

A loud clatter breaks through the commotion, dragging both my attention and that of the guards to a stall that toppled behind the wagon. I catch a glimpse of someone running back into a gap between buildings.

The yelling of the guards pulls my attention back to the wagon. One of the twins—I'm not sure which—jumps off the carriage and runs for an alley down the road from where Leslie and I wait.

Two of the guards run off, chasing the boy, leaving two to protect the wagon. As soon as the guards are out of sight, Kerry and Ash launch themselves to each side of the driver. I didn't see where they came from. Had they been hiding amongst the crowd of peddlers?

The guards, too busy watching behind the cart, are far too late to react to the yells of the driver. Ash and Kerry are already sprinting away . . . in our direction.

Leslie takes a step back and picks up a wooden beam I hadn't noticed leaning against the wall beside her. "You might wanna step away a bit—we'll be running real soon."

She holds the wooden club at shoulder height, standing right beside the corner of the road. Kerry is the first to turn the corner, shouting, "Close," the moment she reaches the alley. The instant I see Ash turn the corner behind Kerry, Leslie swings. The wooden plank only barely misses Ash's ducking head as it passes over him and straight into the head of the guard following at his heels.

The man's feet lift off the ground as Leslie slams his head in the opposite direction. I wince as the man lands on his back, blood gushing from his forehead.

I'm not given any more time to watch as Leslie shoves me. Forcing me to move. I run after Ash and Kerry as they sprint down the alley. A glance back shows the guard sitting up with a hand holding his head. At least he isn't dead.

Ash and Kerry don't take us to their home. They lead us to a place a few streets away that I remember Leslie showing me. It is an abandoned building with five or six exit points. We wait here for a few minutes until the twins join us.

"So? How much we get?" Leslie asks.

Kerry opens the pouch she nabbed from the driver and counts the coins inside. "Ninety thousand."

"Is that it?" Leslie asks, disappointed.

"It's enough to feed us for the next few days, but yeah, I thought they'd have more too," Ash says.

"It will get us through. How about we head to Ari's? I'm starved." Tying off the coin pouch, Kerry tosses it to Ash.

Twenty minutes later, we approach a store with a large window on the front wall. Well, I say window, but it is nothing like the glass ones in New Vetus. No, this window is nothing more than an array of iron bars that let you look inside.

Ash leads us to a similarly reinforced front door. He stops in front of it and turns to me.

"Since you're new here, you should know Ari's rules. First: no stealing. If you ever get caught stealing from her, you'll find nowhere else that'll sell you food.

Second: always keep your hair covered. And finally: do not question her appearance, ever."

"What's wrong with her appearance?" I try to ask, but Ash is already pushing through the door. The others follow close behind.

I scoot through the door before it closes behind them. A counter table blocks off the back wall. On the left side is a selection of breads and on the right are fruits and vegetables, although a very limited selection compared to what I've seen at the ursu Bratchinas. Shelves on the wall behind the counter are lined with containers full of grains, nuts, and cheeses.

As my eyes land on the albanic who is probably Ari, I now understand why Ash doesn't want me asking about her appearance. The woman doesn't have any hair; instead, the entire top of her head is a scarred mess. The jagged, misshapen skin reaches as far down as her ears. One of her eyes looks like the lids melted together, leaving only one eye open to watch us enter her store.

Ash approaches the counter. "Hey, Ari, how's things?"

Ari hums in response. "Can't complain. I see you've another in your group. A recent oust, I assume?" She begins to collect an assortment of goods into a bag.

"Actually, no. She's not from the orphanage. Solvei's from New Vetus."

Her hand stops reaching for a round-shaped vegetable and she turns to me. "Is that so? You lived with those ursu?"

I nod to her, thankful that Ash didn't reveal I'm not albanic.

"I have to know: are they as bad as they say? I grew up in the Theocracy, so I never heard too much until I came here," Ari says as she leans over the counter.

"They used to be nice, but they changed during the war," I say. "Though some were rather cruel even before the war began, some I still wish to see again."

"Well, I'd love to say Zadok is better, but I prefer not to lie when I can. If you're already with these brats, I can't see things being too easy for you," she says, and finishes packing the bag with a few loaves.

I look at the others, but none of them seem fazed by Ari's insult.

"Just this once, thirty-five," Ari says to Ash, whose eyes widen.

"Really? Thank you, Ari," Ash says. He places seven coins on the counter and grabs the bag offered.

As we leave, Ari calls out, "Good luck."

Back in the group's home, I am offered a piece of bread along with some cheese. I refuse. I don't want to feel indebted to them, nor do I want to give them a reason to ask me to help them with that plan of Ash's.

"You can't not eat. Don't feel shy, Ari was nice enough to give us a discount because of you. That doesn't happen often," Ash says.

I lift a plank of wood I took from the streets and ignite it. "This is good enough food for me."

"You eat the things you set on fire? That's sick!" Leslie says. "What's wood taste like?" She leans in, having already scoffed her slice of bread.

"Like . . . wood? I don't know, it's hard to compare," I say. My thoughts cycle back to what was said in the store. "Back in Ari's, she called me an oust. What does that mean?"

"She was talking about the kids that get abandoned by the orphanage. That's what our little group is. Ya see, if ya haven't been adopted by the time you're ten, ya get kicked out. Like everything, being adopted relies on your purity. Some get booted even earlier if the orphanage caretakers believe you are too impure to be adopted," Leslie says with a frown. "You'll never see an albanic darker than Ash because they aren't kept long within the system."

"But you said family is important, right? Surely there are some families with children of darker hair." I remember Leal's fur coat was a different shade than both her parents, which she'd explained as genetics, something I'm still not all that clear on.

"Why do you think orphanages are even a thing?" Kerry says. "I don't know how it was for you, but here, you get to choose your family. Many children born with less purity than their parents get tossed out to the orphanages. I've heard it gets worse the purer the family is. They say the Cano family has tossed out fifteen kids in the last ten years alone."

"Talking about the Cano family, is there anything we can do to convince you to help us against them, Solvei?" Ash asks.

I raise an eyebrow at his question. "Unless doing so doesn't involve making me an enemy of this Cano family, then, no."

I ignore the disappointed look they all give me.

CHAPTER THIRTY-ONE

Found

Kerry and I search through the main road from above. We watch the numerous stalls and peddlers leaving free space amongst the tiled street as they accost the many travelers passing through the city. Far down one end, having long since passed us, is a pure-haired albanic ordering a group of five guards to destroy and scare off the illegal merchants blocking the entryways to the brick-and-mortar stores.

It is strange to see, no matter how many times it occurs. I don't know why they even bother trying to get rid of them; the peddlers are always back not even five minutes after they leave. It is an exercise in futility. Surely the city guards and the Cano family member ordering them around could be doing something more worthwhile.

Kerry and I sit on the hard roofing tiles as we scout for today's prey. I've come to an agreement where I will help with their hits under the condition that I do so with my safety as the lead consideration. I'll help them scout and cover their retreat, sometimes even causing a distraction, but I will never put myself directly in danger.

Even if I hadn't made myself clear, I doubt I'd ever wind up at the forefront, anyway. The swift fingers I've seen from the others are nothing short of amazing. Especially Kerry; I've seen her swipe so many coins now without the owner ever the wiser.

The twins remain as quiet as when I met them. They are short but by far the fastest runners. The trick they pull where one turns a corner and hides while the other twin is already farther away lets them escape from pursuit better than anyone else. Apparently, it was Leslie who came up with the idea. In my time with the group, I've seen her pushing the twins to play pranks on people. She seems enamored with the idea that Demi and Medi could enact the best of tricks, but they are hardly receptive to her ideas. The twins prefer not having to interact with anyone if they can get away with it. Even the others in our group.

"Why do the guards even bother?" I ask.

Kerry follows my line of sight. "Because they are paid to."

Confused, I tilt my head at her.

"The shopkeeps pay the Canos to get rid of them. It used to be effective before most of the city guard got conscripted for the invasion. Doesn't help that there's a lot more traffic through the city now than ever before. Every dog and his wife wants a slice of the gid coming through," Kerry says.

I hum at that, looking over the visitors passing through the city. Few stop for the peddlers from what I've seen. If anything, they get robbed more often than a trade happens. Why would anyone travel through Kelton? Couldn't they find a way around the city to reach the border?

"Hey, why do people even—"

"Look, I think we have our new targets." Kerry points down the road.

Three albanics in identical dark gray uniforms are walking down the street together. I can tell why Kerry thinks they'll be perfect targets. They wear well-made uniforms and are unarmed. If we aren't quick, someone else will rob them first.

Kerry jumps to her feet. "I'm going to get the others. You watch them and meet us at Point A." She runs off as soon as the words leave her mouth.

I turn my attention back to the trio down the road. They've stopped to talk with one of the stall traders. It is odd to see travelers willingly stop by them; usually the peddlers only make trades after bugging people enough that they pay to be left alone. They don't stop for long, soon continuing my way.

In the next few minutes, I watch as they stop every so often to talk to peddlers. Not once do they buy something. As they come closer, I can see that while two of them have white hair pure enough for high-class traders, one has gray hair that rivals Ash's. It is strange to see someone with such dark-colored hair openly exposing themselves. But it has the benefit of scaring off many of the traders despite their appearance of wealth.

They move slower than most, but I need to meet the others soon. Hopefully, they won't be robbed before they reach us. I drop to the roof of an adjacent building and do the same to reach the alley below. The dirty streets pass by as I run to meet up with the others.

They are all waiting for me by the time I reach Point A.

"Two men, one woman. Unarmed. They stop every few meters to talk, so we have maybe ten minutes before they reach us," I say. Usually, it's best to keep the descriptions brief, so we can set up quicker. Not so important now, considering the targets are taking their time, but it can be important when the targets are in a hurry.

"Good work," Ash says. "Let's go with Plan Four. Leslie and I will distract while Kerry, Demi, and Medi will come from behind. Solvei, are you okay to cover our retreat?"

I nod in confirmation. Usually, it just requires me to throw something at any chasers to split their attention enough to give the others time to run. I've never needed to go to the extremes that Leslie tends to. She favors being brutal and has the swing strength to back it up. I don't have that same strength. At most, I'm ready to scare them off with my flames, but I have avoided doing so up to this point.

I carry a few rocks with me as I climb onto the roof of a building with good sight on both the main street and the alley Ash and Leslie will most likely use to escape. I've seen the amount of effort Ash puts into these plans. He has gone through with both me and the others the best ways to approach our targets and the best escape routes when they become aggressive. A lot of thought goes into making these thefts successful without too much danger. The results say everything about how well it works. Nobody has been hurt in the week I've been here, despite the risk they put themselves in.

A commotion in the street drags me out of my thoughts. Leslie and Ash have started their fake brawl right in front of the targets. Ash goes to throw a punch, which Leslie dodges, and she shoves him into the first of the similarly dressed albanics. The man catches the boy and keeps him upright, before the woman tries to stop Leslie from throwing the next punch.

The last man in the group hardly notices Kerry pass by him, swiping his wallet and continuing on as if nothing happened. The twins are less sneaky, snatching the coin off the other two and immediately sprinting away; the uniformed albanics are both distracted trying to stop the fight between Ash and Leslie. Two resounding shouts of indignation ring out as they turn to their robbers. A shove from Leslie and Ash sends them stumbling.

The first man takes a second to realize his wallet has already disappeared before his shout follows suit. He chases after Ash and Leslie as they run down the alley below me. I ready my stone to throw. I pull my arm back before launching it toward him as hard as I can. But the man does something odd. He stops chasing them, instead pulling something from his hip. The man either ignores or fails to notice the rock as it clatters on the ground in front of him. He holds the object up at arm's length from his face.

A crack echoes through the air, like the sound of thunder. I don't see what happens, but only a moment later screams fill the air. I look at Ash, now sprawled on the ground, howling and clutching his leg.

I don't know what is going on. Ash got hurt? How? I look back at our target. The strange, small pipe with a handle is being held above the man's head now. He looks right at me as the crack cuts the air again. A sudden impact assaults my shoulder. My arm jolts backward as if a bat slammed into it.

On instinct, I throw out my flames toward the man who somehow can hit me from this distance. With my flames blocking his sight of me, I throw myself off the roof and run for Ash. Leslie already has one of his arms around her shoulder and is dragging him away.

As my flame dissipates behind me, I turn to see if the man is aiming that thing at us again. He isn't, but I am still unnerved by what I see. The man is grinning.

Why would anyone grin after I attack them with my flames? Even if my flames didn't come close to him, it is still odd. It makes me nervous. The man doesn't move. He just keeps his eyes on me. His two partners join him after only a moment. The woman yells at him with fury, but he continues grinning as he turns to talk to them.

I hurry to catch up to the others and find Kerry has appeared and is taking Ash's other arm.

"Ash, you're gonna be okay. Just push through this until we're safe." Kerry struggles to keep her words from warbling. Tears run down her face as she pushes forward, struggling with Ash's weight.

"Kerry, I'm not gonna die. I got hit in the leg is all, barely a scratch." Ash tries to hide the pain he's feeling, but he cannot stop the wince every time he nudges his leg.

As I catch up, I cast a glance backward once more, expecting them to be chasing close behind, and I ready myself to burn them. Surprisingly, they don't appear.

"They aren't following," I say.

Leslie looks over her shoulder at me. "Nice scaring 'em off. Don't think we could've got away if you hadn't."

After seeing the unnerving smile of that man, I somehow doubt that I scared them off. "We should hide as soon as possible."

"Already way ahead of you. Can you make sure nobody is hiding in the building on the right?" Leslie says. I nod and run forward to make way for them.

I push open the old, rusted door and enter what looks like an abandoned bookstore. Bookshelves cover the floor of the small room, filled with decaying books and cobwebs. There is no sign anybody has been here in a while; the floor is layered in dust.

I step back outside and usher the others in, closing the door behind them. I turn to see Leslie lowering Ash to the floor. It looks like he passed out. Tears trail down Kerry's cheeks as she tries to put pressure on his thigh. Crimson blood puddles around them as it gushes out of the wound in his leg.

"He's losing too much blood. I can't stop it." Kerry tries in vain to push harder against his leg, unable to stem the flow of blood.

"What can we do?" Leslie asks.

"We need a tourniquet, now!" Kerry's voice cracks as she yells.

"What's a tourniquet?"

Kerry scrunches her face in frustration before her eyes land on me.

"Solvei, get over here."

I don't reply. I just do as she asks, approaching her at Ash's side. The blood moves a bit too much like water for my liking, but while touching it does sting a bit, I don't feel the soul-crushing agony that water brings.

Kerry grabs my hands and brings them to his wound. It's so small, but so much blood is pouring out.

"Now I want you to put your finger in his wound and burn it."

"What! I can't do that!" I flinch away from Ash, the image of Gloria's burning body flashing in my mind.

"Please, we don't have time. Just do it."

Kerry's lip wavers as she pleads to me, staring into me with tear-soaked eyes.

I don't know why she wants me to burn him, but I know she doesn't want to hurt him. I lower my hand back over his wound and press my flames inside.

I can only be thankful he is not awake to feel me burning away at the wound inside his body. My flames pass into the wound as directed by Kerry, but I soon find something in his leg that I know definitely shouldn't be there. A small bit of lead and copper is stuck within.

My flame isn't hot enough to melt those metals yet and I don't want to try inside his leg either. Also, I still haven't figured out how to make my flames physical, so I can't use them to pull it out. I have only one option and I don't know if it will hurt him any more than he already is.

"There is metal stuck in his leg. Should I pull it out?" I ask.

"Do it, quickly."

With Kerry's affirmation, I brace myself for what I'm about to do. I push a finger into his wound and try to remove the shard without hurting Ash any more than I need to. I can see the metal piece easily with my flames, but I can't get a good grip on it.

My hands are shaking. I realize my breathing is haggard, so I force myself to calm down. I shove in a second finger, squeeze the shard between my fingers, and drag it out as quick as possible. Blood gushes out faster than before. My entire arm is coated and blood soaks my knees. It stings everywhere it touches, feeling like a thousand tiny pins stabbing into me.

"Burn it, burn it. Hurry." Kerry's voice reverberates in my head. Her shouting next to me only pushes me to move faster.

I push a finger back into his wound and try to fry the flesh. I can't help but remember the way Gloria's skin bubbled the last time I burned bodies like this. It feels wrong.

But, despite how horrible it feels, the blood slows. I finally understand why she wants me to burn the wound. My flames inside his leg give me a perfect idea of what is happening. I can burn closed the small blood pipes in his body to stop him from losing more. Now that I know, I can stop myself from hurting him. I can only lament that I didn't know to do this at the start.

With only the tiniest tongues of fire, I localize the burning of his flesh only to the points I can find the tubes of blood in the wound.

Soon, his bleeding stops entirely, but you can't tell by looking at him. Ash's clothes are soggy with his own blood. Looking down at myself, I realize my own clothes aren't in a much better state.

I take a step back from Ash and Kerry as she holds him tight. My fire burns over my clothes, not hot enough to burn through the flame resistance but enough to incinerate the dirt and blood clinging to me.

Ash looks pale. Far more so than I thought a person could be. Not wanting to step back into the puddle of his blood and dirty myself again, I keep my distance and let Kerry watch over him.

We wait in silence for the next fifteen minutes before Kerry finally speaks. "I . . . I think he's gonna be fine. Leslie, can you help me carry him? We can't stay here."

"Yeah, no problem."

"And, Solvei." Kerry pauses, looking at me with puffy, red eyes. "Thank you. You saved him."

"I'm glad he's okay."

CHAPTER THIRTY-TWO

Closing In

I hold the lead and copper shard in my hand, trying my hardest to burn through the metal. I hoped I could burn hot enough to consume them, but it seems I am still far from adulthood. With all the time I spent in the furnace, I thought I might have sped up my growth. Especially with how strong my flames have been against the creatures and people in the east.

But while the small chunk glows a bright red in my hands, it refuses to be consumed. I'm still far from the level of my elders. Still, it affirms that the beings outside the wasteland are simply weak to fire.

"Y'know, you're gonna be a bloody blessing when winter hits. But right now, can you cool it? You're making me sweat."

Beside me, Leslie fans herself with her hand. A trickle rolls down her forehead.

"Sorry," I say.

A few days have passed since Ash was shot. The others tell me it is a type of weapon that he was hit by: a gun. They say they've never seen one so small, but they are certain that's what it was. The impact I received to my shoulder was nowhere near as damaging to me as it was to Ash. My bullet had flown straight through my body, and while the impact felt like it should have blown me off my feet, it healed as quickly as any old sandworm bite.

I guess I'm lucky not to have a fluid inside my body to lose like Ash does. Really, how do they even live with such vulnerable bodies?

I haven't been able to leave our hole since we brought Ash back. A sudden thunderstorm encroached on the city, preventing me from joining the others as they left for their daily hunts.

Hmm, maybe I shouldn't talk about vulnerable bodies . . .

Either because they are missing two members of their group or no targets are traveling in the rain, the others have had little luck making gains.

The constant pelting of rain on the roof above keeps me awake. I've struggled to sleep at all since the rain started and it is leaving an impact on me. I should be able to limit the spread of my heat more than I have. Leslie would never have gotten so hot if I was still in complete control of my faculties. It isn't a good sign. The last thing I want is to accidentally burn our home, especially as I'm currently using it to hide from the water.

I need to sleep soon, but it's a struggle.

The scratching of the bookshelf above preludes Kerry's return. The first thing she does after dropping past the ladder is check on Ash. He has yet to wake since we returned, but color has returned to his face. I'm told it shouldn't be long until he wakes now. How Kerry knows that, I'm unsure.

"There's even more today," she says after verifying Ash's condition.

"The gray uniforms?" Leslie asks.

Kerry nods. "They're on almost every corner now, breaking into every building they can find. Not just the abandoned buildings either; they're entering merchant-owned places too. They are searching for something."

"How long 'til they reach us, ya think?"

"We're still a bit out, but with how many I've seen searching, probably only a couple of days."

"Who did we piss off? They didn't even have coins in their wallets, just some worthless paper," Leslie says.

I can't help but feel put off by everything that happened. First, that man grins after he was almost burned alive, then a thunderstorm appears out of thin air, and now they are combing the city for us? Over petty theft? Something is screaming at me, something that should be obvious, but I can't think of what through my hazy, tired thoughts. It almost feels like I've forgotten something.

I don't know when I fell asleep, but the exhaustion must have finally dragged me down to the depths of slumber. A hand over my mouth almost makes me shout as I wake, but the heavy footsteps above stop me. I look up at Kerry. She removes her hand and raises her finger to her lips, gesturing me to remain quiet.

Leslie is already helping Ash walk through the back exit. He must have finally woken after I fell asleep. The twins are already gone. I approach the crawl space that we have to climb through to escape. My body locks up in tension as the sound of pouring rain finally registers in my ears. It is still raining and they expect me to go outside.

Ash and Leslie make it through and Kerry's hands on my back are pushing me toward the exit. But I can't. I shake my head and step away.

"I can't do it. It's raining, I can't." Trying to back away from the exit doesn't work. Kerry is stopping me.

"I know you're scared, but I'm not leaving you to them. Not after you saved Ash."

Her hand on my back prevents me from backing away. Every second I take, I'm being pushed closer to the nightmare of a wet crawl space. A crash from above makes me jump. The people upstairs are tossing things as they scour the room. It won't be long before they find the path hidden behind the bookcase.

"Please, hurry up. I don't want them to find us," Kerry says into my ear, pushing me into the hole.

I gulp, swallowing as much of my fear as I can, and climb into the exit. I have only a few meters to crawl, but the trickle of water flowing down the semicollapsed wood I'll have to pass makes the distance daunting. Hurried nudges at my feet force me to push forward regardless. I cover myself as much as I can with Leal's jacket, crawling with the thick leather between my hands and knees and the soggy ground below.

The exit leads to a covered space littered with trash. The moment my head pokes out the hole and relief finally settles in, Leslie pulls me to my feet. Rain in the open air splatters on the ground not a few steps from me. I huddle closer to the wall and tie the strings of the rain jacket as tight as I can.

Kerry is quick to climb out behind me, but I hardly pay attention, instead watching the rain as it continues its everlasting downpour.

Fingers snapping in my face break me from my trance. "Solvei? Come on, we can't linger. Are you gonna be all right?"

I shake my head to clear the chills the rain instinctively brings forth. Snap out of it, Solvei, you've dealt with a little rain before. This is hardly going to stop you now.

"Yeah, let's go."

Kerry breathes out in relief before waving to the others, then heads out into the rain. I start by following close behind them, but the splashes of their steps almost hit me a few times, so I take more space behind them. Where the others run right through the puddles, I try to find any way I can to avoid them. My shoes should keep out water, but I'd rather not take chances.

Once we make enough distance from our home, we gather under a veranda where I can shake off the lingering water from my jacket. I've been lucky so far, not feeling pain anywhere.

"Where now?" Leslie asks.

"We should cross Main Street. Find a place they've already searched over there," Ash says. He must have been awake a while before the uniformed albanics raided our home. "Do you know a good place, Kerry?"

She nods and we are once again out in the rain. I can't tell if it's evening or the clouds just block that much of the sun, but it's dark out. There is only barely enough light to see, which makes the lights coming from the main street all the more odd. It's bright. The street ahead of us is lit as if it's day, while the alley we jog through remains pitch-black.

I catch up to the others, who have stopped before the main street. I step past them to look at what has caught their attention and a pit of dread bubbles within me. Right there before me is a wagon design I could never forget. The tubes curving out of the metal chassis and its large capacity. The strange, no-handled design. This is the same wagon I saw with the Kenna tribe.

These are the people who killed my mom.

There is more than one of these metal wagons; they line the main road as far as I can see. Bright lamps at the front of each wagon light the street. But even worse is that there are hundreds of the uniformed albanics wandering around.

There is no doubt in my mind. They are still hunting áed. They are hunting me. That's why that man grinned; they've found me.

"So, uh, I don't think we're getting past this. What now?" Leslie asks.

Ash turns away from the street. "Yeah. We'll have to find somewhere on thi . . . Solvei? Are you all right? You look like you've seen a void-touched."

I snap my attention away from the uniformed men. "Yeah, I'm fine." Even to my own ears it sounds like a lie. Fortunately, Ash doesn't push it and leads us back into the alleys.

It doesn't take long for Ash and Kerry to decide on a place to lie low. It doesn't have any bedding, nor is it well hidden like the last place, but it puts a roof over my head and keeps the rain out. I increase the heat of the room a bit to help the others dry off quicker. I can dry off their clothes directly, but I hold off doing so unless they ask for it.

Now that I have time to think, I withdraw from the conversation with the others.

They found me. There is no denying it. I have no idea why they want me, but they do. They brought an entire army to find me. Have they already taken out all the other áed they can find? Is that why they have so many people ready and searching here? How many of them are water mages?

"Who the fuck are they? They couldn't be after us, right? A couple of people's wallets could hardly be enough to send so many soldiers. It has to be a coincidence," I overhear Leslie say.

Should I tell them? No. I shouldn't trust so easily. They might just give me to them if they think it'd work better for them.

As it is, I can't stay here. I've already almost been caught and I haven't even seen their water mages yet. My eyes glance to the others. Ash is talking with concern about the events of the past few days. I guess it is time to go through with what he wants. Really, if my only options are going against a family unable to stop peddlers or against proven murderers, the choice is obvious.

The uniformed men fill the streets, so either they are working with the Cano family or the Cano family has no power to stop them. Either case means remaining off their bad side means very little.

I stand up and step toward Ash, interrupting their talk.

"I'll help."

He just looks at me blankly. "What?"

"The Cano family. I'll help you steal from them."

Ash jumps to his feet before the pain that assaults his leg drops him back on his ass. Disregarding the pain, he grins at me.

"Great. When should we proceed?"

"As soon as possible," I say.

"As happy as I am that little icy heart over here finally thawed for us, shouldn't we wait until the gray uniforms stop their search in Kelton?" Leslie asks.

They've been hunting áed for well over a year now; there is very little chance that they're going to give up after only a few days. I don't want to say that, though. I don't want them to know I'm their target. Fortunately, I don't have to.

"No, this is perfect. They are the best distraction we can hope for. The Cano members that haven't left for the war will be tied up with whoever these people are," Ash says. "We can be in and out and nobody will know."

Well, I've set myself to it now. Whatever happens will happen. I can only hope this storm stops sometime soon. I've been lucky so far, but I don't like my chances of fleeing until the rain stops.

CHAPTER THIRTY-THREE

Cano Manor Infiltration

It's funny; I'd thought it was dark earlier. Now I struggle to even see Leslie's back as we rush through the alleys. I am tempted to light up just a bit, so I can see where I am stepping, but the last thing we need right now is to attract attention.

The rain has slowed to a drizzle but does not stop. Leal's jacket has been far more lifesaving than I'd ever expected. I wish I could thank her or just speak with her again. Leal is the only one I know I can trust. Ash and the others have their own goals. Goals that currently coincide with mine, but I know that can change at any moment. I need to be prepared for the eventual betrayal when they no longer need me.

In this dilapidated city shrouded in darkness, the Cano residence sits above all. The mansion shines brightly in the night atop its private hill. It is the only building for kilometers that has its own lawn, a gem buried in dirt and filth. It is impossible to miss any time it enters our sight. Every window and blade of grass on the estate is lit by bright lights found nowhere else in Kelton.

If a building can be beautiful, then this is it. I can't help but feel it is unfair. An entire city of people have to live in decrepit ruins while a single family lives in such excess. Is this what money does? Create discrepancy between who has it and who does not? In New Vetus, everyone has a similar quality of living; well, at least the ursu do.

I never really thought about money as anything more than something that allows you to buy food. I was fine with letting the group have my share from the thefts to let me stay in the relative safety of their home. When I consider how much it costs for them to eat every day, is it possible to ever earn enough to live in a place like this mansion?

Until now, I thought of the thefts I've taken part in as something akin to helping yourself to coal when the rest of the tribe doesn't let you help them with work. It is something I am used to and seems natural. Now I think I know Zadok culture well enough to say it's more like a wake of buzzards clawing at one another to try to get the best bits of meat for themselves.

It is a far different view from what I'm used to, and not one I think I like very much.

People care about themselves first and foremost. I can understand that. I had the choice between my life and Gloria's, and I chose mine. But in the Zadok Kingdom, there are many that take the whole corpse for themselves and don't leave the smaller birds even scraps, so I don't think it is wrong for those smaller birds to steal from those with larger wings.

I am just worried about the buzzards' talons.

"Are you ready, Solvei? Not backing out now?" Leslie says from my side.

I look up as much as I feel safe to, keeping my hood low over my face. The estate fence is right in front of us now. Shabby-looking huts clutter the space up to a meter before it, where the space is oddly empty for what I'm used to in this city.

I nod once at her. There is no option for me. If Ash has a way out of this city, then that is my best bet. I'd rather not risk running into the uniforms on my own; who knows which of them might be water mages.

I walk up beside Ash as he inspects the wrought iron fencing. I don't step any closer than he does, keeping a good meter between the fence and myself.

"This is what I need you for." Ash takes a step back and tosses the stick he was holding at the fence. At only a hand's distance before it hits the black iron, the stick explodes into flame. The burning stick knocks against the fence and falls to the ground, where it lasts only a few moments before it's reduced to embers.

The fence did that? I mean, the flame doesn't feel all that hot, but it is a surprise how quick it activates. The wrought iron bars now glow with bright red inscriptions lining their length. A few seconds after activating, the light ceases and returns the fence back to its unassuming state. Even looking closely, I can only barely make out the lines of the inscription.

"So? You think you can get us through it?" I can feel not only his eyes digging into me, and turning to the others only confirms my guess.

I bring my attention back to the fence in front of me. If all it does is light things on fire, I will be fine, but I don't want to take that chance. First, I throw a handful of flame forward, stripping it of my inner flame and keeping my distance. The inscriptions light up as the flames pass through the iron bars. As the flames reach the other side of the fence, they get sucked into the inscription.

It's a surprising feature, but I suppose it makes sense to stop your own defense system from igniting the grass every time someone throws a stick through the bars.

Should I be worried about my own flames being consumed by the fence? No, its pull on the flames is far too weak to overpower me, especially against my inner flame, which is connected to me far more intrinsically than any control an inscription could hope to achieve.

Also, I have seen an inscription network like this before.

I send my inner flame to wrap around a few of the bars in front of me. I feel a slight but inconsequential tug at my energy. It is nothing I need to worry about. Just like the last time I encountered something like this, I reach through the inscription. Feeling the energy on the other side, I grab ahold of it and pull it into myself.

The network barely puts up any resistance as I drain it of the energy it needs. The fire I can feel through the inscription is far more than what I experienced back at the academy in Fisross. It takes a few moments before I drain it completely. Like back then, I watch as all the lights of the mansion and surrounding grounds dip out of existence. Nothing but my own flames light up the area.

The absorbed fire makes me feel hot. It's like I consumed ten furnaces' worth of coal in an instant, the energy is more than I can handle. I take a few steps away from Ash. My flames return to me and the light cuts out. I know I won't be able to keep my body cool enough with this much heat rushing through me. I'd rather they not burn themselves by accidentally touching me. There's no way I'm spitting out this much energy.

I can't see any of them, but I can still hear their gasps of shock.

"You took out their lights? How?" Kerry asks from somewhere to my right.

"They used the same power source for their lights as the fence inscription. I don't know what they used to keep this thing powered, but I'm stuffed." I pat my belly, imitating how Leslie acts after a meal. Though I don't know how to burp on command.

Leslie snorts. "You *ate* their incineration wall?"

"Yep." Stepping forward, I slap the now-ordinary fence for emphasis. "All good to climb over now."

"Can't you just melt through it?" I hear Ash say.

I would have said no straightaway normally, but the energy rushing through me is incredible. Placing a hand on the iron bar, I heat it up as much as I can. The red glow the metal bar takes on makes me hopeful, but it's already taking too long. It doesn't matter how much energy I have in me if I can only reach a certain temperature.

"Not unless you want to wait twenty minutes," I say. I don't think I can melt through the bars, but I should be able to bend them out of the way if I have enough time.

It takes a few minutes for us to get over the sharp pikes of the fence, mostly because Ash and I struggle to get over. I stress about climbing while keeping safe from the rain, and Ash needs the others' help to get over with his injured leg. The spikes on top of the fence are luckily only for decoration rather than for preventing intruders, their points smooth and blunt. It's like they never expected anyone to get past the security measure that burns on touch. I guess even the eastern races realize how effective fire is against them. Why else would they use fire in their defense?

We glide along the grass of the garden until we reach the mansion. Well-trimmed hedges lining the walls give us a perfect place to lurk.

"We check the windows first. If none of them are unlocked, we'll climb to the second-floor balcony," Ash says.

The first window we try opens with ease. They really didn't expect anyone to make it past their fence.

"Okay, Solvei and Leslie, you two go through that window. Kerry and I will find another window and Demi, Medi, you'll climb up to the balcony. Join Solvei and Leslie if no other is unlocked," Ash says. "Remember, only take what you can easily carry. I don't want to lose anyone because they got greedy. Prioritize jewelry, if possible."

The dry air inside the mansion calls to me. I climb through the windowsill before Ash even finishes his instruction. I take a deep breath, relishing the feeling of air not drowning in moisture. The air outside isn't painful or anything, but it feels like I'm suffocating when I breathe.

Leslie leaps through the window with grace and is already opening drawers and wardrobes before I can blink. I pass through the only door in the room after checking there is nobody on the other side. A couple of couches surround a small knee-high table in the center of the room. There aren't many places to look in this room, only a table with drawers beside the entry door. There are paintings and decorations in the room, but none would be easy for me to carry.

Opening the drawers only returns some tableware. I can probably take some of the shiny knives; they don't look much good for cutting like my hunting knife, but they're made of a metal I've never felt before.

Out of curiosity, I try to burn through it. Unfortunately, even this is too much for me. Although when I open my hand again, I realize I've bent it out of shape. I discreetly place it at the bottom of the pile, taking a few intact knives with me in case I can't find anything better.

"What do you think?" I hear Leslie's voice from behind me.

I swivel on my feet, having forgotten to pay attention to my surroundings. Leslie is striking some sort of pose with her hand on her chin. She's done something to her face, which looks darker than usual.

"Who would've thought these rich families put this stuff on just to make their hair look whiter." She tosses me a small case of a gray powder as she wipes the stuff off her face.

"Should you really be messing around right now?" I ask.

"Why not? Anyone rich enough to afford tan powder isn't gonna be this side of the wall unless they have to. Either they're up north or leading the charge into New Vetus." She continues to rub at her face. "Shit. How do they get this shit off?"

I ignore her and poke my head out the other door of this room. The hallway is empty, so I creep out toward the next room, Leslie following far less quietly behind.

I freeze when I hear the slamming of a door at the end of the hallway. A shout follows not long after.

"Bain, get here this instant. What is going on? Why are the lights not working?"

I hear someone reply, but it is too quiet to know what they say.

Against my better judgement, I approach the voices. It is probably dumb, but I want to know whether they know we are here or not. A bit of risk is fine if I learn whether they are setting a trap for us.

"What do you mean the source was drained?" the voice shouts. "That was supposed to last another two years. Have the pilfers launched another revolt? The nerve to do so while our nation is at war. What of the backup supply?"

Leslie grabs my arm, turning me to face her. She remains quiet, but her raised eyebrow asks everything. I nod toward the voices before approaching the archway leading into a large, open area. A set of double doors sits to my right while a grand staircase climbs the back wall. While not nearly as large as some of the ursu's stairs, it somehow still seems far grander.

Careful to remain within the darkness of the corridor, I watch two men holding candles talk halfway up the stairs.

"I'm sorry, sir, it will take the boys some time to carry the backup source from storage."

"Tsk. Organize the guard. We'll cut down any that breach our estate."

The front doors slam open. I flinch back into the shadows on reflex. Through the entryway runs a woman holding a lantern, rushing until she reaches the base of the stairs.

"Mr. Cano, sir. The Henosis soldiers have knocked down the front gate."

"What! This is the Empire's doing? Fuck! Those bastards." In his rage, the man on the stairs swings his arm into the fancy railing beside him, shattering it and sending stone into the wall at the other side of the foyer. Dust clouds the room from the impact.

"Send someone to the barracks. I want every reserve we have at my front door in ten minutes. I'll grab my sword and meet you with the guard to intercept." With his final word, the man, Mr. Cano, runs upstairs.

As the dust settles, I can't help but gawk as the wall that was there a moment ago is now, well . . . missing. Instead, I can see straight into a large hall with a long dining table.

How is he so strong? I don't think any of the ursu I've met could do that, not even Gerben. He isn't a mage either, unless he has a way to hide the glow of his markings when they are activated. That, or he is a different type of mage than what Leal knew about.

I glance behind me to see Leslie's face gaping with wide eyes. She looks exactly how I feel.

Maybe I shouldn't have agreed to steal from the Cano family after all.

CHAPTER THIRTY-FOUR

Cano Manor Exfiltration

With Leslie beside me, I crack open the window and peek out. There, right out the front of the mansion, are about ten or so guards. The same I'd seen knocking down street stalls this past week.

Leslie and I crouch within a room overlooking the front path of the mansion. We can see all the way down to the gate at the other end of the cobblestone road surrounded on both sides by hedges and grass. Far in the distance, near where the gate should be, I can make out several lights approaching the estate.

"Should we be listening in? Won't it be better to grab some stuff and run while they are distracted?" Leslie seems far more subdued than usual. That display of strength from who I assume is the head of the Cano family must have shaken her more than I thought.

"It's better if we hear what they say. We need to know why they arrived right now. Do they know we're here? Are they here to tell the Cano elder?"

If the uniformed men we've seen in the city are Henosis soldiers, then that means the Empire—the ones holding a nation of ursu by their necks—are after the áed. Aren't they fighting a war right now? Should they really have this many people looking for us? For me?

The soldiers are approaching fast, already close enough that I can see their numbers double that of the guards waiting in front of the mansion.

A slam from the entrance doors somewhere to my left announces the arrival of Mr. Cano. He storms up to the guards, who split down the middle to allow him to pass. He stops, facing the approaching soldiers as the man from the foyer, Bain, approaches his side.

"Lieutenant von Dunnell, why do you trespass on my property?" Mr. Cano says loudly into the open night air.

A figure at the front of the approaching soldiers raises his hand, and as one, they stop. It's kind of eerie how synchronized their steps are.

"Wynn Cano, I thank you for being as accommodating to our search as you have. Unfortunately, what we search for has eluded us. I believe now is the time to extend the search to your residence." The man who steps forward is rather tall for an albanic. Each step he takes with confidence as he walks away from his soldiers and approaches Wynn, the Cano family head.

"What nonsense. I allowed you to strip the woodwork of my city because of the agreement between our nations, but do not think for a second that I am here to bend to your whims. Should you remove the presence of yourself and the soldiers behind you, I shall grace you with ignorance to this slight. Otherwise, I'll have you and your men slaughtered where they stand."

Almost as if timed with his words, guards rush in from the gate behind the Henosis soldiers. I don't have a perfect angle to see, but there are at least fifty guards approaching. Half the Henosis soldiers swivel and hold their guns toward the approaching guards.

Guns aren't something I'm all too familiar with, but I've seen how damaging they can be from a distance. Both sides hold long arm-length guns that I once thought were oddly shaped cudgels. Tensions rise as the Cano guards surround the Henosis soldiers.

"Is this really how you want to do things? You'll be making an enemy of the Empire. I'm sure even someone as dull as you can understand that isn't the smartest idea." The lieutenant's gaze turns cold, and he walks toward Wynn until they are a body length apart. He seems completely unfazed that he's surrounded.

"This is your final warning. Leave." Wynn has his hand tightly gripping the handle of the blade at his hip, ready to unsheathe in a moment.

The two men glare at each other for a good five seconds before the Henosis lieutenant sighs. He makes a motion with his hand over his shoulder before the world becomes deafening.

My head throbs from the combined sound of twenty guns firing at once. Before the guards can even retaliate against the shots fired from the soldiers, a wall of water rushes around the Henosis, blocking much of the return fire.

Through the distortion of the flowing liquid, I see many of the soldiers rising above to take a shot before dropping back to cover. On the guards' side, after they take their shots, they are left stranded without cover. After the initial salvo from the guards, they become sitting ducks, unable to return fire while receiving bullet after bullet from the soldiers.

Barely ten seconds pass before all the Cano guards are lying dead or incapacitated on the ground. The wall of water around the Henosis men disperses.

Wynn is staring slack-jawed at the scene around him. He'd swung at the Henosis soldier a few times before he realized what was happening around him. Lieutenant von Dunnell simply brushed each swing aside with an ease that reminds me of my sparring sessions with Auntie.

"Wha—How?" Wynn stutters. While he is lost staring at the surrounding dead, Bain steps forward with a bright amber light shining through his sleeves. He throws his arm forward, and spears of stone hurtle out of his hand and fly toward the leader of the Henosis.

The man dodges to the side and deflects one from the air with the side of his sword. With speed I've only ever seen from my elders, he runs at Bain, plunging his sword straight through his chest.

"You bastard. The Zadok Kingdom won't forgive this." Wynn flies into a rage, rushing the lieutenant.

The man smoothly slides out of the way of his swing, putting his leg out to trip Wynn before tugging his sword out of the now-dead Bain. Wynn's sword continues to swing into the ground, launching much of the cobblestone path flying from the impact.

"You've quite the bit of enhancement there. Must have cost you a fortune. Is that where all the money in this city goes? Too bad it's wasted on you." The lieutenant dodges another swing and dances behind Wynn. "I'm surprised Zadok even knows about the ritual. If my task wasn't so important, I'd take you back to Henosis myself. I've heard it's far more efficient to perform the ritual on a living target than the dead. More painful for you, but efficient nonetheless."

"Mongrel, you'll regret this day. The Cano family will tear down everything you know." Wynn throws himself at the lieutenant.

The loud laugh he receives in return only makes Wynn push more strength into his swing, caring little about form. The wild downward slash is easily redirected, and before I know it, blood is everywhere, splattering over even the glass of the window I am peeking through.

Wynn Cano cut his own leg off. Actually, no. It's more like his leg exploded. The lieutenant's skilled redirection let the man mutilate himself. From how they fought, it is hard to tell if the lieutenant even has much strength himself. He obviously didn't need it against Wynn.

It is a pitiful sight now. Wynn's sobs and cries are loud but incoherent. He curls up on himself, holding his now-defunct limb.

"There will be no retribution for you, I'm afraid. Your family, as well as the rest of the Zadok Kingdom, is inconsequential. If they call for retaliation, they would be nothing but fools. Your nation is less important than a child that can spit some fire." With his piece said, the lieutenant brings his sword down on the sobbing man's neck.

I snap out of the trance I've been locked in, watching them. There is no time to waste. I should have run when I heard the lieutenant say they were going to search the mansion. There's no way he isn't looking for me.

I grab Leslie and pull her back out into the hallway. "Find Ash and Kerry. We need to leave now."

I don't look back, just run into the foyer and sprint up the stairs. The second-floor hallway hides me just as I hear the entrance doors slamming open. Behind the third door I slam open there is finally someone, a woman looking out to the front yard through a window. She isn't anyone I know. I close the door and find the next before she can even turn around.

The next door to the back of the house doesn't have anyone visible, so I move to go to the next room before I spot movement from the corner of my eye. The twins pop out from a large wardrobe, seemingly hiding before they knew it was me running through the hall.

"We need to go now; they are gonna search the house." I push them out toward the balcony at the back of the room.

Thankfully, they realize the seriousness of the situation and hurry to climb down the side of the building. I follow close behind, tying the hood tight over my head.

The dark clouds in the sky radiate a deep red hue. Light from the Ember Moon colors the overcast sky above. The darkness recedes just enough that I can see the garden filtered through red.

Ash and Leslie are already waiting for us at the bottom, so as soon as we touch the ground, we're off running toward the place we entered. Sneaking might have been a better idea if we weren't limited by time. The soldiers haven't reached the back of the premises yet, but I don't doubt they will surround the place soon enough.

Yet it won't be that easy to get away. The sound of a gunshot rings as if it's been fired right beside me. I don't know where the bullet lands, but they have to be shooting at us. I throw out a wall of flame to obscure us. I don't want them to hit the others while they are climbing the fence. Once I make myself known, the shots stop only to be replaced by shouting.

I keep the wall up while I climb over myself. Only when I drop it do I see the number of soldiers running toward us, not just on the mansion side of the fence but the city side too.

Where do they all come from?

Before I can freeze for more than a moment, Ash already has my hand and is dragging me through the alleys. Without it even needing to be said, the others split up and run in different directions. They throw stones at some of the pursuing soldiers before throwing themselves out of sight. I'm sure they'll run through the complex maze of alleys and abandoned buildings where the adult albanics have no chance of following.

A minute passes with no soldiers spotting me and Ash. A sigh of relief that I let out comes too early, as a heavy crashing reaches our ears. Looking back at where we came from, the same place as the noise, I spot sudden rushing water knocking through buildings and tearing down weaker walls.

I squeak in fright and jump on the nearest roof I can find. Ash braces against the wall below me and I feel the entire structure wobble as the water passes underneath. I'm so thankful it doesn't collapse under me.

I look down to see Ash steadying himself in the moving water.

"Uh, what the fuck is going on?"

"Can we find the others first? These aren't the Cano guards."

Ash nods and goes to move but stops when he realizes I'm not following.

"Are you coming?"

"Yeah, I'm just waiting for the water to drop a bit." The water is moving downhill and we're near the top, so I'm hoping it eventually drains away. It takes a good minute for it to happen, but the water dries out.

"Sorry," I say.

He waves it off and goes to step out into the adjacent alley before pulling back at the last second. Through a gap in the wall, I watch as a soldier runs past, coming within a body length of where our exit is. Shouts and heavy footsteps reach my ears. That minute was enough for them to spread through the streets. And with the water having torn through a bunch of the buildings we could have otherwise escaped through, we are left without many options.

What do we do? There's no way I can use the crawl spaces we use to get around now. If the flood did not destroy them, they'll be drowning in far too much water for me to move through without hurting myself.

The longer we wait here, the sooner we'll be found. That lieutenant has already proven himself willing to go to any length to find me, whether it be making an enemy of an entire kingdom or destroying people's homes. Assuming the flood was caused by a water mage rather than some incredibly unlucky coincidence.

Ash keeps an ear to the wall, waiting until the sound of footsteps disappears from the alley before leading me out. He leads me through the city with expertise. It is surprising he can find so many paths despite how damaged the buildings have become. He knows exactly which buildings and alleys have the least amount of damage. His memory of the city is incredible.

It takes a while, but we finally reach a safe enough distance by dodging patrols and moving through buildings when we can. The planned meeting point to regroup with the others is only a few blocks away. The damage doesn't reach this far out, the flood likely having crashed through some other part of the city.

The rain stops for the first time in days. I'm not willing to risk dropping my hood, but it is a good omen. Hopefully, the others grabbed enough to fund our escape from Zadok. I trust they are competent enough to have done better than I did, at the very least.

The tension from the night flees my shoulders. It looks like we're finally in the clear.

I push open the door from the abandoned sewing workshop we pass through, out to the street that leads to our meeting spot.

Suddenly, I'm knocked on my back. My head spins and I look to my side. A man, one of the Henosis soldiers, has Ash pinned to the ground with his knee in the boy's back and his gun held at his head.

What? But we were safe. We'd almost made it back. Why'd they find us now?

I look up at the soldier above me, staring right down the barrel aimed at me.

CHAPTER THIRTY-FIVE

Tore Hund I

Tore Hund had served many commissary chairmen since he swore his oath near two hundred years prior. None had come close to the wisdom of their predecessor, yet he faithfully fulfilled his role with naught a word.

He followed the chairman at two paces' length, as he has done for each that came before. They strode toward the continae before them, each soldier and official shrinking from his presence. This wasn't just any continae, this was The Continae. The central governing citadel of Flehullen, capital of New Vetus.

The tall entrance arched high over the heads of the ursu as they moved aside for Tore and the chairman. Tore very much loved this building. It was one of the last remnants of the nation and people he cared for so deeply. Back in the revolution, he and his comrades bled so much to lay the foundations of this monument. It was a shame the nation had fallen so far since.

The commissars were rarely good men, the chairman often the worst. Many times in his life, Tore lamented the state of his people. He disagreed with many orders he was given, but he could not disregard them. Even these resistant thoughts were the most he could manage a century and a half since he . . . changed.

Most would say improved, but the sacrifices made were not worth the strength. Not to Tore.

He followed the chairman to a room at the back of the second floor of the continae. The guards posted at the door stepped aside for the chairman but gulped up at Tore and took an extra instinctual step away.

The chairman strode into the room, eyes firm on the table ahead of him. Tore ducked under the lintel and ignored the trailing eyes of the guards. He rose again on the other side but not to full height. Shoving his head through stone was never a fun thing to do.

The men, already at their seats, stood and quietened as he entered the room. As the chairman took his seat with Tore crouching behind him, the men followed suit. Tore disliked these meetings for a myriad of reasons, the greatest being the memory of what it should have been. Now the conference was nothing but a butchered remnant of what the original chairman envisioned.

The original intention for these meetings was to be a place for the commissars of differing specialties and divisions within the nation to debate and propose legislative changes for the betterment of the country and its people. The original role of the chairman was to be an unbiased overseer to manage these meetings and the ideas that occurred within.

"I very much hope you all have some good news for me," the chairman said in an even tone that did nothing to hide the anger in his eyes.

Now? These meetings were nothing but a farce for the commissary to appease the chairman, and Tore was the stick, the implied threat if they failed their duties.

He hated this role, but he had no choice. He was as much in control of his body now as he was a hundred and forty years ago. The first order he received from the second chairman was not something he was likely to forget.

"Chairman Vernados, we have held the Empire at Brua. The contracted front has benefitted our defensive effort immensely. We expect to hold the line indefinitely," the Commissar of Military Strategy announced.

The chairman did not seem pleased by the news. "Hold the line? What are your plans for reconquest?"

The commissar hesitated for a moment, eyes flickering to Tore before speaking. "None, Chairman. The corridor of Brua benefits our defense, but the same could also be said for the enemy's. Any offensive will cost us twice or three times the lives of what we will inflict upon the Empire."

"That is inconsequential. Organize an offensive by the end of the month."

"But, Chairman, winter will soon hit. It would be impossible for logistics to support—"

"Are you questioning me, Commissar?" The chairman's eyes narrowed dangerously.

The man straightened up, realizing he'd overstepped. "No, Chairman Vernados. I'll get on it right away. I won't fail you," he said before leaning back in his seat.

"If you fail me, the only one you need worry about is Hund." He motioned to Tore looming behind him. "Anyone else have something for me?" the chairman asked the room.

Another man stood up, placing his cigar on the ashtray before him. "Yes, Chairman Vernados. I believe I have news you would enjoy very much."

Raising an eyebrow at the Commissar of Reksha, the chairman urged him to continue. "Well? Don't leave me waiting."

"Of course, Chairman. On investigation of the burning of Morne, our agents discovered an invading force from the Zadok Kingdom."

The chairman growled at the man. "How is that good news?"

Unlike the first commissar, the man was unfazed by the chairman's anger. "An interception force was assembled posthaste. They slew the Zadok soldiers with minimal losses."

That brought a smile to the chairman's face, the sharp grin almost feral. "What, did Henosis not share their little toys?"

"It appears not, Chairman. In fact, I don't believe they've progressed much at all since we pushed them into the little corner of the continent."

"Good. After we deal with the Empire, we'll have to remind them of their place. Talking about toys, how goes the reproduction of the expropriated artillery?" The chairman turned his attention to the Commissar of Industry, the anger in his eyes calmed for the moment.

"Good, Chairman. We have managed to recreate the mechanism to a suitable level."

"Oh? How far are we from producing them for the field?"

"We could do it now, Chairman, but it would require our mages be returned to the research division. The inscriptions required for the artillery are a bit too complex for a common mage to inscribe."

"No! Those mages are imperative for defending our entrenched positions," the Commissar of Military Strategy interrupted.

The chairman looked between both of them for a moment. "A third of Commissar Dov's mages will be returned; the rest shall remain on the front line."

Tore had seen this all too many times before. He knew he wasn't the most intelligent ursu, but he had enough experience to tell Dov, the Commissar of Industry, was lying through his teeth. If Tore had to guess, it was likely that they hadn't replicated the weapon near enough to be useful.

Tore wouldn't say anything. He rarely did. He was forced to follow any order of the chairman and protect him from any threat, but he never went further than that.

After the war for his people's freedom, he'd declared his loyalty to the man who would become the first chairman. He was the man's sword during a period of immense civil infighting. Tore had proven himself during the war against Zadok and fought alongside the chairman to create a nation amongst the conflicting interests of the ursu.

Even before the Void Fog changed him, he was the greatest warrior the ursu had seen in hundreds of years, but the Void Fog *had* changed him. And now, he was restricted by the thoughts and resolutions he'd set for himself so long ago.

His undying loyalty to the chairman was twisted by the incomprehensible fog, and he'd been left unable to deny orders from not just the chairman he'd declared himself to but any proceeding ursu that took his position.

Tore assumed he had another century ahead of him, his life extended by the strength he'd obtained. In that time, he hoped he would manage the willpower to eventually fight against his old resolutions that were now deeply ingrained within.

The conference finished up and the chairman was the first to leave. Nobody moved from their position at the table until Tore left the room as well, lowering their heads as he passed.

Tore waited until they were alone before his deep voice had the air quivering. "I should fight."

The chairman stopped and turned to look up at Tore. He was the only ursu Tore had seen that didn't fear him, having been served by Tore so long he knew the ursu would do anything he ordered.

"No. You won't leave my side. I'm not about to let myself be stabbed in the back while you have your fun." The chairman returned to his walk.

Tore didn't reply. He wanted to enter the war, but he would not disobey. He was sure he would find it frustrating if thoughts of his fealty weren't so pervasive. Any thought that opposed his dedication to the chairman took far more effort to sustain than normal. If he didn't constantly put effort into keeping his thoughts divergent from instinct, then he was sure he would have devolved to nothing but a sharp-toothed hound.

The current chairman was one of the least intelligent men Tore had had the displeasure of serving. He hadn't reached the position he was in due to capability or trickery as the others, no; he was placed there by the previous chairman. Raised to have the same beliefs, brutality, and paranoia as his predecessor but none of the ability. The short ursu continually made decisions that harmed Tore's people.

So many talented ursu were sent to the gulags because of the chairman's fear. A fear that was both warranted and unnecessary; sure, many of them would attempt to assassinate the chairman should they be given the opportunity, but it was unreasonable to believe that they would ever succeed, not with Tore protecting him. Due to the chairman's paranoia, New Vetus now lacked any proper elites—besides Tore himself—to defend the nation.

Tore knew if he'd been allowed, this war would have been over from the start. If the chairman had sent him to fight right away, so many of his people wouldn't be dead, feeding the enemy's strength.

The ursu of today were soft, unused to war, and comfortable with peace. They had the arrogance, but not the strength, of their ancestors.

Tore could do nothing but lament not being sent to the battlefield. Even if it was him alone, the war would be over.

There was no stronger race than the ursu. Each averaged two and a half to three meters tall with the strength to crush stone.

Tore Hund's strength far surpassed that. He stood at an intimidating five and a half meters. Only the tall ceilings of the Flehullen continae could contain him. His strength was immeasurable, so great in fact that he struggled to differentiate between a gentle touch and a stone-crushing grip.

A three-meter sword sat in a sheath at his waist. It was the largest sword he could get forged for himself after his growth. The ton sword would be hard for most to lift, but on him, it felt small. It was like using a kitchen knife when he'd grown up wielding a longsword.

If he was truthful with himself, the sword was unnecessary. He'd beaten the strongest in the world long before he'd lost himself in the strange world within the fog. It was a memory he often thought back to, tinged with remorse like so many others, but he never truly understood it.

Most believed the Void Fog to be a completely random disaster. Appearing without reason nor direction. It would just appear one moment, consume everything in its periphery, and leave once again. It was as horrifying in its unpredictability as it was in the damage it brought.

The light-devouring black fog did not destroy things; they simply disappeared. Buildings, people, even the earth were gouged away. There were stories of a mountain losing half its mass by the passing of the fog.

Many believed that the Void Fog obliterated everything it touched, leaving nothing. Tore knew better. He'd once been consumed himself, after all. He knew nothing the fog consumed was destroyed. Instead, it was changed.

The Void Fog was far more a mystery to those who escaped its clutches, for they had seen what was inside.

To Tore, the fog appeared like its own entirely contained world. His time within was both terrifying and incredible. The laws of the world seemed not to apply. Time flowed backward. Steps traversed leagues, while leaps cut momentum. Things there one moment would disappear the next.

The creatures within were familiar yet changed. Gifted with new abilities and strengths yet cursed with weaknesses or faults that would have them dead in a moment outside. But they lived. Likely sustained by the very fog itself.

Tore had seen structures in the fog. Buildings twisted far from any original purpose they may have had. Architecture from places he could hardly imagine.

Escape was difficult. In fact, Tore to this very day still struggled to understand how he managed it. Of course, he knew what actions he'd taken to escape, but how it let him escape was something he struggled to fathom. Luck was the only thing he could tie his freedom to.

But the Void Fog hadn't been done with him yet. Even after escaping, it had its clutches in him. It changed him and led him to create disaster amongst his own people and the downfall of the man he swore himself to. And eventually the death of his wife and daughter.

CHAPTER THIRTY-SIX

Mercure

D on't move," the man above me orders, the barrel of his gun pressed into my forehead as I look up at him.

Ash is in much the same position as I, gun held to his head and pressed to the floor. From the corner of my eye, I see a third soldier approach Ash.

"Now, now, kids. We just need to check something, then you'll be free to go," he says as he pulls a canteen from his chest strap. A single drop falls on Ash's exposed skin before the soldier stands again and looks over at me.

What should I do? Can I stop them from checking me somehow? Maybe I should try to burn them before they get the chance. A glance over at Ash has me throwing that thought out for now. The gun is still firmly held at the back of his spine. I can't act now unless I want to get him shot.

The man and his canteen approach with slow steps. My eyes dart around the room, looking for anything I can use. There don't seem to be any other soldiers than these three. If there are, they are still out on the street.

"Chill, girl. This won't take but a moment."

I try to hold in my scream when the drop hits my cheek, trying my hardest to hide what I am. My efforts are in vain, though; the steam and loud sizzling that come from my face give me away without doubt.

The eyes of the men in front of me widen. "Jonas. Flare, outside. Now!" The soldier turns his attention back to me. "Now, now. Don't you move a muscle."

I can't let that man get outside. If he gets a signal out, the water mages will be here in a moment. I don't know why they don't just try to kill me themselves, but I can't go against the water mages.

The only thing that stops me from attacking immediately is that Ash is still in danger. I look over to see that the soldier on top of Ash is distracted, looking at me. His gun is lowered and not pointed at Ash.

This is the best invitation I can hope for. I launch my flames at the soldier above Ash. I'm not passive with my fire as I have been in the past. Instead, I put intent behind it. I don't just want to use my fire as a distraction or to scare them off. I want them to burn.

And burn they do.

The gun, made with a wooden body, bursts into flames easily. Almost as easily as the soldier holding that gun does. His screams fill the air as I launch myself toward the door and send a scorching wave into the man with the canteen standing behind me.

A bullet rips through my chest and hits the wall in front of me. I stumble but push through the pain and out the door behind the soldier called Jonas.

I try to scorch the flare out of his hand before he can fire it, but I don't reach in time, my flames only an instant too late.

I failed. I wasn't quick enough, and now this place will swarm with soldiers before long.

An instinctual feeling through the edges of my fire pulls me. My flames pull on their own, soaring after the projectile faster than I've ever moved them before. I can feel the burning within the flare pulling my flames to it.

I grab ahold of the flare and suck all the energy from within, extinguishing my tendril flames at the same time. My fire is visible in the air to any looking, but it is far better than letting the flare explode.

I can't see the now-defunct flare as it falls back to the earth below, but a bang snaps me away before I can be certain it won't explode from the impact with the ground. The soldier, Jonas, holds his gun up at me. He's already fired a shot—which missed, fortunately—and is now struggling to reload his weapon. I burned his fingers when I hit the flare gun.

I don't want to give him time, so I throw myself and my flames at him. I cling to his uniform so he can't escape my fire. Each swing of the stock of his weapon hurts as my flames spread around us. The energy I drained from the manor earlier fuels me as I try to burn through both him and his weapon. After engulfing him in my flames for only a few seconds, the soldier is already throwing away his weapon and rolling around on the ground trying to stop the flames that I won't relinquish.

I hate this. I hate the screams. I hate the way his skin bubbles under my blaze. I hate that I have to feel it all. But there is no choice, it is either me or him. Never do I want to do this, but I want to live. I don't want to be scared that any moment one of these people can drop out of nowhere and toss a bucket of water over me.

I don't want to die.

So he has to die.

The crack of a gun being fired almost knocks me off my feet. No, wait, that's the bullet that does that. Another tearing its way through my solid-flame body. It rips me from the smoldering form of the man once called Jonas.

The other soldier, the one that dropped water on my face, holds his gun at me, standing with his back to the door. I don't move. I don't want to kill anyone else.

"Please, just leave. I don't want any more," I plead.

The man looks down, the body of his buddy at my feet. I should have expected the anger that crosses his face. I would have sighed if the pain of the third shot through my chest didn't hurt so much. In a way, it is fair; I should hurt for killing others. But I hate the pain. I won't sit down and accept their retribution. I want to live. Even if that means I will have to kill thousands, I'll do it.

Not bothering to move, I throw some flames toward him. I stop myself from sending my inner flame with them, not wanting to feel another die at my hand. But the man dodges, rolling to the side. Without my inner flame controlling the fire, I'm unable to change its trajectory to follow him.

He fires another shot at me, this time hitting my upper arm, piercing through with ease.

What am I doing? I can't take it easy just because I don't want to feel his death. Resolving myself, I grasp him. He's unable to dodge me this time, now that I have control. I try to burn through him as fast as possible, not wanting him to suffer for longer than necessary. I try to ignore the screams and the feeling of my flames burning under his skin while he still struggles on the ground.

I shouldn't feel bad. He was trying to kill me. I gave him an opportunity, which is far more than they gave my mom.

A hand grabs my shoulder and I spin, ready to burn whatever soldier I missed. I pull myself back from burning Ash's face off just in time as he takes a hurried step back.

I drop my hands and extinguish the surrounding blaze. Despite the intense energy still smoldering within, I'm exhausted.

"Are you okay?" I hear Ash's concerned voice.

"Yeah," I say. "We should meet with the others and get out of the area."

We are back in the group's original home. The bookshelf that hid the secret room lies knocked on the floor in pieces. The basement area isn't in good shape either, the beds torn up and thrown around, the table and chairs now broken. Really, we are only here until the search cools down outside. Having already been searched, it is as good a place as any to hide.

We are sitting around on the floor together. The others' gazes hold square on me as I try to pretend they don't exist. The ceiling has a rather interesting pattern ingrained in the wood.

"Solvei, I think it's time you explained. Who are those soldiers? Why are they after you?" Ash asks.

"They said they were from the Henosis Empire," Leslie says. "Why are you so important that they'd take an army away from the war to find you? Did you piss off their emperor or something? Maybe you burned the hair off his head?"

"What? No! I didn't even know they were from Henosis until today." Isn't the Henosis Empire far to the east? Why have they been looking for áed so far from their homeland? "I don't know why, but they've been hunting áed. They killed my mom and half my tribe."

"How? I saw you today. You brushed off like three bullets as if they were nothing," Ash says.

"They have water mages. Lots of water mages," I explain.

"Okay, great. So they want to kill you for . . . reasons, but why did they attack the Cano head?"

Ash turns to Leslie at that. "They attacked the Cano family? Is that what those gunshots were?"

"Oh, yeah. It was an absolute slaughter," she says, shaking her head. "They wiped out the entire Cano guard in seconds. Wynn Cano was played with, like a child, before they killed him. And that was after we'd seen the man blow up a wall with his strength. I didn't even know it was possible to get that strong."

"Shit. So if the guard is gone, who is in control of the city? Henosis? This is gonna make Mercure's job so much harder. Let's hope we have enough to pay."

I look at the pile of stolen goods between us. Most of it glimmers in the light and some of the stones make me salivate a bit when I brush my finger over them. Some sort of gems with an incredible taste that I have to whip myself away from.

I have no idea what the collection of jewelry and other shiny things is worth, but I am sure it far surpasses everything else we have stolen since I joined their group. If this isn't enough to pay Ash's friend Mercure, then I doubt he ever planned to smuggle anyone out in the first place.

In the early afternoon of the next day, we leave our home for the last time. After meeting with Mercure, we won't be returning. Instead, we are prepared to leave everything but one another behind to head north.

The Henosis soldiers are everywhere, but there are so many people around the main street, they can't search everywhere. They set roadblocks to check the cargo of anyone passing. It appears they know I am young, because they splash a small amount of water on any child they see after detaining them.

The ground has grown dry again, which means we can take some of the tighter detours through the city. While the sky is still overcast, it has yet to rain again since late last night. I can only hope the weather stays as good as it is.

We take a long time to reach the woodworking warehouse that Mercure uses as a front. Kerry carries the bag of jewels while the rest of us watch over her.

We agreed not to tell Mercure that I am the target of the soldiers currently putting the city in semi–martial law. I'd been worried about telling them last night, thinking they would sell me out to save their own heads, but I am stuck at the moment, so I can't just run away. I am forced to trust them.

It is relieving that they have yet to break that trust, but the stress I feel about the possibility they are just waiting for the perfect time to betray me won't leave my mind.

A solidly built man leads us through the warehouse to a back office where a thin stick of an albanic sits behind a desk.

We've kept our hats secured tight over our heads, as is required anywhere we don't want to be tossed away in but a moment.

"Do you have it?" Mercure says without looking up from his desk.

Ash grabs the bag from Kerry's hands and places it on his desk. "Here."

Mercure finally looks up, not at us but at the bag on his table. His face remains apathetic as he opens it and inspects the jewels. "Quite unlucky timing, you being at the Cano estate at the same time they were wiped out," he says without looking up. "I heard one of the Henosis water mages destroyed a good portion of the old upper district. I'm surprised you got out."

The others and I remain still until he finishes his inspection.

"Well, all looks good here. Half of this would have gotten you out of the country until today. Unfortunately, security in the city has been raised. I will now be taking the lot." He finally raises his eyes to dare any of us to complain.

I see the others fidget a bit, but we already expected this. Of course, we had hoped to keep some so we didn't have to start with nothing in the northern states.

"I have a proposal," Mercure says, bringing my attention back to him. He eyes each of us a moment and I swear his eyes linger on me longer than the others.

"I want to know how you got through the Cano security. If you tell me that, I'll only take half of this pile as I would have before all this."

I tense and gulp, sending a glance to the others out of the corner of my eye. Crap, when they tell him it was me, he'll either want to use me himself or he'll give me to the Henosis. The teenagers beside me I could work with because they strongly desire to leave the country. By helping them, I was helping myself escape.

This man doesn't have any goals in common with me. He will either use me for whatever use I'd have, or he'll sell me out to the Henosis. He won't let me go if he knows.

Do I try to run now, before he can try to stop me? Without the others around, I don't know how well I'll be able to hide in the city. Is it better to do as he says for now? Go along with whatever he asks of me, so I'm not put up on the execution block?

I scream in my head. There's no good solution that comes to mind.

"I'm sorry, but there's not much I can say," Ash says. "Really, we just got lucky."

"Hmm, lucky indeed." Mercure hums, staring at us a bit too long for comfort.

Wait . . .

Huh?

I turn to Ash. He didn't sell me out? But didn't he want to start a new life? They'd be able to create a perfect life for themselves with that much money. Why give that up?

Ash notices me staring. The smirk that covers his face after seeing me is so self-satisfied that I feel like smacking him. But he didn't betray me.

I assumed he and the others would sell me out the moment they were given the opportunity. Was that wrong? Can I actually trust them?

I feel like crying at the revelation, but I am interrupted as Mercure rises from his seat.

"Come, then. I hope you lot ate before you arrived."

In a dark corner with no windows or lights, Mercure leads us to several wooden boxes a bit taller than my hip.

"Hop in. They'll be your homes for the next few days. Make sure to ration your food and water. Wouldn't want to die from a touch of hunger after going through so much to get here, would you?"

CHAPTER THIRTY-SEVEN

Serron

The crate jostles once more and I try to reorient myself into a comfortable position. It is an unending challenge, though. Without being able to stretch myself, I will never find comfort.

I've been stuck, alone, in this wooden crate for far too long now. I have to stop myself from gnawing at the interior of the box, my flames edging to burn my way out. Charred markings already cover the walls I can see, from times I got too restless.

The space within the box is so cramped, it feels like I am constantly crushed by the proximity of each side. I can't imagine what it is like for the others; I am the smallest of our group, but we'd all been given crates the same size. I worry for Leslie the most, as she is the tallest and I can't imagine she'd enjoy sitting still for so long.

Something whacks against the crate. I can feel the impact through the wood at my back.

A creaking noise fills my box and I look up to see light breaking through a new gap. The lid of the crate snaps off with a crack and I see a stranger's face.

The woman steps away from the box, giving me room to stand up.

"Join your friends, we'll be moving soon. Also, I probably don't need to remind you to never remove your hats."

The rush of fresh air makes me breathe deep. I stand and extend my arms far from my body. It feels so unnatural to remain still for so long; finally having my movement back is incredible.

The other five are already together and stretching amongst themselves. I hop over to them, feeling great now that I can stretch my legs. Also, the fact that they didn't sell me out when I expected them to improves my mood. I feel slightly guilty for doubting them so long, but it is a humbling feeling to know they care enough not to throw me away for their selfish benefit.

I can't say for sure I would have done the same. And I now feel terrible for it.

"Hey, Solvei. How are you feeling?" Ash asks.

"Better than you look." And it is true—each of the others looks horrible. I won't be surprised if they haven't managed a wink of sleep since we started our travel within the confines of the crates. Each of them makes a pained face every time they stretch. I am right about the crates being tighter for them.

I look around and take in the sights. We are clearly not in Kelton anymore. The buildings have a similar architecture as what I've seen in the city where I spent the last couple of weeks, but they look new and well cared for. I can't see a single collapsed or obviously abandoned building around. The city I find myself in isn't as clean or impressive as Morne or Fisross, but it is an incredible improvement over Kelton.

"Where are we?" I ask.

The lady who broke me out of the box is the one to answer. "We're in Serron, north of the wall. It'll be a month before we can get you to the northern states, but you won't have to hide in a crate for any of it."

"Praise Belobog," Leslie says without moving from her spot on the ground. She's stretched on her back with arms wide.

I can understand how she feels. There's nothing I want to do more right now than stretch my flames as far as they'll reach. I know I can't, though; it's best the woman leading us up north doesn't think there is anything strange. I may trust Ash, Leslie, Kerry, and the twins now, but I still need to be careful around others.

"Now, brats, it's my job to get you past the northern border, but past that you're on your own. Call me Ivory and let me do all the talking as we travel. Understood?"

Her voice is followed by a few *yes, ma'ams* and nods from us.

Satisfied, she continues. "Good. Now, we'll be together for a while from now on, so I want you all to follow a few rules. First, you will always follow my orders. Second, you will stay together—no one wanders off by themselves. Third, no complaining. And finally, don't give anyone a reason to believe you shouldn't be here. Pretend like you grew up here."

"Okay . . ." Ash says, as put off as the rest of us. "How will we be moving?"

"We'll walk. If anyone asks, we are a family traveling to trade our harvest," she says. "Well, my new nieces and nephews, I hope you've stretched enough. We best be moving."

We are already at the outskirts of the city, so after Ivory climbs onto the pholo-pulled wagon—not inviting anyone else—we walk north.

* * *

A few days later, we arrive at a town. Well, saying "arrive" is not really correct. The homes, storefronts, and other assortments of structures litter the landscape between here and the city we've traveled from. Never a true town or village, but not decreasing in the density of construction. The buildings look poor in their construction, but it is still a significant improvement from the layered trash heap that was Kelton.

I call the place we enter a town simply because the quality is far greater than what we've seen until this point. The ground is a proper cobblestone path rather than compact dirt.

The people we pass rarely wear head coverings, unlike their near-universal use in Kelton. Instead, their hair is on clear display, long and tied in odd ways to show off their rather pure white color. Those with the whitest hair almost always have the best-looking clothing.

I struggle to find many of the darker-haired albanics as we move through the bustling town. Are they all stuck between the wall and the border to New Vetus like my friends, or do they just not come out to the forefront? Either option is rather disgusting. It means they cordon all their "lesser" albanics to the space between the border and their main line of defense or the dark-haired are too fearful to show their faces amongst the usual crowd. I don't know which is worse.

A caw snaps my attention up to the roof of the stables as Ivory ties away the pholo. A magpie rests at the edge of the covering. It caws once again, looking down on our group as a shadowy mist seeps from its dull, red eyes.

"Come, now, let's grab some dinner," Ivory says. "I have a friend who'll let us stay the night."

As the others follow her down the street, I look back at the bird. The eerie black smoke spreading from its eyes disperses in the light breeze. It caws again before flying off.

I've fallen behind the others and quickly catch up, remembering Ivory's rule.

We walk with her for five minutes or so until she has us stop in front of a two-story house. She tells us to stay here before she knocks twice, then pushes her way through.

Her muffled voice reaches our ears, but we can't make out what is said. It sounds like she is happy or jovial, but the few crashes and bangs we hear seem to undercut that. A man's yelling has us eyeball each other before the house goes quiet.

A few minutes later, Ivory returns alone. "All right, my cousin will let us stay in his shed. He's not as happy to see me as I thought he'd be, but that's fine; we got somewhere to sleep."

The beds she lays out for us aren't particularly comfortable. In fact, I'd rather the cruddy little things we had back in the basement in Kelton.

"What do you think it's like outside Zadok?" I hear Ash whisper after we lie down. Ivory takes a spot at the far side of the room by herself.

"Have you seen the places we've passed? I hope there's more like this where we're going. I want to live somewhere we don't have to worry about the roof collapsing," Kerry says.

"I heard they have to deal with creature attacks from the Titan Alps," Leslie says, rolling to face us. "Solvei, you're the only one of us that's been outside. What is it like?"

I tilt my head to look at the ceiling, thinking about the places they might want to know about. "Well, New Vetus had a lot of enormous buildings. But ursu are a lot taller than albanics. They have these massive feasts every week that were a spectacle to watch. You'd be surprised how much food they prepare, but I guess it is the only time in the week they eat."

I pause for a moment to parse the memories of the wasteland, the good and the horrid.

"My home, the wasteland, is rather bare. There's sand as far as the eye can see. Sometimes canyons or valleys break up the monotony, but really the wasteland is boring. There's nothing to see if you don't know your way around. But still, I have a lot of good memories of my tribe out there."

My chest tightens at the memories surfacing, so I try to push through and move on from my family.

"Mom used to tell me of the Agglomerate. She called it the home of áed. I've never been myself, but she described it as a mountain of glass that glistened in the sun. It's somewhere I've always wanted to see."

"Do you plan to travel for it once you're out of Zadok?" Ash asks.

I shake my head without checking if he can see or not. "No. I want to find it eventually, but it'll take too long and I'm not sure if the water mages are still scouting the wasteland. I'd rather stay away from wherever they've been."

"Well, you are welcome to stay with us for as long as you'd like. Without your help we wouldn't be leaving, after all," Ash says, to the murmured agreement of the others.

"I think I'd like that," I say. It'd be nice to create a place for us to live. Hopefully, the northern states are as good as Ash believes they are. "What do you want to do when we get there?"

"I want to earn a place for us to live, something more than just a roof over our heads. Maybe I'll be able to get an apprenticeship for a gunsmith or construction, I don't know."

"What a boring answer," Leslie says derisively. "Me? I want to get my hands on a gun of my own. Ya think it'd be possible to get me one of them Henosis weapons?"

"I want a dress that doesn't feel like I'm wearing a potato sack," Kerry says.

"Chocolate."

"Steak."

The two voices I hear almost make me jump. I realize it's the first time I've actually heard their voices. I can't help but stare at them through the darkness, but I can't see their faces.

There is quiet for a moment after their words before Leslie chimes in. "Yeah, definitely. Can't wait to try some sweets and meat. When was the last time we had any?"

"We nabbed some lollies from that young mother not long before we met Solvei, remember?" Ash says.

"Yuck, you can't possibly call those things sweets, they were so sour." I can't see her through the dark, but I can imagine Leslie sticking her tongue out and cringing in disgust.

We continue to bicker and talk for a while before quieting to sleep. It feels nice, almost like I'm a part of a family again.

I was so hesitant to let them get close because of the distrust I placed in them. Despite living in the same room as them for weeks now, I've never really become close to them. I never talked to them the way they talked amongst themselves. It was never that they didn't try to bring me in, but more like I was resistant to their attempts.

After Ash proved he wasn't willing to sell me out, I've become more open with them. I know that. Whether it will be a good idea, I'll have to see, but I want to make this work. Having people I can trust and talk to again would be nice.

When I'm certain the others are sleeping, I rise from my bed. The Ember Moon will show herself soon and I want to watch. I don't feel tired at all. The pace we travel is much slower than what I grew up with.

On the other side of the house from the shed in which the others are resting is a tree that is perfect to watch the night sky from, its leaf cover already discarded to the grass below. I could climb the shed, but I don't want to wake any of the others, as I doubt I'll be able to do so stealthily.

I pull myself to a branch that lets me look over the roof of the house. Lights can be seen near the center of the town, but mostly the night is dark.

The moon is already missing from the starry sky. It won't be long until Eldest Ember shows herself.

As I sit here waiting for the darkness to recede, a flock of birds flies overhead. It's hard to make them out with the lack of light, but the sound of their squawking and wing flaps reaches my ears as they fly from the town center over my head.

I look back to the lights of the town. One by one they go out. It must be time everyone's heading to bed.

I sit there, watching as most of the lights extinguish. Strangely, lights that I thought were stars slowly extinguish as well. I must be mistaken; they are probably just distant houses on the other side of town.

The stars continue to disappear. A chill runs through my arms and I heat myself in retaliation to the feeling. Is it cloud cover? It seems to spread too fast for that. The pace at which the lights disappear picks up, climbing well into the sky ahead of me.

I jump to my feet, feeling the oddness of the entire situation. I am about to jump off the tree when the sky lights up in the redness of the Ember Moon.

No, only some of the sky glows red. A massive portion of the sky ahead of me remains as pitch-black as I've ever seen. It doesn't glow with the color of the moon as clouds usually do; instead, whatever is in front of me seems to suck the light out of its surroundings. Only at the edges between the darkness and the red sky can I see that the blackness is a mist. A fog spreading over the town.

This is the Void Fog.

CHAPTER THIRTY-EIGHT

The Void Fog I

A scream tears through the night air as another albanic notices the encroaching darkness. I can't help but stare at the fog as it consumes everything in its path. Light doesn't pierce it, leaving a gaping hole in the world.

I don't think I've ever seen something so unnatural. Even the Titan, while terrifying, still felt real. This blackness has no substance; it doesn't fit with the world.

There is a reason people call it a void.

My eyes ache looking at it. I can't see anything in the fog, and the more I look, the more it feels like my eyes just don't work. Even the darkest night doesn't come close to this. The black of night is just another color as intense as any other in the face of the Void Fog.

I step back from it, forgetting where I am. My foot finds nothing solid to stand on and I'm falling through the air before I know. The loss of balance forces my eyes away from the fog, right to the vivid red moon above. It's like looking at the sun, it's so bright.

My arms come to cover my eyes as I hit the ground. My neck aches from the impact, but everything else is fine. I can see the light through my hands, but it quickly dims to normal.

That was . . . strange. I look up but keep my eyes away from directly looking at the Void Fog. I run around the house and slam open the door to the shed, planning to wake the others up.

It seems I don't need to bother; they must have heard the screaming. Ash and Leslie are already on their feet with the others struggling to get up.

"The Void Fog appeared in town," I say. "It's spreading quick. We need to go now!"

Ash seems to comprehend my words, so I rush back outside to see how much time we have. I've only been inside the shed for a second, but as I exit once again, I know the situation is bad. I can see the house in front of me, but everything behind it is missing. Lost in the black void.

Bits of the house start disappearing and I know we don't have time. The others won't be able to run out the door quickly enough.

I run back inside and incinerate the back wall as fast as I can. Ivory squeaks in surprise, but I don't have time to care.

"It's too quick. Everyone out the back!" I yell, and start shoving the others to the new exit I made.

Ivory is hesitant to step through the residual flames and gives me a dumbfounded look but follows close behind.

We run away from the void, weaving through the streets, racing to keep out of the fog's grasp.

"I grew up around here, I know a shortcut." Ivory takes the lead, pushing forward and leading us behind a house and down the hill.

I glance back, but the darkness is all-consuming. I can't tell how far away it is. That some of the ground behind us is still visible is the only indicator we still have any time.

I notice far too late where Ivory is leading us. Ahead of me she jumps along a few boulders half-submerged in water. The inert creek spreads far to each side of me, and I halt immediately. Water splashes from a few of Ivory's footsteps, showing not all the rocks are above the water.

The others don't follow her; instead, they stop to look back with worry at me. I twist left and right, noticing a bridge a short distance away. I wave off the others and sprint away.

"I'll meet you on the other side. Just go," I shout over my shoulder.

I don't look back to make sure they follow Ivory. I have myself to worry about. The world is growing dark. I don't know if it's because of the Void Fog or because the Ember Moon is hiding once again, but it makes it hard to see in front of me.

Flames ignite around me to give light, but it does nothing to show how close I am to the fog. The void sucks in any light that comes near it. It's enough to outline the bridge ahead, but I can't even see the ground below me.

I extend my flames to cover the ground, carpeting it so I can see where I step and won't trip when I really can't afford to.

I push to run faster than ever, throwing myself forward with every step. The bridge speeds toward me with each step. Not a few paces away do I find I'm unable to see my own flames at my side. They are still there. I can feel them, but I can't see them.

I forget to breathe and launch myself at the bridge.

I stumble as my feet touch the wooden crossing, and I gasp as I make it. I continue to sprint over the bridge, feeling the wood beneath my feet and flames.

But something is strange.

I can't see.

I can't even see my own flames burning before my eyes.

I can feel the bridge turn to soil once again and use the carpet of flames to guide my way.

No matter how far I run, my sight doesn't return.

I'm gasping and choking as I try to keep running despite my legs' protests. I can get enough air, but my legs just don't want to run any longer.

I push through, fearing the fog is at my heels. I push until my legs collapse underneath me from exhaustion.

I wait to be consumed. Sobs churn up from my chest and bubble their way out my lips. I've done so much to keep moving. I don't want to die now.

I want to refuse the world, but I can do nothing but wait for the inevitable end.

Wait.

And wait.

Why am I not dead?

I stand up. I can still feel the soil beneath my feet. Burning my hand in front of my face, I find I still can't see.

Am I dead? Is this death? I expected the Eternal Inferno to be . . . hotter? Or am I stuck because I have nobody to send me off?

That would suck. A lot. Will I never get to meet my family again?

With nothing else to do, I walk.

This can't be all there is. There has to be something here somewhere.

Only a few steps and I find myself walking on wood once again. My flames spreading over its surface tell me it's the same bridge I ran over earlier.

That can't be right. I ran far from it. I should be ages away by now. But the wood smoldering under my flames doesn't lie. I'm back at the bridge.

Wait . . . am I inside the Void Fog? Am I not dead?

With that thought, I turn and run away from the bridge again. Maybe if I run far enough, I'll find the edge. I'll escape and meet up with the others and continue our journey north.

Again, I soon tire and slow to a walk. I'm sure I ran far, but it still doesn't end. I take my time to recover so I can continue again soon, but I keep walking while I do.

My foot lands on wood once more. The bridge is there again, new scorch marks and all.

There is no way I am running in circles. I may not be able to see with my eyes at the moment, but my flames are decent enough to feel the ground around me. I'm certain I wasn't turning at all.

A caw rips through the surrounding air. Not unlike the call of a magpie, but more of a warped musical warble. It is loud but sounds distant. I can't imagine a small bird being the source of the noise.

Silence returns for only a moment before a cacophony of near-identical caws whispers in my ear. They are quiet but clear. Thousands of individual birds adding their own warble.

I flinch and spin on my feet. It sounds like they are right behind me. The unnatural ripple of subdued caws continues for minutes, tickling my ear and sending me spinning. I can't make heads or tails of the direction. One moment it sounds like they are ahead of me, the next they are behind.

I take a step away as they sing their last. My foot lands on something hard. Stone, I realize. I didn't feel this with my flames. It was dirt until I took the step.

I walk back, expecting to find myself on soil again, but the stone doesn't leave. Each step lands on the flat stone tiling reminiscent to that of ursu cities.

What is going on? Is the world broken?

I keep my attention on the flames carpeting a ring around me. I don't want to miss it the next time it happens. The stone remains the same as I walk, never changing.

I trip on a step that wasn't there a moment ago. The slight negligence that results from my surprise is enough for my flames to transition over the new staircase in front of me.

Somehow, I failed to see the change as it happened. It's like a lapse in attention is all that is needed for the world to change around me.

I climb the second step and notice the world, while black, isn't the same void it was before. There is a tiny, minuscule bit of brightness, or maybe it's more accurate to say less blackness.

Another step seems to brighten everything just that little bit more.

I'm walking up the stairs at a proper clip now. I can see them slowly appear in front of me with each step. The light doesn't originate from any one point but rather from everywhere, at every angle and every tiny spot.

I see an end to the stairs ahead now. The brightness of everything around me is almost too much after being in the void for so long.

The last few steps brighten everything in sight, and I'm forced to cover my eyes.

Blinking rapidly to adjust to the change, I drop my hands. The scene before me is, well, it's impossible. Or it should be.

A massive continae looms ahead of me. The spherical, decorated top, snapped and disconnected from the building, hangs suspended seemingly by nothing but air.

I blink and rub my eyes in disbelief at the half-floating building. When I look again, it's gone, as if it was never there to begin with.

The platform I'm standing on is at the top of a tall pyramidal structure. A glance down the stairs on the other side of what I climbed shows it descends into the dark fog.

The blackness of the Void Fog surrounds everything, but also in contradiction, it lights everything I can see.

I don't blink; instead, I turn to see a massive mountain has appeared behind me, from where I climbed. It towers far in the distance, magma gushing down its side, and I realize half the mountain is missing.

I keep my eyes open on it this time, not willing to let this place play any more tricks on me. It stays for a while, but soon the fog creeps around the mountain, wrapping it in its black embrace.

I can't tell if it's there or not anymore. The Void Fog is too dark to see through.

This place is freaky. I want to leave, so I descend the stairs to where I think the closest wall of fog is. As I walk down, I watch the blanket of black mist along the ground recede to the familiar sight of sand.

A single step onto it brings a wave of nostalgia. I look back. There is no surprise that the pyramid is gone. It creeps me out how everything flashes in and out of existence around me.

I trot forward, keeping my eyes peeled for anything that might pop up in front of my face. My foot hits the sand, and something flies out and bites at my foot. The teeth sting a bit but it's nothing bad.

I struggle to pull it off, but a strong-enough squeeze dislodges its teeth. It's a sandworm, but it's far stranger than I've ever seen. It's got bigger teeth and a wider mouth. I've never seen one attack immediately like this did, and it spat itself out of the sand faster than I've ever seen.

A bite out of the worm makes me gasp. It's so much sweeter than I've ever tasted. I swallow it almost whole, relishing the taste that is far better than I've ever experienced from any other sandworm. It is bursting with energy, so much I don't know how it fits it all in its small size. It's nearly comparable to the energy I ate at the Cano residence.

I go to keep moving, but the moment my foot touches the ground, another worm flies at me. I don't deny a free meal, only hoping I'm fast enough to catch them before they latch into my shin.

Three more sandworms follow suit. The energy and taste put me into a good mood and I skip my way through the sand, waiting for more to jump out.

I hear a rustle of sand behind me and turn, hoping to catch the worm before it nibbles on me. The worm I see makes me freeze. It's just a *little* bigger than the sandworm I expected, towering four times taller than myself.

I don't know if it missed me or if there was something else it targeted, but the colossal-worm reenters the sand underground with hardly a sound. I can hardly feel the movement of the sand underfoot from its movement.

Why is a colossal-worm here? There are none of the normal signs around. Where are the sunken holes in the sand? Where is the discolored sand?

This isn't the time to wander. I am in a damn colossal-worm's hunting ground. I don't have the time to do anything but run. And that's exactly what I do. I sprint as hard as I can, spreading my flames, trying to disturb the surrounding ground to make it harder for the thing to track me.

Colossal-worms are one of the most dangerous creatures I know. Even the elders always have trouble fighting them, preferring to avoid them when possible. The outer skin of the worms is fireproof, so my elders have to rely solely on their weapons to take them down, and it's not like they are easy to cut either.

I pump my legs as I mentally compare sizes. Why is it so big? It was double the size of the ones I've seen my tribe take out in the past.

The fog opens up ahead, and I can see my haven in front of me. Everything I can see is green, but it isn't sand so it shouldn't be able to follow me.

I cycle my legs, one after the other, but why does it feel like I'm getting farther away? The harder I sprint, the smaller the patch of green ahead seems to shrink.

The ground opens up to my front and side. I throw myself away immediately, but the worm bursting out of the ground still throws me in the air. The worm knocks me to the side, away from the green patch I need to run to. I'm lucky I'm not swallowed in a single gulp. The interference my flames caused to its senses saved my life. If it was any closer, I'd be dead.

My back lands on something soft. It's definitely not sand. I look around quickly to see I'm surrounded by the green I've been running to. How am I here? I still had a distance to run before I could have made it. There's no way it threw me that far.

My eyes catch the colossal-worm twisting and squirming on the green, not grass but something else. The worm can't dig itself underground without the sand. It is helpless.

Will it die here without the sand? Should I try to kill it while it can do nothing but wriggle?

I decide I should take the opportunity given and take my space from it. My eyes remain on the worm as I back up. I'm glad I don't look away, because before my eyes, the ground beneath the worm and only beneath the worm morphs into sand, letting the giant creature dig its way out.

I look around the deep green hillside where I now find myself. It's about time I find somewhere to rest.

CHAPTER THIRTY-NINE

The Void Fog II

The area is absolutely drowning in moss. I couldn't tell from a distance, but the area is filled with small huts along its slope, each house covered by green moss and overgrowth. The dense moss hides any other artificial construction, leaving the village looking like nature warped into the shape of people's homes. The perfect right angles of each large mossy square are the only distinction this isn't natural.

I walk to the closest hut. The soft, spongy ground crunches under my feet. An opening that might have been a door at one point is now only recognizable by the rectangular shape of vacant moss. I take a step through the opening into a surprisingly still-intact home. A table, couch, and bench counter all remain in good condition, if you ignore the growths climbing up and over them all.

A hearth sits at the far side of the room, and when I go to approach, I find myself unable to move. My legs move forward, but I can't seem to get enough grip on the ground to push myself forward, like something is pulling me back.

I try to back up, to get out of this hut and see what is happening. The same thing happens. I'm rooted to the spot. An attempt at spinning back to face the door has me tripping over and falling off my feet. My hands come up to brace for the impact with the ground, but it never comes.

I crack an eye open to see I'm suspended in air, the ground only a finger length from my face. My left arm comes forward to press against the moss below, but my right doesn't leave my side despite my attempts at moving it. It's stuck there, but I can't see what stops it from moving.

A prick of pain snaps my attention up to my leg above. It's not quite enough to hurt, but it still feels like a pinch. There on my thigh, biting into me, is the tiniest spider I've ever seen. I might even call it cute if it weren't for the fact that it's trying to eat me, as futile as that is, considering the size difference.

I quickly heat the skin it's biting into. There is no need to kill it; the littlest bit of heat should be enough to scare it off.

The little thing poofs. Gone. Wha . . . Did I kill it? But I just heated it the tiniest bit, nowhere near enough to kill anything.

My free arm spins, trying to dislodge me from whatever is keeping me suspended. My left arm gets stuck. It's caught on something in midair, nowhere near the rest of my body. Frustration mounts as I can't pull my arm back from the awkward position, and I just burn through whatever is holding me.

My face slams into the ground, no longer held back by the suspending grasp. A groan ekes out of my throat as I get my feet under me. This hut is too much. I push toward the exit, ready to look somewhere else, but my legs won't move; whatever it is has grabbed me once again.

My arm swings wide, burning through anything holding me back, and I run out the doorway before it can grab me again.

Again, out on the spongy ground, my legs work properly. Each step isn't made impossible by some invisible force.

I'm tired. Hours must have passed since I first saw the fog. The huts would be a good place to sleep, but that strange force is not something I want around when I rest.

Between the huts is a single tree surrounded by overflowing moss. Unless I want to risk going inside again, I don't think I'll find a better option. The soft moss welcomes me like a mattress as the branches above obscure the void in the sky.

Maybe this whole Void Fog stuff is all a dream and it'll go away when I wake.

Nope, it's still real.

I got some needed sleep, but now I'm stuck on top of some insanely tall obelisk rather than the soft field where I fell asleep.

On hands and knees, I shuffle to the edge of the flat stone. I peek over and can't help but flinch at such a long drop. The pillar below me is a part of a series of equally tall obelisks that tower above the black mist far below.

I need to escape, but I can't see how I'm going to do that if I'm stuck so far in the air. The world seems to change each time I stop paying attention. Maybe I can get that to work for me. It's worth a shot.

I look up at the void above and close my eyes. In my mind, the picture of the towering pillars transforms into the Void Fog with a great big door in it. The image repeats in my head as I forcefully try to get the fog to let me escape.

My eyes open and the pillars remain.

I slump in disappointment for only a moment before the surrounding changes become apparent. The obelisks are no longer straight. They twist and intertwine in ways that shouldn't be possible. Most I can see should collapse under their own weight, mine included.

I close my eyes and try again. The world changed the first time; maybe I'll get something easier to work with this time.

I peek out again but movement under my knees makes my hands grasp for something to hold on to. My platform has shrunk and I'm able to hold on to the edges, but that doesn't freak me out. What freaks me out is that the pillars are now moving. They've split at the bottom and now walk like huge stone creatures.

The ground underneath me lurches to the side and I'm almost flung off.

"I'm sorry, I won't try to force any changes again," I yell out. Maybe my attempts to force changes pissed off the Void Fog.

If the void is conscious, it doesn't respond.

The neighboring once-obelisk's long leg impacts the platform I'm on, sending me flying. I squeal and brace my arms in front of my face as I tumble down into the Void Fog below.

There is no impact; instead, my back is suddenly sliding along flat ground. It didn't feel like I changed directions, but I have definitely switched from falling vertically to sliding horizontally. I try to sit up, but I'm yet to stop sliding.

The ground around me is white for as far as I can see. It's strange seeing an almost perfectly white ground against an infinitely black sky.

The sliding never seems to stop. I just keep moving along the ground as if there's an angle I cannot see. It's getting colder. Each second spent sliding seems to cool my flames and chill the surrounding air. I amp up my heat, trying to counteract the cold, but as I do, stinging pain rips through my back. The pain of water digging into my spine stops me from increasing my heat. The chill returns but the pain leaves.

Is the ground underneath me . . . ice?

I'm tempted to immediately close my eyes and hope for a better environment, but after the last attempt to force a change, I'm hesitant. I'd hate for the change that is all this ice switching with water; just the thought has me shivering as much as the cold.

This is getting ridiculous. How long am I going to slide?

I pull the scarcely used knife from my waist and stab it behind me. It screeches as I pull it through meters of ice before jerking to a stop.

My leg wobbles as I try to steady myself on the ice. My second foot joins the first and I rise to stand.

A loud, earthshaking howl knocks me on my ass again. A huge white fox as big as the colossal-worm is behind me, right in the place I just slid through.

I try to back up, but the ice stings my hands on contact. The fox looks around as if unsure of where it is. Its eyes lock onto mine and I can't pull them away. I can tell there is more intelligence in those eyes than any animal has a right to; its gaze is calculating, inspecting me up and down before turning away, deciding I'm not a threat or at least not worth its attention.

The fox shakes its head, and the long fur shimmers. As it moves, its coat shakes and seems to tremble with increasing intensity. The vibration parts the air around it, and black particles of mist fall off the creature.

My eyes don't miss the moment the fox disappears from existence. It looks like the very air is pushed away, only for the Void Fog to replace the beast. The void compresses, then disperses into the air around.

Am I seeing things? Is all of this just inside my head?

I spin in place, making sure that there is nothing else around me. I saw that. I actually saw it that time. The fox disappeared not when my attention was misplaced, but when I had all my focus on it.

What's different about it? Did the fox force the change? How?

I shake my body and shiver in imitation of the fox. Nothing happens, except feeling like a fool. It's silly to think a bit of shaking could force the fog to change.

It's getting colder. This isn't the time to think about the strange fox. I need to find a way off this ice, or at least somewhere to warm up.

My flames slow with the temperature. I want nothing more than to stoke, to burn hotter in retaliation, but the ice under my feet stops that. My inner heat rises as far as I can push it without affecting my skin temperature, but it is nowhere near enough.

My movements become sluggish. Each step is like trying to walk while buried in sand, which isn't helped by how slippery the ice is. Every time my leg comes forward, it is a battle to keep it from sliding out underneath.

The horizon doesn't change: no buildings, no rocks, no new features, just the same ice and void as far as I can see.

The cold is soon too much. My leg refuses to move as much as it should and I tumble down on the ice again.

It's too cold. I stoke my flames enough to keep my movements free, but the ice melts underneath.

I try to regain my feet before the water can burn me, but the ground disappears underneath me.

I'm falling, drowning, I can't breathe. My arms, legs, and tendrils of flame lash out, trying to grasp anything to save me from plunging into the water. There's no air to breathe. My flames spread, searching for something to breathe that just isn't there.

A sudden calm washes over me. Breath doesn't come to me, and neither do my limbs or flames follow my thoughts, still stretching farther than I'd thought possible to find any small bit of air. My thoughts are clear, despite the gasping breaths and reaching flames.

There is no water here, only the darkness of the Void Fog. No, that's not quite right. There are stars all around, little lights dotting the normally endless black of the void.

I'm falling, but I'm not sure which way is down; everywhere looks the same.

My flames sputter, not finding the sustenance they need to continue burning.

Some stars are moving now, swaying back and forth as if they are living creatures swimming in the darkness.

The lack of air is getting to me. My searching flames die out, and all that remains is my form, but that won't last long—the physical flame is only a bit more resilient than my other flames.

The stars spin, rolling around me as my mind decays.

Thoughts are hard.

Light dims.

I gasp deep as I finally find that sweet nectar, my flames reaching and snatching away as much air as they can.

Warmth embraces me, and after a few minutes of choking and struggling to regain my breath, I relax. Beside me is a pool of lava. The boiling rock emits an inviting warmth that pulls me to its shores.

I've had enough. This is all too much, I don't want to be here anymore. I want to go home. It doesn't matter if home means being with Ash, Leslie, Kerry, and the twins, or my tribe; I just don't want to be here anymore.

Every minute I'm being pulled and stretched to my limit. I fear what the next place is going to hold. I glance around warily, wondering what this new place might hold in store.

I'm underneath that huge half volcano from earlier. The top of the mountain arcs high over my head, suspending hundreds of thousands of tons of rock above. An incredible amount of magma drops from the looming mountain, free-falling thousands of meters through the air before splashing down into the lake of volcanic rock before my feet.

I lower my foot to the lake and dip a toe in. It's not too hot! Last time my tribe visited a volcano, I'd been too young to enjoy the heat with the others. But as much as I'd like to just ignore my problems and relax, this is hardly the time. I need to get out.

There is something I have to try. Back while I was struggling to breathe, I noticed that the Void Fog seemed to appear, compress, then spread after my flames extinguished. Whether it was my mind playing tricks on me in that air-deprived state or it actually was the same thing that happened to that fox, I need to find out.

A ball of flame appears in front of me, about the size of my head. I move it around to see if that does anything. Nothing. Next, I have the ball extinguish. As it poofs out of existence, a few black particles spread out from the center of where the ball floated.

It works! I can finally change the world around me.

Trying it proves difficult. I can hardly extinguish myself—that would be rather counterproductive.

I create another ball in front of me, planning to experiment with ways to create the same effect without extinguishing the central fire, but a cacophony of synchronized warbles drags my attention to the sky above.

There, flooding the sky above, is what must be millions of magpies. Their individual caws mangle together into a constant droning buzz. Every part of the void above that isn't covered by the mountain is now layered by innumerable birds.

Okay.

I look back down and create the flame again. I need to test this quickly. There is no way I want to be here if they start to swoop at me.

Thinking back to what the fox did to create the phenomenon, it shook its body with speed, right? Could I do that with my flames?

The ball in front of me pulses back and forth as fast as I can force it, but I just can't seem to get it to move fast enough. I need to try something else. What is it that the fox and my flame both achieved in common that caused the fog to appear? Where does the fog come from?

An idea comes to mind. I take the ball in front of me and force it to push a hollow sphere of flames from it in every direction, leaving a space between the outer shell and the inner ball. Something happens even as I force the outer shell to extinguish.

The ball of flame is missing, but I can still feel it for barely a moment before I feel it extinguish as well. It is strange, like my flame both doesn't move and travels an infinity away.

It works! Yes!

It's a good thing I figured it out, because I'll be attempting it very soon. The swarm of birds closes in, much of the mountain above now obfuscated.

One bird swoops but completely misses me and flies straight into the falling magma. I can't help but stare at the fireball that was a bird not a second ago. It missed me by a full body length. Was it even trying to hit me?

My answer comes in the form of thousands more swooping birds, all with just as bad aim as the first, but with millions of them I'll be mauled eventually. A claw cuts through the top of my shoulder, sharper than a magpie's talon has any right to be.

Fire wraps around me, covering every part touching the air. In a swift push,

I create a shell around me, which disappears as soon as it leaves contact with my body.

The retched noise of a million birds ends and the sky turns blue. The moon hovers above and the rock returns under my feet.

I'm . . . out?

I can't see the Void Fog no matter how much I look; instead, all that remains is a scarred landscape, as if a massive scoop has been taken from the land. The ground is smooth, curving upward to a ledge above each side of me. The path left by the Void Fog is immense.

I'm out. I almost cry in relief.

There's nothing left for me to do now but climb my way out of the scar of missing land. My arms are all torn up. It looks like I was scratched by far more of the birds than I thought. Well, it doesn't matter; I am out now. I just need to find where the others went.

Over the ledge, there is a definite line where the fog traveled. Buildings only half-consumed by the fog remain, cut down the middle with the interior rooms showing. It's odd, but nobody is around. Did they all run off?

I walk north, hoping to find a clue to my friends' whereabouts. The crossroads between streets are behind me when sudden pain in my knee drops me to the ground. The bang of the gunshot echoes in my ears a moment later.

My flames burst out to defend me, but I'm forced to pull back before they hit a wall of water that suddenly forms around me. A pit grows in my stomach; they found me. A man walks forward from behind a building, hoisting a long gun over his shoulder. I know this man. He's the lieutenant from the Cano mansion. The man who killed a person I'd seen knock down a wall with a flick of his hand. A murder he achieved with ease.

"Finally. I don't think you could imagine how difficult you were to find, little áed."

CHAPTER FORTY

Teine

feel sick. I don't know when it started, but my flames now churn like they're trying to eat something that isn't there.

Maybe it's because I haven't been allowed to move around in days, or maybe it's the constant proximity to water, even if it is hidden within the bars of my cage.

They caged me, steel bars and all, like an animal. They don't treat me like one, nor do they treat me like a person, more like an object or oddity.

I am trapped again, this time in a smaller and colder cell with a physical lock rather than a mental one. I absolutely hate it. These people don't pretend it's for my benefit, but there is no difference between now and what Gloria did to me.

The door in the room hosting my cage opens, and an albanic enters wearing that same heavy silver suit all the others in this place wear when they approach me.

I wait until the albanic is only a few steps away from my cage when I launch a surge of cinders around them. I try to roast them alive inside that frustrating suit, which my fire struggles to do more than slide over. They don't react to my actions, simply holding some metal box into the flames. I try to burn through that too, hoping to damage whatever they brought with them.

A minute of trying to burn them shows no results, but I don't stop. I want to put everything into my flames, but I can't. The fear I might melt through the steel bars and open up the water stored inside holds me back. The albanic needs to die, but I don't want to die to achieve it.

"Eleven hundred kelvin. Deviation of less than three percent. I don't think we could have asked for a better sample," a feminine voice says from the silvery bodysuit.

She was testing my flames? Indignation fills my chest and I snap my flames away from her, trying to keep her from getting what she wants.

She closes the distance and stands above my cage. I watch my reflection in the visor of her suit as she stands over me. The pitiful sight only makes me more frustrated. I don't know what she's looking for, but I don't like it. A wall of flame curtains the bars, obscuring her sight.

"Subject twenty-two is ready for transport to the testing facility," I hear before the steel bars move underneath me.

My flames drop while the albanic pulls my cage toward the exit of the room. I stick my hand through the bars to try and stop one of the wheels, but I just jar my finger for the trouble and fail to make the woman's job hard.

She pulls me out through a garage door and through an open warehouse to the crane used to bring me in here. Two other albanics join the woman there and soon have my cage hooked up. I search around, hoping to find something made of timber I can burn, anything to give them trouble, but I'm disappointed to find nothing.

They hoist me to the top deck, out to see the sun and sky for the first time in a week. I've seen a shipwreck before, but never would I have thought I'd be on a ship while it was in the water. I still don't want to be, but this is where that lieutenant took me after he had me caged.

The damn cage isn't even tall enough to let me stand up. It is bigger than that box the others and I used to pass the wall in Zadok, but it still isn't huge.

They push me along the deck until we reach the far back of the ship, where a cubic building sits alone above deck. Just being out here, where I can see the water spreading over the horizon, is enough to make my legs rigid.

In through the roller door, a clutter of strange-looking equipment occupies much of the floor space. In prime position at the center of the room is a huge metal orb. Outfitted with an incredible number of pipes, the sphere looks somewhat like the design of the vehicles they use instead of wagons.

The cars—as they call them—can hardly reach speeds anywhere close to that of a train, but it is still enough to outpace walking by far. It took only a few days before I found myself at the docks after the lieutenant caged me.

Dim, glowing inscriptions cover the orb and piping. I've seen inscriptions in New Vetus, Zadok, and even in my tribe, but these are far denser, drawn with an accuracy I can hardly fathom.

They push my cage right up to the open door of the sphere. It is obvious they want to put me in that thing, but there isn't a chance I'll go willingly.

The bars clang against the hard metal of the sphere as they line up my cage to the opening. Clamps snap shut and tighten the cage in place, closing any gap I might have hoped to use as an escape.

There are more albanics in this room. Some aren't even wearing the silver armor that protects them from my fire. I lash out at them, trying to burn them while I can, but before I can reach them, the two following my cage shove me into the orb with long poles.

My struggles hardly matter. One of the T-shaped tips of the poles catches me under the arm and the other curves around my waist. I'm forced in before I can stop them or stretch my flames toward the workers.

A hiss sounds before the door slides down and locks me in. A slam of my arms against the door does nothing. It's as if the door isn't even there anymore; the seal is flush.

The inside of the orb is perfectly circular, about as wide as I am tall. A pedestal in the center of the capsule holds a ball. It's double the size of my hand but has inscriptions lining it that are far more intricate than even the exterior or interior walls of the orb I'm stuck in.

My first thought is to burn it, but it sucks on my energy with greed and I quickly pull back. I still want to break it. Whatever it is, I'm sure it's expensive and difficult to make. So, I kick it. Unfortunately, I'm not that strong and just fall on my butt.

"In a moment, we will start the machine. Your task is to redirect the energy of the outer sphere and input it to the inner sphere while making absolutely sure to keep the energy distribution consistent along the surface." The voice comes from above, sounding like the man is speaking within the capsule, but there is nothing there except the glow of inscriptions.

"Start."

The glow of the inscriptions on the outer sphere grows in intensity. Four major points start assaulting me with an incredible amount of fire. It feels great, so I take it all for myself. It doesn't take long until the inside of the orb is as hot as the lava I felt not long past.

A sound halfway between a horn and a whistle blares around me right before a spray of mist rains down from above. The water burns across my skin and I scream out in pain.

"No energy detected by sensors C-one through -sixteen. Failure to follow orders will be punished. Distribute energy across the surface of the central sphere."

Everything burns, and not in a good way. My skin stings like millions of needles stab all over my body. Not wanting to feel that again, I push some of the energy into the ball in front of me. Out of spite, I still don't push all the energy I gain from the walls.

The same loud beep cuts through the heat and makes me shiver. I flinch back as another spray burns through my skin. I pull away, trying to hide from the mist, but there is nowhere to run in this cramped sphere. Steam blows off from my body and I choke on the moisture in the air before I can let out another scream.

"Difference between sensor values greater than maximum limit. Insufficient sum of detected energy. Punishment administered."

I sob from the pain. My arms and chest are partly black and charred, and my face doesn't feel much different. I hate this. I hate them. But I do as they want and spread the energy I gain from the capsule over the ball. I'm scared of the agony that water will bring, so I put more than I need to, putting in some of mine and making sure the flames are as perfectly spread as I can.

"Energy levels adequate. Timer start." The voice fills the sphere once more.

Timer? How long do I have to do this for? I don't want to be here anymore. I want to leave. I want Mommy.

My head snaps up at the thought. No. They already killed her. There's no going back. I am on my own, and that means I have to look after myself. If I'm to get out, I have to do it myself.

Once, I let anger and hatred fuel me, but I was blind to the mistakes I made while consumed by rage. Gloria was cruel and evil, I still believe that, but a city didn't deserve to burn because of her.

The Henosis Empire is worse. They are far more evil than Gloria ever was, but they are also far harder to deal with. They have water mages, soldiers that can do more than punch through walls, and who knows what else? There is an army at their bidding, an army that beat the ursu. How can I fight that?

I can't just blindly burn things around me as I did last time. No, I need to be patient. I'm not sure why they are doing all these tests, but for now, they aren't killing me. Lie in wait, that's the only thing that can be done. For however long I need, I'll wait until I get the opportunity to get back at the people who killed my family, who started the war that split me from Leal and took her father, and who trapped me, locking away my freedom.

The energy rushes through me for almost ten minutes before finally cutting off. The glowing inscriptions dim as I sit unmoving in the sphere. They take another fifteen minutes before they open the door to the orb and usher me back into my cage.

I don't fight—there's no point yet. I need to wait for an opportunity. Attacking at every moment will do nothing but tire me out and keep them wary.

The next few days are hard. I have to force myself to follow their instructions and not fight back when everything inside me screams to burn anything that would.

The testing continues; every day I am led back into that capsule and they add more instructions that I have to follow while also maintaining the tasks I've previously been given. The inscriptions lining the spheres are now nothing more than guides for the manipulations they require I perform.

It is similar to the inscription networks I've been able to infiltrate at the mage academy and Cano residence, only the Henosis know I can do so and have blocks in place that cut me off from controlling any more of it than they intend. I am to accurately and efficiently control the system only so much as they allow.

I haven't been able to figure out what the purpose of these tests is. They have very specific requirements a lot of the time, using an exact amount of energy in an exact distribution while reducing thermal interference to an exact level. It is extremely random, while also completely intentional.

By the time the ship docks at land once more, I can control the entire process by myself. The albanics around seem so pleased by the fact, and I have to remind myself that now isn't the time. I have to strangle down the indignation caused by them congratulating themselves for a good job. My opportunity will come. I don't know when, but it will.

It has to.

I am glad to be back on land, even if still in the clutches of the Henosis. Every day I spent over the water made me more nauseous. Hopefully, now that I'm separate from it, I'll feel better.

My cage is lowered from the back of the car and an albanic, still in that full-body suit, pulls me through the gate around what I can only assume used to be a train depot. Rails line the area, with many leading within the structure ahead of me. Railway carriages are parked neatly in much of the free space of the open area before the depot.

What is strange is that the Henosis soldiers have fortified the area with so much defense it's hard to imagine it is only the train yard they are defending. Spotlight towers and the tall fencing seem brand new next to the rust-damaged rails. Albanics with clearly exposed tattoos on their arms stand on guard.

The albanic pulls me through a wide, steel sliding door, likely intended for trains to pass. He chains the door closed before retaking my cage and leading me farther into the building.

We pass a railcar with one of those strange spheres integrated within. The black steel makes the entire thing intimidating to look at, unlike the bare silver of the one on the ship.

There are a lot of albanics moving around in here, many without the protective suits, but that doesn't mean they aren't defended. Amongst them, both as guards and workers, are mages; black ink markings decorate their exposed arms and faces.

My cage is dragged past all the workers, guards, and machines lying around and taken through a large ceramic door. Simply passing the threshold, the temperature of the air rises exponentially. I'm surprised the albanics leading me can even handle it, despite the suits they wear.

My breath hitches as I catch sight of the áed ahead of me. My cage rings as the bars lock against the cell of the woman burning with no care of controlling her form.

We are soon left alone, the large ceramic door creating an echoing clang as it shuts.

The two of us just look at each other. It's been a long time since I've met someone from the Agni Mountain tribes. Unlike all other áed, they prefer not to control their forms and ignore all the benefits of a more physical body. Although I guess they never need to bother when they spend most of their time within the magma flow in their village.

She is tired. It's obvious just from a glance. Her flames are static, barely moving; she sees me but is slow to comprehend. She rises with sluggish movements and pulls herself to the link of our confines.

She struggles to speak, but her words still come. "I am Teine, of the Logi tribe, and who might you be, young one?"

"Solvei, of the Vatra tribe."

"Ah, that's good. Cyrus will come for you, then."

I don't have the heart to tell her he is already dead.

"Child, give me your hand." Teine puts her arms through the bars for me.

Not thinking too deeply about the request, I take both her hands in mine. The nostalgic warmth rushes through me, tenderly touching and healing the charred marks on my face and arms. It's been so long since I felt such comfortable warmth of Kindling that I almost lose myself in it, but the intimacy of the act makes me aware of just how bad her state is.

"Stop." I jerk my hands away from her. "You don't have enough strength to be doing this!"

Her inner flame is running on fumes. I can't imagine they've been giving her much to eat if she's in this condition.

Teine looks down at me with a soft smile. "I've seen too many of my family leave before me. My own child taken from me. I do not wish to live without them, so please let me do this one last thing so that my death isn't worthless."

Her hand remains reaching through the bars, but how can I? I don't want to watch anyone else die. She should want to live, to move on and have a life that her family could be proud of. If not, then why have I pushed so hard until now? Was it selfish of me to live on with everyone I love gone? I refuse to believe that this is something her family would want for her.

"Child, I understand your plight, but I am old. I have lived a long life and I want to be with those I love again. You don't have to do anything, just embrace the warmth and think of your family."

I sniffle but lift my hands. My eyes don't lift from the ground as she grabs my hands. I do as she says and imagine it's my mom's warmth, her loving flames hugging me close. Heat floods my body, my inner flame entwining with hers, and my chest scalds as she pushes more of herself than ever should be done in Kindling.

I try to grip her arms tight, not letting her go, but I feel my fingers slip, like I'm losing my grip on her arms, but her own hands hold mine tight.

My head pulls up only to see her outlined form decaying into an intangible mass. Her body's frame loses its physicality and becomes natural fire.

"Please, when you escape, give my family a beautiful pyre." The last of Teine embraces me and I feel her entirety seep within.

"I will," I say, feeling the warmth continue to burn through me.

A tear drops and disperses into black smoke.

CHAPTER FORTY-ONE

Tore Hund II

When Tore learned of the plan the military strategist decided on, he couldn't help but despair. There would be no winning any fight in these conditions. The man should have organized a reconnaissance-in-force mission and taken any lackluster gains to show off to the chairman.

A full offensive, especially one that involved a landing, was the definition of stupidity in the current circumstances. Winter was showing itself to be hellish this year, and while ursu are comfortable in the cold, it was unreasonable to expect them to fight while wading through semifrozen wetlands.

The weaponry the enemy had was a whole new field to Tore. No more did the common warrior need to be within striking distance to butcher each other.

The Zadok Kingdom had inferior versions back in the war almost two hundred years ago, but they had been almost completely ineffective against the ursu's naturally thick skin. Now Tore wished he had taken them more seriously. Who would have imagined that a person with no training, no experience, and most of all, no body enhancement could ever cause so much widespread death simply because they had the right weapon?

If only countries could settle their disputes by throwing the elites at each other. The death count of innocent lives would be reduced by incomprehensible amounts. Or, even better, settle their disputes peacefully. Not that he was naive enough to believe that could happen.

The offensive plan relied on far too many external factors going perfectly in New Vetus's favor to ever possibly succeed. Mostly, it hinged on the strategists of

Henosis being idiotic. Considering the speed with which they annexed half of New Vetus, idiotic they were not.

Tore didn't even have the full details of the plan, but he could already see countless points of failure. If there were Henosis ships in the southern sea. If the Henosis army didn't push forward after New Vetus's fake retreat. Even if Henosis had slightly more units than expected. Any of these would doom the entire offensive.

What's worse is that, should this plan fail, it would leave the New Vetus front line vulnerable to a counteroffensive. With all ursu troops pushing south for a flank from the sea, any piercing attack could reach Flehullen before the units could be scrambled to intercept.

In a way, it wouldn't be the worst thing. Should the Henosis reach the capital, the chairman would have no option but to let Hund off his leash. If he could enter the battle, then he would finish this war before the chairman could call him back.

Tore had been right.

The ships transporting the ursu across the southern sea were intercepted by Henosis destroyers and sunk. Simultaneously, the front line didn't just follow the retreating ursu, they stormed past and crushed many of the defensive positions that had yet to be fortified.

Henosis now controlled a direct path toward Flehullen.

Tore followed the chairman into the continae conference room, once again making sure he didn't scrape his head against the fragile ceiling.

The Commissar of Military Strategy knew what was coming for him. All in the room could see the nervous twitching and terrified expression. The man couldn't take his eyes off Tore once he entered the room.

The chairman took his seat with a slump. "Commissar Misha, I would usually have you sent to the gulag for your failure, but we do not have time for that today."

The relief on the man's face was palpable, but it came too early.

"Hund, crush him where he stands."

Tore sighed, which sounded like more of a growl to those around him. He would make this quick. He stepped forward to the man now trying to back away in vain, relief wiped away by the terror. Tore reached forward and grabbed the man around the chest. Like squishing a grape, the effort required was no different. He applied pressure on the man's head first, feeling no resistance at all under his large thumb. He died in a fraction of a second. Tore crushed the rest of his body, trying to keep the blood spray to a minimum.

He pitied the man. Sure, he'd doomed the nation's defenses, but nobody deserved an end like this.

The silence reigned as each commissar stewed on the death of their comrade. The chairman, entirely unfazed by the death of his subordinate, took his seat at the end of the conference table.

"Everyone sit," he grouched when he realized the commissars were still standing, distracted by the bloody remnants at the side of the room.

The ursu hurried back to their seats, not wanting to be the next to anger the chairman.

"Now, does anyone have a suggestion to solve our pest problem?"

Each and every one of the commissars' eyes glanced upward at Tore, but none of them were willing to make the suggestion. Quiet ruled the conference room as the seconds ticked by, each commissar not wanting to be the one to propose the only answer any of them knew would work.

"Commissar Dov, I gave you those mages you asked for. What do you propose be done?" The unlucky Commissar of Industry was called upon first.

Tore did give credit where it was due. The man could hide his nervousness and fear remarkably well. "Chairman Vernados, the Henosis army will be here in a matter of days. Should we not have Hund eliminate them?"

"You would like that, wouldn't you?" The chairman's mood soured. "You think I don't know I'd have a knife in my back the moment I let my guard down around any of you miserable fucks?"

The chairman rose from his chair and narrowed his eyes at the remaining commissars.

"All of you will take yourselves and your families and join the front lines. Those who don't will be hanged, including your children." He marched to the exit, turning only before leaving. "Dov, take those mages with you, their families too."

Tore took one look at the shocked and horrified commissars before he turned to follow the chairman out of the room.

Upon exiting the continae, the chairman climbed into the carriage for the ride back to his residence. The carriage was new. Usually, he would walk the fifteen minutes it took, but his paranoia had only amplified after hearing about the power of high caliber weapons.

The carriage was supposedly bulletproof. Whether it was or not, Tore couldn't say. It didn't look like much to him, but he supposed he was grateful to have a wall between himself and the chairman for the duration of the walk. It wasn't like he could join the chairman inside the tiny carriage.

The streets were rather bare. Word that they had lost another major battle and the Empire was on its way had likely spread. Many ursu hesitated to leave their homes with a threat so close.

The lack of people walking the street also made the assassins so very obvious.

He tried to ignore them, hoping if they acted quick enough, he might fail to protect the chairman. The first assassin passed the carriage and threw a small box underneath while it moved. Tore struggled against the rising desire to protect the chairman, pushing the urge down as far as he could.

The moment the explosion went off, time slowed for Tore Hund. All he could think of was that the man he'd sworn his oath to was in danger. In that moment, the chairman wasn't Vernados; he was Torben, and Hund would do anything to keep the man alive.

The explosion crept outward from its origin underneath the carriage. Hund was already too late to stop the explosion, but he could still save the chairman.

He tore off the side of the carriage, giving him access to the man inside. He couldn't just snatch him up and move away from the explosion, as the whiplash would kill him. Instead, he lifted him ever so lightly and kicked the carriage out from underneath. Using his body as a shield, Tore blocked the explosion from impacting the chairman. The carriage he'd kicked aside slammed through the building opposite, collapsing the structure.

Tore set his old friend down, watching as the man gasped for breath and looked around with wide eyes. The dust settled and Hund's eyes fell on the assassin, dead from his own bomb. He turned his head to watch the second assassin throw his own box toward Tore and the man before him.

Hund lifted his arm and grabbed the bomb out of midair, clenched his fist as the explosion went off in his hand. Smoke billowed out from his palm, but otherwise, there was no damage.

The second assassin's eyes widened at the sight and he stumbled backward before sprinting away. Hund's hand dropped to the sword at his hip as he launched forward.

Only after the cobblestone street was painted crimson did Hund realize there was no need for the blade. His reaction was excessive against an ursu that had probably never seen so much as a brawl, but that someone would try to kill the chairman—the man who had done so much for the ursu people—infuriated Hund.

He twisted his wrist, flicking off the lingering blood from the blade, and sheathed it.

Hund turned to check on the chairman and make sure he was unhurt but spotted another ursu with a briefcase. The man stared with wide-eyed horror at Hund, before dropping the case and running off. Hund let the man go, instead crushing the briefcase and making sure the third bomb was dealt with.

He returned to the side of the chairman only to find he was not the man he thought. A nauseous feeling rose within his chest when he discovered he'd protected this despicable man at the cost of ursu courageous enough to go against him for the betterment of their people.

Tore sighed in frustration as he realized this attempt would now only amplify the chairman's paranoia. If there was any chance he might have sent Tore to fight in the upcoming battle, this had shut that down completely. Tore applauded the ursu who attempted to remove the current chairman but also despaired at their failure.

With nearly every able-bodied ursu having been sent to war—besides those necessary to keep the nation operating—there was hardly a chance for an uprising. Tore was relieved he wouldn't have to kill his own people again, but that was only because the Henosis Empire was doing it in his stead.

Every possibility before him led to tragedy, and yet the only person who could change that simply wouldn't. The hatred he felt for each succeeding chairman was filtered through his fealty for the original, but he felt nothing but resentment for the man kicking the corpse before him. The body was hardly recognizable, shredded by his own bomb.

Tore lifted his hands, urging them forward to wrap around the body of the chairman. He tried his utmost to finish what the assassins started. The man was right there, just barely outside his grasp. He could squeeze just the tiniest bit and all the nation's issues would be over in a moment. All Tore's people would be saved. He would be free to remind the neighboring states why ursu were once feared.

But it was for naught. He was physically incapable of killing the chairman.

Tore lowered his arms, severely disappointed in his own lack of conviction. The man before him remained completely unaware of the murderous thoughts running through the mind of his bodyguard.

"Ha! I knew I was right not to trust those lousy incompetents. I'll make sure they regret this. Hund, if any of the commissars or their families survive the battle, give them a most painful death. I don't care if they are children."

Tore remained silent, the inner turmoil and frustration not once bleeding through to his expression. His desire to fight battled with his instinct as he followed the chairman to the decriable safety of the man's lavish home, while the rest of Tore's people were left before the jaws of the enemy.

He could only hope Henosis would assume control of Flehullen rather than lay it to waste.

CHAPTER FORTY-TWO

The Source of Despair

Once we load you into the capsule, you will wait until you hear the buzzer to start the process. You will not do it any sooner if you do not want more punishment," the bastard says.

Yesterday, they moved my cage once more, this time loaded up on the train behind the railcar with the capsule. I traveled on the flat train car with nothing but the bars of my cage blocking the wind until I was unloaded here, amongst thousands of roaming Henosis soldiers.

The man standing over my cage, Colonel Olipho, is the leader of the silver-armor-wearing people. I recognize his voice as the one I always hear within the capsule when they have me doing the menial fire manipulations.

I hate all the tasks they give me, but I can't help but be surprised by the difficulty of the challenges they lay before me. Ever since I managed to control my flame without a connection to my body, I never considered I could improve my control in any way that wasn't pushing the distance of separation. But the tasks I am forced to do for these people require a level of control I'm barely able to manage.

Controlling ten different threads of fire at specific individual temperatures is far harder than separating a ball of flame from my body. Begrudgingly, I have to admit that the tasks they've set for me have grown my control in these few weeks far more than I could have hoped for by doing my own practices.

Teine's passing is a reminder that Henosis hasn't only caused disaster for me and my tribe. Many tribes were killed or captured for whatever sake they think legitimizes their cause. They brought tragedy to New Vetus, transforming the once-welcoming people to spiteful.

I'm not the only one whose life Henosis destroyed. Leal lost her father, lost her home and education to them, and I went and destroyed her second home. Teine lost so much she wasn't even willing to continue living.

I just can't imagine anything but evil causing so much tragedy. They are the true definition of the word.

"Ah, so this is the one that caused us so much trouble, is it?"

My head snaps to the voice. I was so lost in thought, I didn't even hear the man approach. He is tall for an albanic. With wide shoulders and a straight back, he stands tall over my cage. The confidence he exudes surprises me, considering he stands before me without protective metal armor.

I could burn him in an instant, before the water mages can react, and it would be so satisfying to get some retribution for all the pain they've caused me. But I hold myself back. Burning him won't give me an escape. At most it will be momentary gratification before I'm punished.

The mages around my cage seem rather prepared as well, tensed to jump in at an instant. It's hard to say if I'll be able to kill the unprotected man before I'm stopped.

The speaker is old. Age lines wrinkle his forehead and a neatly trimmed white beard adorns his jaw. The man stands there for a moment, inspecting me. I stare right back, not wanting to show weakness to this man who doesn't show a hint of wariness at being near me without protection.

"General Mudra, you shouldn't be so close to the subject. They tend to be rather temperamental if you don't have the proper protection." Olipho steps up beside the man. "And yes, the subject has proven adequate to enact the required process. We are ready to send the weapon at a moment's notice."

Weapon? Is that what the capsule is? I don't have a clue how it might possibly be one, but maybe I can use it against them.

"You best hope so. You understand what will happen to you should this fail? Your ineptitude so far has cost us greatly; far too many of my mages were lost in the wasteland expedition. Mages invaluable to this invasion." The man glares at Olipho. "Luck is the only reason the war is going so well. I'm sure you've been taught the impact an elite warrior can bring to the battlefield. They have been holding back, I'm sure of it."

My fists clench and I have to hold back my flames from lashing out. These two are the cause of everything?

"How can you be so sure, General? They have all but lost already. Would they not have sent out their best soldiers long before the war reached this point? It would have been the best opportunity to send them in during the stalemate of the isthmus."

Is that all they hunted us down for? They killed so many áed for a weapon they don't even need. They've won this war already; even from my cage, I can tell.

Flehullen is their next target. The capital of New Vetus. If moving on the heart of the nation doesn't count as a victory for them, then I don't know what would.

"Call it a hunch built upon experience." General Mudra turns to the capsule train. "I'll be sending one of the new railway guns. Use it as bait when the time comes. You have only one chance at this. Don't fuck it up."

One chance? Will I die using the weapon? He not only took away my family, but now he wants me to kill myself for his goals? No! I won't do it!

Flames erupt around me. In barely an instant, they engulf the evil general in front of me. Strengthened by my fury, the flames burn hotter than I've ever managed. Every portion of my consciousness pours into incinerating this albanic in front of me.

I try to increase the intensity of my flames as much as I can, raising the temperature and exploding the amount of fire that circles the man. My only goal is to burn this man to ash before the mages can put a stop to it.

The general takes a calm step toward me, and before I know it, I feel a crushing pain through my head. My flames redirect to the hand gripping my head through the bars, but they barely seem to do anything. I try to crawl away from the pain, but the man holds me in place.

"You will stop or the pain will only get worse." The voice enters my ears, calm but clear.

As if to emphasize his words, the man squeezes harder and I can't handle it. I cut my flames, hoping for an end to the crushing pain.

He lets go and I scuttle backward, cradling my head and glaring daggers at the man between my arms. He looks unhurt. Much of his uniform is scorched, but not a single point on his body is damaged. His skin doesn't even look red. I had the opportunity but wasn't strong enough to do anything to him.

"You two!" I hear the general's commanding voice, but he's looking at the mages beside him. "Your reaction speed is lacking. Because of your clear incompetence, your squad can expect a thorough rediscipline exercise in the coming days."

I try my hardest to kill him and he barely acknowledges me. It's infuriating. The inferno roiling within me wants nothing more than to obliterate the general from existence, but it's impossible. I can't hurt him. I'm not strong enough. Glaring at him is the only thing I can do. Anything more would just get me punished or killed, so I push the fury churning within me through my gaze.

When the general turns back to me, he raises an eyebrow. "Are her eyes supposed to be smoking like that?"

At his words, Olipho's armored body faces my cage once again. "No, at least I haven't seen that in any of the other áed. I'll have to look into it."

"Do as you will. Just make sure the weapon is ready for the offensive. Infantry corps are expected to commandeer all rail to Flehullen within forty-eight hours. Be prepared to move out." The general then marches out of sight.

Olipho waits until the general is out of sight before commenting, "Subject twenty-two, if you had done that to anyone else, I'd have you bathing 'til every inch of you is charred. Fortunately for you, General Mudra is a grumpy old prick and needs to be taken down a step or two. Don't do it again."

I just glare in return to his words. If Olipho wasn't wearing that annoying armor, I'd have tried to roast him too.

Besides those few words, he pays me no mind and walks off, leaving me alone.

Even up to this point, caged and unable to escape, I've never felt this helpless. After failing to hurt the albanics around me, I blamed it on their metallic armor and told myself I'd be able to hurt them when they didn't have it to rely on. Just wait for the perfect opportunity. That had been my plan.

But even without that defense, I was unable to hurt the root cause of all this. I placated myself after the first tests in that capsule because I wanted to wait for a chance to escape. Escape and get back at those who've caused so much misery, but primarily I just wanted to give myself an opportunity to escape. And yet, I threw that away in anger to avenge everyone, only to fail.

They spoke over me as if I'm not a person. They don't care what I know, as long as I'm forced to do as they want, and I realize now there is no escape. I believed there would be the chance. That if I was patient, if I waited for the right moment, I could escape, and then an opportunity would fall in my lap to take my vengeance.

My opportunity came, at least to avenge my family's deaths, but I was powerless to do anything. Maybe I've become so arrogant because of how everything burns so easily outside the wasteland that I just assumed I can get through any problem by burning through it. I can't. Facing that brute of a general washed away all pretenses of strength I thought I had.

There will be no escape. I am still not as strong as an adult, and even they weren't able to escape the Henosis. Teine's despair is enough proof of that. An escape through my cage, assuming I can actually melt through the metal, would just result in me dousing myself in the water within the tubes. Should I somehow avoid the water, trying to get through the mages guarding this military outpost would have me dead in moments.

And now, the only solution I thought I had—patience—is destined for my death as well. I haven't the faintest idea what the weapon will do when I'm forced to operate it, but the general specified there would only be one chance for it to work. The only reasons I can think that might be the case are that operating the weapon will kill me or the response from the ursu army will kill me.

It's hopeless. I can't see any way to get out of this. My only possible hope is that Olipho never gets the order to send me into that death capsule.

My knees pull to my chest and I hug them tight. Why can't everything just go back to the way it used to be? It was so great when I didn't have to worry about anything but how to not disappoint my elders. The desert is boring, but it's so much better than this. I wish I could just open my eyes and wake up from this nightmare.

I can only thumb Mom's marble tied around my neck and be glad they haven't taken it away from me.

CHAPTER FORTY-THREE

Moribund

I lie on my side in the corner of the cage, idly scratching a finger along the steel bars beside me. The metal underneath is as uncomfortable as ever. I try to angle myself to lie between two of the bars, but it just makes it feel like it's digging into my body.

It's hard to distract myself from my circumstances. I've been trying to remind myself of good memories, usually falling back to the days with my tribe, with Leal, and I am surprised to note that even thoughts of the five from Kelton have wormed their way in. But every time I think about the times I miss, I'm forced to realize that those times are over. I'm never going to see any of them again.

The capsule weapon sitting innocuously beside my cage is a constant reminder of my pending death. My attention can't help but drag back to the machine any time my thoughts wander. The amount of time I've spent just inspecting the capsule and train it sits on, you would think I'd have it memorized. But any time I look away, my thoughts twist the visage of the machine into something far more terrifying. I have to keep looking at it now. If I don't, I'm sure my fears will overwhelm me.

Hunger pangs within my chest, but I refuse to beg them for something to eat. It's not much of a resistance—heck, it's less self-preserving than anything—but I don't want to give them the satisfaction.

A whistle sounds through the camp, and in an instant, the area is bustling. Albanics surround the capsule train and many run back and forth, and all the while, everyone is yelling.

A massive cylinder of metal on a railcar rolls down the tracks before it clanks against the capsule railcar, and albanics connect them together. The simplicity of its shape belies its immense size. The long metal barrel hangs above the train carriage far ahead of its mounting brace.

I don't know what it is, but it looks dangerous.

A crew of six albanics with reflective metal armor circle my cage before one of them addresses me. "Finally, we get to see all our efforts pay off." I recognize the giddy voice as Olipho. I've never heard him sound so happy. "Remember, enact the process at the sound of the buzzer. Any delay will result in continual punishment until you do as instructed."

Before I can prepare myself, they move my cage right up to the capsule and have their sticks pushing at my back. I put as much effort as I can into staying away from the machine, but the curved heads of their poles lift me from underneath my arms and legs and shove me in despite my struggles.

My feet stumble and I try to throw myself out, but the door is already sealed behind me. Fists slamming into the door and walls achieve nothing.

I slump, my back sliding down the curved wall. The ball in the center of this capsule looks different. The platform holding it up is nowhere near as thick, more like a thin pole now.

I'd hoped beyond hope they would decide against sending me out. I don't want to die, especially not for the Henosis.

Suddenly, a terrible idea hits me; if I am going to die anyway, then why not take out these bastards while I can? I don't want to die, but I have to be real for a moment. There is no good luck coming my way, no miracle coming to save me. I am going to die. And if I have to die, I want it to be on my own terms.

My body jerks to one side and I realize they must have started the train. With not much time to waste, I throw as much energy into the ball in front of me as I can, following the guidance I've been led through in the prior weeks to enable whatever is in this sphere before me. I can feel a massive difference from before; I have no idea what it is, but it reacts to the energy I'm pumping into it. I throw as much energy as I can spare before reaching to the power sources lining the walls of the capsule. My flames reach into the inscriptions to find that energy I know is always there . . . and find nothing.

They've blocked off my connection to the fire source, so I can't get enough strength to finish the process. I lift my hands to my head and slam it into the wall behind me. Of course I won't be given the opportunity to start the weapon just like that. It would be far too easy if I could just end things.

The heat in the orb before me cools, and whatever is contained within returns to a stabilized state. I'm drained. I can't do that again if I try. Not without the energy sources powering the process.

The palms of my hands push into my face as I wallow in dismay. I was determined to die, but even though I resolved myself, it meant nothing in the end.

Nobody will be avenged by my actions. I won't be able to give a proper funeral to Teine's family, nor will anyone perform one for me.

I'll die achieving nothing.

Within the spherical capsule, I roll around with each motion of the train. I don't care anymore to resist what happens to my body with each curve in the rails.

My mind remains blank, unthinking for the hours of travel. Time just passes, and I couldn't be more glad. Unthinking of those I've loved and lost. Unthinking of those I hate. And unthinking of the future before me. Everything that happens just passes my consciousness like wisps of smoke. I could grab at them if I wanted, but I don't. I leave them to blow away in the wind.

The hammering sound of a bang snaps me back to consciousness. The capsule lurches and shudders from what can only be an explosion. I struggle to breathe as I realize the train isn't moving. All goes quiet for a minute before another thundering bang slams me into the wall as the train pitches.

The buzzing noise I have been dreading blares in my ears as the train returns to a stop. The pod shudders as another, more subdued, bang resounds, dissimilar to the previous two.

I ignore the buzzing. There is no chance I'm just throwing away my life. Try as I might to keep that thought at the forefront of my mind, the moment the water sprays down on me from above, I can't help but break down. I let out a scream but can only hold on for a moment before the pain has me going through the process once again. Reaching into the walls, I find the energy sources are once again available to me.

I twist and weave the flames powered by the walls into the orb before me, relieved only momentarily that the water stops before the situation kicks in. I'm going to die. Either painfully by the spray of water or by the unknown of the weapon I'm about to set off.

I don't understand what is happening within the orb, but whatever is in there is becoming unstable. It feels like I'm edging ever closer to a cliff but not quite tipping.

More and more energy is pumped into the ball, and I can feel the moment it reaches the tipping point. I keep throwing more energy at it like the Henosis want. The moment I stop, I know, will be the moment everything will end.

The capsule jumps and I struggle to keep in control of the flames pouring over the orb as an impact knocks the train on its side. Each second, it gets harder to supply the orb with enough energy to keep it from escalating out of control, but I still want to believe I have a chance. I don't want to give up, no matter how slim my chances of survival are. If I can do anything to survive, I'll do it.

The train tilts once again, and before I know what is going on, the thick metal of the capsule above me tears open. Besides the light of day, above me looms an enormous giant of an ursu. The fear overwhelms me, and I finally cannot support the energy needs of the orb.

Everything burns white, then black.

CHAPTER FORTY-FOUR

Tore Hund III

Tore watched as artillery laid waste to the city that had been his home for over a century, completely unable to do anything despite having the power to do everything. The sniveling, cowardly, rat of a chairman had him sit at his side as he hid within his lavish manor.

Only when the sound of explosions through the city ceased did Tore know that they had finally lost. A lone soldier ran through the damaged streets to the chairman's manor. The man barged in to let Tore and the chairman know that the continae had been lost and that the enemy demanded the chairman's presence for an official declaration of surrender.

The chairman was not happy to hear such words. He pulled his own sword and clumsily swung his blade at the messenger. It was fortunate that the messenger was quick and dodged the unskilled swing. The man backed up before making a bolt for the exit.

"Bastard. Kill him, Hund." His anger leaked through his words.

Tore winced at the order. The poor man likely never wanted to be the messenger in the first place. Unfortunately, orders were absolute. As he was accustomed, he made the man's death quick and painless, though it may not have looked that way with how much blood covered the manor path.

"Hund, we are leaving."

The last thing Tore wanted right now was for the chairman before him to surrender. If the man did that, then there would be no future for his country, unless the Henosis Empire was stupid enough to remove power from the chairman completely, but even by the time that happened, he didn't believe he wouldn't be dealt with. As long as the chairman didn't become subservient to the Empire, there was still a chance for Hund to be unleashed.

So when the chairman had Tore push through the escaping ursu to the exit to the city, his anticipation grew. As much as he hated having to toss his people out of the path of himself and the chairman, it would be the tiniest of sacrifices for what might happen.

The chairman wasn't the only one trying to escape the city; there were thousands of people flooding the western exit. The enemy was seemingly allowing the citizens to emigrate.

The moment Tore reached the border of the city, he announced his stipulation.

"The moment you take another step out of Flehullen, you will have surrendered your rights as chairman to the next most applicable commissar."

Tore's sudden halt of motion and his words had the chairman spinning on the spot. The man looked flabbergasted that Tore spoke to him as he had; he was unused to Tore making any more input than necessary.

Of course, when the words finally registered in the chairman's brain, he was outraged.

"What nonsense! I am the chairman, and you will do as I say and protect me regardless of where I decide to go."

He spun on his heel and took another step.

Vernados never saw the blade coming. The man, now paste, unfortunately splattered over many of the escaping ursu. Tore felt slightly bad for the mess, but the euphoria of freedom was overwhelming. He took a moment just to breathe in the air that now tasted so much better for no other reason than it wasn't stained by the breath of these inferior chairmen.

He would be locked down soon enough, once they decided the next chairman, but until then he had free rein to wipe out this invasion.

It wouldn't be the fastest way there, but he didn't want to destroy what remained after the bombing of his city. He crouched before rocketing through the air toward the continae.

He crashed down on one of their armored cars, crumpling the scrap of metal under his weight. Tore rose, lugging his sword in one hand as he stared down at the army. Albanics, hardly a fifth his height, swarmed and pillaged the citadel he and his old friend built a century and a half ago.

He moved, the common soldiers unable to keep up with his speed, nor could they defend against his attacks. Whether it be by his sword, foot, or fist, the Henosis soldiers died in droves, their bodies bursting from such overwhelming force.

Hund tried to minimize the strength he used, not wanting to damage the roads while removing these nuisances. He could kill thousands in minutes, but that was not his objective. Or, at least, not a primary one.

He wanted to terrify these men. Scare them out of the city until he could take care of them more easily and with less mess. He also wanted to bait out any of their stronger warriors. Taking out the elite would be important if he wanted to have free rein on their troops without worrying about his own people in the back.

The best way to do this was to create a spectacle. He walked through the enemy troops, splattering as much gore over himself as he reasonably could. Many bodies were tossed in the air to both show off the difference in strength and attract attention from any that had, until now, failed to notice him. Really, it was all just a messy job, but it worked. Soldiers were running, petrified at the sight of him, and Tore could see a single soldier with a confident gait strolling against the crowd of panicked men.

"I'm happy to see you ursu finally have someone worth taking on, but you took a bit long, don't you think? The war is already over."

Tore glared down at the skinny man. "You are right. This war is now over."

"Well, if you've come to battle until death, I'll be glad to have this duel." The soldier straightened his pose and drew his sword, pointing it at Tore. "I am Lieutenant von Dunnell. May I know the name of the only warrior that seems of worth amongst the ursu?"

Tore considered the man before him. He recalled many warriors in the past with attitudes identical to this man. They never lived up to their own confidence. In fact, they usually never accepted the loss when it cut their legs off. Tore couldn't imagine this man would be any different.

"Hund." He did still respect those who attempted to retain their honor in battle. Even if he considered it a naive way to treat war.

An explosion rained debris from the continae above, followed a few seconds later by a bang in the distance.

Tore never looked away from the man before him as chunks of stone slammed down on his head. Likely trying to use the sound and falling rock as a distraction, the lieutenant dashed to Hund's side, trying to get his rapier in the back of the giant ursu's knee.

Hund brought his own sword down to knock it away. He barely felt the contact between his heavy one and the lieutenant's thin poker.

Von Dunnell jumped back after his failed attack.

"I see you have more speed than your body would indicate."

The lieutenant readied his stance again for another attack but stopped at the sight of his sword. What he'd thought was a deflection left his rapier completely out of shape. The sword was bent a good sixty degrees in the middle.

Lieutenant von Dunnell looked up from his weapon in shock, barely quick enough to save himself. He threw himself backward. Hund's sword tore through the arm he'd been slow to pull back. The lieutenant stumbled and fell to the ground, hardly able to comprehend his missing limb.

As always, Hund thought, it was the arrogant ones that had the most to learn. Unfortunately for this one, he wouldn't get the chance to learn from this fight.

Hund approached the downed lieutenant. The man's eyes widened as he tried to back away with his sole remaining arm. Hund's sword came down, ending the brief battle and von Dunnell's life.

Tore stood around for nearly a minute, waiting to see if any other would challenge him before the slaughter began. He looked up to the damaged continae, just in time to watch another projectile crash into the dome roof. The top half of the continae crumbled from the explosion that shook the building, yet Tore could do little but watch. For all his strength, he lacked the talent to keep the building from collapsing.

With one last glance at the damaged continae, Tore sent himself hurtling through the air once again.

He landed with a cratering impact near a train holding one of the largest cannons he'd ever seen. The albanics operating it ran, terrified, upon his arrival, each scattering in random directions.

Hund crushed the cannon before chasing down the fleeing soldiers. He returned to the train to investigate the strange secondary railcar attached to the cannon. As he approached, he felt his fur standing on end. It was strange, not a feeling he'd felt in over a century. Whatever was causing it, he'd need to deal with it immediately.

The railcar with a strange sphere integrated amongst a mesh of steel piping was lying on its side, knocked over from when he destroyed the cannon.

The fur over his body continued to stand on end as he got closer. Digging his meaty fingers into the sphere, he pried it open. Tore didn't know what he was expecting, but seeing a terrified young áed staring back at him was at the bottom of any list he might have made.

The girl's eyes emitted a heavy, dense, black smoke. It was something he knew almost intimately, being as much a part of him as it would be for her. Soon too; of that he had no doubt.

It was only because of Tore's enhanced reaction speed that he could even comprehend the events that followed. An orb the áed seemed to push all her fire into suddenly exploded into a blinding white light. His feeling of wariness surged alongside the light.

Something blinding expanded at a rate he could never escape from. The energy multiplied at an exponential rate, ready to consume him and everything else in the surroundings.

Tore, for an instant, thought this was going to be the end. Death had finally grasped him.

But the blackness erupted from the girl. It consumed the glowing white substance still expanding, before accelerating farther, encasing everything in its impossibly dark embrace.

Tore felt the touch of the Void Fog once again. It calmed him and soothed his old body, but the mixed emotions he held toward the chaotic mist refused to allow him to relax.

The girl sat before him, looking lost and petrified. Her body flickered with orange flame, reflecting her thoughts and emotions.

Tore didn't want the girl to make the same mistakes he made all those years ago. If she didn't set her mind straight for the challenges ahead, she would become trapped within her own mind.

It was time he gave his wisdom.

CHAPTER FORTY-FIVE

Return to the Void Fog

'm back in the Void Fog? How did I get here? I was about to die and then I just appeared within this darkness. Or am I actually dead, and being dead looks a lot like the Void Fog?

No, I thought I was dead the first time I experienced the mist, and now, I don't know why, but I can just tell that this is the Void Fog.

Like last time, I can't see my hands before me. Oddly, the moment I think that, the fog disperses, giving me a clear view of my hands and the rest of my body. I'm about to clamp down on my body's flames that have embarrassingly slipped from my control during the high stress in the capsule when the immense ursu appears before me.

Any thought of controlling myself slips my mind as I look up at the giant before me. He's bigger than twice as tall as any other ursu I've seen. The same ursu I saw tear open the thick metal of the sphere I was in right before . . . whatever happened.

The sheer presence he exudes is enough to have me shivering in terror. It feels like I am looking at the Titan all over again. This is a being that can cause incredible damage simply by existing. A natural disaster.

"Settle your mind, child. I shall not harm you." His deep yet soft voice reverberates through my chest. It feels like I am being shaken by each word.

"Many trials lie before you. Should you leave the void with your mind intact, you must do as I say." The huge ursu takes a seat before me and continues, his voice heavy with controlled power. "Consolidate your thoughts, direct them solely toward your greatest desire. Only then will your mind remain through the changes to come. Determine your true desire and verify within yourself that you shall never regret the consequences of fully achieving that desire." His voice sounds somewhat sad as he speaks the last words.

"Do not fear the changes. Do not hate the changes. For they are a reflection of everything you are and everything you will become. Do not make the same mistakes as I; live for yourself and not another, lest you watch the world you love decay around you."

With his words given, the large ursu does something that looks like a flex of all his muscles at once, creating a ripple within the Void Fog, and he disappears. Now the space where he sat is as empty as everywhere else in the void.

I'm not sure what that man was talking about, but I don't want to stay for the fog to send me to all those dangerous places again.

I try to do what I did last time, sending out a shell of flame around me to create that weird effect that takes me out of the Void Fog. The moment I try to do it, the fog seems to condense around me. Outside my flame shell, the fog seems to flicker and weaken, but the strength of the void grows to a point of near suffocation.

It won't work. I don't know what's different this time, but I won't be able to escape the same way as before.

Well, it doesn't matter that much. Because of the Void Fog, I am alive. I thought there was no chance of survival after they forced me to enter the capsule, but now I'm alive and free. It doesn't matter that I'm trapped in the Void Fog. I've gotten out once before, I'm sure I can do it again.

I plan to walk until I appear in one of the odd locations hidden by the fog, but upon taking my first step, I know something is different. Wrong.

The fog grows dense around my body and I can feel it trying to worm its way in. I can't keep my form from reverting completely to fire, and nothing I do brings it back under control.

I struggle against the fog, but the more I move, the more restrictive the fog becomes. Sudden, intense emotions wash over me for no discernible reason. Love for my family, hate for the Henosis, helplessness, terror, anxiety, hope. All the most intense feelings I've felt in my life flood through my mind.

I find I can no longer feel my body or the flames that should be attempting to burn out at the Void Fog. My thoughts are the only thing I have, and yet they are barraged by memories, both good and bad but all intense. I feel everything as I did when everything happened.

The sorrow and grief of losing Mommy.

Terror in the presence of the Titan.

Joy as I spend time with Leal.

The uncertainty within the furnace.

Burning hatred after Gloria's betrayal.

Suspicion and distrust as I interact with Ash, Leslie, Kerry, and the twins.

Being happy yet ashamed that my mistrust proved misplaced.

Confusion in the Void Fog.

And finally, the complete hopelessness in the grasp of the Henosis.

The Void Fog rips through my consciousness, taking and exposing all my inner thoughts and memories, and forces me to experience them once again. My thoughts begin to fray, latching on to each of the feelings that comes with them. Some parts of me want to reminisce in the good times with my family, while others want to chase my hatred for the Henosis or cower in fear of the world.

I can feel my mind peeling in thousands of directions, all wanting their own paths, all with their own desires. The giant ursu's words are replayed in my mind and I finally understand this is what he was talking about. I need to take control before I lose myself.

I clamp down on each frayed part of my consciousness, untangling them from the winding they attempt to create for themselves, and bundle them back within. What is it I desire most? I love my family, but they are already gone, and no desire I have for them to return will ever be achieved. My hatred for the Henosis is severe, but the ursu's words echo in my mind. I don't want my life to be defined by a desire to avenge.

No, what I really want is the freedom to live. It always has been, even after I was forced to travel alone after losing my tribe. I never gave up. Not once did I give up moving in the desert despite the seeming futility. I want to live and never be at the mercy of someone else's whims.

I don't want to be caged.

Never again do I want to be trapped.

I want to be free.

Something changes. I can feel the fraying fragments of my mind, bundled together in a figurative hand. They tighten, weaving together into an impossibly tight rope. It is incredible yet terrifying. My mind warps and I can feel an instinctual need—a want, no, a true desire—to survive and remain free no matter what. The rope of my consciousness won't fray even should I want it too.

The feeling of my body returns to me, and I know I have changed. Something is different within me, but other than the rope of my consciousness, I'm not sure exactly what.

I try to send a flame out to see if anything is different with it. The flame appears before me, sending away the void that blocks my vision. The flame doesn't look any different from usual; it doesn't seem stronger, though it feels odd. It feels closer, more intrinsic to my thought, which is strange because as an áed I am already as close to fire as I can get.

Still within the darkness of the Void Fog, I feel a massive force slam into me. The booming of an explosion washes over me and I'm knocked on my back. An intense wind blows over me and I huddle down, hoping for it to stop.

It does.

The Void Fog twists the landscape around me once more. Now I am within a cave with glowing inscriptions lining the walls. With a touch, I try to send my flame within the network, but I find the inscription rejects my flame as it tries to worm its way in. The inscription doesn't react in any visible way other than to stop me from entering.

The cave has three passages leading out from the cavern. The inscriptions wrap the walls down each, highlighting each path with its bluish-white light. I choose a passage at random and soon my legs have me walking through tight, glowing walls as they close in around me.

I still find the underground claustrophobic, and while I'm glad I'm no longer in the pitch darkness pelted by the strong wind, I would rather be back at the lava lake under the volcano.

Passing the next turn in the cave, the world opens up to a clear, endless space. I spin to find the cave is no longer behind me; instead, the memorable volcanic magma-fall greets my eyes. It's surprising, but I'm not about to question the fog changing things positively for once.

I sit down beside the burning lake, enjoying the warmth it emanates. The Void Fog is strange. That's not a new revelation, but I find it strange that I don't feel trapped here like I did last time. The black mist doesn't suffocate me anymore; it feels more comfortable somehow. I don't feel the fear of what the area might transform into around me, even though I know I should.

I'm even tempted to go for a swim in the lake before me, but I don't want to chance losing my clothes, so I hold myself back. Instead, I relax for the first time in what feels like ages, lying down at the shore of the lava. Without the birds blotting out the sky—even if the sky is just the blackness of the Void Fog—this area is much better. I just hope I won't be taken away from here the moment I close my eyes.

How did this all happen? At one moment, I thought I was gonna die from the Henosis weapon, and the next the Void Fog had engulfed me once again, changing me in ways I can't fathom. Where did it come from? Why did it happen? Did the weapon do what it was supposed to? Did those Henosis men intend to unleash the Void Fog?

I don't know anything about the mist or what was in that orb they had me pumping heat into, but I don't think they are the same. They must be linked somehow, but they feel so different that I just can't accept that possibility.

Did the Void Fog save me?

Is it conscious?

I look around, expecting to see that giant ursu again. He appeared right before the darkness overtook everything, so maybe he is linked somehow?

Does the Void Fog want something from me? Is that why it changed me? The thought incites a deep, instinctual resentment stronger than anything I've felt. Just the thought that something might try to use me, to take away my freedom, is comparable to the indignation I felt when I found out how Gloria thought of me. It's inexplicable that I feel this way about the *possibility* that an entity I don't even know exists *might* want to manipulate me.

This is the change in my mind, isn't it? Even the possibilities feel as horrible as if they're actually real. There is a worry that my mind has been angled to follow the wishes of the Void Fog, but it contradicts heavily with my feelings now. If I am under its influence, why would I feel so strongly against doing what it wants?

My consciousness rope still pulls heavily in one direction. Actually, I feel far more aware of my soul than before. The bound rope of my consciousness is a far more physical thing within my mind than I would ever have been able to picture before. Looking closer, I see that each strand still has its own thoughts and desires, but none are given room to travel far out from the general direction of what I feel is my desire for freedom and survival.

Within the rope is one particular knot of thought and emotion, trying hard to twist away from the rest but heavily overpowered by the binds over all. Pulling at the knotted strands brings an intense hatred toward the Henosis, the general, and Olipho to the forefront of my mind. I may be resolved to live for myself, but my resistant thoughts remain.

I still hold the full force of my resentment within me, but any suicidal thoughts I might have considered before to achieve vengeance are now gone, clamped down and unable to be accessed. I'm not disappointed to see them go, but it shows that my thoughts may not be complete. I'll need to be careful that these partial thoughts don't put me in danger in the future.

I snap back to the world around me, trying to push down the hatred I drudged to the surface. The landscape hasn't changed; the volcano remains arching above. It is strange—I've stopped paying attention a few times now, which was usually enough to twist the surrounding landscape, but nothing is different.

My thoughts on the men who caused all the pain and suffering in my life don't disappear. Instead, they amplify as I think about the horrid loss of control they caused in my life. I want nothing more than for them to be right in front of me so I can burn them alive for all the terror and pain they've caused me, my family, and my friends.

The Void Fog thickens before my eyes, wrapping me in darkness and taking the lava lake away from me. I don't know how to explain it, but I feel the darkness move around me. It moves, all the while remaining still. My head is traveling at the speed of a train while my feet are still. I feel like I'm spinning, but the ground under my feet is solid.

Everything lurches to a stop and I jerk against the motion, but I was never moving, so the attempt at keeping upright just sends me sprawling.

I stand once more and the Void Fog thins. Before me, looking around in confusion, is the general of the Henosis army. At his feet is the mutilated body of Olipho.

CHAPTER FORTY-SIX

Retribution

Why is he here? I can't imagine the man would be anywhere nearby when the weapon activated, so how is he here? Olipho too. He's dead? A massive chunk of the man I've only seen in the metallic armor is now missing from his upper body. He lies motionless on the ground between me and the general.

The old albanic finally notices me, and he frowns at the sight of me. The general walks toward me with that same confidence that infuriated me last time. He is so assured of his own superiority, not even heeding those that oppose him.

"Tell me, why did the bomb not explode? Where are we?" He sweeps the corpse of Olipho out of his path with a boot and approaches me.

Does he seriously think I'll tell him anything after what he's done? The pain and hatred amplify simply looking at him. My flames expand around me trying to scare the man, but he doesn't flinch.

"Careful, girl, it would be wise not to anger me."

Anger him? A short, gasping laugh leaves my lips. I couldn't care less if I anger the man who caused me so much suffering. Everything that has gone wrong in the last years traces back to this man. He's already tried to have me kill myself for his own plans, not to mention the cage he forced upon me and so many other áed. No, I want him to be angry. I want him to feel the same pain he has inflicted.

"Why?" There's only one thing I want to know from him.

He stops and narrows his eyes. "Why what?" he grunts.

"Why did you do it? Why hunt áed? What reason do you have for all the murder and war?"

"Why not? Both the áed and the ursu had something I needed, and I had the power to take it, so I simply took it. One hardly needs a better reason for war."

I knew he wouldn't be repentant, but to hear the blatant disregard for the lives of my family is infuriating. Momentarily forgetting the last time I met him, I flare out. My flames surround the man, trying to cook him alive.

With a clear lack of haste, the general sighs before pulling the sword from his hip in a slow, deliberate motion. Something within me screams to move, to jump out of the way, but I can hardly move before the man's sword has swung through my body, dissecting me right through the middle.

Two things run through my mind at that moment: one, my flames still don't hurt the man, and two, the sword passing through me doesn't hurt anywhere as much as it should. In fact, the blade passes through my torso with hardly any resistance at all. My upper and lower body split for only a moment before the flame burns together as if nothing happened.

An attack that would have killed me not long ago now hardly does anything.

The general has sheathed his weapon, but as I remain standing, his eyes marginally widen. Even if I can survive his swings, it doesn't make it any easier if I can't burn him. Regardless of my lamentation, I keep my flames around his body, trying to burn through the skin that just doesn't want to burn.

His eyes narrow again and that instinct returns. I try to jump away and I wish to be outside the general's range. Nothing happens for a time and I look up to find the man is now a hundred meters away, glaring at me across the distance. What happened?

The general sprints at me, closing the distance extremely quickly. I dodge again and try to get as much space as I can. This time I watch as it happens: the Void Fog splits us apart.

I finally realize what's going on. The Void Fog is following my will. It has been since I arrived for the second time. I wanted the warmth of the lake and it popped out in front of me. I wanted my vengeance on the general and Olipho, and they showed up. Now the darkness separated us because that's what I willed.

How can I use this? I picture in my mind the lava lake appearing underneath the general. Success! It's extremely disorienting as the world morphs outside my perception even with my eyes glued to the area around the general. He falls into the thick, molten rock now smoldering underneath. Unfortunately, a simple kick against the magma below sends him to the shores. At least now he's stopped coming after me. He looks around and up at the volcano that appears from apparently nowhere.

Okay, lava doesn't work. Is there anything that can actually hurt the man? I'm safe at the moment because of the apparent improvement to my body and the fact I have enough control over this fog, somehow, that I can keep my distance despite the general's insane speed. There is no way I can hurt him either. My fire is useless; he just shrugs off the heat. Is it even possible for this scenario to end in any way other than a stalemate?

While I try to think of a way to end this, the general has given up on attacking me; instead, he is chasing the thick Void Fog in the distance. I understand why; I tried the same thing to get out of this place when I was first here, but he still doesn't realize doing so will not help him. In fact, as he runs away from me, despite the distance he covers with each step, he seems to get closer to me rather than farther away. For a moment, I just ponder this confusing place.

It doesn't take him all too long to figure out that he isn't getting anywhere.

"How are you doing this?" His commanding tone demands an answer, but I'm too busy relishing his struggle. I may not be able to hurt him, but watching him flounder is a satisfying placeholder.

My lack of answer must infuriate him as he launches at me with an arm extended. His blade is sheathed again. After failing to hurt me with it, does he intend to grapple me to death?

An idea pops into my head as he flies toward me, and I grin as the world twists again. The general crashes straight through the front wall of the green, moss-covered hut. I cast a glance through the hole he made in the wall and see the man stuck suspended in the air with his arms extended.

He struggles within the mysterious grasp, and I take the opportunity to run up to his side and take his sword from the scabbard. As I tear the sword out, the general pulls his arms into his chest, out of the hut's invisible grasp. The walls collapse over us.

I flinch away, but I'm not fast enough. The general grabs my arm and I fly into a panic. I tug and scratch at his hand, burning it as much as I can, but his grasp doesn't loosen. My feet kick at him while the landscape morphs around us. The pyramid, continae, ice field. I take us to so many places, but none dislodge his hand from my arm.

My breath comes in rapid gasps and my arms tremble. I can't get out of his grip. I'm trapped. The general lifts me in the air by the arm and sneers at me. My body jerks away and my eyes slam shut. I want to go home again. I want to be back in the wasteland where I can be free again.

One last time, I pull with all my strength against his grip. Surprise and relief flood me when I crash into sand. I quickly will the Void Fog to separate us again and hold my chest as I calm down.

The desert surrounds us. While I know it's still within the Void Fog, I am happy to be back. My eyes drop to the arm the general held, where the strange sight of unbound flame replaces where my arm should be.

It takes me far too long to realize that the flame is my arm and not my inner flame. Like when the sword passed through me before, my arm has lost much of its physicality. Normally, my body is limited to its default shape, fingers, arms, legs, and all that stuff, but now my arm lacks its definite outline. It's hard to distinguish what is my inner flame and what is my body.

I try to mold the fire of my arm like I would my inner flame, but I find far more resistance to change. That isn't strange in itself, but the fact that it changes at all, even if slowly, is incredible. In a few seconds, my arm returns to normal, my fingers reforming from the flickering flame that took their place.

"How long must you keep this up?" The general's voice resounds across the silent sands. "I do not have time to deal with this." He readjusts the sword back into its scabbard.

Damn, I hoped the blade would have been left behind.

Okay, so my form is much more flexible now, how can that help me beat him? It's great that he won't be able to hold onto me as easily, but it doesn't help the deadlock. I could just leave, but I don't like the idea of leaving this man to his own devices. My flames writhe with hatred for the man, but even without that, I can't leave him. He will just continue his path of destroying the lives of other áed.

If I knew he'd be stuck within the Void Fog forever, I would ditch him here. But I could figure a way out, so there's no reason to think he won't as well, especially considering his strength.

The general takes a step toward me, and I follow with a step back. A sting in my ankle makes me jump, but it is only one of the sandworms, the hyperaggressive sandworms of the Void Fog rather than the slower normal ones.

"Fuck!" I look up to see the general with a worm of his own lodged in his ankle.

It's surprising the little things can even get their teeth into his skin, considering how poorly my own flames have done so far. He kicks off the pest and charges toward me, only to have three more of the worms latch onto his legs. I simply have the Void Fog separate us when he gets too close for comfort.

Two more lunges and six more sandworms later, the general becomes visibly sluggish. His stance doesn't have the same stiff confidence as before, each move is slower than before, and he even stumbles after his last attempt. How is he getting tired already? There's no way someone with so much strength could fall after only a few jumps. Is he trying to trick me? Does he want to bait me into close range? Well, I won't fall for it.

The general yells out a frustrated cry and swats each of the worms chomping at his legs. He pulls the sword from his waist again, but I don't know what he plans to do with it when he can't even get close to me.

"Fuck's sake, girl. This farcical nonsense has gone on long enough." He pulls out some strange, steel, cuboid rod about as long as his finger from a pocket along his belt. "I needed this for later, but you've given me no choice. Just know I will comb the deserts and eradicate your kind."

I narrow my eyes at his words, and he pushes the small bit of steel into the pommel of his sword. Almost immediately, I feel a strong wind blow into me, forcing me to take a step back to hold myself steady.

The air around the general's blade is now distorted, making the blade look wider than before. A constant gust pushes out of the sword, sending up a cloud of sand around us. Soon the sand is thick enough that I can't even see the general. I take a few steps back, expecting him to try to attack through the smoke screen, and I'm glad I do. His sword swings right through the space I was only a moment ago, blowing away the sand for just enough time for me to see him before I lose him again within the rising sandstorm.

The sand whips against my face as I try to take distance from where I last saw the general. My newfound instinct screams at me to move as the howling blade appears to my side. I'm able to jump back just enough so that only my smallest finger is cut by the blade, but the damage it leaves is anything but small. An overwhelming pressure engulfs my hand, and the entire upper half of my forearm is blown away.

My arm explodes in agony. It feels like I shoved my arm in a river of water. The time my leg was crushed under a boulder was nowhere near as excruciating, despite leaving me in the same limbless state. My arm is gone. My inner flame erupts from me, not caring that his body has already proven resistant to my fire. I spread it as wide as I can, trying to find him and burn him.

He passes through my flame behind me while my inner flame grasps at him. I will the Void Fog to separate us once more. The twist in space around me separates my control, and the flames disperse around him. With a moment of respite, I scorch off the worms assaulting my legs.

I've lost sight of the general again, and while it's exhausting keeping my flames up so long, having a way to see him coming is crucial.

As he swings his sword through my flame once more, I have enough time to tell the darkness to move me away only enough to dodge. The blade cuts the air in front of me, blowing enough air to knock me off my feet. My back hits the sand, but I'm still within range to control the flames now engulfing the general.

I feel many of the sandworms biting into his legs, some even latched to his back. They are helping me with the old albanic, so I avoid burning the little things while I twist my flames around him. I feel as he stumbles and moves toward me again. Stepping to the side, out of his path, I watch through my flames as he follows my movement. How does he see me?

I have become so accustomed to him being immune to my flame that I take far too long to realize the fire surrounding him is actually burning his skin. It's ever so slight—only leaving slightly red welts on his skin—but it's enough to have me push all the remaining energy I have into incinerating the man.

A vortex of fire roasts the general as I dodge more of his increasingly faltering strikes. The sand whipping around is still too thick to see, but I can feel the rage plastered on his face. The small bit of desperation, pain, and fear that sneaks its way through his normally grumpy expression has me basking in the malicious pleasure. It is oh-so-satisfying to see this bastard who caused so much pain for so many finally feel some of that himself.

The general collapses to a knee, grunting as he holds his arm over his eyes, trying to block out the flames. I see the weakness he shows and dig my flames into his eyes, amplifying the intensity in the small area where I can concentrate the heat.

He lets out a loud warrior's roar, pulling his arm away from his face, and grasps his sword with both arms. The air ripples as he swings his arms and launches his blade at me. It closes the distance in but a moment. Even my new instinct's warning hardly blares in time.

I try to dodge, to will myself away, but I'm not quick enough. The blade slices through my hip, and excruciating agony fills my being. I don't even feel when I slam against the rocky ground underneath.

All I feel now is a chill. I'm too cold and empty. A glance down shows a good chunk of my torso is gone, along with one of my legs.

Breaths come in ragged gulps as my body shivers against the cold. I'm so tired, my flames hardly want to burn anymore. The sandstorm is gone, but so is everything else. Only the darkness of the void greets me.

CHAPTER FORTY-SEVEN

Final Pyre

I t's cold.

I don't have enough energy for my fire to do much more than smolder.

My body is freezing.

The Void Fog engulfs me completely. There is no ice field, no external chill that should make me this cold.

I want to be warm again.

The agony of my body stops me from looking down. I don't want to see the horrific sight I know is there.

Take me somewhere fervid.

Heat engulfs me. I can't help but cry at the intense warmth soothing my pain. I cannot breathe, but I find it doesn't matter. My flames reach out, grasping at as much heat as they can take, restoring much of what was lost.

The weightlessness holds me for a long time. I don't care about anything but the comfort surrounding me, the heat permeating me, healing my body.

I open my eyes and see nothing but a bright orange filling my vision. An attempt at moving my body is met with difficulty; the liquid all around me moves with a lot of resistance. While it feels like I'm being crushed by a thousand tons, it also engulfs me with so much heat I can't help but soak in the feeling.

The Void Fog must have transferred me to the lava lake. Nothing else could be this empowering. I spread my flames through the molten rock and find that it is much easier to do so within this liquid than in air. My flames pass through the lava, mixing with the heat and traveling farther than ever.

I can see almost everything in this magma lake as if it were right in front of me. That also includes what is left of my body. I'm missing an arm, a leg, and a large portion of my lower torso. There is no way I would have survived if it weren't for this molten bath I've found myself in.

With my body in the state it's in, how will I survive once I leave this lake? I won't be out in the desert where there are an infinite number of sandworms to eat. Could I try to stay within the Void Fog? Something about that idea just doesn't sit well with me. I feel comfortable here for now, but how long will the darkness remain on my side?

In the fight against the general, I was able to revert my form away from the normal physical flames of an áed's body. It is the only reason I wasn't butchered by the man's blade. But the ability reminds me a lot of what Elder Enya was capable of. It might be instinctual, but I can feel a much greater intimacy with my flames. I feel like I can twist them in more ways than before, my body included.

Can I transform into a bird like Elder Enya? If I can grow myself some wings, maybe I won't need to worry about my lost limbs.

Normally, I control my body's flames to be more solid than normal, which has the effect of hiding the glow of my fire. Now, I want to do the opposite, push my flames to be as malleable and nonphysical as possible.

I find my body obeys far more easily than I expected.

My arm slowly disperses into wisps of flame, flickering about before my body. It is strange. My arm has completely lost its form, but I can still feel it as if nothing has changed. It's not like what my inner flame feels like when I move it around. It feels so much closer. That's not to say my inner flame isn't an intricate part of me, just that my body, even in this form, is on a different level.

My arm is slow to change, but soon I have a wing forming in the shape I remember Elder Enya always took. A sudden thought stops me halfway through forming the wing. If I can change my body this easily, can't I just regrow my limbs this way?

So I try. Immediately, I realize it won't be easy to do this normally, but I'm fortunate enough to have this massive lake of heat ready to supply the energy I need to re-form my body.

Creating new flames for my inner fire is easy. Creating them for my form, not so much. It takes all my concentration, and the energy drains rapidly from my reserve as I re-create my torso and limbs.

I stretch my arms and legs within the restrictive molten rock and am satisfied to feel no difference between the sides. It's like the limbs were never gone.

I move my arms through the lava, trying to make my way to the edge of the lake. As comforting as it is to relax within the warmth, I can't sit still now. I need to know what happened to the general.

My new arm works just fine to pull me out. The relatively cold air hitting me as I breach the surface nearly sends me diving right back in, but I push forward. I rise to my feet and a wave of exhaustion rolls over me. I was able to put it off because I could run on the heat provided by the magma, but now that I'm out, the full brunt of the past few days slams into me.

I need to get this over with and get out of the Void Fog before finding a place to rest.

I send my will to have the general brought before me. What happened to the man after he almost killed me with that throw is something I need to know.

The general's prone body appears before me. Red burns line the entirety of his body and his eyes are gone. It's not a pleasant sight, so I send my flames forward to consume his corpse, as my uncle instructed I do with all my kills.

My flames pass over the man's body and I flinch back when he jerks at their touch. He's still alive? Quickly, I increase the distance between us, preparing for another surprise strike.

A few seconds pass where he does little more than twitch and gasp in choked breaths. There are still many of the sandworms chomping at his legs. He must not have bothered to swipe them off.

At a distance, I concentrate my blaze toward the eye sockets and try to end him as quickly as I can. Despite being able to do so before, I find it extremely hard to burn through the flesh. It takes a few minutes of watching the man's pained grunts and twitching before I finally burn into his head and he finally dies.

It is a relief to know the man is dead, but it doesn't bring back my family. I am both satisfied and not. He won't be able to cause the same grief he inflicted upon me on someone else, but I feel like his death was too quick. I only hope it was as painful as it looked.

The Void Fog brings the other cause of strife before me. The man is long dead, someone having cut right through one side of his body before the Void Fog engulfed him.

I send my flames over both, ready to consume them for their strength. Olipho burns quickly, but the general's skin is resistant even in death, and I remain seated by their corpses for a long while before they are consumed.

In the time it takes to eat them, I mess around with the new control I have over my form. It seems I'm unable to take on a nonphysical form while I'm still hiding my flames. The types of modification to my flames are in the complete opposite direction from each other, which prevents me from doing both at once. Which is strange, because I'm sure I remember Elder Enya being able to change into a bird while retaining some physicality.

As my fire burns its way through the general, I realize that his body is probably the most nutritious meal I've ever had. Back in the tribe, besides parts we could use to make tools or clothing, we would always consume every scrap of the creatures we killed. Uncle said after we took the nutrition to support our bodies, the rest went to increasing the strength of our bodies.

It wasn't something I really understood because it was never an observable improvement. But now, I can feel it. There is so much energy stored in the muscle, fat, and bones of the general that I can feel my . . . everything improving with each bit my flames take in.

I guess it is understandable to take in more strength from those that are far stronger. The closest I've felt to this was when I was given a bit of a colossal-worm one time. But even then, it was hard to tell as we shared it amongst everyone in the tribe.

Once I finish absorbing the bodies, I know it is time to go.

I build a shell of flame around me, intending to try again now that the Void Fog had its way with me. Same as the first time, my fire pushes away from my body and immediately disappears, replaced by the outside world once more.

Again, I find myself in a long scar through the landscape. The scar is much thinner this time, but it appears to travel in a long, straight line as far as my eyes can see. If this is the path the Void Fog traveled, consuming everything in its path, it must have moved much farther than back in Zadok.

I notice a commotion at the edge of the scar above me, where the disappeared land tapers back to untouched. There is little chance anyone in the area will be a friend; more likely, they will be soldiers assuming the Void Fog didn't take me far from where I began. Knowing that, I move away from them, backtracking down the curved crevice until I find somewhere that lacks people.

Nobody has come for me yet, but I don't want to leave anything to chance. As soon as I climb over the ledge, I run away as fast as I can without collapsing. I push my body through the exhaustion so I can find somewhere safe to rest.

All around me is farmland. I run through some type of grass crop growing in the organized fields. Far too soon I find myself unable to run anymore. I trip over my own feet and land amongst the grass. Unable to get up, I drop my head and give in to sleep.

It is dark when I awake. An eerie silence encompasses the land. No birds, no bugs, not even the breeze makes a sound.

I rise above the grass and look around. There is nobody. No one has come looking for me. Is it finally over? With the general dead, I don't have to keep looking over my shoulder, right? The water mages aren't going to look for me; they think I died in that weapon. And without the general, they have no reason to continue searching for other áed.

It is over.

I've lost so much and gained nothing, but it's over.

The grass passes around me as I walk. I feel a sense of catharsis now that I'm free. The men I hate are dead and the áed will not be hunted, but . . . I am in the same place I started. Not physically, of course, but I don't know what to do from here on.

I'm lost and alone once more.

No. What am I thinking? I have a way out of that. Ash, Leslie, and the others—I can join them. I know where they have gone, not exactly, but I'm sure I can find them if I travel north. And Leal too; maybe I can find her somehow. I have options now. There's no reason for me to be alone. I'll head to the northern states and find where the others went.

But first, I have a promise to fulfill.

I glance over the extensive field of grass. Highly flammable grass. I promised Teine to give her and her family a send-off, and if I'm going to offer them their parting without knowing their names, I should at least make their pyre bigger than any other.

I run through the grass until I find the perfect spot for it: an old, worn barn built for ursu proportions sits amongst the grass at the top of a hill. The large doors creak open with a push, and I make sure there are no people around to either be hurt or stop the pyre. Originally, I planned to take some of the stuff I found inside to create it, but I soon realize—why not just use the barn itself?

So for the next hour, I cut some of the grass and lay it around the wooden walls of the barn, ready for the Ember Moon to come. Sometimes I wonder if the eastern races make these things intending to let them burn. I mean, why else would they make these buildings from wood?

When the light of the moon finally disappears and only the stars remain, I run around the outside of the barn, igniting every pile of grass I've left around. Once done, I run through the fields of long grass, hoping to start a widespread fire.

The barn burns quickly. A tower of flames rises high into the sky even without me needing to interfere. I couldn't have hoped for a better pyre. Eldest Ember must be delighted with my effort.

Soon, the sky tints with her color, and I walk through the burning doors of the barn surrounded by burning grass as far as I can see. I push my inner flame into the fire, amplifying the already strong blaze. The fire spins into a vortex under my control, but it isn't enough for me. I flip the control of my form, forcing it into as intangible a state as I can manage.

In the time I have, I can't spread far, but those few flames I mix with feel ever so much closer than I could have imagined before. With my inner flame spreading through the fire far and wide and my body merging with the superheated central inferno, I create the best path for my kin to the Eternal Inferno. It is sad I do not know their names to help them through, but the intensity and size of this flame should allow any to see, no matter the distance.

I wish a goodbye to Teine, who could not push on through the death of her family. I didn't know her long, but I want her to reunite with her family, something I hope I can do myself one day.

It is a sad moment as I think about all the áed who have died, but it is also happy in a way. At least I have survived to give them their path forward. I want there to be finality with this pyre. This is my third one and I want it to be my last. There will be no more loss in my future if there is anything I can do to stop it.

Using the new strength Teine's sacrifice and the consumption of the general's body has given me, I push as much power into the flames as I can, spinning the inferno with intensity and heat. I enhance the fire with every part of my being until the orange color twists into a yellow and burns in a vortex reaching heights far greater than before.

Life will get better.

About the Author

J. B. Oro is the author of the Young Flame series, originally released on Royal Road. He is a massive progression fantasy and xenofiction fan. Oro finds that the more unassuming and visibly contradictory to their strength characters are, the better.

Podium